The Teaching of Blackbeard

Jeremy Birch

Published by Intuity Design

First published in Great Britain in 2016

This book : ISBN 978-1-78280-916-6

Contact us : books@intuity-design.co.uk

Dedication

To Judith, Peter and Helen, who have tolerated this Bristol lad's interest in a particular corner of history.

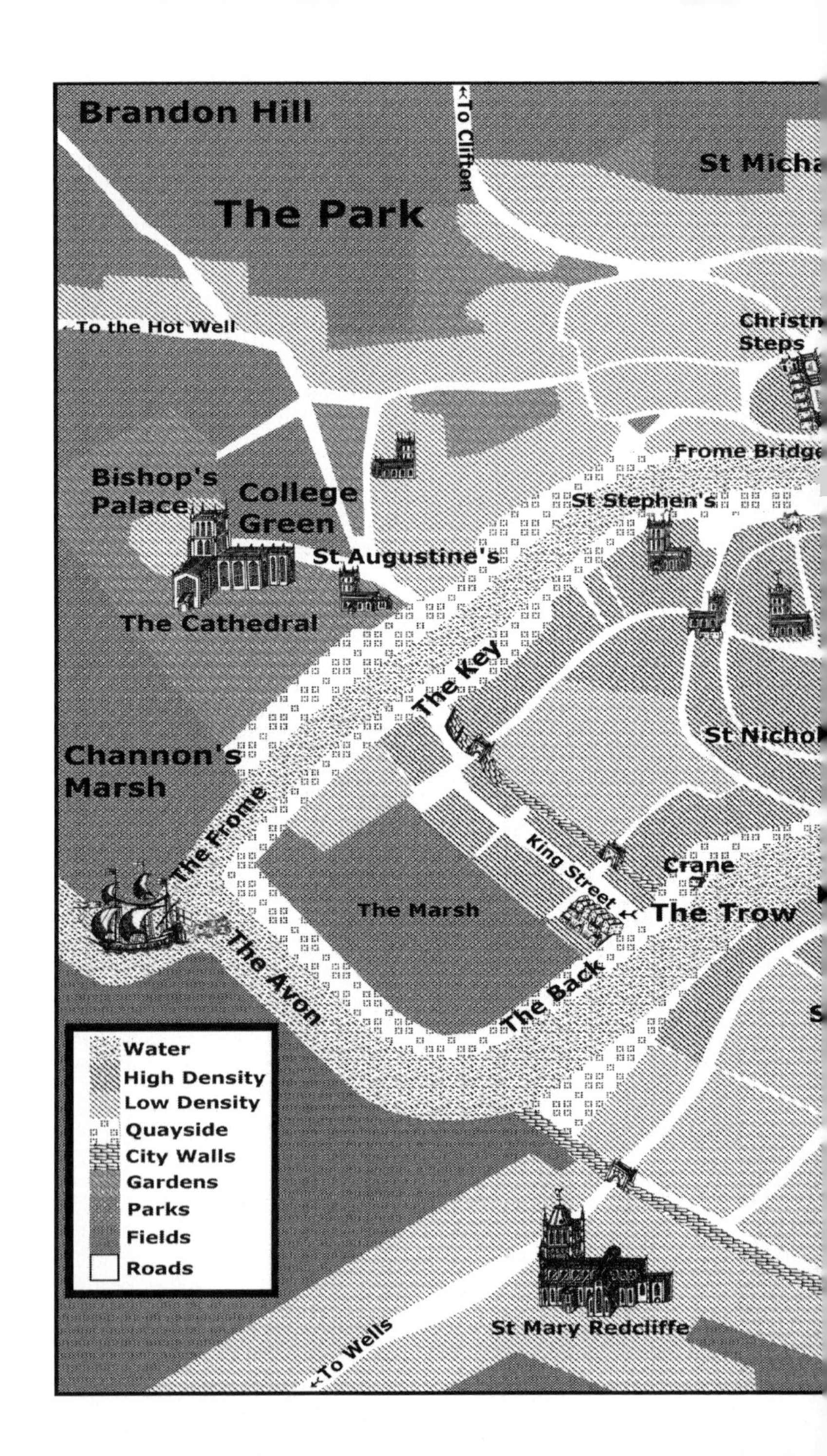
Brandon Hill
To Clifton
The Park
To the Hot Well
Frome Bridge
Bishop's Palace
College Green
St Stephen's
St Augustine's
The Cathedral
The Key
Channon's Marsh
The Frome
King Street
Crane
The Marsh
The Trow
The Avon
The Back
Water
High Density
Low Density
Quayside
City Walls
Gardens
Parks
Fields
Roads
St Mary Redcliffe
To Wells

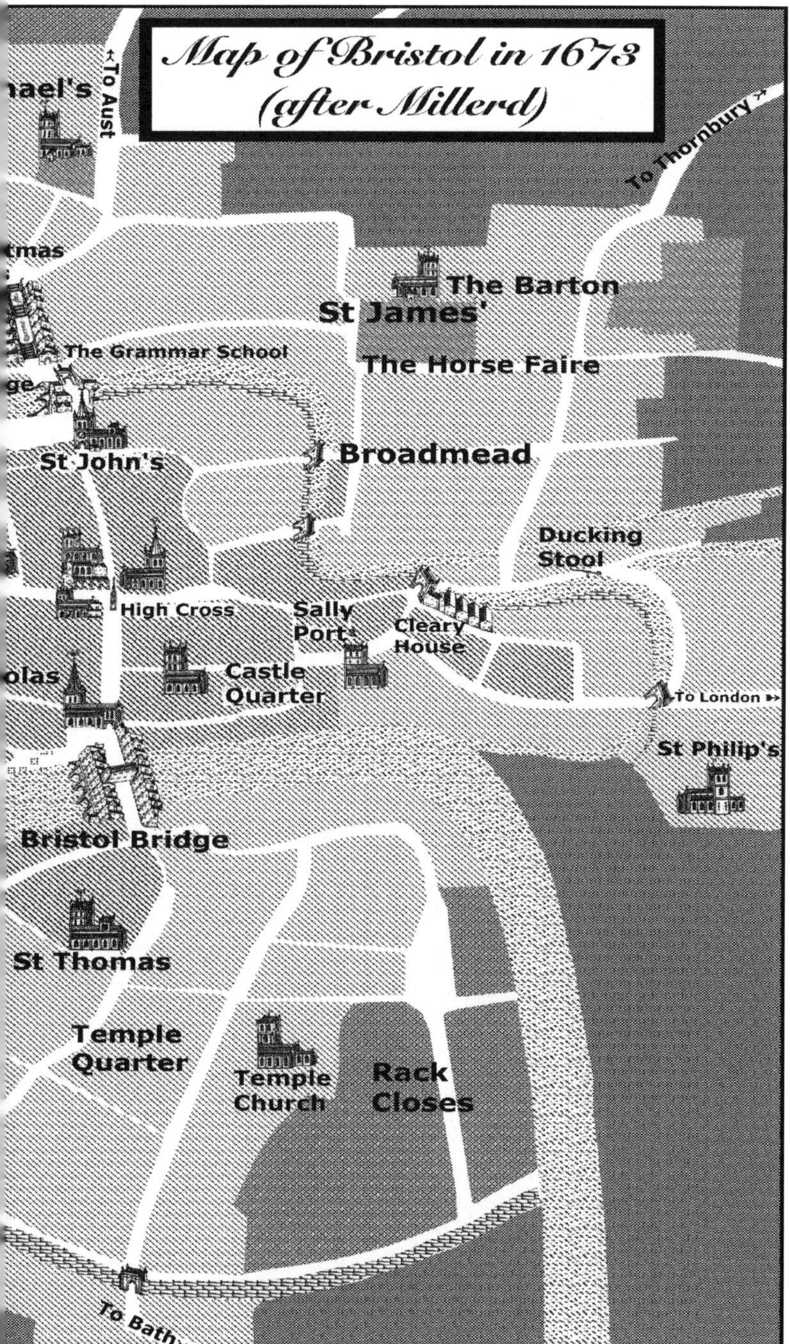

Map of Bristol in 1673
(after Millerd)
To Aust
To Thornbury
...hael's
...tmas
The Barton
St James'
The Grammar School
The Horse Faire
Broadmead
St John's
Ducking Stool
High Cross
Sally Port
Cleary House
...olas
Castle Quarter
To London
St Philip's
Bristol Bridge
St Thomas
Temple Quarter
Temple Church
Rack Closes
To Bath

Contents

Prologue: The Log of Discovery

This book is the story of the most infamous and maligned pirate Blackbeard, and of his childhood friends. Before we get to that, however, I must tell you how Long John Silver led me to find this story in its hiding place, where it had lain undisturbed for more than a century.

Around twenty years ago, I was walking around Bristol with my wife and our young son, in his pushchair, when we happened upon a garage sale. We would not normally have stopped, as we were both averse to having unnecessary junk in the flat, and there is quite enough necessary junk with a modern child to make such a small space into an obstacle course at the best of times. Our son was gloriously asleep, in the way that only babies can be; it was a hot day and homemade lemonade was on offer in sparklingly clean glasses, and we were flagging from lugging the buggy up the city's hills, leaning forward to the point where the chair was almost at shoulder height; so we gratefully stopped.

As we drank the refreshingly cold, tart liquid, we idly sifted through the variety of jetsam, junk and detritus that was on sale for a few pence. Amongst all of this half-forgotten tat was a box containing a porcelain cream jug of the Royal Albert type. As we had already inherited a teapot of the same series, it seemed a happy chance to add to the set for minimal outlay, but the vendor was quite insistent that we could not have the jug alone and we had to take the rest of the contents of the shoebox with it, at no extra cost. I could see in her eyes the look of a tidy person desperately grasping an opportunity to shed some unwanted trash onto anyone foolish enough to show an interest. We acquiesced, and put the box under the buggy as carefully as we could to prolong the sleep of our son, and continued on our way homewards, much refreshed.

Later, all of the usual routines having run their course, including multiple sessions of feeding, changing, washing, and "chuggling" our son, the bedtime story read until his head started to loll, and he had once more relapsed into the untroubled sleep of the infant. We finally got around to fishing the box from under the buggy, an operation that was necessary so we could fold it up and reach the front door of the flat without risking life and limb.

We took the box into the kitchen, and my wife carefully, almost reverently, scrubbed the jug to within an inch of its life until there was no chance of any ancient milk remaining adhered to its surfaces. While she was so engaged, I sorted through the remaining items in the shoebox, which had originally contained the sort of leaden school shoes that I had worn, and wantonly destroyed, as a child.

Inside this somewhat stained and foxed container was a variety of scrambled wrappings which concealed: a spoon from Austria, with a flag upon the handle; a selection of dust and balled-up, desiccated woodlice; a battered silver cup just about large enough to hold a cream egg, though it was beaten almost flat; a pair of pince-nez glasses that fell apart when I tried them on my nose; a sixpence from the 1950s, and pieces of broken, corroded and unidentifiable metal.

I quite happily disposed of all of the above, with my wife's blessing, and proceeded to flatten out the papers in which they had been wrapped, being a bit of an over-keen recycler. Most of the papers were torn from quite old editions of the Bristol Evening Post, dating back to the 1970s, bemoaning the performances of the city's sporting teams; some were undateable, but one was quite different from the others. I found that it held a mint Victorian penny, quite crisp unlike all the others I had ever owned which were worn black and nearly featureless. I happily slipped the coin into my pocket, as something that my son might appreciate one day for its rarity if not its value, and then I flattened out the papers in which it was wrapped.

To my surprise, these were not more of the local rag, but a handwritten letter that must have been contemporary with the coin that they had held. It was addressed from the "Hole in the Wall" pub, where I remember having had several birthday meals when I was a child (shod in diving boots), my parents having been fans of the Irish coffee and steaks that were served there; but the letter dated from long before such culinary innovations were known in Bristol. Its contents were unlike those of any letter I have ever written, so I felt it needed to be kept, and possibly investigated.

I give the letter in full here so that the reader may understand my interest in it, and follow my investigations more easily:

The Hole in the Wall,

Bristol

The first of October, 1880

Dear Father,

I have spent some days in the port of Bristol, where I have come for the waters in case they can help shift this dreadful cough of mine. I trust that Fanny is not pining for me; please tell her that I am much improved, and that I will meet you all soon, at your house.

To while away the hours, I have been reading the "History of Notorious Pyrates" and have been much surprised how many of them were reputed to hail from this very city. I had been put in mind of pirates by a treasure map I drew for young Lloyd during our voyage, and desired some inspiration to spin a tale for him.

I have been making some enquiries to discover how much truth there is to the tales, and if any evidence of that former skulduggery is still to be found behind the appearance of respectability that I see all around me. I have found that practically every quayside, street and inn has some link to those bloodthirsty villains of old, and I am most taken with it, at this safe remove. I have discovered inns where the great pirates Roberts and Hands were known to have drunk, and I have been shown so many places where Blackbeard is reputed to have stood, that he must have been more millipede than man.

The inn at which I am residing is wonderfully evocative, and it has inspired me to conjure a yarn that encompasses the feelings this all engenders in me, of those days gone past, before the age of lighthouses, transatlantic cables, telegraphs and such wonders as we use every day.

This is not the most important thing I have to relate. On asking my questions about the old buccaneers, I was directed to another inn, not far from this one, and there I enquired of the landlord if he knew anything of the days of the pirates. He looked earnestly at me but said not a word, other than to ask the reason for my question. When I said I had a mind to write a story that involved such people and needed to know more about the truth of them, he gave me a look with his twinkling eyes, but remained mum.

When the other guests were taken once more with their dominoes he led me into a side room and told me to attend whilst he looked out something that might be of interest to me.

I sat down with my drink, a murky liquid they refer to as "zider", but finely refreshing nonetheless, and he disappeared upstairs, from whence I could hear some thumping and banging as if large items of furniture were dancing around the room. When he eventually returned, somewhat dishevelled, dusty and flustered, he carried a large object wrapped in a blanket. Before he put this down he extracted from me a solemn promise that his establishment would not be named in any of my writings, and the existence of this bundle must be kept secret. I was happy to give my oath to this as I was doubtful that anything I may write of this kind could ever find an audience.

The landlord placed the bundle upon the table in front of me and then unwrapped it with some reverence. Inside there was a large book, about the size of Grandfather's Bible, but bound with uncoloured leather of some great age, there were also two loose sheets of paper, one bearing the traces of a seal. Around these was a layer of oiled wrapping that crackled when he moved it, and which bore some rusty coloured marks. 'These might be of some interest to you, take what notes you like but nothing else may leave this room,' he said, and left me with them, his eyes still a-twinkle.

And what was in this mysterious and revered bundle, you might ask? The book turned out to be a ship's log written in two hands, the first being a fine copperplate which ran over a great many pages and titled "The Log of Revenge," which showed the day to day running of a ship of that name from the beginning of the eighteenth century. It soon became clear to me that the log was of a pirate ship and when I later referred to Captain Johnson's history, I found that such a ship had been under the command of the infamous Blackbeard, so it would seem that the fine scribe was none other than that freebooter himself.

Father, as you can guess, I was eager to know as much as I could of this blackguard's story; I read for hour after hour, and made what notes I could. Where his log abruptly finished with a dedication to one John Porter, another less sophisticated hand began its account, and it was the log of life in the very inn in which I sat, starting two centuries ago. The author had been born there, then grown to run and own the establishment despite being but the illegitimate son of a serving maid, and had known the boy who became Blackbeard. But many other characters of interest came across the pages, so many that I can hardly credit that such a lowly man crossed the paths of so many who are now famous, and notorious. From this I think that I have identified the true person behind "Captain Johnson," and his motivations for publishing that account, the background to a famous castaway, and much more besides which fascinates me and makes me most certain that I must write something about that time.

You can imagine that by the end I was boiling over with

ideas and inspiration for my tale, so that I could hardly stand it, and I was desperate to get to writing before that mist evaporated in the light of the rational sun. As I put the bundle back together I realised with some shock that the stains I had seen upon the wrappings, were the blood of the very pirate about whom I had read, and frankly for whom I now felt some empathy. I called the landlord and he could see that I had been quite affected by what I had read, and said, 'I trust you will make a good story of it, but remember your oath.'

He removed the bundle and again I could hear some great disturbance above my head, before he returned, shook my hand and wished me good luck in my venture.

I said, 'I am most grateful to you, you must guard these things most fiercely for they are truly unique and precious.'

He replied, 'I do that, dear sir, you are but the second outside the family of landlords to ever set eyes upon it, to my knowledge. We shall continue to guard it until opportunities arise to reveal it to the benefit of the original author. We do this because the original owner, my ancestor named Hawkins, made a solemn oath to keep these things safe and to ensure that no one could use them to disparage or defile the memory of Mr Teach. I saw something in you that made me think that here was a man who could do justice to Teach's spirit, and his ilk. I am rarely far wrong in my judgement of people, and I am not wrong now. I wish you luck.'

I thanked him profusely, and returned to my room with my head spinning with ideas that I needed to mesh together into a story. I must depart from here tomorrow, so I will spend the next few hours getting my impressions down before they blow away. I will work it up as soon as I reach Braemar, if Fanny will indulge me, and I will soon be able to show you all the fruits of my labours.

Father, perhaps you can help me to get the nautical details correct? You know far more about the sea than I ever managed to grasp on our summer voyages. I have at least found the names of my heroes and villains, a setting to start with and the feel of the thing, and that is half the battle won.

I must sign off now, as I have quite forgotten to eat anything and have consumed more than I ought of the local brew, and what with all this excitement it is nearly midnight.

As always, your loving son

Lewis

In those days, when we were new parents, before the advent of internet search engines and on-line encyclopaedias, there was precious little time to spend looking for answers, and soon the novelty letter found itself stuck between the pages of some book on our shelves, and it was forgotten once more.

*

Some years later, a series of coincidences led me a few steps further forward. My son was at primary school, and I still read to him every night. We had progressed from Mog and that greedy Tiger, through the first of that schoolboy wizard's stories, and now as part of a literacy programme, Bristol's primary school children were given a copy of a book to read, which had a link to the city. The hope was that this link would make more children enthusiastic about reading, and the history of the city, and it was successful in our home at least.

The book concerned was "Treasure Island". I gladly read it to my son, a chapter or so each night, and we were both quite taken with it. I had never read it before, although I had of course seen dramatisations during my own childhood. I can't recall at exactly what point in the story I had my revelation, but one evening I stuttered to a halt, and the book dropped from my hands as my mental gears finally started to mesh. I was brought back to the story when my son's small elbow was sharply such between my ribs, urging me to continue with the story.

The elements that were coming together were: Robert Louis Stevenson had written a book about pirates, many years after that species had become extinct in the Caribbean. The story had the treasure hunters departing from the port of Bristol, and this was rumoured to be because the author had started to write the book in the city, inspired by its pirate heritage (one of our football teams is even nicknamed The Pirates). Could the letter I had found so long before be written by RLS himself? It had been five or more years since I had last seen it, we had moved house and produced a baby girl in the meantime, so I feared that the letter had been lost along the way, by accident or design.

I searched until midnight, when as I was being given stern looks by my wife, and I was despairing of ever finding the letter, out of an old copy of the National Geographic slipped the yellowed pages for which I had been searching. When I read the letter again, I saw that it could be interpreted as being the work of RLS, if I took the story he meant to write as being Treasure Island, and the date fitted with that mentioned in the introduction of the book that I had been reading to my son.

This was quite exciting, even my long-suffering wife agreed, but there was no more I could do that night. When

I looked again at the letter the next day, I was even more certain that I was right. It was signed Lewis, and that was the name by which RLS had been christened, before he romanticised it by using the French form of spelling. I referred to another book that I owned, about the lighthouse building Stevenson family, and that confirmed that RLS was the black-sheep of the family, having turned his back on the business of surrounding the deadly rocks of the Scottish coast with indomitable lights; which was probably just as well as his chest was very weak and not up to the exploits of the men of the preceding two generations. The family referred to him as Lewis to avoid confusion with his pioneering and domineering grandfather Robert, who had died in the year that RLS was born.

So even after he had adopted his nom-de-plume, RLS might have used the name Lewis when corresponding with his own father Thomas. It explained the non sequitur reference to lighthouses in the letter, too. The clincher, for me, was that the name of the original owner of the log was Hawkins, and Lewis had claimed to have found the name for his hero. Was Jim Hawkins inspired by that humble Bristolian innkeeper, or his ancestor?

At that time I was led no further, we had a potentially interesting letter with links to Bristol and one of the world's most famous adventure yarns, so it might have had some value. What I really wanted was the treasure whose existence it indicated: where was the X marking the last resting place of Blackbeard's own diary?

*

Some months later, at a fundraising quiz at my son's school, my wife introduced me to another couple sat at our table, parent's of a boy in his class. We chatted a little between the frankly bizarre rounds of questions, and I learnt that they were the tenant landlords of the historic

Llandoger Trow pub in the centre of Bristol, and they lived above the shop.

When we were all a measure more tipsy, there was a round of questions on literature, which cast its net pretty wide, from Enid Blyton to Barbara Cartland, with one question being 'In which novel does Admiral Benbow appear?'

There was a certain amount of consternation, no one having heard of such a naval gentlemen, but our table-mates had a confident air about them. 'Treasure Island' was the whisper that they gave in unison. At the end of the round, when the answer papers had been swapped with another table and exasperated sighs of 'Of course, Treasure Island!' were heard, the husband lent across and said, 'Of course, you know that the Admiral Benbow was modelled upon our very own pub? Apparently Stevenson visited it and was inspired to start writing his book that very night.'

I was somewhat befuddled by this time, 'in my cups' as they used to say, so I was not very swift on the uptake. In the middle of the night, with dreams fuelled by too much cheese and red wine, I suddenly awoke with a concrete certainty that the Trow was the inn referred to in the letter I owned, and that meant there was just a chance that Blackbeard's log really existed and was at that moment lying peacefully within the fabric of that pub, pickled in cigarette smoke.

On Monday morning, I traipsed off to school with my son holding my hand, playing our game of making words up from number plates, to pass the time. I had brought with me a copy of the letter. I saw that the landlord was in the playground when I arrived, waiting for a teacher to take over supervision of the half-ling horde, so I sidled up and greeted him. After a brief exchange of pleasantries and review of the quiz evening, I said that I had something interesting to show him, and handed over the letter.

He read it through, with growing interest, and then exclaimed, 'This is incredible, is this real? So Robert Louis Stevenson not only visited the Trow but read there a log written by Blackbeard himself, and it is that which inspired him to write his book? So what happened to the log afterwards?'

I said that I did not know, but the letter implied that it had been put back into some secret hiding place within the fabric of the inn, somewhere upstairs. At this his face fell, 'Ah, well it has been heavily remodelled up there several times since the 1960s when it was sold by the family who had owned it for generations; I doubt anything hidden there could have survived. That letter is over a hundred and twenty years old, anything could have happened. The Trow was hit by a bomb in the war, the book could easily have disappeared that night without anyone knowing it even existed. Anyway, I am only a tenant landlord; I cannot go around ripping up the floors on a wild goose chase. But it is interesting, I will keep eyes and mind open and see if anything crops up.'

*

Again, there was no way forward and I just had to let it rest. Occasionally I would talk again with the landlord, but neither of us had any more clue to the whereabouts of the log, and we had to leave it at that. We could not risk any publicity, or there might be hundreds of treasure hunters, or pirate nerds, ripping the Trow apart with their penknives, or worse, in a vain hope of finding the log. It was rumoured that Blackbeard had left a large cache of gold and jewels in North Carolina and the log might indicate its position. I believe the whole of Bath,NC makes a mighty play upon Blackbeard's association with the area, and this would lead to quite a lot of unwanted interest should the letter ever be published.

So we come to the final lucky coincidence. One of the things we liked to do when the kids were young was to visit the City Museum, at the weekend. There are stuffed animals, a gypsy caravan, dinosaur bones, a fine array of pianos, lots of wide staircases for the kids to attempt, and a cafe with a welcome assortment of cakes. We never really bothered with reading the information cards apart from when one of the kids really, *really*, wanted to know who was that funny man in armour, so it was just a genteel playground for them, and a respite for us. Occasionally we would be able to look in on an exhibition when the kids were sated with staircases and sugar.

On the visit in question, there was a display of famous artists who were linked to Bristol, from Turner to Banksy, by way of some more obscure figures, who may not have been that well known in their own households. There was a depiction of Edward Colston, after whom so much of Bristol is named, on his death bed with a young black maid kissing his hand, which felt a little tasteless given his reputed links to the slave trade.

In the middle of the exhibition was the altar piece that William Hogarth had painted for St Mary Redcliffe church in 1755, which had been donated to the museum two hundred years later. Unlike the other works by Hogarth which are more widely known, such as the Rake's Progress and Gin Lane, the altar piece of the Ascension is as reverent as the others are satirical.

Alongside this was a portrait, described as being 'possibly painted by Hogarth at the same time as the altarpiece, a portrait of a justice of the peace named

Hawkins, shown with a book of Law'. The man in question is well beyond middle age, though the fashion of the period dictated that any man of position wore a white wig and that made ageing him by his hair impossible, but his face certainly bore the lines of time. He looks at the viewer directly with a certain twinkle in his eye, and has his arm resting on a thick book. In the background there just can be discerned a fireplace, and above that a portrait of a heavily bearded man, with two objects lying upon the mantle beneath that might be cutlasses.

The implication was that Mr Hawkins used to be a bit of a lad, very hirsute, but had become a fine upstanding member of the legal profession. At this point, childhood patience was exhausted and I was dragged away for another tour of the stairs, before we returned home, and prepared for work and school the next day.

Something nagged at me, and it was not for another few days of unconscious pondering that I could put my finger on what was irritating me. At the next opportunity, I revisited the exhibition, and made a beeline for the possible Hogarth, and my first glance confirmed what I had suspected. The book that his right arm rests upon is a heavy tome, but not bound in the fine leather which might be expected of a legal text, but a rather rough and ready hide. The title is only barely discernible beneath his fingers and the shadow cast by them, with only 'The L' clearly visible. But my suspicious, and perhaps prejudiced eye, saw that the next letter was not an 'a' but in fact an 'o'. Could this be a book entitled 'The Log …'?

I went to the cafe, to sit down with a hunk of rich chocolate cake and a coffee, the combination of which made my heart feel like it was trying to leap out of my chest. I examined the copy of the letter which I had come to carry with me as a matter of habit. I read it through several times, then searching all my pockets for a pen I found none so I dashed to the gift shop and purchased one inscribed 'Why not visit the Mummies of Bristol?' with which I started to circle parts of the text.

I was looking for coincidences, trying to sift possibilities out of the mist of distractions, and I thought I had found something tangible at last. The log had been apparently dedicated to one 'John Porter,' and the landlord of the pub many years later, who had shown the log to RLS, was a man named Hawkins. He was certainly not the man painted by Hogarth, he could not have been born until many years after the painter's death, but there was the name Hawkins as was shown on the portrait.

The current landlord of the Trow had implied that it had been a family business up to the 1960s. It was well known that the pub was named after a type of flat bottomed boat that used to shuttle between Llandogo in Wales and Bristol, and that it had been given this name by its first owner, a Captain Hawkins, in the 1600s. So it seemed possible that the landlords for two centuries afterwards were named Hawkins. If that was the case, then the man running the Trow when Blackbeard died in 1718 must have also been named Hawkins, yet the name given in Lewis' letter was John Porter. Perhaps, just perhaps, his full name was John Porter Hawkins. And that might be abbreviated, especially due to the limited space available on the painting, to JP Hawkins. Had the museum staff mistaken his initials for his title?

Wired on semi-lethal doses of coffee, chocolate, sugar and fat, I went back somewhat shakily to examine the portrait once more. If I now read it correctly, this man who was officially believed to be a respectable member of society, a justice of the peace or JP, was in fact the proprietor of the Trow, and he had been a close acquaintance and confidante of one of the most notorious pirates of the age. It probably tickled Hogarth's sense of disrespect for pomposity to cast such a man as if he was on par with a magistrate, and to put his secret in plain view. If my conjecture was correct, then the book beneath his elbow was none other than Blackbeard's log, and we had confirmation it existed around 1755, and was held in the Trow. That being the case, how was a casual observer, or seeker after truth, meant to discover it? Hogarth was known to use symbolism in his satirical works, could he (or someone like him) be using the same tricks to convey a hidden meaning in this painting?

I once more examined the background of the portrait, and determined that this was meant to be the real clue. How would you describe it in isolation if Mr Hawkins was not there? There was so little to be seen of the painting above the mantle that I would have had to call it 'the man with the black beard,' and given that there was precious little man visible, it was only really Blackbeard. It was not a portrait of the man, but of his nom de guerre. To make it all the more certain, the swords were placed beneath in very much the arrangement of the bones on the traditional, and possibly apocryphal, Jolly Roger flag. So was Hogarth stating that Hawkins *was* Blackbeard, or was there some more subtle message here?

The reported dedication of the log, *to* John Porter rather than signed *by* him, indicated something beneath the surface. As there was no superfluous detail in the background, just a wash of black and brown, I had to assume that what was there was there for a purpose, and I needed to discern what that purpose might be. Why, for instance, was the log shown in the portrait if it was not known to exist? Perhaps this was the public declaration of its existence, to show to those willing to decode the image that Blackbeard had recorded his adventures in a book, and that it was in the possession of Mr Hawkins. Maybe this painting originally hung in the Trow but its significance had been forgotten over time, and now separated from the inn, its meaning was concealed.

I knew from RLS's description, or at least his inference, that the log was hidden in a hard to reach place involving the shifting of furniture and perhaps floorboards, and it is reasonable to assume that this same hiding place had been reserved for it from soon after its arrival in Bristol. So was the last clue to this trove hidden in the portrait, which must have dated from late in JP's life when he wanted to pass on the secret to perpetuity in some way that did not rely on word of mouth or the longevity of human memory?

I could not see what was hidden there for me to discover, so I lackadaisically went round the rest of the exhibition once more. The descriptions of the portraits commented upon whether the sitter stares confidently out at the viewer, or askance at some glorious distance we cannot see, or averted, and stated how this was a form of code to reveal the personality of the sitter: bold, visionary or modest. JP's portrait stared challengingly out at the viewer with the nearest to a twinkle in his eye's that I have ever seen conveyed by paint, perhaps asserting his worth despite his lowly commercial position, but also challenging us to break the code of the painting.

So what about the infamous pirate in the background, surely he would have at least as confrontational an aspect as a purveyor of beer and cider? But no, from the tiny and indistinct image concealed under varnish that had suffered from smoke and time, I could see that infamous criminal had his eyes averted, and not like the modest maidens of other neighbouring images, but strongly staring down to the left of the portrait. Standing as close as I could without causing the museum guides to haul me away, I could just make out that there was a subtle asymmetry to the mantle, where on the right hand side was shown a carved rosette, on the left hand side there was a blank, black square. Was this what Blackbeard was looking at, in surprise or annoyance?

From a guess at the proportions, the void indicated could only be large enough to fit a seaside postcard slid in diagonally, certainly it could not hold a great tome like the log in the painting, or as it was referred to in the letter. Perhaps there was a handle there that released a catch which would make the fireplace swing out revealing a concealed room? This seemed implausible, and given the remodelling of the Trow in recent years, well beyond belief. Feeling that I had at last gained some insight, I returned home to my paternal duties.

Not long afterwards, my son was invited to the Trow to attend the birthday party of his classmate, the son of the landlord and landlady. All the usual party games and food were present and correct, and the kids certainly enjoyed themselves, despite the rather unusual setting of a function room in a pub. Towards the end, when the children had slowed down their orbiting of the room, and were reaching the nirvana afforded by tiredness, happiness and cake, I had the opportunity to have a conversation with the host.

'You might be interested to know that I think I have found a clue to the hiding place of that book we were looking for?'

After a moment of perplexity, he recalled our previous discussion of the letter, and drew me into a quiet corner.

'Really? I thought you had given up on that as being hopeless. Well, what have you found?'

I told him about the painting I had seen, and what I had deduced from it, but his expression seemed to imply a healthy degree of scepticism, 'What makes you think that the painting had anything to do with the Trow, or that the subject of it was some coded message for those seeking treasure? It all feels a bit far-fetched to me.'

'Well, I admit that I might be completely wrong, but this is the only lead I have had in years. Tell me, are there any original fireplaces left in the Trow?'

'Several, we have not been allowed to remove them, even when they are in frankly inconvenient places, because they are deemed to be of historical interest. I will show you them later once these darling forces of chaos have been collected by their parents.'

An hour later, we were stood in front of one of the fireplaces in the lounge bar of the pub. It was certainly impressive, ornate and black with a hearth large enough to hold a roasting pig, but it certainly was nothing like the one in the painting.

'Not this one? Well, we have plenty more for you to look at.'

In all there were eight fireplaces, from the grand one in the lounge to a tiny Victorian one up in the eaves, perhaps where the most junior member of the household shivered in Dickensian winters. The one that caught my eye was in the part of the inn that would have been the living space for the landlords of old, but it was now stranded in the middle of an area used as a restaurant in the 1980s, and now somewhat surplus to requirements for the pub. I stood as far away from it as I could get and compared it with the image I had in my mind's eye, as I had no copy of the painting to which to refer. It looked to have the same proportions, and if JP had sat somewhere in the middle of the room while Hogarth stood where I was, then the overall composition would be about right.

'I think this must be it, but there is some difference from the painting.'

I went over to the fireplace and examined the mantle in detail. Where I was expecting to see a carved rosette, there was instead a fairly crude rendition of a sailing ship about four inches across, facing a similar one on the other side. The painting had indicated that the left hand detail was important, but push, pull and twist as I might I could not find anyway to reveal a secret compartment, and indeed tapping the whole area showed it to be very solidly built. I was just about to give up in despair when the landlord pointed at the moulding just below the ship, where I must have slipped and scraped the finish with my fingernail.

'What's that, there seems to be some mark there?' he asked

I thought at first he was objecting to some damage I had inadvertently inflicted, but then I saw where he was pointing. There indeed seemed to be a long line of marks in the upper side of the moulding in such a position that it could only be seen by someone standing with their feet in the hearth, which presumably was not a common thing for most of its working life. I worked at it a bit more with my thumbnail and managed to scrape away an inch or so of a black, waxy material. This revealed a slightly lighter layer, with marks that were now clearly writing left in the darker finish. The word I revealed was 'Pirate'.

I whooped, this surely must be a sign that we were getting close, and by now my host had lost his reluctance to damage the fixtures and fittings, and had fetched a butter knife from a drawer. With this implement he rapidly revealed a line of text stretching a few inches to either side of the carved ship. This read:

'The Pirate fired another great broadside'

And indeed we could now see that the ship above did seem to be in the act of firing its cannon, and might conceivably have been flying that notorious flag at its masthead.

'But this is not much of a clue; how can we find the log from that? It certainly is not in the fireplace, that seems to be as solid as a lump of granite,' he puzzled.

I pondered, I was not going to give up now after my hunch about the painting had paid off. So what was I missing?

'The sentence is not complete, there is no full stop, yet they carefully put a capital letter at the beginning. Perhaps there is more to be found further along?' I conjectured.

So we worked our way along but found no hint of writing for the whole width of the hearth. We were about to despair again, and wondered how we were going to conceal the damage we had caused, when we reached the other upright in the vicinity of the second boat. And again we cheered, for we found the text continued:

'… and cached her beam end where she lied.'

'It is pretty awful doggerel, I must say; even our kids could beat that, and the spelling is atrocious!' he exclaimed.

'What if it is not bad English? Perhaps it is a coded message, maybe even the bad spelling is deliberate? Don't forget that it dates from before Dr Johnson and his idiosyncratic views on spelling, so this might have been acceptable to even the pickiest linguist of the time. Let us copy down the words and think about how they might be interpreted,' I suggested.

We made a copy of the writing and then concealed it again with a black crayon from his son's pencil case. We returned downstairs and sat around a table at the back, two couples examining a single line of text, as if it was the most obscure crossword clue. My wife suggested we treat it just that way, and asked if there was a dictionary or thesaurus in the pub. She then flicked backwards and forwards through the books, looking up every word in the line while the rest of us worried away at the text, like dogs harrying a flock of sheep.

'I have something, I think: that use of the word "cached," we have all been reading it as if it said "catched" as in "caught," but what if it *is* deliberate, and means "cache-d" as in "stored away in hiding," isn't that what we are looking for, a secret cache?' my wife asked.

'Brilliant – you must be right!'

'Ok, I'll give you that, but what about the rest of it, what gives us a direction?' said the landlord.

Then his wife spoke up, jabbing her finger in the middle of the first phrase, 'Where did you find this writing? It was on a fireplace wasn't it? And what might be a different word for a fireplace? Why a grate of course! So this is saying that the Pirate used another *grate*, not the one where you found the writing.'

'Terrific, so which of the other seven, or one that has been lost, is the one that we are looking for?' worried her husband.

'Right – if that phrase refers to another fireplace, then what does broadside mean? It can't mean letting off a lot of cannon, so perhaps it means that there is a grate that is asymmetric, one with a narrow side and a broad side?' I proposed.

'Great idea! Except we have looked at them all and there is not one of them that is noticeably wonky, so that can't be it,' said our resident sceptic.

Again we fell to pondering and flicking through the books; the children were curled up exhausted on sofas so we had the liberty to continue, for a while at least.

'But of course! There are eight grates, and seven of them are original and irritatingly symmetrical, and they would have been here when JP sat for Hogarth. But the eighth is far newer, merely Victorian. What if there had been an older grate there and it was replaced by the cast iron job we see now? Shall we have another look?' suggested the landlord, brightening up.

So we traipsed back up several flights, and stood rather awkwardly in the tiny attic room that contained the small fireplace in question. It was dimly lit by the bare, hanging bulb, but fortunately as our host used the room as an office, there was an angle-poise on the table, which he now directed towards the wall.

'There, turn the light a bit to the right. Is it my imagination or is there a mark as if the wall has been re-plastered? Let's look the other side. It is the same again, but much closer to the grate. So – was the original fireplace wider on the right than it was on the left? In which case the "broadside" is the right hand side,' my wife stated.

'Ok, so what do we do now? The log cannot be in this fireplace, and I presume anyone who re-plastered it would have noticed a great lump of book hanging out of the wall, so where is it?' I asked.

'Let us look back at the text to see which words we

have covered … "The Pirate" well that is just to show us that we are on the right track; "fired another great broadside," that gets us to where we are standing, at the right hand side of a rather unassuming fireplace. "Cached" means that the thing we are looking for is hidden here, so what does "her beam end where she lied" mean?' puzzled the landlady.

'Beam-end is a term meaning the sides of the ship, I looked it up earlier, though it normally was used when a ship had turned over onto its side,' my wife explained.

'The other bit is interesting, wasn't this always the bedroom of a member of the family or staff of the inn? So quite possibly a maid slept here, so this is "where she lied," or lay at least, I trust the odd spelling in this case is just to make an awful rhyme! If that is so then the bed would have to be to one side or other of the grate, and we think it is the right hand side.'

'And beam end, that might mean it is hidden at the end of the beam, beneath where the bed must have stood?' guessed the landlord.

'Genius! How I hope you are right!' I shouted.

So between us we moved filing cabinets and chairs out of the tiny garret room, and stacked them precariously at the head of the stairs. We found a wrecking bar in the cellar left over from some previous renovation, carefully peeled back the lino to reveal the floorboards, which showed great age but no sign of modern interference, and proceeded to try to lift a board some eighteen inches to the right of the previous grate, a position in the middle of where a fairly narrow bed might have been in the past.

With an agonised squeal of wood sliding passed ancient nails, we managed to get it moving, and with a combination of the bar and our hands we managed to tug six feet of lumber out of place. We put the angle poise on the floor and pushed its head down into the dark aperture, shining it towards the outside wall of the building. At first we saw nothing, but then with an exclamation, our friend reached right in, so that he almost disappeared into the cavity, and came back up coughing and streaked with dust, holding a small piece of what may have been an antediluvian blanket.

'I think something is there, I could not get a proper grip on it, but here is what it was wrapped in. Someone smaller needs to go in to fetch it out.'

My wife, who is considerably more petite than the rest of those there assembled, held up her hand to volunteer, despite being in some of her smartest clothes. She removed her jacket and placed it neatly upon the desk, then we helped her down into the hole and she worked her way forward, until she seemed to be so far in that I thought she must be dangling over the traffic outside. There was a muffled cry by which we assumed that she wanted us to pull her out, so we grabbed her ankles and dragged her back, trying not to stretch her too much in the process. She came out spluttering, caked in the grime of years, but triumphantly grinning: she had a large book in her hands.

*

From that night, it has taken me several years to pull together a sensible way for the wider public to read the logs. First of all we needed to take a fair photographic copy of every page, before there was any chance that the paper could degrade or any mishap befall it, and of course we had to do this in total secrecy with only the internet and library books to guide us. After the copy had been taken we determined that the log must be carefully and reverently preserved, so we invested in a substantial fireproof container just large enough to hold the log and some desiccant material, and hid it again within the fabric of the Trow. I will emphasise here that it is not in its original place of concealment, the container is free of metal and is substantially indistinguishable from the surrounding building. Don't go looking for it, you won't find it, and the current owners of the Trow would not appreciate any DIY archaeologists, or nighthawks, ripping apart their premises.

I have spent a considerable amount of time decoding the somewhat spidery writing of Porter, and the more florid script of Teach, and have expurgated some details which did not make for a good story or which might lead to a certain area on the other side of the Atlantic being pock-marked by treasure seekers. I have corrected the spellings for the most part into ones of which Dr Johnson might have approved, apart from certain speeches by Jack and Co. which remain essentially untranslatable *Brizzle*.

I have included the original letter by RLS, and this extended prologue, to give some framework to readers who are separated from the action by three hundred years or more, and I have added some explanatory notes in the text and at the end.

I have grown fond of the characters you will find in these logs, all of them faulty, proud, deserving of some sympathy, and some disdain. The luckiest and most fortunate of all is the one that goes unrecorded by history, apart from in an obscure painting attributed to "possibly Hogarth". The others were not treated well by Fate, and though their names live on, emblazoned on t-shirts and mugs across the Caribbean, the spirit and circumstances which drove them have been forgotten.

So I now humbly present to you the logs, in a form that

I trust will in turns inform, horrify and delight you. The log of course contains much that would not interest the casual reader, having course settings and soundings, observations on the weather and on minor matters of crew discipline, and I have removed those from the version that follows. Please note that all of these details of navigation and housekeeping are present in the original, and meticulously kept, as you would expect of the son of the grammar school master. Teach always used his mind before his fists, and without knowing this fact we would merely see a character from a Mummer's play, like St George or the Turk.

The Log is Blackbeard's journal, not a formal document, and reflects his state of mind. Teach was not taken completely unawares as the end approached, he may not have known the day of Maynard's attack but he sensed he was in the closing chapter of his life and had sent much of his crew away hoping that they might survive its final full stop. He surely anticipated the end, for why else did he finish his log and seal it up and send it to the Trow if he expected to write in it again?

I have rearranged the telling so that Porter's account of Teach's early days proceeds the story of the pirate's last years, the reverse of the order in the Log itself. I trust this makes it easier for the reader to form a true impression of the characters that cross these pages. Otherwise what you read hereafter are the words written by Porter and Teach.

For myself, the lasting impression I have formed is astonishment that a city of around twenty-five thousand souls, could produce in one generation Teach, Hands and several other infamous pirates, raise Woodes Rogers, sponsor Dampier, host Selkirk and Abraham Darby, kickstart the industrial revolution and massively increase the slave trade.

The City of Bristol is now twenty times the size it was in Blackbeard's day: what great or terrible things could be achieved in the city if that spirit of independent enterprise once more pulsed through its streets?

Part1:The Log of the Trow

1:Small Beer

My name is John Porter Hawkins, and I write this to complete the story of my close friend; to show that his heart was not as black as it is reputed to be. I hope to redeem him, his tarnished name, and that of our mutual friend Woody. To do these things I must tell the story of how I met Teach only a few steps from where I sit, and ultimately how I received the log in which I now write.

*

I was born in the spring of 1679 to the yeasty breath of beer, on a trestle table at the back of the Llandoger Trow inn. My mother, Mary, had been carrying flagons of beer to the Welsh, just arrived off their boats, when her pains came on. She spilt that ale everywhere, mixing it with her own earthier brew. The landlady helped her into the back room and shooed away the men.

I know this tale to be true, it was often told to me as the reason for me being called Small Beer, until I was big enough to shut the mouth of anyone saying it. Baptised in beer, they said; it was the only baptism I ever received, thanks to the hypocrisy of those who aim to save souls but who will not touch those who have no father's name.

I grew up at the inn, on the dockside, in the hurry and bustle of the port of Bristol, second only to London. Through the doors of the inn came every man of trade, from dock and deck hands to the agents, merchants and owners. Those whose clothes were torn and dirty from labour, and those who wore silks and held lace to their noses to block out the stink of the trade that made them rich.

When I was young, the merchants grew fat on the profits from selling wool cloth to the French and Spanish, when we were not fighting them, and richer still on the wine and brandy they brought back, even when we were at war. That wealth is nothing compared to the fortunes which have since been made from buying and selling black skins.

As a kid suckled on milk and weened on beer, I saw those men swirling through the doors of the Trow; I witnessed merchandise being examined, prices being agreed and silver crossing the board in exchange for ale, port and brandy. Rarely were the doors shut, except for when the wind brought rain to the back of the hearth. Even in winter, the snow stood no chance against our furnace-hot fire; like some magic curtain, the heat held back the forces of nature from the threshold.

Many men we saw at the beginning and end of every shift, more returned each week from ferrying goods to Wales, or to France. Others were gone so long that I would wonder if they had wrecked on some rocky coast, been taken by pirates, sunk by enemy frigates, or swallowed by some great monster in the rolling deeps. Some never returned, often for one of these reasons.

Of the people I saw each day, most vital were my fellow merchants of mischief. Our gang of ruffians roamed between the sailors and traders, showing respect only to those who could catch us, snatching apples from the market stalls and cheeking all who caught our eyes for these larcenies, but doing no real harm to anyone.

As children we ran around the port, between heaps and bales of goods, around pyramids of barrels, across the decks of the ships lined up three deep at the quayside, past the windows of the rich merchants and the hovels of the poor, playing tag across the sides of Brandon Hill between the lines of drying cloth, until we were parted by our chores, lessons, or the night watch.

We were not the worst of boys, but preferred to act like we were beyond redemption: the Devil's own scallywags. I was valued for supplying large jugs of small beer, and small jugs of anything left unconsidered at the Trow; all of it gratefully received by a dozen thirsty throats.

We patrolled our territory from the broad quay to the backs, around the marshes and the customs house, from the tall masts to the local trows, ducking and dodging whenever our names were called or our collars grabbed. Across cobbles and mud we ran, through the markets and warehouses, hiding in haylofts or under tables in straw-strewn inns. Our gang was of ragbag ruffians, ragamuffins and riffraff, who were really scholars, the sons of merchants and cathedral choristers in drab. We never questioned the bona fides of our members: once they had fought their way into the club we united in loyalty around them. We did not use each other's given names, or care too much about backgrounds, just how we fared in a scrape and how we shone in triumph.

I must have been ten years old when I was inducted into the gang. I remember seeing tousle-headed boys increasingly around the Trow, ducking behind barrels and bales outside or walking nonchalantly past in groups, but always surreptitiously glancing at the door. After a week of this surveillance, my curiosity and irritation were unbearable. I was collecting pots when I saw a hand creeping over the edge of a table, searching the surface for bounty. I slammed one tankard down on this five-fingered marauder and poured slops from a jug over the end of the table.

'Ouch – you blinking rascal, there's no need to have done that, I was only after what had already been left.'

Up popped one of that ragged crew, dripping, sucking at his fingers then clamping them under an armpit.

'There is a lot more of that I have to spare,' said I, as I went to hit him, but he was swift and agile, fending off my fist and then clouting me hard enough on the ear to sit me down.

'Now, now, young sir; we could use a handy boy like you, one with connections to such a venerable business as the Trow,' and grinning he offered me the very hand that had felled me, this time in friendship.

'Edward Drummond at your service, though the gang call me Teach, after my father's profession. It is normally me that hands out the lessons, but I have learnt a bit from you today young master, and no mistake.'

He was a year younger than me but already taller and broader, with a fine head of black curls, and an engaging grin.

'What should I call you – I have heard you named Small Beer but I reckon that does not please you very much?' he asked.

'They call me John, born in the Trow and lived here every second of my life so far,' I replied.

'I can see you are much more than small beer, so the boys will call you Porter, if that suits you John; for I can see you are a stronger brew altogether. Let me introduce the rest of the gang.'

At this, from corners and shadows, from behind piles of lumber and slate, appeared the rest of that ragtag crew.

'This is Butch – his old man works in the Shambles. This one's Fuller – his folks work with cloth in the Temple and he can whiff a bit sometimes, but none at all his fault.

Crusty, his Dad's a baker; Crane – his family have worked the dock crane for generations, and least of all Spadger, who hops over the Cathedral wall at the drop of the hat, when he is not required to be singing like a linnet. There are others, but some boys have to work, you know! Lads, this here is Porter and if you don't like him joining then I will learn you where to find your teeth! A man can get thirsty speechifying, so why don't you fetch us all some small beer, Porter, so we can seal our pact?'

Not quite knowing why, I complied with this suggestion, finding a half jug and bringing it to that mismatched gang of boys. They were trying to look brigand-frightening in their handed down clothes and torn chorister's britches, all wanting to look worse than they were, hiding their brave and true characters behind scowls that might suit the worst of vagabonds.

'Here's to me babber Porter; why, what with Butch, Crusty and Porter, we shall feast like kings and not one farthing spent! Let us talk of devilish deeds, of gold and treasure seized upon the Main, of galleons and top gallants, of trophies, broken treaties and revenge. But first, and most importantly: how do we go about recruiting a young purveyor of baccy?'

So it was that I met the boy called Teach, who later became a legend, for all the wrong reasons.

*

Each day the gang, with or without a few of its members, would include the Trow in its round of the city, cooling its feet, and wetting its throats with a jug of what had already been left, could be spared or would never be missed. Whether Simon the landlord knew of this, or minded, is not clear to me now. He may have recalled similar deeds from his own youth, or thought it a small price to pay for preventing a multitude of minor offences by the gang, or others. With us being around, there was no need for him to worry about other youngsters causing trouble, and even the sneakier criminals, tricksters, cut-purses and lifters of other people's goods, were less prevalent than before. The boys, the "Quarterdeckers" as they became known, had a fearsome reputation and certainly their appearance would put off most uninvited attention.

For the most part this was camouflage and bluff, like a cat doubling its size by setting its hair on end, deterring any who did not know that this muscle-bound beast was mostly soft fur. Oh, we could fight if we needed to, and we were never bested, but few people were ever unwise enough to offer us the challenge.

Butch was tall, broad and barrel-shaped, with arms and legs twice as thick as Spadger's, having helped his father for some years by carrying carcasses and hewing them with cleavers, but he was a gentle and simple soul, to belie his appearance. Crusty was smaller and rotund, fed on endless bread, and a fair amount of cake; he wasn't as fast, but he was formidably solid.

Spadger was a tall chorister with an Adam's apple which looked like no chewing had occurred, and which spelled the end of his career in the choir, his voice haphazardly on the edge of breaking, first up in the rafters then down in the cellar. He was gangly and lightning fast with a slap to the ear, which was his trick for keeping ahead of the younger boys whose voices were still sweet. Crane was muscled and always alert; Jasper in his broad-banded smock was even quicker to sting than Spadger, though he was often absent due to helping at his father's mill to the south of the river. Various smaller and grimy understudies were able to stamp on toes, kick shins and bite hands when needed.

Above this hierarchy of bruising rivalry was our captain Teach, who could scowl peace into most antagonists, failing that a growl often succeeded, and only the truly belligerent would hold on to find out if the threatened attack was as bad in reality. It was.

Teach held us together through firm leadership, the occasional glower rather than cuff, and provided for our wants, mostly by placing a tax on our members, a loaf here, a jug there. When a boy needed a helping hand or a kindly ear, then it was privately provided, without letting his bluff and scary appearance drop in public. He was our lion, our mascot, our schoolmaster.

*

I was educated by three teachers: my mother taught me to read passages from the Bible in the mornings, between laying the fires and serving breakfasts; Simon taught me figuring so I could keep tally of deliveries and of drinks I dispensed, which allowed me to know what would not be missed; and I was taught the ways of the world by Teach, on the streets of Bristol. All of these lessons I greatly valued, and I would not be the man I am today without them, but the greatest of these teachers was the last.

Being with the Quarterdeckers showed me the invaluable support of true friends, how to stand up for what was right, and how to assess strangers quickly and fairly. Teach thought ill of no man until he had demonstrated himself unworthy of that trust, even though most people marked Teach down as a rogue on first sight. He would become a friend for life in seconds, until he was betrayed and then he would become a perpetual enemy. He would forgive innocent slights but punish any spiteful act with his fists, or worse with banishment from his trust, and exile from the gang. To see the look of sorrowful anger upon his face when his trust had been broken, was truly terrible: you knew that cutting the ties of friendship cost him dear, but he left himself no option to forgive whilst he remained the leader of the gang.

One incident illustrates this beyond all others. There was a beggar in the port known as Umble Jack, who plied his trade in such a quiet way that few ever knew he was begging at all. He inhabited a pile of rags that had once been naval clothes, inside a barrel at the end of the Backs, where trade was not so urgent as to have him moved on. He had lost more limbs than he could spare in the service of the King, and he could only displace himself from his hovel by a few yards, and that with ponderous difficulty. Somehow Jack maintained a humble dignity, repose and respectable aspect. Teach had of course got to know Jack in our tours of the docks and had spent a lot of time talking to the old man about the sea, the navy, half-dreamt of foreign lands, and all the perils of warships, pirates and unsympathetic captains. I say he was old, in truth he had become this wreck of a man whilst under thirty years of age, and was still shy of forty, and unlikely to reach it. Teach took pity upon him and provided him with a regular portion of our harvest of provisions, not as charity but as 'Payment for an education in all things oceanic,' as he said.

One day, at his perch outside his tun, Jack was espied by a former shipmate who had risen to lieutenant, a rare thing when most posts are bought by the gentry for their spare sons. This man was shocked to see the state of Jack, and astonished at his humble pride. He could not stay long, as he was hurrying to an official meeting, but he gave Jack his purse, containing more than a guinea, promising to return later.

Jack, who rarely had more than a penny to his name, did not know what to do with the glittering coins, and indeed most of those who supplied his needs could hardly make change from such wealth. As he sat staring at the flashing disks in his hands, one member of the Quarterdeckers, Curry the stable lad, happened past. He too was fascinated by the shiny objects but not at a loss in how to use them. Quick as a whip, he grabbed the coins and strolled away laughing at Jack's foolishness. There were no witnesses to this crime, it having taken place at the quieter end of the Backs.

Later, Teach stopped by for his regular chat with Jack, bringing him bread, ham and beer supplied by his quartermasters. He saw that Jack was holding an empty purse, bereft not at the loss of the money so much as the waste of his friend's gift and the betrayal by Curry. On enquiring how Jack had come by this purse, Teach rapidly discovered the wrong that had been done and dashed off to right it. He first went to the Haymarket, Curry's place of work, only to find the villain had spent the day enjoying his new fortune by losing at pitch-and-pay, pell mell, box and dice and cards, getting riotously drunk and even trying to engage one of the market harlots.

When Teach found him, Curry was at the Horsefair and laughing in his drunkenness, but when he saw the look on Teach's face, he ran as fast as his legs could carry him after such indulgence. Teach pursued him at a leisurely pace, thinking the punishment more fitting that way, letting Curry's conscience cause him more harm than any punch or kick was likely to do. The villain ran to the Key, then along and up Christmas Steps, across to Brandon Hill. He finally collapsed near the cathedral, bedraggled, soiled from his own fear and guilt, quivering for what he feared Teach would do to him. Teach stood over Curry, looked hard at this sorrowful figure, and just held out his hand for the little money that had not been squandered.

'Give me what's left and let me never see your carcass again, you mangy fly-bitten nag, not fit for making glue,' he demanded.

Taking the last five shillings that had not been spent, Teach strode off without a backward look, having cut Curry from his life forever, even though they had been as nearly brothers as if they had fed from the same breast.

Teach hurried back to Umble Jack and awaited the return of the naval gent, who came back before nightfall. Teach explained to him that Jack had little use for largesse and in truth it would bring him more harm than good, but suggested that an account should be opened for him with various tradesmen, paid in advance, that would see to his needs. Despite Teach being a third of his age, the lieutenant understood the wisdom of this arrangement. From then on, various pedlars and sellers from baskets would stop at the barrel to provide Jack with all he could use, even an occasional shave or a nearly new coat or blanket each winter. Teach acted as trustee to ensure Jack was never again done badly by. As for Curry, he could not stay in a city where Teach had cursed his name, so he soon left as cabin boy on a ship bound for the Americas, never to be seen on Bristol's streets again. Umble Jack has carried on for many years, long after his protector and patron had been lost to legend, happily telling any who would listen that he lived in luxury thanks to the greatest of pirates.

*

The Trow was a bustling hive, the newest inn of the port, in a row of five gabled houses between a gunsmith and a tobacconist. It had a kitchen serving food at any time, to match the pattern of the tides and the demands of sailors, porters, carters and merchants. It was built soon after the return of the King, and the consequent removal of rules prohibiting most of what it provided. It was new, well run and better sited than either the Hatchet or the Shakespeare, which are somewhat older. It offered day round food, and of course drink, a place to do business or shelter from the elements, a bed for the night or a base from which to mount an expedition to Wales, or to the ends of the Earth.

Within these walls collided the three divisions of men who made Bristol thrive: the sailors, the merchants and the lowly people who serviced their needs. The merchants grew fat on trade, bought fine houses away from the stench of the docks and rode high until their ventures sank in some distant ocean. The sailors fought the sea, the weather, pestilence and the Spanish, French or Dutch, depending on the political season. The stevedores and longshoremen hauled goods hither and thither, only conscious of the weight on their backs and the pennies it earned them. The Trow happily provided food, drink and a place to sleep to men wearing canvas or silk: their money was all the same to us.

On a typical day, we would be active before dawn laying fires, feeding the carters who brought produce to the port and our door, and the porters who loaded and unloaded the ships. If the tide was rising, merchants would arrive to await ships that had been sighted at Pill, trying to strike deals before the merchandise was landed or inspected. If the tide was turning, sailors would grab their last meal ashore before casting off and riding the tide down to the Channel. Betwixt times, we had merchants celebrating a good deal, or commiserating a bad one, hiring for the next venture, or trying to cover the losses of the last. These men had run the city since Good King Harry, becoming aldermen and mayors, leaving fortunes to praise their worthiness throughout posterity in the many almshouses of the city. They had risen when the grip of the priories was broken by the first Cromwell and now they wielded all power in the city that was not enforced by the Crown, after the death of the second.

There were rooms set aside for the merchants, with coffee available as well as port, sherry and brandy. The bustle of porters and sailors were excluded from that rarefied world, but only by wooden partitions. Deals would be struck that amounted to the earnings of many lifetimes for the porters, feet from where they agonised over a farthing for a tankard of ale.

We didn't have many foreigners drinking our beer, the merchants kept a tight hold on trade and only wanted their own crews to bring back the spoils from other lands, thus multiplying their gains, from selling our cloth, coal and lead abroad. So it seemed to me that all the wide world must look and talk like Bristolians, or our Welsh cousins.

As the merchants grew richer, we saw signs that the world's people did differ, but these were only token slaves kept in silks to belie the word slavery. They did not mix with us common folk, but were kept in their own gilded cages, and often died young from an ague that might not even confine one of us locals to bed.

Although the whole world was brought to our door, the world we knew by sight, rather than by reputation, had a tiny boundary. From the horse and hay markets on the road to Gloucester, to the marshes, from the Shakespeare and the Templars' church over to the hot springs below the cliffs, our kingdom could be crossed in under an hour, or much less at the pace the Quarterdeckers moved.

In the early years, we did not often wander beyond the city and into the fields of Somerset and Gloucestershire, all we knew and desired lay within the bowl of those hills, and the bounty they attracted by road and sea. Only on rare occasions had we gone outside the belt of our kingdom, to pick blackberries or to scrump apples, to find a hill pristine in its snowy robes, or by cadging a lift on an early cart to visit the distant villages of Westbury or Stapleton when it was too hot in the city, then lolling back across the fields and meadows.

*

One day we made a different venture, due to a chance conversation at the Trow. Slate Jones, captain of the Fair y Fenni had that week been delayed by bad weather and had missed his deal for the return leg. His boat carried slate and coal from South Wales every week and usually returned there with a cargo of cloth and coarser wines, but the delay had meant he had to sell to a market already sated and could not afford to buy goods for the return.

He drunkenly asserted, 'She will be bobbing like a cork without some ballast, and if the weather is bad again she will be in trouble. I would gladly carry anything on this jolly trip back, having only earned half pay for the month!'

Another captain, Jenkins by name, and known for being sharp with his money, chipped in, 'I have done well this time, and you can carry some of my load if you like, but for no fee or share of the profit mind, just to help out a fellow sailor in need?'

'Right you are, Islwyn, that will save my neck long enough for my wife to wring it! It will be a thin time until the next run, and I don't know how we will cope if I am late again!'

This left Slate with two headaches, one from the cider

and the other from not having earned enough to feed his family.

Teach overheard Slate bemoaning his bad luck, so he suggested, 'Captain Jones, would you carry us down the river a-ways in exchange for a shilling? My friends need some country air, and you could be of service to us?'

Slate readily agreed to the boy's suggestion. Thankfully the tides meant Slate was sober by the time we set off next morning. We boys, with all our chores done, brought our provisions of bread, roast pork, beer and cheese to the Backs in time to help shift Jenkins' cargo aboard the Fair y Fenni, before pushing off. We made way by a combination of oar, sail and the falling tide.

Within half an hour we had gone beyond the cathedral, then turned the corner at the hot well; we were soon moving past the great cliff of St Vincent's rock, topped with woods and fields full of grazing sheep, and on the other side of the sinuous brown river were the forests and quarries of Abbots Leigh. The wind was with us as we turned the corner towards the gorge and the boat fair bolted along before it, only half laden as it was.

At Pill, we managed to pull into the harbour from where the pilots joined the largest vessels to navigate them upstream, and there we took our leave of Slate Jones. We made a meal from some of our provisions, then took to our feet to return across country. We turned inland following the course of the stream that flows into the Avon at Pill, then bore south along the ridge on a cart road across the fields that feed Bristol. There were large woodlands on either side, fishponds concealed within them from when the monks were in control around the city. All that remained of the monks were the fish and some names, Abbots Leigh, Whitefriars and so on. Now the forest held an odd folk who coppiced trees to make hurdles and wattle, or burned the wood to make charcoal. The air was filled with the hanging smoke from hundreds of those slow fires, the owners rarely seen, and secretive in their habitual ashen blackness.

After an hour, we reached the part of the woods facing St Vincent's rock, and turned from the road to reach the cliff edge. There we ate the rest of our vittles as we overlooked the river which lay hundreds of feet below. The tide was nearing its lowest ebb and all but the smallest of boats had departed. There we found the remnants of some ancient fort, so we naturally fell to a game of King of the Castle. Teach played the game in good spirits, both becoming King and being deposed, knowing his standing with the rest of us was never in doubt and indeed it was enhanced by that modesty.

Afterwards, we descended a narrow wooded valley to the tow path, which we followed along the Avon, turning east across the meadows of Somerset whilst keeping clear of the marshes, until we hit the road from Wells. We directed our weary feet north again towards the city walls, past St Mary's with its cut-off spire and in through the Redcliffe gate. Once on home ground, we sped up, jostling along the bridge, lined with fine houses on both sides and almost no sky visible overhead where they stepped out to meet each other. We reached the Backs, and were then home at the Trow, great adventurers all.

*

After that first time, we often repeated our little journey by water, stopping at Pill or Sea Mills with its ancient harbour reputedly built by Caesar to chase the grandfathers of Slate Jones into the fastnesses of Wales. We would take hunks of nearly fresh bread, rinds of cheese, ends of hams that were more bone than meat, all wrapped in a scrap of sail cloth and slung over our shoulders on a hempen cord, with a flask of something refreshing to aid the digestion.

Other towns use their woods to provide fuel and they have thinned the forests to within an inch of their leafy lives; at Bristol we have the use of coal from the rebellious miners of Kingswood and from the bowels of the green hills of Wales; we are warm and the trees remain to brood at the edges of the fields, and it is those woods that provided our playground.

When we walked up from Sea Mills, we pretended to be adventurers in the New World, the first English Men to set their feet in that unmapped forest, constantly alert to the hushed sounds of painted enemies hiding behind the trees. We played out the roles of Discoverers and wild Indians, chasing and hunting between the great trunks, skirting the bright openings where some mighty oak had fallen, coming in surprise across a track or cottage, stalking the footprints that we found. When we tired of this game, we would wolf down our provisions, perhaps sleep for an hour or two on the dry leaves if the weather was warm enough, then followed Teach as he led us unerringly back to either the Clifton Road or the Aust Road. Both of these cross that great common, known as the Downs, where all may graze their sheep and kine.

When we came upon the Clifton Road, we crossed near the top of St Vincent's rock and saw the start of the fine houses being built thereabouts for the richest merchants who desired to be away from the bustle and smell of the docks, despite it being the source of their wealth. If instead we came by the Aust Road, we would pass the remains of the Royal Fort upon the hill, then the gallows and gibbet that stood to warn of terrible justice awaiting any who should steal from the city, then down the steep hill to St Michael's and the two long runs of Christmas steps to the

Frome bridge and the city walls.

When we made such trips in the autumn, we would return with pockets and bellies full of the forage that we had found, with blackberry stained hands, arms grazed by brambles, our jerkins stuffed with cobnuts in bunches and chestnuts liberated from the urchin-like shells. We might have taken from the orchards any fruit that had happen to fall, but we were always wary of being seen to encourage that fruit to drop before its time: theft from the branches could lead to us hanging from that dire tree upon the hill above the city. If God placed this manna in our path on our desert journey, we were destined to take it and to give thanks, though not before we were out of sight of the farmer.

We would make such journeys three or four times in a year, and fill our hours in between with our recollections of battles fought, maidens rescued, and treasures won, or in planning for the next jaunt.

Our days turned thus: the boys who had lessons or chores attended to them diligently for the morning, then they escaped from their parents' or teachers' notice and joined their fellows at whatever corner served that day as our guild house. Often this was a quiet corner of the Trow, but when too many boats were riding at anchor there would be no safe place for me and I would need to escape my duties, so then we moved our court to the hay loft, barrel store or wherever else we could be boys, undisturbed, and unheeded.

After assembling, we exchanged any tidbits of intelligence on comings and goings, of captains sighted entering or leaving the harbour, or leaving another man's harbour as matins rang out, when the master of the house was away. We noted where we might gather fine provisions overlooked by their owners, or where our appearance might earn us a clipped ear, or worse. Teach would lay out our course through the streets, guiding us around the shallows and reefs, into good channels where we might fill our holds with prime cargo, being unafraid of both piracy and taxation. We would then set sail, trusting in our pilot, and reap the true rewards of the urban venturer.

There was never any malice, nor true theft: we mostly asked for what was taken and were never wisely refused. What was lifted unbidden was surplus to requirements or readily spared. We did not keep this bounty, we gave most of what we gathered to those who could not sail those dangerous waters for themselves, like Umble Jack, orphans, or widows awaiting the return of their drowned men. We may not have been blessed by all, but the blessings outweighed the curses as a tun does a firkin. For some of the boys, their absence was welcomed by their parents and keepers, for they were growing and riotous. Some boys were missed, and others punished for chores undone. Yet the rewards of adventure and friendship trumped the burden of duty, and the rumours of the kindnesses we performed softened the blows dealt to us in punishment for our laxity.

By day or night, sunshine, rain or ice, the bustle went on and the merchants grew richer, and more grand.

*

It was around this time that we first met a new friend. One of my chores, when trade was light, was to help my mother wash the sheets and cloths of the Trow. She would boil them all up with good Bristol soap, as approved by Queen Bess herself, made from olive oil from sunny climes and caustic ashes, and then carry them all to dry on the racks of Brandon Hill. As these were fine cloths, or at least finer than most could afford, we daren't leave them under their own cognisance, so I acted as shepherd to this fluttering flock of linen and wool upon the side of the hill. I was left with a fist of bread and a flask, and frittered away my day by dreaming that the flapping sheets above my head were the sails of a ship bound for Bordeaux or Bermuda, laughing at the puny waves and relishing the tempest.

I would exchange friendly words with others who came to peg out their own greyer flocks, women whom I saw every week, or the lads who helped them. Boys might run around between the walls of cloth, sticks in hand, fighting the Spanish or the French, or lie back watching clouds drift between the flapping sheets, a sweet grass stalk to each mouth.

It was whilst following this trackless pursuit, and dutifully ensuring my flock did not take flight one way or another, that I first met Woody. His father had just moved the family from Poole to the great harbour of Bristol, wanting to be captain and owner of larger and richer ships. Their maid had come out with the washing and young Woody had been sent along to keep out from under his mother's feet while she put their new house in order. His father was bargaining to find a ship to share and sail in, making himself known to all the agents and merchants. Woody's younger brother Charles was less of a handful and had been left to play with his top and whip at home.

Although this boy was dressed more finely than myself, I could detect the same spark of jest and mischief in his eye. Soon we were chasing around between his sheets and mine, boarding ships, calling down blazes upon each other and damning each other's eyes, like the finest of buccaneers. When, at last, we were both winded, we collapsed on the ground beneath our flapping charges.

‘My father is the great Captain Rogers, and I am his son Woodes. Who has been acting pirate with me this fine morning?’ he enquired.

‘John – call me Porter, my mother is maid at the Trow, the greatest of all inns,’ I proudly replied.

‘Tell me Porter, what do you find for fun, apart from playing pirate around the washing?’

So I told him of my adventures with the Quarterdeckers, and his eyes shone when I spoke of our trips down the river and through the forests, all the while sharing with him my scant provisions of bread and beer. I told him how the captain of us all, our guide and teacher, was the inimitable Teach.

‘I would dearly like to meet your Captain Teach; he sounds like a fine fellow.’

I vouchsafed that there was not another like him in the city, nor probably in all Christendom, and I still believe that to this day.

Later, we folded and stowed my sails and carried them back together to the Trow. I pointed out the grander buildings, he commented on the rig of the ships. When we arrived, we found the ‘Deckers thirstily waiting, having lapped the docks several times already. I made my introduction to Teach. He and Woody eyed each other and saw what a pair of likely rogues they were, both a cut above the harbour rats, with the ambition and drive to make much more of themselves. They clasped hands and smiled broadly, and their pact was sealed.

‘Lads, this here is Woody, son of a great captain harboured in this city, and a welcome addition to our crew, if he will but sail with us,’ Teach announced to the gang, and they readily cried their approval of this suggestion.

Woody knew far more about sailing and ships; he had been out to sea with his father, rather than just along the Avon, and Teach would defer to him in all things naval. Teach was a natural leader of men, having the charm and energy that calls upon others to follow, he could drive and cajole, or flash a look that threatened force, without often using it; but mostly we followed him because wherever he led we were bound to find adventure.

Woody soon became Teach's lieutenant, and our pilot whenever we travelled by water.

*

Woody and Teach were a strong team, taller than the rest of us, quick to assess a situation, but slow to judge people badly. They found adventure around the port, as often as not they did someone a good turn as they circumnavigated that world.

One evening, the 'Deckers were prowling around the Marsh, watching merchants and courting couples promenading along the avenues of trees, observing games being played at the bowling green, and generally enjoying the serenity of inaction that came at high water in the evening, when all boats are ready to depart but await the tide and wind to do so.

One young man was endeavouring to impress his girl, wearing his finest wig and hose, the brightest buckles and the gaudiest blue silk half-coat, when a bilge rat of our acquaintance, called Dipper, happened to jostle them, knocking the girl's parasol to the ground. In profusely apologising, he pushed the article into the man's hands and turned away towards the Key. Teach saw this and immediately pulled us into a huddle.

He said, 'Dipper has just taken that young man's purse; if we catch him quickly I reckon we can share a fine meal from another man's dishonest labour, and be counted heroes into the bargain. Woody, you take the youngsters and stroll a tail on him. Porter, Crusty and myself will await you at Swan Lane; Woody, make sure you drive the sheep towards his shearing.'

All understanding our roles, we went about our mission in silence.

We cut up Marsh Street, through the gate and onto Swan Lane where we merged with the shadows at the water end. Behind us we heard the young gent exclaim that he had been robbed and the cries of distress from his fair lady. We had not been in place more than two minutes when we heard running on the cobbles to our left. Dipper charged around the corner only to find Teach's leg left untidily in his way. Dipper went sprawling into the mud of the lane at our feet, sliding a fathom or more before coming to a halt.

'Where are you bound to in such a hurry, young master? Has your Mam got your supper ready, or are you late for evensong? Or is it that you have a hot pie about your person and you need to take it somewhere to let it cool off? Perhaps we should take a look for a pie, lads?' Teach enquired genteelly.

'Ize not 'fraid view, Teach, your just pissen wind, I dun nuffin and got nuffin t'say,' replied the muddy Dipper.

'Now Master Dipper, for a boat stuck in the mud you are putting on a lot of sail, and some might say you need to trim your rig before your hit the rocks, or the other way about.'

'Youz just a bluffer Teach. Ize under the wing of Masher and you daren't touch I.'

'It so happens that I am no more concerned by Masher

than you are about being descended from a rat. Now hand over that pie before it burns you.'

'Wadya mean pie. Ive no pie, neever wud I give you un.'

By this time, Woody and the younger boys had gathered at the end of the lane, cutting off any hope of escape for Dipper towards the Key.

'My apologies, Master Dipper, I must have been mistaken. Let me give you a hand up so you can be on your way to church,' offered Teach.

Teach bent over and clasped the rascal's hand, placing his boot upon Dipper's foot, holding it hard against the ground, and then firmly pulled upon his arm.

Dipper squealed, 'Youz breakin me foot, less I go!'

'Master Dipper, I am doing you no harm, in the same way you did not lift a purse from a gent not five minutes ago in the Marsh. Of course if you did find yourself to be carrying that particular hot pie then I would gladly relieve you both of it and any discomfort you may be feeling in your ankle.'

'Yurtiz, damn you. Masherz gonna hear of this – you don't steal from a lifter and walk free.'

'Master Dipper, I do so hope that we won't have to call you Master Limper from now on. Please pass my regards to Mr Masher, and make sure that you steer clear of the Marsh, if you have any ambition to dance at the May fair again.'

Dipper rose unsteadily to his feet and hobbled away, smeared with mud, snot and worse. He turned at the end of the lane to shout 'Youz nuffink burra gurt bully, jeswait for Masher to fillet you.'

He then moved off as fast as he could when Teach took a step towards him, and he was chased away by the sound of the 'Deckers laughter.

'That is a fine looking purse filled to bursting. What do you intend to do now, Teach?' asked Woody.

'Follow me and you shall see,' replied our captain.

We trailed behind him to the corner of the Marsh, near King Street, and there we found the young couple much deflated, he all fury, she all desperation. Teach walked up to them and appeared to enquire what pained him. The gent used wild gestures and invective to damn the citizens of the Bristol for their dishonesty and thievery, before he was stopped by Teach holding up his hand, producing in the other the purse and enquiring if, perchance, the young man recognised it. The man gasped and seized it from his hands, opened it and hungrily assessed the contents, then whooped and clasped Teach to his chest before swinging him around. The girl kissed Teach on the cheek, before blushing prettily, and then hugged her beau with both arms. Before Teach could leave this happy scene, the young man opened his purse once more and extracted several gleaming coins which he forced into Teach's reluctant hands.

Teach came back to us where we were lurking at the corner.

'Here, my hearties, is the bounty of honesty. We have two whole guineas, whereas that worm Dipper has nothing but a muddy hide and a limp. Now we can tour the harbour like kings.'

He rewarded us all for our help in this adventure by paying for two ferrymen to row us full round the docks, from the Frome bridge to the King's Marsh, each one of us with a pie in hand and a jug to pass around, with all those on the quayside applauding us in our pomp and celebration. We still had enough left to pay for several more days of jollity, and for Umble Jack to remember us in his prayers.

*

Subsequently I learnt that the couple at the centre of this affair were not the unworthy Lords that they had seemed. The lad was Tom Jackson, who had only recently prospered by the death of a wealthy uncle, until then he had been a poor apprentice cobbler. The girl was Sarah Woodcot, daughter of the widow weaver who lived next door to Tom's master's shop. That purse, and the clothes they wore that day, represented their entire fortune, and the money was their stake to buy a house and business of their own. Without it they would have been out on the street within the week. By Teach's actions, they had learnt a valuable lesson in humility, and gained a second chance. Dipper and Masher would have caroused that fortune away and cursed the two lovers to a life of struggle and dirt, lower than any of our own. Teach must have known or suspected this: he knew everyone around the harbour and much of what happened in the city.

As for Masher, he continued to loom in the shadows without taking revenge. He may not have believed Dipper's tale of lifting a lifetime's fortune in a single purse, or he may have relished the way in which Teach had taught the weasel a lesson. No doubt it might have been stored away on a tally of grievances, to be settled at a moment of his choosing, but that day never came as Masher was soon dropped out of this world on the end of a rope for a minor act of thievery, closing a hempen loop on his nineteen years of life.

2:The Moat

The 'Deckers would often walk through the new quarter that had sprung up within the castle precinct in the thirty years since Cromwell tore down the walls; the only significant new building for a hundred years since the merchants gained control of the city. This new area was densely populated, chaotic, with the moat bounding it on two sides and the docks on a third, only the western side was open to the city. All kinds of crafts had sprung up there to provide goods for trade, or to service the needs of citizens and sailors. All that remained of the once great castle, which had held out against armies under siege for many months, was the moat, a section of wall along it and its name borne by the new streets. We found this new warren ripe with adventure, as such tightly packed areas often are.

One day, we were wandering around the meal market towards St Peter's when we heard a muffled whining and scratching. We searched for the sound and discovered the source to be beneath a grill set into the ground, made of old corroded iron. When we tried to pull this grill up we received a yap in reply. We could not hope to move the grill nor break through it and it did not seem to belong to any extant building. A dog must have fallen into the moat, which is fed by the Frome and hence is moving water, albeit also an open sewer, and been swept along unable to escape until it reached the bottom of the concealed steps below the grill. Now trapped, cold and fearful, it was weakening fast.

'There is nothing for it but to follow the same route in and rescue the poor mutt. Who's up for a paddle in the moat?' asked Teach.

'Blige Teach, I bissen gerrin in thur, its as cawd as a

snowman's arse and a sight too smelly for swemmen' said Crusty, and several others readily stepped back to avoid volunteering.

'I will take it on, Teach' said Woody, 'just hold my coat and show me the way.'

'Good man, Woody; never afeared of shit nor shiver!' Teach replied.

So we went out of the former castle grounds by the Newgate and headed along the Weare looking for an access to the water, but found none to our liking. In the end we decided to make use of the old ducking stool to lower our volunteer into the moat. Woody stripped down to his shirt, removing coat, waistcoat, shoes, stockings and britches and was then lowered into the moat with a gasp, wisely keeping his head as high from the water as he could. He executed a side stroke back towards the gate seeking the lower end of the steps on the far side of the moat, then disappeared from view.

After a few minutes Woody could be seen again holding a very sorry parcel of dirty fur. He shouted across to us, 'I cannot swim with the dog and it is too far gone to swim on its own; what shall I do?'. Teach thrust Woody's clothes into my arms and sprinted back through the gate, to appear again soon after at the window of a new house backing onto the moat from Tower Street. He had grabbed a basket on his way through the house and was using his own coat as a rope to lower it down to Woody, who then gratefully placed the dog in the basket before swimming back to us.

When Woody reached us we fished him out, trying not to get too close to the filth that stuck to him. He discreetly removed his shirt, and put on his remaining dry clothes, with a wall of 'Deckers hiding him from public view. We then strolled back through the gate, thinking ourselves to be mighty heroes and wondering what had become of Teach. We found him at the front door of the house whose window he had used. Beside him were a mother and daughter, who was holding the bedraggled but much relieved dog.

'Ahoy mates, let me introduce Mistress Cleary and her daughter the fair Hannah, and their prodigal companion Charlie. By chance I chose the very house from whence he came, and possibly used the same window from which he fell into the moat. These are the Quarterdeckers, dark in name and fame within this fair city, but mostly pretty of face! And this is Woody, who ventured forth to Charlie's rescue.'

'I am wordless in admiration of your deed, kind sir' said Mistress Cleary, though she was also lost for words due to the odour coming from the dog and Woody. Miss Hannah was less effective with her words, but very admiring in her glances, Woody's bare chest being clearly visible within his coat.

'Won't you all come into our house so we can reward you with some refreshment after your labours?'

To a mixed chorus of 'it was nothing really,' 'Thankee kindly' and 'reckon cannava nuvver brekfuss', we trooped inside.

*

Mistress Cleary's house became a regular port of call for the 'Deckers, and more so for Teach and Woody. There was always a bun or a slice of bread to hand, Charlie was ready to leap upon the laps of his rescuers, and Miss Hannah blushed charmingly to our captains, and was ever polite to the crew.

Over the next couple of years our numbers began to shrink: Spadger's voice finally broke and thus he was no longer of use to the cathedral choir and returned to his father's farm in the Mendips; Jasper and Crusty were needed in full-time work; Butch and Fuller were apprenticed and bound that way for seven years until they could be masters of their trades; and I was needed more and more at the Trow. Woody was learning navigation from his father, when he was ashore, and Teach was to be found in the library when he was not being captain to our crew around the town. His father wished him to follow in the schooling trade, which Teach made a show of doing whilst being determined to be more than just a schoolmaster.

For much of the time, Teach and Woody still roamed the port, keeping up acquaintances, checking that all was well with those they had aided, hearing more from every ship that came in that fired their blood for the sea. They still called by the Trow, and when I needed to avoid Simon's eye, we retired to the cellar which was convenient for both its seclusion and its contents. Bristol, being an old town that had seen feet before the Romans came, is full of old tunnels and cellars of buildings long fallen and forgotten. Even as close to the Marsh as we were at the Trow, there are fine cellars that run across the burrows of years gone by. For Simon this meant a large and free storage space, extending under the street and neighbouring houses unannounced; for us it was a ready source of adventure should we need it. On one occasion we found that only a thin partition separated us from the basement of the adjoining tobacconist, and with only a little persuasion we were able to remove a brick at the base and managed to extract a small amount of tobacco from a bale stored on the other side. Having covered our tracks, using some handy mouse droppings to explain the chewed corner of the bale, we happily repaired to the Marsh to try out Teach's new clay pipe, to the accompaniment of much coughing, spluttering and tears of laughter.

Another time, we found in the darkest, dankest recess of the cellar, where the brickwork dated back to the days of the monasteries, a rotten wooden panel. With the application of Woody's knife we were able to cut this loose and look beyond. What we found was another cellar with arched brick vaulting, stacked with barrels, which must have belonged to the White Hart, the inn opposite the Trow that competed for the attention of the Welsh sailors. As the hole was too small to take a barrel through, and the landlord of that establishment was renowned for having a violent temper, we replaced the board and consigned its memory for future mischief making.

*

Around this time I lost my mother, who was at the time some thirty-five years of age. She had been born just before the Great Plague, which killed her father, and she had spent much of her life working at the Trow. She had been caught in the rain coming back from Brandon Hill with the laundry, had developed a fever and taken to her bed in the eaves of the inn. Within the week she had gone beyond knowing any who spoke to her, and then she was dead. Simon paid for a decent burial at St Michael's; he said she would enjoy the view from up there. I was sixteen and orphaned, with no estate and precious little to my name apart from my mother's Bible and the clothes that I wore.

Seeing that I was cast adrift on the sea of life, Simon, Captain Hawkins, took me under his wing. 'You are a likely lad, John, and handy about the place. I know it is hard, I lost both my parents to the Plague and I know full well that you need an anchor right now. So I propose that I adopt you as my second son, brother to Roger who has been away on the briny these dozen years. How would that suit you, Boyo?'

It suited me just fine: I moved into the room set aside for Roger rather than staying in my cot in the eaves; I dressed more smartly, washed more often and learned all of the Trow's business as if it was my own concern. My friends Teach and Woody were now welcome upstairs, not just in the yard and cellar, and they spent much time pumping Simon for tales of the sea, even though he had only plied the same routes as Slate Jones and his brother Welsh captains.

Our lives span on: Teach was now helping his father at the Grammar School, setting young boys' feet on the path to a righteous mercantile future; Woody was learning navigation and business at his father's elbow, and I was apprentice publican in all but indenture. Woody was walking out with Miss Hannah, but always with Teach as companion and chaperone, which satisfied Mistress Cleary's concerns. No one would seek to harm Hannah in Teach's presence, tall, dark and glowering as he was. Other gangs of youngsters took over where the 'Deckers had left off, but Teach kept them on the right side of the gallows with fatherly advice and a well-timed slap or two. We felt ourselves to be men in waiting, though what we were waiting for was as yet a mystery to us.

*

The arguments in favour of the slave trade I heard played out again and over again in the Trow, in the context of the immoral injustice of the London monopoly and how this restriction in trade impacted upon the merchant's rights as free men to profit from a legal trade, to the benefit of society as a whole. As for the slaves, they were timber, cattle, black gold, cargo, goods; like so many bales of tobacco. Simon allowed this form of argument to take place in the Trow as it was preferable to the fiery debates of religion, monarchy and political affiliation that had led to such strife and killing in his father's day, which could still easily erupt again.

Woody's father wanted advancement for his sons and decided that Woody needed to be on the sea before he could hope to become admiral of his own fleet, so he found him an apprenticeship with Captain Yeomans. The good captain ran with the Bristol fleet to Newfoundland, that land discovered by our adopted brother Cabot, where seas of fish threw themselves into our waiting boats, to make the city rich and fat. For months at a time, Woody was away off that distant coast, returning tanned and hardened. He would carry a strong odour of fish until he had been scraped, scrubbed and washed in Bristol's best soap, guaranteed to clean your skin, or to take it clean off.

Teach would visit Miss Hannah just as regularly when Woody was away, to stop her pining and worrying for her beau, with no other motivation than loyal friendship to both of them. The rhythm and routine of sailing to Newfoundland and returning again had settled into our bones by the time of Woody's fifth voyage. It was then that the fleet was caught in a terrible storm in mid-ocean, with boats losing masts, or sinking under great waves with the weight of all those fish eager to return to the sea in their salt barrels. The fleet was driven apart for days, and being knocked off course could not reassemble or find each other in those great grey wastes of water. When the expected day of return passed, no great surprise or shock was experienced as delays were common, often due to the bountifulness of the banks of cod, which might mean even heavier and slower boats than usual. But when the remnants of the fleet were first sighted off Pill, a messenger came galloping to the Key:

'The fleet is broken and lost, our boys have gone to Neptune,' he shouted, unleashing a panic and great dismay. The wives of the fleet all ran to the Key to seek news from those who returned; the owners anxiously awaited a tally of their vessels; the merchants wanted an account of the barrels of fish landed; the bankers sought their debts to be repaid.

Amid this mob awaiting solace, I could see Miss Hannah ashen with worry, by her side was Teach, all solid reassurance. When the first boats reached the harbour we could no more hear the news than we could hear a fly in a tempest: the mob was so dense and anxious, and rumour loud and rife. Teach brought Miss Hannah back to the family's room at the Trow and I fetched our best Bristol sherry to calm her, then I went where I knew I could gain intelligence of the fleet: the sailors' bar. Sure enough, not forty minutes after the first boat reached the Key, the ragged remnants of the crew of the Lady Susan came in.

'Giss I ginormous zider, me babber, for Ize bin drinkin brine aw dis month pass,' said the first, and having slaked his thirst, he doused it again to ensure it stayed slaked, then related what had happened:

They had fished together off the banks for a fortnight, cutting, gutting and salting down the fish into barrels for fourteen hours a day, the weather fine and the sea like a mirror. With no wind to turn towards home, they just kept on fishing, packing more and more into each barrel until even those kept for water were being emptied and used for more fish.

The wind at last picked up westerly and they broke for home, sailing low in the water but none the worse for it. Then the wind turned and became the mightiest gale he could remember or imagine, with every ship on its own wave, mountains and valleys of water greater than the hills of Wales, and the boats began to founder. Those captains who were wise, cut their sails, dumped their cargo back into the depths and put out sea anchors to keep the bows into the waves. Those too inexperienced, or greedy, delayed taking these measures, and were lost to the deep. When the wind eased they could only see one other boat within the horizon, and smashed pieces of wood covering the surface of the sea. They reset their rig and limped to the other vessel, then set course for home. By the time they reached the coast of Ireland they had gathered a cluster of five boats, but no other had been sighted, and he doubted that any were still in God's sweet air.

'Cappin Yeoman wuz a steady 'and, but Ize not seen 'ee for weeks, Gawd blessem; 'ee was a gudun.'

I conveyed this news to Miss Hannah and Teach upstairs and she shrieked in anguish with her hands clasped to her belly, and fainted clean away.

When she came back round on the settle, she cried in despair for some time before we could calm her at all: 'My darling Woody is gone and I am ruined and undone'. After some gentle enquiry she confessed:

'I am carrying his child, and my reputation will be ruined: no good man would ever have me now.'

'I would, Miss Hannah, with all my heart,' said Teach.

'You cannot mean it, dear Edward, you surely would not take another man's bastard child and its tarnished mother?'

'Indeed I would, more eagerly than a ship with a following wind takes to the sea, or a drunken Welshman to song.'

So this plan was settled upon and proposed to Mistress Cleary in the presence of Simon and his wife Jane, then announced to Teach's father with no mention of Woody's contribution to the affair. All were happy and agreeable, though some were deceived, and plans were laid for this event to be formalised the following fortnight.

Those two weeks went by rapidly, with the preparations being made for the wedding. On the Saturday we repaired to the church of St Nicholas, where there were only a small number of us: myself, Simon and Jane, Teach and his parents, Mistress Cleary, the 'Deckers and the priest. Miss Hannah, now Mistress Drummond, was both happy and sad at the same time, smiles covering an inner sorrow. Teach was all attention to his new wife. We returned to the Trow where Simon laid out quite a feast, although it was just the same fare we served up to the better paying customers: bread, wine and spit roasted pork; the spit dog had been running all morning to turn it. We soon needed to return to our duties at the inn, so Teach and Hannah went to her mother's house where a modest dowry chest had been delivered by sled earlier that day. Teach, of course, needed to make a show of taking Hannah to be his wife, to allay any suspicion on the issue that was anticipated but unannounced. I do truly believe that he respected and dearly loved Hannah, and she too thought much of him, even though she had chosen to give her heart and body to his friend, avoiding Teach's guardian watchfulness, and hence causing the problem of whose fruition we dared not speak.

*

It was on the fifth day of their marriage, when Teach and Hannah were walking across the Frome bridge towards her mother's house, hand in hand and reconciled to their destinies, that the cry was heard 'The fleet is back from the dead'.

The crowd around the Key formed so suddenly that none of us could get near to the rider who had brought this news, and so guesswork and rumour again took the place of fact. Two hours later, through the mist that lay upon the river, we could first discern shadows approaching upon the rising tide. At the head of this line of ghosts was a ship with a high prow, and at the bowsprit stood a figure we knew well: it was Woody. As they came to the Key, we could hear his voice call out 'Three cheers, for the greatest man in Bristol – Captain Yeoman'. And what was lost in the weak voices of the crews was made up for by the massed crowd along the Key, raising their voices in hope and surprise to that great man of the sea. Again there was no way to reach the ships, so Teach and Hannah continued to Mistress Cleary's as a likely port of call for Woody, and I ran back to the Trow.

A few minutes later, Woody strode in, tanned and crack-lipped but full of vim.

'Ahoy, Porter, is there any ale for a mariner in need?' he asked.

I gave him a flagon of our better beer and then inquired what had happened to this prodigal fleet.

'You heard that there was quite a blow when we were returning from the Banks?'.

I replied that we had the story from the five boats which we thought were all that remained of the Newfoundland fleet.

'Thank God some others got back, we were afraid that we had lost twelve but now it seems it was only seven,' and he continued to lay out the tale.

As the wind blew up, the Captain had ordered the lines

to be cut and the sails to be drawn in as fast as could be; he had seen bad weather more times than most men have seen the altar at church. They put out a sea anchor to drag the boat straight and heaved half of the cargo over the side, using the rest more for ballast than in hope of a profit: better half a load arrives back in Bristol than a full boat lies at the bottom of the sea. They called to the others to do the same, some heard, some acted of their own accord, but others were guided by greed rather than wisdom and tried to outrun the storm. He saw boats with snapped masts, rigging in the water dragging them broadside on to the waves, then being rolled, turned over and gone, nothing but empty, angry sea remaining of them. Soon the wind and waves drove them apart and they lost sight of each other. All that day, the mountains of water toyed with them, ready to drown them in a moment, then that night there was nothing but the violent movements of the boat and the fear of being engulfed by an invisible black hand and dragged to the base of the ocean.

On the second day, the clouds parted, the wind dropped to a kitten breeze and the sea fell to a gentle rolling. They then saw a few clusters of boats lashed together, scattered within the offing. Yeoman's ship had a whole mast and he put on sail to reach the nearest group. Two ships, the Princess and the Mary, were tied together but in bad shape. Their decks had been washed clean of gear and several hands had been lost to the waves. The Captain shared out some of his dry provisions and fresh water, and instructed the others on how to prepare for the journey home.

Yeomans then visited each other boat in turn, assessing the damage and assets, seeing how the crew fared and convinced them that they would all see Bristol again. In the end, he had gathered twenty boats with sound hulls, half with workable masts, and five boats that were worse than sieves. They took everything of use from these last, then scuttled them so that they would not cause any mischief in future to some unsuspecting voyager.

These ragged survivors proceeded to make what sails and rigging they could from the canvas and line they had salvaged. With these they made enough sail for the ten masted craft, and lines to throw to the rest behind. With quite an amount of their catch remaining, all they needed was a favourable wind and some fresh water. Few of those who returned would ever want to eat salted fish again.

The good captain asked each ship to use its spare canvas to catch any mist or rainfall and funnel it into the rapidly emptying water casks, by which means they managed to have just enough to stay alive. There were a few hours of rain on the tenth day that brought them back from the dead; they gave thanks for the rain and Captain Yeomans.

So they limped back to port, with little to show for the venture but losses, empty barrels, cracked hands and lost friends.

'But here we are, and a pint of ale makes it feel more of an adventure than purgatory. I am hogging the news, what has been happening here in port while we have been out boating?' asked Woody.

I told him how the merchants had worked to break the monopoly of the slave trade, how there was talk of turning the Marsh into a square of fine houses, and about the return of the first part of the fleet.

'And how are my friends Teach and Miss Hannah getting on without me? Pining I trust?', he enquired.

I could not decide what to say, and he sensed my hesitancy.

'Why, what has happened; all is well with them, is it not?'

'To tell you the truth, we all believed you to be lost, and there was such an urgency to Miss Hannah's anxiety, that Teach stood in for you and now they have been wed these five days.'

'Perish the Devil – was he so eager to take the future of a dead man? I will see him in St Michael's yard for this.''

He dashed out, furiously bellowing, dodging round bales, sleds and sailors, vaulting over pigs who were foraging for food in the gutters, rushing headlong to Mistress Cleary's house. I was eager to know what was happening, but could not leave my post with thirsty crew of the fleet coming through the door every second. Perhaps half an hour had gone by when Teach came rushing through the door, streaming water, running for his life.

'Help me Porter, Woody is after me and will not listen to either me or Hannah. I could not stop him short of spilling his blood, and I would never do that, so I had to leap from the window at the back into the moat, but still he pursued me; I am only a few seconds ahead of him,' all the while he was leading the way down to the cellar. Despite the only light coming from the top of the staircase, Teach navigated to the furthest reaches and that rotten panel we had found years before, which he lifted aside and squeezed through. 'Now put this back in place, roll a barrel across, I will do the same from this side, and forget you have ever seen me.' Once this was done I hurried back upstairs, and had just drawn a pint of cider for another crack-lipped member of the fleet when Woody ran in, dripping water and with a large knife clutched in his hand. He grabbed me by the throat and pushed me hard against the barrels.

'Where is that dog? I know he will be snivelling here, I

mean to take back the life that he has stolen from me, and any who obstruct me will answer to my steel!' he demanded.

Before I could react, he saw the trail of water leading to the cellar and he chased those footprints down. I could see from his eyes that he meant what he said, and as I did not want to see one friend kill another, then be dangled from the gibbet above St Michael's, I hurried after him with the casking mallet from the bar. He was already following the steps around the barrels across the cellar, and I had no time to think, so I knocked out the spile of one of our largest barrels and lifted its bung. Within seconds the torrent of ale jetting out of the tun had produced a frothing flood right across the cellar floor, washing away all trace of Teach's footprints.

Woody let out a shout of rage and rushed at me, but he did not see in that dim light the spile amongst the beer. He slipped, and hit his head on a barrel as he went down. Simon came bellowing down the stairs, demanding to know why I was letting all the fleet go thirsty, but when he saw Woody come at me with the knife he forgot all about his anger, and the spilt beer, and hurried to my side just in time to tap Woody smartly on the head with the mallet as he came back up again. This finally felled him, and he lay in an inch or more of ale upon the floor.

Woody was not in a much better mood when he came back round to the sound of my mopping up any beer that had not already sunk into the floor, but he was now disarmed, trussed up with his own neckerchief and too woozy to make much trouble.

'You Judas – why did you waylay me?' he shouted.

'Because you were going to kill a man who has never been anything other than your true friend, and the protector of Hannah,' I explained.

'Bah – how can you suggest his actions are honourable, he has stolen my girl and my life from me! He shall swing for this, I swear it!'

'He was precisely honourable; it was you who left Hannah in a position of dishonour and ruin, by leaving her carrying your child and unwed.'

'What … she is … what have I done?'

He broke down into gasps, trying not to cry or sob, exhausted from all that had happened to him.

*

We tried to find Teach, but failed to do so that night: he must still have feared that Woody meant to kill him, and in the process cause even more unhappiness in the four lives most concerned. The harbour was all a-bustle with the preparation for the Beginning to sail, and that also confounded our search.

The next morning, as I took the air along the quayside, getting away at last from that overpowering smell of souring beer at the Trow, I passed Umble Jack's abode and he beckoned me over.

'Young Porter, Ize summon for ya, I duz it frim whoz bin so kind to I' and he palmed me a packet as if he was just shaking the hand of a benefactor, my hand between both of his filthy own.

I raced back to the Trow to examine what I had been given: it was a small purse holding a tightly folded sheet of paper and eight guinea coins. I unfolded the note, and for the first time I saw the scholarly writing of Teach upon it.

'My friend Porter, I am most grateful for the assistance you gave me today, and even more grateful for proving

that you are indeed my truest friend, and ever have been. I can but hope that Woody's madness will pass with time, but as yet I cannot see how I can undo the harm that I have now inflicted upon him in the very act that I thought would save Hannah and her child from penury and dishonour. Nor can I believe that our friendship can mend after his attempt to slaughter me without asking one word of explanation for my actions.

I have this day take a place aboard the Beginning, which sails on the morning tide, bound for Guinea and the Americas, where I will seek what fortune I may. I do not intend to return to Bristol, which has become too hot and too sour for me, and Hannah is free to believe me dead. I will leave the name Drummond behind. Let no action that I take now ever bring dishonour to the name of my father, or to Hannah's son should he take that name.

I have made such arrangements as seem fit for my messenger Jack to continue at least in the humble state to which he is accustomed, and I have left what aid and comfort that I can afford for Hannah, which shall be brought to her attention discreetly. You may also give her half of these coins, the rest I request you to use to entertain the Quarterdeckers at the Trow, even Woody, if he allows and merits it, and to remember me to them.

The boys need a captain, and an anchor to keep them clear of the shoals of life, and if I cannot be that captain any more then I trust that you may provide a safe anchorage for them whenever they are caught in a storm. They are all good men and boys, and will serve well if they don't lose there footing to the waves of adversity. I trust you to help them now that I can no longer do so.

Fare thee well, my boy, and be the good man you have always been. If we should meet again, there would be no happier man than me, but I reckon on joining my dust to that of some distant land.

Yours, forever in friendship,

Teach'

I sprinted out of the inn, headlong along King Street towards the Key, splashing through the filthy central gutter to avoid the varied obstacles of sleds, bales, sailors and wandering pigs out on parole. I looked in vain for the Beginning at her moorings, and on inquiring I heard that she had left on the tide with a favourable wind two hours before. By now she would be nearing the mouth of the Avon and beyond the power of any mere man to recall. Her next anchorage would be off the West coast of Africa. I considered ways to get a message to Teach, but I did not know what name he was signed under, nor where or how to send it.

I turned from the Key in despair and went directly to Mistress Cleary's house, where I found Hannah alone in a state of high anxiety.

'John, have you any news of my dear Edward? I cannot sleep or eat due to the fears I have for him,' she enquired.

'I have news, but none too good. Please sit down and take what comfort you can from this,' and I handed her the purse and note that I still clasped. As she read, she gasped, smiled, and finally cried out as the paper fell from her hand. 'Is there no way that we can recall him, to say that he is forgiven?'

'None – the ship has gone beyond us and I cannot think of any way to get a message to him. It sounds like he has decided it is best if he leaves and never returns, and you must act accordingly,' I said.

At this she wept bitterly for many minutes, calling out 'Oh, Edward' several times betwixt.

We were then joined by Woody, who had to bear Hannah's anger and dismay, which he did with the patience and forbearance of the true penitent, and when her spring of emotion at last ran dry, she handed him the letter to read for himself.

'What a foolish but honourable man, always eager to be a friend to us all and tripped up by it. He is too good for us, too good for the whole world,' said Hannah.

'I shall try to make amends, but as Porter says, there is little we can do and it seems Teach is determined to disappear, so we may have to live with that decision,' Woody replied.

Hannah agreed, and set her mind resolutely to the future, her child, and how best to form a family around it, and she may have wondered how long it would be before she could be married to the father of her child.

That is how it stood: Teach had left us, and for all we knew, we would never hear of him again. He had settled some of his limited funds for looking after Umble Jack, and others who had benefited from his help in the past; he had left more for use by Hannah and her child, though Woody resented this greatly, and he had gained his father's agreement that any money he should inherit would pass on to her. This last act was as sure a sign of his cutting his lines as any we could expect: he would come back to penury, if he ever did return.

The city, for the most part, did not mark his absence and loss, beyond those who loved him or were beholden to him. If any event of that day was remembered, it was the departure of Captain Barker upon the Beginning, and the start of the business which would grow Bristol's fortune beyond measure, after years of fighting the London monopoly.

3:Beginnings

In the following months, we occupied ourselves with the drudgery and minutiae of our lives, and with the signs of expectation. We, who were not involved in high finance and big trade, were hopeful of new of Teach, and expecting the arrival of Hannah's baby.

The merchants were extending the alms houses near the Trow in the new year, a rare sign of piety amongst their much greater expenditures on their own mansions, when we received our first information from abroad. It came in the form of the returned Beginning and a letter brought to me by one of the senior hands.

Having read it, and been shocked by what it said, I proceeded to Mistress Cleary's to find there Woody, Hannah, her mother and Mistress Woolley, the midwife. It was clear that Hannah was soon to be confined upstairs, yet I could not wait.

'I do not know if you want to hear this now, but I have received a letter of great import to yourselves,' I announced.

'John, if it is news of my husband, then I am eager to hear it, whatever it is,' Hannah replied.

Woody winced at her use of that term, but with both her mother and the midwife present no other form of words was suitable. So, I read out the letter to all those assembled:

'To whom it may concern, this day in Port Royal on the island of Jamaica, I have to record the death of one of the crew but newly arrived upon the ship Beginning, out of the city of Bristol. Said person, known as Edward Drummond, had caught a malady from the cargo and had been in high

fever for some days before succumbing. He was only briefly lucid, in which time he gave the details of the addressee of this letter, and no more.

He has been buried in the yard of St Catherine's of this town, at the expense of the Captain below signed.

May God reserve a place for him in Heaven.

Your servant,

Capt St Barker

witnessed Mr Ed Teach esq'

Hannah cried out several times during this recital, and Mistress Cleary was near a faint, but I managed to catch Woody's eye and he took her out to join Mistress Woolley in another room, for the sake of Hannah.

'Do not distress yourself, Hannah,' I whispered so none outside the room could hear, 'this is Edward giving you your freedom: he is no more dead than I am, and I can be sure of this because he has placed his signature below that of Captain Barker. The whole letter, apart from the signature, is in the same hand as the note that he sent to me upon his departure. He has stepped firmly aside so that you can marry Woody and bring up your child respectably. Although he may never return, he is very much alive, well and as full of his tricks as ever. I am sure that he only intends you and I to know this, for he is not sure of Woody, and I think we must keep the truth of the matter secret from him.'

'Oh John, I am heartily glad if what you say is true, and although my sadness at not seeing dear Edward again is beyond measure, it is compensated by knowing he is well and up to mischief. I am sure you are right and this must remain a close secret between us until Edward releases us from it,' she determined.

She cried for a few minutes, realising that her close friend, and husband, would likely never return. This bitter emotion was slowly replaced by happier thoughts. When Woody returned from the next room, she was quite composed, if tear-stained.

'Dear Woodes, although this is most sad and bitter news, and I know that it will be some time before any of us is truly happy again, I realise now that we can be married with honour and without recourse to the law, or a long wait, and I think we should do so with some haste, for the sake of our child,' she urged.

'Hannah, I am bitterly sad at this loss, but also rejoice at the freedom that it gives us. But let us now concentrate on the matter in hand. John, please recall Mistress Woolley, and we will repair to the Trow to leave Hannah in her artful hands,' he coolly responded.

Woody did not seem to be excited by the happy consequences that this sad news might have for himself and Hannah. Instead, he was eager to talk about other developments and plans: the square to be built near the Trow on the grounds of the Marsh; the new trade to Africa and the riches it would bring; and his hopes of increasing his father's shares in shipping into a whole fleet of his own. By the time we were in the Trow, he was gabbling away as much as some of our more loquacious customers do on a few pints of Somerset cider, yet he was stone sober. Perhaps it was the excitement of imminent fatherhood turned into other avenues. By now it was past sunset, and we settled down to await events, Simon allowing me to remain with Woody rather than serve our customers. The Trow was not very busy, all spare hands were helping to unload the huge cargo of the Beginning: tobacco, rum, sugar and cotton, piling it up, loading it onto sleds and dragging it away to the cellars of a hundred happy merchants. If these hands did have respite tonight, it would not be at the Trow.

Some time after midnight, when all had sunken into a stupor, a scruffy little messenger arrived: 'Ize a message fur Mr Rogers; Missus Cleary give I it.'

Woody gave the urchin a penny in exchange for the paper, quickly glanced at it, then screwed it up and cast it into the embers of the fire.

'Well, I am to my bed. I bid you a good night. Mistress Drummond and her *daughter* will keep to the morning,' and so saying, he rammed his hat onto his head and strode, only slightly weaving, out of the inn. I did not say a word, having sat with him through his vigil; I really had not expected such an attitude to be displayed at its conclusion.

It was late the next afternoon before I was free to visit Hannah; the Trow had been busy since dawn with the sailors and porters who had finished unloading the great ship, now with pockets full of coin and with demanding thirsts. When I reached the house beside the Newgate, I immediately sensed that all was not right.

'Mistress Cleary, please tell me that mother and child fare well! Is there anything amiss?'

'They are doing well enough in themselves, but it seems my Hannah is to be left a widow with a dead man's baby to bring up,' she said. She had never been very clear whose child Hannah was carrying and had chosen to see it as Teach's when he had married Hannah.

'Why, what do you mean? Surely Woody is to marry her in the near future?' I blustered.

'So we all believed, but he came this morning and soon after left, with Hannah crying in her room,' she explained.

'Please take me to her, Mistress Cleary.'

Indeed, I found Hannah looking both exhausted and distraught, with her baby daughter beside her in a crib. That which should have been one of the most joyous of days was instead full of tears.

'Oh John, what a cursed wretch I am!' she said, as soon as her mother had withdrawn.

'Why, what has happened to take away your happiness today?'

'Woodes came this morning, and he was very cool and formal with me, I who had loved him and borne his child. He stated that it was all my own fault, designed to entrap him, and he had no intention of taking on either me or my ill-starred daughter. He even suggested that she was Edward's child and not his own. He said the only guilt that he felt was any part he might have played in driving the baby's father abroad, and for that alone he was giving me this *settlement*.'

As she spat out this last word she flung a small purse onto the floor, where it spilled forth a small number of coins.

'He said that this concluded his business with my family, and he wished me a good day. It took me a few moments to realise the full import of this and then I fainted, before waking to be the bag of nerves you now behold. Oh! What am I to do, abandoned by two husbands and left with a nameless child? How can I give my daughter a live worth living when I fail in my own at every turn?' she despaired.

I was dumbstruck – I knew Woody had been acting less than paternally the night before, but I put this down to the strain of this new and unexpected experience. Now it seemed that he was already turning over the idea of this abandonment even during our vigil. Whether he would have acted differently had Hannah given him a son, I cannot say. He had clearly severed all ties to Hannah in his mind and heart, and by doing so exiled himself from the companionship of the 'Deckers forever, if I could not reverse his decision.

I gave what little comfort I could to Hannah, without saying what was on my mind, then hurried over to the Rogers' house at the foot of Brandon Hill, where my hammering at the door brought a flustered maid to meet me.

'Young Mr Rogers is not seeing anyone today, sir,' she said.

'His eyes must be faulty then; he is bloody well seeing me,' I asserted, as I pushed past her, ignoring her offended squawking as I searched that unfamiliar house for Woody. I found him consulting his navigation books at the window of a room on the third floor.

'What are you up to Woody? You must have gone mad!' I shouted.

'Not that it is any business of yours, Porter, but I am studying for my master's certificate and the noise that you are making is distracting me,' he calmly stated.

This was too much for me, I crossed the room and dragged him to his feet by his lapels.

'What have you done to Hannah, you dog?'

'I realised I have no wish to align myself with that strumpet, or to raise Drummond's daughter. I have my position to think of, and binding myself to such a lowly person would be a great hindrance and disadvantage to me, and would damage the name of the family,' he remarked.

'This is nonsense. You know damned well that you fathered that child and took away all honour from Hannah; it was only to restore it that Teach took her as his wife. If you do not marry her and adopt the child, then you are the blackest scoundrel in Bristol and you will be unwelcome in every house where I am known.'

'There is no point in discussing it. I am decided; my father has a wife in mind for me who will be quite advantageous, and my studies await. I am sure I will flourish without your patronage, Porter. Good day to you!'

I stared at him for a few more seconds, this man that used to be my friend and playmate, then flung him back into his seat in disgust, dusting off my hands to remove all trace of his filth.

'Never cross my path again, Rogers, or you shall regret it most sorely. Do not expect any kindness from those that love Hannah or Teach, and there are many of them. I damn you for the fool and coward that you are.'

I stormed out, raising yet more flustered squeaks from the maid, and fairly rocked the house as I slammed the door.

So it was that Hannah had to live meagrely as Widow Drummond, bringing up Edwina with the help of what little had been left to her by Teach – she had given away Woody's blood money to the poor, being too disgusted to keep it for herself. I stood as godfather to the girl, and the rest of the Quarterdeckers were uncles to her, making sure to always bring round bread or bacon, candles or soap, flour or butter, or whatever might be wanting in the house, as well as little knickknacks to please Edwina. We heard little of Woody and shunned him completely. He was off with Captain Yeomans and the rebuilt fleet for most of the time, and it was well that he did not encounter any of us that had borne witness to Hannah's tears.

*

The port became rapidly busier and richer, with the merchants showing their wealth in ever bigger and grander houses, rebuilding their guild house in King Street, dressing in silks more often than in good Bristol wool. We saw two ends of the trade, with the shoddy goods to be traded in Africa being loaded into the large and strangely shaped ships, and then months later we saw the same ships return ladened with sugar, rum, tobacco and cotton from the America's – all grist to the mills of Bristol to be refined into products we shipped and carted around the country.

Over two years passed, with various 'Deckers completing their apprenticeships, becoming full masters of their trades. Some were taken on as partners in the business, married into the families of their masters, or even bought out an elderly master, or set up in their own premises, having thus decided the course of the rest of their lives.

One mid-winter day, when the cobbles were crazed and sparkling with frost, and ropes on every boat hung like strings of diamonds, a weather-beaten sailor came to the inn with a sealed oilcloth package addressed to 'John Porter, the Trow, Bristol'. Inside this package I found a bundle of papers and a few coins of strange design. I gave one of these to the sailor, and thanked him for bringing the parcel to me.

As it was a quiet day, I was soon able to take the papers to my room to examine them in privacy. I have them before me now, so I will transcribe the relevant portions here.

'Port Royal, Jamaica, August 1702

Dear Porter,

I trust that all is well with you and all my friends at the Trow. I realise that there is no way for you to send any reply to me so I will refrain from asking you questions that may not be answered, for both of our sakes. I will hand this package to a trusted sailor who will carry it to you but who will never divulge its source, a task made easier by his muteness. This subterfuge is necessary, I assure you, to preserve the illusion of my death which is necessary for Hannah's happiness.

Please give the enclosed coins to her to help with the child, after you have given my messenger a token of our thanks. Since you assisted me in escaping Woody's wrath, much has happened. Of course you know that I shipped out with Captain Barker on the Beginning. I was initially just a deck hand, but after the first few days at sea, as we sailed towards the coast of Spain, I was employed to supervise the preparations of the cargo deck because I had the skills to run the ledger on the work done there. There was a team of ten men fixing shelves and eye bolts to the main woodwork, with no purpose that was obvious to me, but it needed to be done carefully so that the cargo of cloth, wine and trinkets was not damaged.

It was a fast ship yet it still took more than a fortnight to reach the African coast, much of this time being spent preparing the decks. We anchored off Elmina, and in that hot and steamy atmosphere we could hear the calls of strange birds and animals in the forest beyond, and smell an odd, earthy sickness from the shore.

The captain and his agent went ashore each day in the long boat, sometimes with ledgers and at others with samples of goods and trading gifts. After a few days of this, we were ordered to move the ship into the harbour using a combination of the wind and rowing tugs. We offloaded all of the goods that we had brought with us onto the quayside and prepared to take on a new cargo. It was soon after this that we found the source of that strange smell that pervaded the coast, as out of a low building, in fact more a huge roofed cellar or dungeon, a long line of manacled black ghosts were marched towards us. I had never seen more than a couple of black people together before, but now there were hundreds of them shuffling towards us, men, women and children, but they had no spark of life to show that they were more than cattle and they were driven as such. From this crowd rose the stench we had but previously sensed only weakly, the miasma of disease, and death, and insanitary conditions they had been kept in for God knows how long, and the odour of despair throughout. They were filthy and rank, looked to be half starved and several were too weak to walk and were dragged along by the rest of their coffle, whereas the overseers who drove and whipped them were neat and clean being either white men in good working clothes or people of an Arab appearance in long white flowing robes, and all well fed.

The Captain was shocked, not at the enslavement but at the quality of the goods he had been sold, and protested most strongly believing that he was being swindled when the best goods were going to his competitors from London. He was assured by the local trader that these were prime stock and would soon plump up on good rations. It was standard procedure to keep them like this to break their spirit and make them compliant with their new masters' wishes, and hence enhance their value; it did not pay to pamper such cattle as it would spoil them forever. Barker argued back that half of them looked to have cholera, and so it went on for some time.

Eventually, a deal was struck, the locals drove the goods to the dockside where they were coarsely washed with sea water, shaven, then inspected by the ship's surgeon in the most intimate of ways to eliminate any with defects, sickness, bad teeth or bad attitude. Those who passed this most humiliating examination were manacled again into groups of six and marched to the gangplank of the ship, the rest were sent back to the stinking pit from which they had been brought, to await a less careful purchaser. Any man that struggled against his condition and confinement was soundly beaten, those who followed soon learnt meekness.

It was now that I saw the true purpose of our labours on the way from Bristol. As we took each coffle down to the cargo deck, we laid them out six to a shelf, alternating heads to feet as tightly as they would go, with three layers of shelves one above the other and slots between for things to descend from higher shelves onto those beneath. Barker had bought so many that we could not fit them all in lying flat so many had to be lain down on their sides and then turned every few hours so that they were not permanently damaged by this arrangement, which would reduce their value at sale.

All through this hauling and shelving we heard barely a murmur from the cargo, as they were in such a lowly and cowed state that they barely acted as if they were alive. They were so low in condition, so dispirited, so afraid of reprisal should they struggle, or resigned to and ignorant of their fate, that for the most part they were like sacks of grain. After more than a day of this stowing in a breathless, steamy hold, the smell of the cargo had grown again to a sharp and sickly stench. I saw now that the shelves allowed all bodily products of those above to rain down on those below, and if there was any illness on one shelf it would rapidly spread. They could not bathe or go to the jakes, all happened where they lay and fell on those beneath, to be washed away with hoses when we remembered or could no longer bear the smell, which would raise a hopeless groan from the cargo. Throughout the voyage, we would remove any that fell ill from their shelf and they would be cast overboard as having no value to compensate for the risk they presented to the rest of the goods. We would wash down each shelf and its occupants once a day with sea water, which only briefly removed the stench. Once every few days, each coffle would be brought up and danced to keep them alive and stop their limbs from failing: ten minutes in the fresh air before returning once more to that pen, that animal shed in which we kept them.

We watered and fed them only sufficiently to keep them alive, after all the more we put in the more we would need to clean up later and the more lively and rebellious would be our charges. Captain Barker was determined to beat the London slavers at their own game, had a margin to meet and cared nought for the bundles that made up the cargo beyond the profit they represented to him, so long as sufficient survived until we dropped anchor off Jamaica.

Most of the crew acted as if this was all normal and to be expected, no worse than the loss of cargo to water damage or weevils, and I fell in with this general feeling: to do anything else risked my own skin. But at night, I would often awake in a sweat, dreaming that I too was chained on one of those shelves, struggling for breath between my neighbours in that fetid air, half crushed by those around me as the ship was rolled by the waves.

Even though the ship was made to travel rapidly, to reduce losses and avoid pirates, we still lost one in five of the cargo due to sickness or madness, but at least this gave some space to their neighbours and the death rate reduced as we travelled further.

At last, we arrived in Jamaica, and we offloaded the cargo into large holding pens like so many cattle. Again the ship's surgeon went through them all, separating the sick from the healthy, but at least now he was treating the ill to help maximise profits. They were all washed down with water and lime, and shaved again to remove the lice that had infested them all. They were fed on fruit, bread, fat and meat to put some flesh on their bones, then kept dancing for hours, and moving piles of rocks from one end of the pen to the other to build up their muscles again and get them trained to the whip. All of this in the interest of making them saleable merchandise.

As the day of the auction approached, we aimed to get the males demonstrably fit and to this end we dressed them only in coarse white trousers and had them oiled to emphasise their muscles. The females were dressed to make them look modest and obedient, but also to demonstrate their fecund shape, suitable for breeding up a larger herd. On the last day, Captain Barker came along to inspect progress, he having been preoccupied with the cleaning of the cargo deck and its refit for valuable goods to return to Bristol, as well as bargaining for those goods and entertaining some of the wealthier dealers before the auction. He was examining the line of females when one of the male slaves grabbed a pair of shears and rushed screaming in some barbaric tongue at Barker, with the weapon held above his head. He was within a couple of paces of the Captain when I stopped him with the heavy staff that I was holding in my role as a guard. He fell sprawling at Barker's feet and was quickly pinned and manacled by the other crew, before being given a double dose of the drugged drink that we used to keep the slaves quiet and obedient at auction: he would be incapable of attacking anyone for days.

This was no sign of mercy towards him, it was only to avoid bruising valuable goods so close to the sale; if he had attempted this on the voyage he would have been dropped over the side without a qualm. Looking back, I realise that Barker must have been pawing the slave's wife or sister, but this meant nothing to us or any white man on the island. It was for my action in saving Barker from this likely lethal attack that he granted me the favour of certifying the death of Mr Drummond.

The auction was the greatest shock to my sensibilities. The lots of men, women and children were pushed onto stage with no eye to family links, friendship, or even a shared language. They were displayed and examined like so many cattle, or at best in a few cases like race horses: their limbs, ears and teeth were checked, muscles squeezed, even their private organs revealed to display virility and fecundity, but throughout there was barely a murmur from the drugged slaves, no fire in their eyes, just a dazed and resigned look. Even when the children were separated from the mothers, there was no cry of distress, instead just a dull sense of loss.

Barker was overjoyed at the prices. We had brought the first new slaves of the season and the plantations were desperate to replace those that had died over the winter through disease, rebellion, overwork and ill-use; we were weeks ahead of the London ships and had the market to ourselves; there was a great need for new fit and breeding stock.

I left the auction to fetch my kit from the Beginning, leaving behind the screams of anguish and the stench of burning flesh as the newly purchased slaves were branded with their masters' marks.

I had only signed on for the outward legs of the voyage, so I took my share of the proceeds and secured my death certificate from Barker, which I then put into the care of a tar who did not know my real identity but who nonetheless owed me a favour. I left the Beginning as they started to refill the cargo deck with sugar and all the other goods that likely will have made a handsome profit in Bristol; again bought at low prices because it was the start of the season and there were no competing bidders.

I was at a loss for what I wanted to do next, but I was certain that I never will ride on a slave ship again, nor aid the trade that runs them. My nights are still filled with dreams of those silent, dead brown eyes, looking at me, a challenge to my soul.

I found work around the harbour helping with local trade. Very few roads there are fair enough to take carted goods, as we did out of Bristol, so most go around the coast in smaller boats, or are distributed from there to neighbouring islands. Sometimes I just ran the ledgers for what was loaded and unloaded, at other times I was sent to haggle over contracts and prices, and all of this because I have my numbers and letters where most around me only have the learning in their calloused hands. Of course I lent my weight, joining the tail of the rope when the sails needed to be raised, aiding the navigation and taking soundings: no man can rest idle on a small coastal craft.

So I wasted my life for a couple of years, unable to return home without unwinding the lies I had so carefully woven, trapped in a life that bored me. I was rescued from this little life by the news that England was again at war, and the call came for every Englishman to do his duty by hurting the interests of France and Spain, wherever they were to be found, and particularly in the Americas.

I have signed on with Captain Henry Jennings of Jamaica, on his ship Bathsheba: he has letters of marque from the Governor and we are therefore free to attack and take any enemy ship. We sail today as privateers of England, and may find glory and fortune, or just death.

I send this packet to you so that I may be remembered. The gold is for Hannah, but please make it seem that it has come from your own pocket, Porter. The secrets told here are for you alone.

In good faith, your friend,

Teach'

I was surprised and dismayed at Teach's description of the trade: all we knew of it in Bristol were the riches and activity that it brought, and a few silk-coated and bewigged black footmen that the merchants kept. It now struck me that this might be as much to distract attention from the real conditions that slaves were held in both on the ships and the plantations, or to assuage the merchants' consciences of any blame so that they could delude themselves as much as anyone else who saw these pampered members of that tortured tribe. It was also a conspicuous exhibition of power and wealth.

I passed on the gold to Hannah as if it was from some good fortune of my own: a lucky wager that had paid off to my surprise and delight. She was biding well, and Edwina was flourishing, already on her feet; but I could see that Hannah was weighed down by a sadness that no gift could dispel, and this made me angry at Fate and Woody. What could a mere cellar-man do to relieve this grinding, hopeless misery?

4:Hell and High Water

There had been much bustle in the port with the new trade, and even more following the call to take up arms to protect Queen Anne's interests abroad against France and Spain. Several merchants took the opportunity to raise letters of marque for their vessels, allowing them to act as privateers should the will take them and the opportunity present itself, so that they could fill up any empty corners in their holds with goods seized from competing foreign vessels, sometimes even ones with which they had dealt honourably in the recent past.

Slave ships took to this enthusiastically as they were already armed and designed to move swiftly, and certainly had ample storage space for valuable goods, even if it meant the slaves squeezing up a bit more. They could afford to try their hands at this legalised piracy should they come across a Spanish ship carrying gold back home to fund the war, especially as this was far more profitable than carrying cotton back to Bristol. One vessel that we heard was dispatched for this very purpose was the St George, captained by the renowned circumnavigator William Dampier. He set off to plunder gold vessels and towns along the coast of South America, with the blessings of both the Queen and the shareholders, including Woody's father: an exercise in the boundless greed we witnessed many times.

The merchants had a busy year, many gaining most of their profits from the triangular route, now that their normal trading partners had become the mortal enemies of England. Their cellars were packed with sugar, rum and tobacco enough to make many fortunes and they just awaited the arrival of winter for higher prices and even fatter profits to roll in. Mr Colston extended the Queen

Elizabeth's Hospital out of his own pocket so that it might hold almost twice as many boys in search of an education. It was at this point, with all our harvests gathered in and all anticipating a plump and roasted Christmas, that a judgment came upon us, and the greatest wrath fell on Bristol and London alike.

I remember being asleep in the Trow early on the morning of the twenty-seventh day of November, when I was awoken by a noise I trust that I will never hear again, like the cry and wing beats of some avenging angel sweeping across the city, rattling every tile and slate, every window and door. Suddenly from a dead calm, we were embraced by a wind greater than I had ever known, or even heard reported by those who sail the high seas. In my room, the suck of the wind was enough to pull dust from between the floorboards, and relight the embers in the grate before scattering them across the hearth. I dashed from my bed and emptied the wash jug over the embers before they could set the whole room alight. Another gust made my ears pop so that I was dull of hearing for some time, and disoriented me in that screaming darkness, the rush of air inside the room enough to make it feel like I was on some exposed hill. Now plunged again into a darkness that resonated with the remembered sight of flames, I struggled to find my flint and strike a spark for my candle. I approached the window to discern what might be happening outside, but all I could see was a wild blackness, rain driven hard against the pane so that it could hardly run down it; no more was visible by my feeble light.

I could hear ropes and cables singing in the wind, masts clashing together, hulls crashing against the quayside, and a clattering of tiles flying from roofs and shattering against distant walls. Incredibly, after each lull the wind came back stronger and wilder than before, rising to a banshee pitch and filling all the senses.

Rain and hail was now lashing the Trow like musket shot, and even as I stood there trying to make out anything beyond the window, a diamond pane exploded from the leading and the wind came in harder, pulling the rest of the window apart like a gossamer web; it collapsed in a twisted tangle of glass and metal sending splinters everywhere. I fortunately had turned aside as the first pane was shed and did not suffer more than a scratch to my cheek. I gingerly felt for my clothes and boots, once more cast into darkness, then pulled across the shutters as best I could to keep out the furious tempest. As I reached the door, I heard Simon calling for me and we rushed together down the stairs lit only by his candle to close shutters on all the remaining windows before the Trow could be wrecked by the gale. As we hurried about this business, a hammering came at the door.

'Let me in, for the mercy of God, let me in; I will not last long out here,' we heard over the storm.

It took both of us to open and hold the heavy door so that our storm-blown visitor could enter without the raging elements taking the door as kindling. He fell through in a heap of water and torn clothes, and had to wait there until we had used all our might to get the door closed again. Then we knelt to where our new guest was lying on the floor, sparkling with hail and fragments of glass, and we found it to be Slate Jones, who was in a desperate state. Simon gave him a goodly measure of brandy (seized patriotically from a French ship, of course) and let Slate recover a while before enquiring what ailed him.

'My boat is foundering at anchor in the harbour; this is no mere storm but a judgment upon us all and the End of

Days. The tide is coming up and will not stop until it is over the walls and has washed away the town. It is Noah's flood over again: plead for God's mercy, and run for higher ground, boys!'

Simon thought the Welshman was raving, but when we looked from the last window before we shuttered it, we could perceive that the cobbles had disappeared under water and we were adrift on the sea, which was lapping at the steps of the Trow. Now perhaps it would be better if the inn really was a boat and not just named after one!

'Quick John, down into the cellar and block all the bung holes, then bring up any dry goods and candles you can find down there. The drink will stay fit in the barrels for days even if they are afloat on the sea, but the rest will spoil,' Simon ordered.

So we left Slate to his brandy and ran down to the cellar. By the time we had secured the barrels and lifted all other goods up a few steps, there was water coming through the walls and rising from the floor. As we got the last of the goods onto the ground floor, the cellar was ankle deep in water, which was rising fast.

'I don't know if we may last the night, but we have light and food and drink, and tobacco to see us through, God willing,' he said.

The three of us sat there in vigil, with candles lit, strong drink at our elbows, ready for Neptune to come through the door, or for fire, war or pestilence to drive through the walls, listening to the mayhem happening outside. All the while Jane was fast asleep upstairs. But then I remembered Hannah, her mother and child, and our friend Umble Jack out on the harbour side, and could remain no longer selfishly in the flickering safety of the Trow.

‘We cannot sit idly here while others are in peril: if we stay it is our own souls that are in danger,’ I stated.

‘Right you are, Boyo, worse things happen at sea, they say, though the sea is knocking at our doors, so we might very well find out tonight,’ responded Slate, standing up.

‘You are right, John, let us throw ourselves on the Lord’s mercy and see what we can do to aid those who cannot help themselves,’ said Simon, joining our band.

So we left that safe harbour, carrying the closed lanterns that normally hung besides the front door to welcome our guests, a length of rope tied between us and another coiled over Slate’s shoulder, with a long bar to use as a lever or ram should it be needed. The tide was already knee deep and still rising, King Street was a canal between the Back and the Key. We were not the only ones abroad, other parties of sailors were endeavouring to save their boats, or just cutting them free so that they did not sink at their moorings, or trying to rescue the most valuable stock, or their purses fat from the cargoes they had sold, but most were hammering on doors, either begging for shelter or warning those asleep inside that the Day of Judgment was upon them. Barely a house was whole, windows were smashed, chimneys toppled, tiles scattered, thatch waving as if it was back in the fields from whence it came, slates scything across the streets then exploding in splinters.

Bells on the steeples rang in alarm, or just at the whim of the wind, stone spires crashed down to the street or through the chapel roofs. In the distance, on that darkest of nights, we could see flames like the edge of Hell – these were houses whose damped down fires had relit and scattered, or been overdrawn and scattered into the thatch, or windmills whose sails had spun faster than their bearings could take and the axles had set alight, they surrounded us as far as we could see in that torrential rain.

Through this world of wind and flood, fire and hail, we three strode now through thigh deep waves yet we were stood in our own street. We first set our heading towards the Marsh, now reclaiming its former character, but where we expected to find Umble Jack there was nothing but open water. We knew Jack could not hope to run from such a flood, or swim through it, and all three at once knew that this adventure was a game no more, but instead a deadly trial for all abroad that night. When despair made us turn about, we heard faintly on the wind:

'Ahoy, Ize adrift immy barrow, Ize bound fer Merical, jeerme?'

I could just make out a darker shape upon the waves out beyond the Marsh, it was Jack's home a-bobbing and a-spinning. We tried thrice to cast out a line to Jack, but between the wind, the darkness and his shattered limbs, he could never catch hold.

Slate was at the head of our rope, and now he said, 'To redeem my earlier faint heart' and plunged into the churning waters. A second later, we saw Slate reappear, stroking strongly towards Jack. We could not clearly see what was happening, but after few moments we heard his voice over the gale crying 'Haul away, boys' and felt a tug on the rope.

We pulled as strongly as we could with our uncertain footing upon cobbles that lay beneath a yard of boiling sea, rain lashing our faces, lanterns clenched in our teeth. At last, we could see our lights reflected off the gleaming rim of the barrel, Slate behind kicking with fury, and we landed them like some wooden whale. We looked inside the bobbing barrel to find Jack half drowned, but with a grin on his gargoyle face.

'Porter! Zit you? Fort Ize a goner! Bless you awl!', he managed to say.

We towed the barrel back to the steps of the Trow and moored it there. Slate gently reached in and lifted Jack in his arms as if he was only a child, and carried him in to the inn. There was Jane, now fully awake and dressed, acting hostess to many another drowned rat, all thrown together by the storm into our safe harbour, like so much flotsam. Simon refused to allow Slate to come back out with us again, he was soaked, half frozen and near done in. So we left him there, with Jack recalling their adventure on the high seas of Bristol, to all those assembled about the fire, fuelled by brandy and the admiration of all those stranded sailors who had run from the storm.

We set off again, keeping close to the walls of buildings lest we be swept out into the harbour or hit by falling debris. We wore our thickest coats and a pair of old Roundhead helmets, which normally saw service as a spittoon and for receiving ashes knocked out of pipes, on either side of the grate at the Trow, their previous contents hurriedly swilled out in the sea lapping at the inn's doorstep. We were heartily glad of these as shards of glass and tile rained down upon us from every side, the wind gathering its rage again as it howled in fury at all those impertinent enough to be outside that night.

It seemed to be many hours before we reached the Newgate, but it cannot have taken even one hour to make the journey. The flood was nearing its peak and the water was at our waists, when we spied Mistress Cleary's house, or what remained of it. A chimney had fallen and accounted for much of the roof, the sea was lapping at the cill, the windows blown to splinters, and no lights showing anywhere.

We could raise no answer from hammering at the door, and it was too stout to force even with the bar we had brought with us, so we climbed in over the window ledge into the calmer pool beyond. There I saw only floating items from the parlour, including a spinning top beloved of Edwina. We struggled to pull the door open against the water, and mounting the stair we called up above. We heard a querulous voice from the next floor: 'John, is that truly you? Oh please hurry!'

We rushed up the stairs as well as we could, encumbered by our helmets and heavy coats, more soaked and chilled than any fish, following Hannah's voice. We found her in the wreckage of her mother's room on the topmost floor. The chimney had crashed through both roof and ceiling, then landed full square upon the bed where her mother had lain sleeping. Hannah had cleared what bricks and tiles she could from her mother, and was holding her hand, but by our lantern's light we could see that Mistress Cleary was no longer with us, her shattered shell to frail to hold out against the fall of rubble. 'Hannah, come away now, let your mother rest here till the storm has passed. Where is little Edwina?'

With a torn and empty look, she led us back down to the middle floor, which was still and calm and whole. Edwina lay sprawled in her sleep across Hannah's bed, luxuriating in the space and calmly sucking her thumb.

Simon said, 'Let us drop anchor here for the night. We would be risking everything to try to return to the Trow in this.'

So we settled down around the smoky embers, the fire no longer drawing well with the chimney gone, both Simon and myself dressed from a trunk holding Mr Cleary's old clothes, Hannah collapsed in grief and exhaustion beside Edwina, and we barricaded the window lest any item should yet fly through it and cause more sorrow.

The night screamed on, the storm slowly losing its fury, and in that snug dark room we all finally slept. I had no idea of the time when I was awoken by the sound of Edwina crying out, anxious at the unaccustomed dark, and as I stirred so Simon also awoke, grumbling upon the floor.

'Shall we see if the world has been washed away, if we alone have survived this night?' and so saying we shifted the dresser from the window and stared out at the scene so revealed.

The tail of the storm was still with us, but no worse than a strong breeze and showers of rain. That which had passed in that night could have been none less than the hand of God, or the sweeping tail of Satan. What should have been a bustling view of traders and sailors, carts and sleds, market stalls and foraging pigs, was all a sea and that strewn with wreckage and flotsam. The water we had struggled to wade through had fallen back to perhaps a foot in depth; we could see doorsteps standing proud of it, but there was as yet no dry place to stand in the street. The raised area of the old castle had fared better, the water was even now running off its sides as if it was some great beast emerging from the ocean. No building appeared whole, each bore marks from the flood and storm: broken windows, dangling shutters, shattered trade signs, missing chimneys, torn roofs, and the wan and terrified faces of the occupants peering out in fear. I could see both St Peter's and St Nicholas had lost parts of their adornments, and could smell enough smoke to know that there was more fire damage than just the odd fallen chimney.

‘You remain here for a while, Mistress Hannah needs you. I Must get back to the Trow to see all is well – I will send someone with any food we can find before long,’ said Simon as he pulled on his saturated boots once more and crept out, endeavouring to leave Hannah asleep. I rested at the window with Edwina for company, quietly pointing out the most extraordinary consequences of the tempest, waving our reassurances to neighbours cut off by the flood, and all the while I tried to forget what awaited us upstairs.

By this point it must have been nearing ten o’clock, but not one church bell rang to greet it, no hands turned to mark the hours, and all was cast into confusion. Another hour passed and Edwina was growing fretful, and indeed I had become most hungered when we saw a figure splashing through the street. I descended directly and struggled to open the door most swollen after its briny immersion, letting a good measure of tide flow out from the house, to join the ebbing sea. Before me stood Slate Jones, beaming across the basket he carried.

‘Truly it was a lucky day when I met you Porter, for last night you saved my life and redeemed my self respect, and now this morning I see that my boat is still afloat but adrift across the harbour, when I thought all was lost. I have brought breakfast for you all, and will return once I have secured the y Fenni.’

I took the basket back to Hannah’s room, where she was now just stirring.

‘Oh John, why have you brought us a picnic, what a strange idea? Let me just call Mother…’ and the smile on her face vanished to be replaced with a look of the utmost misery on recalling the events of the night before. She rushed upstairs, with me following, leaving Edwina to burrow delightedly in the basket of provisions. I caught up with Hannah just as she saw her mother's body amongst the rubble, looking merely asleep but certain never to stir again, now that the rain had washed away the soot, grime and blood. Hannah let out a piercing cry and near collapsed into my arms.

'My poor mother, how peaceful she seems … Oh, what have we done to deserve all these blows from Fate?'

I took her, half led and half carried, back to the basket, and we then fed, heartened by Edwina's smile, chatter and sense of adventure, despite the dreadful events outside that snug room. I then made a more careful inspection of the house, near the conclusion of which Hannah joined me in the kitchen.

'It can be repaired, but you may not live here until it is sealed and dry again. There is still a lake of water in the cellar, no roof nor chimney, and only one window that bears service. Come to the Trow, if it still stands, and you may have my room.'

She gave me a smile fit to break my heart, with tears in her eyes, and nodded her acquiescence.

'I am sure you are right in what you say, John, and we may make it all good again if we have faith and our hearts are true,' she said.

Hannah then went upstairs alone and was gone some time. When she returned, she stated simply, 'She is now ready for her grave, washed and bound. We must inform the wardens and they shall take her to St Michael's as soon as they may.'

We bundled up what we could, mostly clothes and the family Bible, a jewel of her mother's and some letters. Without hesitation or tear, she lifted the basket and led

Edwina downstairs. I followed with a larger bundle tied up in a sheet. At the front door, she hoisted her daughter onto her hip and strode out into the flooded street without a backward glance, seemingly happy to leave that cursed house, confident that I would follow her to the Trow, or to the depths of Hell.

All along the way we passed shattered houses, debris from roofs and churches, and things out of place. The prow of a long boat appeared from Small Street, where it had been washed and stranded by the flood; the pinnacles of St Stephen were driven like daggers into the churchyard and through the aisle; window shutters and shop signs lay tangled in a corner where an eddy had gathered them like some outsize magpie's nest; straw was strewn about to make the city look like a stable; and everywhere a foul and slimy mud appeared as the sea retreated to its normal bounds.

We reached the Trow and were greeted there by Simon, Jane, Umble Jack and Slate Jones. Jane embraced Hannah, eased Edwina from her grip, and led Hannah upstairs, because she could see the last of her strength and resolve was ebbing away. Jack set to entertaining Edwina, doing things seemingly impossible for a man with such a small collection of limbs, or things only possible for such a man. She watched in horrified fascination, confused completely by his strange words, before deciding it was all a great comedy, clapping and laughing for more.

Simon sent word to the warden's, who replied that Mistress Cleary would be the first of many they retrieved that day, and she would be fitly treated; such was the respect that Simon and the Cleary's deserved. Slate secured his boat once more, which had fared better than many that had ridden at their moorings until they smashed against the quay or submerged. Now he had two of his men using a pump to draw water from the cellars of the town, with the Trow being his first call, lest he appear ungrateful, and Mistress Cleary's second on their long, long list, to great but reasonable profit to himself, some compensation for his lost stock.

Some days after, we attended a rushed burial at St Michael's, Hannah, Jane, Simon, Edwina and I, and then some weeks later a memorial mass was held with a wider circle of friends and well-wishers, Hannah having no surviving relatives of which we knew. Through all of this, Hannah's only concern was for the welfare of her daughter.

*

That winter was hard for all of the city, much of the fleet was damaged and several ships lost with all hands. Jasper's windmill had caught fire; he said it felt that it was about to take wing as the sails buzzed around like a humblebee before the blazes started and the axles jumped, but it was all reparable with time. This and hundreds of other mills having been damaged, along with wrecked grain stores and flooded cellars, meant that flour would be scarce for many months. Great ships had been driven ashore along the Severn, one had even be stranded fifteen miles inland on the Levels, and having turned turtle was now being used to replace a barn that had been demolished by the winds. Sheep and cattle beyond number had drowned that night in Gloucestershire and Somerset, along with many people whose homes were set beside their fields, so the only meat we had expectation of was from the flock upon the Downs and from those urban pigs that had survived by swimming to higher ground. Much of the dried provisions put by for the winter had spoiled or been lost to the waves, it would be a lean Christmas and a sorrowful New Year.

Many of the churches had lost their pinnacles even if they had kept their roofs; strips of leading had flown like ribbons from them and none were sound against the rain and wind any more. So much straw and hay was lost that if it was not for the livestock having drowned, they would surely have starved before spring came. The great trees that shaded the promenade of the Marsh were felled as if by a single axe blow, the new square would look bare and stark for many years to come. The supply of timber was a welcome if smoky source of fuel when the snows came, and much was used to rebuild and repair the houses, although in later years this green wood twisted and buckled the roofs that they formed.

Ships in the King's Road had been driven aground and shattered, but the greatest damage and the widest consequences happened in the houses of the merchants. All year they had been storing up their goods, the sugar and tobacco in particular, waiting for the high prices of winter. Yet now they had lost in one night all of their dreams through the inundation of their cellars. The sugar had dissolved, the tobacco become most foul, and their imagined deals had evaporated. They survived the winter far better than those hundreds and thousands without adequate food or shelter; they still had much of their gold and silver, and some good credit, and resolved to make up their losses as rapidly as they might. To this end they endeavoured to redouble their efforts on the triangular route, their surest source of income.

It was declared by Parliament that the Storm had been 'a Judgment by God upon the Crying Sins of this Nation' and it 'loudly calls for the deepest and most solemn humiliation of our people,' which meant holding a national fast for one day in January. How one day of fast was meant to atone for such a sin that would have merited such loss of life and property as we had just experienced, was not stated, nor how a day with no food might improve the situation of those who already faced starvation. It was not determined which particular sin our nation, and Bristol and London in particular, had practised that justified the Storm in the mind of a loving God.

Those who had already suffered hunger for two months would not benefit a jot from the merchants going hungry for one day, even if they were observant of this national humiliation. And the greatest sin we surely practised was redoubled in order to refill the stockrooms of the merchants, by putting more ships than ever before on the course for Africa. All of us felt the impact of the Storm for years afterwards, and the city still bears the scars in places where the money has not been available to patch roofs or replace pinnacles.

A London man advertised for accounts of the storm, and he published a book based upon these stories. It was thus that Mr Defoe first came to our attention, although his name was not borne by the title page. I have here a copy of his book, which bears his signature as he gave it to me some years later, and it brings back that terrible night more vividly than anything published in the Post Boy, even though that paper must have mentioned the Great Storm in almost every edition for a decade.

*

It was crowded and hectic at the Trow: we had Jack lodged with us for some weeks until he was fit enough, at which point he insisted on taking up residence in a barrel in the cellar, and by that time we had become so entranced by his humour and limbless prowess that it was May before, at his own decision, he returned to the home comforts of a new barrel at the site of his former abode and the joys of waking to the dawn. Edwina loved him as a pet, and he loved her as a niece and spoiled her as much as a man of his meagre means could afford. There were plenty others lodged with us while their homes were repaired or rebuilt, including Hannah and Edwina, and this made the inn more chaotic and lively than a carnival from dawn to midnight.

The repairs to the Trow itself were swiftly achieved, and all through that winter it served as a warm beacon of hope for those whose own homes, livelihoods or hearts would take far longer to mend. Due to Simon's wisdom and rapid action, we had not lost one drop or morsel of our stores, and once the cellar was dry, you would never have known that it been flooded to a depth of yard, if it were not for the mysterious salty rime that appeared on the walls no matter how many times it was scrubbed away.

Hannah's home took far longer to repair: there was little money available and a lot of other demands on the time of all craftsman and labourers, who accordingly were able to charge more than twice their normal rates, but not to Hannah if they ever wanted to drink in the Trow again. We had prevented any worse damage occurring by virtue of Slate and his men pinning canvas across the hole in the roof, the windows were boarded and the cellar pumped dry. It was almost a year before it was fit for Hannah to return there, so for that twelvemonth mother and daughter remained at the Trow and became part of the family.

I lodged in my old attic room once more, and Hannah paid for her lodging (at her insistence, not Simon's) by tending the bar, cooking and serving food, and helping in a hundred other ways. With so many people to feed, warm and comfort, we were all run near ragged. But this flurry kept us all occupied and our minds off the circumstances that had brought us to this point, and we were glad to help all who came to the door. We were also glad to retire to the private parlour for a meal together when time afforded it, and our beds offered dreamless silence which we welcomed.

Through this we became a large and happy family, with our new additions Jack, Hannah and Edwina, and all of the visiting uncles of Slate's crew. We never had much time spare, and when we did it might be just a few minutes grabbing food at the end of the common board. Edwina spent her meals making faces at Jack, who could return them tenfold with his terrible gurning, making her scream with laughter and try harder to compete. This left Hannah free to talk with the adults, and most often with me. Slowly, throughout that winter, we built a fire between us, at first just the barest flicker of warmth fighting against the cold sadness in her heart, but then growing brighter steadily as the weeks passed, burning away at our reticence and reluctance, she being afraid of another disastrous entanglement, I not wishing to tread where I was not welcome, or to usurp the role abandoned by Teach and Woody.

So we came to be more than just colleagues or friends, devoted to seeing each other each day, dependent upon it, yet the Trow was so busy that we barely had a moment to be alone, and we could not act upon that surety. It was not until June came that we crossed the Rubicon, and I can never be sure who it was that made us ford that river, who connived at it, plotted it, or celebrated it, beyond us two.

Simon had contracts for supply with brewers, farmers, bakers and all manner of tradesmen: the Trow was a big business despite its appearance of being a family table at which a passing traveller could dine. After that hard winter, stocks of all goods were low and there was the spectre of hunger around the Avon, prices had outrun the purses of many who had survived the storm, even when the goods were available. Simon was thinking ahead and he wanted to secure his supplies for the next winter, not knowing if we might have another storm or anything else that would but his stores under strain again, so he sent me to negotiate with the farmers and stockholders for miles around. For one such trip to Ham and Pill, Slate offered to convey me, as he had many times before with the 'Deckers, saving me some hours getting there by land. He suggested that Hannah might like to come along with us, as she had never yet travelled outside the city and might enjoy the break from serving beer and swilling pots.

So early on a June morning, we boarded the Fair y Fenni as the sun rose over the Mendips, rosy light on the spire of St Mary's reflected on the waters of the harbour, amid the emerging blues of the sky. Slate handed Hannah down to me and we moved to the prow to be out of the way, as the crew cast off and the boat slid downstream.

The blackbirds started their chorus, the gulls awoke where they lined the roofs and raucously cried in complaint at their more tuneful neighbours. Then they wheeled across the dock in pursuit of the boats falling towards the Severn, first dark scimitars across the water, then peach crescents raked the sky, grace in motion. There was only a light breeze, but the tide was on its ebb so we were soon sweeping down as part of the rippled mirror, the sun edging higher behind us, deep shadows alternating with pink glints ahead.

We glided past the broad key, then the cathedral, with the green mass of Brandon Hill behind, the stone turned ruddy hues by the young sun, then out towards the hot well. Hannah had never been afloat before, nor outside the narrow boundary of Bristol, and the magic of that morning lifted her spirits, her face taking on the look of joy and fascination that I had often seen on her daughter's when she was watching Jack's conjuring and juggling. All shadow of her worries, her abandonment by Woody and Teach, losing her mother and home, and Edwina's future, melted away like the mist upon that dawn river.

From the stern came the sound of Slate singing hymns to the God that gave him that day, full of the joy of living at that moment, slipping along between the walls of the great gorge. Hannah's eyes sparkled as they reflected the ripples on the river, and she leaned forward, eager to see what new wonders might appear around the next bend. I thought that she had forgotten that the rest of us existed, as if she was one of the gulls swooping along ahead of us, low over the water. She had nothing more than the experience of each heartbeat and the gentle breeze on her face, but then she spoke.

'Isn't it just wonderful, John, to be alive this morning? Isn't it beautiful?' and she turned to me with such a look of joy in her eyes that it made my heart ache to see it.

We landed at Pill in the y Fenni's row boat, then waved Slate and his boys farewell as they glided off into the morning. Thus returned to mundane reality, we had to devote ourselves to our mission for Simon. We visited several farmhouses around Abbots Leigh, and there haggled for a guaranteed supply of lamb and beef, cheese and butter, and thus occupied the better part of the day.

We returned through the woods overlooking the gorge, on the route the 'Deckers had taken years before, at last coming to the peak opposite St Vincent's rock, and there we sat a while to rest in the shade of the trees, to watch the tide rising again far below, lifting the ships up river.

As we sat, Hannah leant against my shoulder and said, 'It has been such a lovely day, John, riding downriver in the dawn, walking back through the forest, being with you.'

Perhaps she could hear the thumping of my heart, or the catch in my breath as she said this, for she went on, 'You have been so kind to me, so dear,' and she kissed me chastely on the cheek, then as I turned towards her, as much in surprise as emotion, she took my face in her hands and kissed me softly, sweetly, brooking now word, no objection, until we lay in each other's arms upon the ground.

'Hannah, I don't know what to say.'

'Say that you love me as I love you, then no more words are needed.'

'Indeed I do love you, I think I have since first I saw you, that day Woody and Teach rescued …' but before I could say another word, she drew me down into the dry leaves, and we did not rise again until the sun was far down in the West and we had to hurry back across the meadows by the light of an early moon.

There was no inquiry at our delay, Simon and Jane exchanged glances and smiles on our late return, perhaps gaining a clue from the odd leaf still clinging to our backs. Edwina was even slightly sad to see us back again, to break up her play with Jack, to take her to bed, her tired and reluctant face showing over Hannah's shoulder as she was carried up.

Things did not change dramatically after this, but looking back I can see that Simon made certain that there were times in which I and Hannah could be alone, or sent on errands together, and we took these opportunities to grow our bond, in words and looks, and more rarely in deeds of intimacy and love. Thus we spent that glorious summer and fruitful autumn, becoming as close as any man and woman can be, each as dependent on the other's breath and heartbeat as their own.

*

We often had to supervise the repair of Hannah's house. It had not progressed rapidly after the initial precautionary sealing of the breaches in its hull, as we could not afford to pay rates that competed with those paid by the merchants for their homes and warehouses, but by September we had managed to air and dry it out, washed and lined the walls to remove the mark of the tide, replaced rush matting, cloths and cushions that had rotted, leaving only the devastation of Mistress Cleary's chamber. Hannah, who had eagerly addressed the former tasks, and prolonged their execution by perfecting the results, was daunted by that room and near fainted away on seeing the bed again, the shadow left amongst the rubble where her mother had lain. She sobbed upon my shoulder for many minutes before drawing again on her resolve and turning to the room once more.

'It must all go, even the bed; I cannot bear to see these things every day, and if we are to live here then this room must not be a blight upon our happiness.'

I hoped that this "we" might include myself, but I dared not ask if it did. My heart pounded hollowly in my chest until she said, 'Come on, John, let us clear our home so that we may live here openly in the sight of God.' She squeezed my hand to confirm our bond, and my heart almost burst with joy.

We emptied the room completely, all cloth being thrown out because it had been soaked by the storm and grown fusty, the bed was dismantled and sold for a fair price. The trunks were emptied and only a handful of keepsakes retained, including a chain of garnets that had been passed down since the Tudors reigned, and the mariner's quadrant by which she remembered her father. By the end of this, the room was stripped bare ready for the roof and ceiling to be repaired, and for life to return to the building, making it a home once more.

Hannah remained for some minutes, holding the garnets and the quadrant, standing erect and determined like a portrait of Queen Bess I have seen, before leaving the room to the mercy of the builders.

There only remained the ghost of Teach across our path to future happiness, and Hannah must have sensed that I was uneasy on this score, for one day as we returned to the Trow, she stopped me, held both my hands and looked earnestly into my eyes. 'John, dearest John, you must know that I never lay with Edward as his wife, our marriage was a gift from him to my honour, and to protect the name of Woodes, who I had mistakenly believed was betrothed to me. You are more husband to me than either of them were, or could ever have been, and though I have been widowed and abandoned, I have never yet truly been a wife. That is a duty I only owe to one man, and that is you.'

Overcome with emotion, I could not hope to match her eloquence, but merely said, 'My love, let us be married before any further misfortune can befall us.'

She wept to hear this, and kissed me, to the delight of the dock workers who saw us, and to the scandal of the few who pretend that passion has no part to play in a respectable life.

*

We were married a year to the day after the Great Storm had torn so many lives asunder, and brought us together. Simon stood in place of Hannah's father, Edwina was her bridesmaid, Slate was my best man, his crew and many of the Trow's regulars, and most of the Quarterdeckers our witnesses and supporters. As a wedding gift, Simon and Jane bought us a new bed to go in Hannah's house, finely carved and stuffed with the best wool and down. We took over the middle floor of the house and gave the top to Edwina, who felt no shade of the past in that room, indeed had a thrill of being so high up as if she was in the crow's nest of a gallant ship. We had ensured that the chimney could never fall upon the bed again, with shorter brickwork and a stout oak beam running right across the room, with the bed on the far side out of all danger.

One last incident of that glorious day I recall clearly: as we walked back from St Nicholas, having avoided St Michael's for all the death and mourning we had known there, we strolled around the now treeless Marsh, Hannah and myself at the front, Simon and Jane holding Edwina's hands as she chatted away. Slate and his boys carried Jack in style in a makeshift sedan chair, the 'Deckers and their wives promenaded behind, all very grand. When this procession reached the last corner of the square, soon to be renamed for Queen Anne, we encountered none other than Woody. There in fact was no way for us to avoid him, he was backing away from a patch of ground marked out with strings and pegs, with a periwigged man who was juggling rolls of paper. He walked flat into me, turned red-faced to berate or strike his attacker, but then froze to see me and Hannah, and our long entourage.

'What do you think you …. why, Porter, what a surprise to see you here, and with Miss Cleary too; you seem to be leading a rag-tag parade!'

'It is our wedding day, and I would have you show some respect to my wife.'

'*Your* wife? Well, you do get around, don't you Hannah?' he saw me clench my fists, and the set of Simon's jaw, and so hastily, if insincerely, retracted.

'I beg your pardon, I am sure; I had no idea. May I offer you my congratulations on this most happy day? It is a great day for me as well: this gentleman is Mr Draycott, the renowned architect. He has designed a mighty and spacious building for me to take up this prestigious position on the Square, which will no longer be the playground of riffraff but instead be the preserve of those who have been a success. It may take some time to construct, but I am assured it will be the envy of all who see it. This will be the grandest square, the place for the very best of Bristol society. You are currently standing in my withdrawing room; oh it will be grand and the source of much jealousy. I have set my sails for greatness, and this house will be the symbol by which people will recognise that I have achieved it. Well, I cannot stand around all day idly chatting; Draycott, pray explain again the merits of stucco over common stone?'

Thus dismissed from his *illustrious* presence, we walked on, and Edwina ran up to us and asked in a loud whisper, 'Who was that horrid man, Daddy?' to which I most happily answered 'He is no one to us dear, and be glad of it.'

I for one did not think any more about this incident, but I heard some years later that Butch and Crusty had returned that evening and carefully repositioned some of the pegs and string, so that the rooms were out of true and not as large as intended, and the front door always stuck badly, despite letting in a bad draught.

*

We settled into a happy married life, living at the

Cleary house, working one or both of us at the Trow, bringing up Edwina to have a fine mind and strong character, with sympathy enough to see how much better a man Umble Jack was than many a silk-clad merchant, her true father included. She has never been told that her father is really that "horrid man", instead she believes in the legend that Teach is her sire. She always and only calls me Daddy, and I am heartily glad of it.

In due course, Hannah bore me two sons, the first called Simon, the second Jack in honour of those firmest and truest friends. Slate would not have any Bristolian bear his Welsh name, nor did he like it enough to use it for himself, 'So why should a new pink baby be saddled with it, Boyo?' he had asked.

We carried on thus, happily, surrounded by love, and watched the city repair itself and become notably richer than it had ever been before. As it turned out, it was several years before the new Queen's Square was ready for its illustrious residents, and even as they took possession of their fine homes, the star of Clifton was rising over the attractions of the old Marsh.

5:Departure and Arrival

Woody completed his apprenticeship with Captain Yeomans and was then all set to take over his father's business, and control his ships, eager to make money from the African trade. He married Sarah Whetstone, the daughter of an admiral, and with his sponsorship became a full-fledged freeman of the city, and was in high standing. The Admiral was a friend of Woody's father, and it was now clear that Miss Whetstone had been his intended for many years before; his relationship with Hannah being only a way of whiling away his time until Sarah was available for marriage.

They had a grand society wedding, with all the grandest merchants and city fathers in attendance, and so it seemed that Woody was set on his course to power and fortune. They took possession of that grand house on the West side of the square, perhaps never knowing why it felt oddly mean in its dimensions, and irritated by its sticking doors.

The next year, Captain Rogers died and left all his assets, ships and business to Woody, making him initially rich and an object of jealousy and hate for his younger brother, whom he condescended to allow to work at the family firm. To grow this wealth, he sought letters of marque for several of his vessels, and aimed to profit both as a privateer and from the triangular trade. He renamed a ship after his father-in-law, fitted it for slaves and despatched it to Africa, in hopes of a tidy profit, but it fell into the hands of the French when fully laden, and this started his long fall into debt and ignominy. Watching this from afar, we could not feel sad that such hubris had been struck such a poetic blow.

Late in the year, we had word that Mr Drummond, Teach's elderly father, was gravely ill and wished to see

Hannah and Edwina. We visited his house on Denmark Street, where we found his wife bravely entertaining the many well-wishers drawn from his old classes, while her husband faded away upstairs. Mr Drummond greeted us weakly, but he smiled to see Edwina who was by then seven years of age and full of life: it was evident that he believed her to be his grandchild from his words, and the smile on his pain-ravaged face.

'I will not keep you many minutes as I have a long journey to embark upon, but I wanted a last chance to see you. I know that Edward wanted his inheritance to pass down to you, and I acquiesced to this wish at the time, and now gladly accept it. But I must also have some consideration for my dear wife and her needs, as Edward would surely not have his mother in the poorhouse because of the needs of his child. I have not fared well in recent years, and I lost much during the Storm both in property and investments I had ventured on boats that sank and stock that spoiled. After this house, there is but a little living for my wife and some trinkets of no value to any one else. So I must make it clear now that all I can pass on to you is ten guineas, and any of Edward's possessions that remain here. In the fullness of time, when Patience and I are reunited forever, you shall then have what remains, though it may be very little. I hope that you can accept this frustration of Edward's will?'

He was obviously quite exhausted by this speech, and also anxious for it all to be settled.

'Do not worry, we are happy and content, and though we may not be rich in money, we have a home and work, and the love of our friends, enough to feel wealthy beyond compare. You have shown us more consideration than we deserve, and you should rest happy that we are satisfied with our lot,' said Hannah, tenderly holding his hand. He smiled and closed his eyes, patted her hand gently, and did not wake again.

We heard later than evening that he had passed away, and that we could return after the funeral to collect the few things left to Hannah. We visited a week later to be met by Mrs Drummond's tear streaked face. Hannah firmly refused to take any of the money previously mentioned, saying that Edward would surely want his mother's greater need to take precedent. We did accept the basket of goods from Teach's room. At home, we spread the contents out across the table to better examine them. There was a selection of oddments that he had collected over the years: the purse that had been handed to Jack then stolen by Curry, beech mast from the woods, an arrow head from Stoke Leigh camp, a hymnal given to him by Spadger after his voice broke, a scrap of slate from the y Fenni, a battered tankard that bore the mark of the Trow, and his best hat, which he had worn to church. We kept all of them as a shrine of remembrance for our long lost friend.

*

It was soon after this that Mr Dampier came upon the scene. He had been a well-respected naval captain, who had sailed around the world but then fallen foul of a court-martial due to being too keen with the Cat and too mean with the bounty. He had been disgraced and ruined by the trial, and arrived in Bristol seeking some way out of his troubles, in particular wanting to use his friendship with the wealthy Captain Rogers to start some new venture profitable to himself, and glorious to his name. Finding that the father was no more, he turned his attention to Woody instead, assuming he had large reserves of wealth, but in fact by this stage much of the estate had been squandered through ill-luck and mismanagement.

Woody was also eager to start some new business that

might reverse his misfortunes, so he put what money he had into it, and worked his contacts including the grand Admiral Whetstone, Mr Dover and Mr Goldney in his new house overlooking the city. From this they formed a company with two ships, the Duke and the Duchess, with which they aimed to become the premier privateers by attacking Spaniards wherever they might find them, and particularly out on the rich routes around the Spice Islands and the East Indies.

Dampier knew that part of the world well, having aimed to intercept Spanish gold off Manila on his previous voyage, which ended farcically when his worm-eaten ships ran aground off Chile. The Bristol merchants were keen to take gold off the enemy as they had lost several slave ships between them to foreign action, and they fitted out the Duke and Duchess to be fast, fit and furious. Woody claimed the honour of being captain of the Duke, with Dampier under him as an adviser, the Duchess being put in the care of another captain called Cooke, whose honour had never been called into question, nor had his ability to bring a ship and cargo home safely been doubted. The pair of ships set off and were gone so long, without any word, that most concerned believed them to be lost, a failed gamble that the financiers could probably afford to bear.

*

Industry had begun in the city, with Mr Darby's brass works at Baptist Mills, and Mr Goldney's iron works, but the merchants looked down on these men because they were both Quakers, one of the many non-conformist groups that made their homes here. Despite this prejudice, those same merchant's happily took Goldney's money to fund the Duke and Duchess.

That grand expedition, which aimed to raise the fortunes of its many investors and the reputations of

Woody and Dampier, had departed in the middle of the summer of 1708, aiming to catch the Spanish between South America and the Indies. We did not hear from them again for three whole years, apart from the rumours that before they had even reached Ireland the crew had mutinied: an inauspicious start. There the crew were replaced by whatever squalid troop of ruffians could be assembled or pressed into service, before heading out into the silence of the ocean. It seemed that all of Woody's ventures had an element of chaos and farce about them.

The triangular trade carried on, and the longer it made money, the more it grew, with the only major losses being to French and Spanish naval action, as with the Whetstone Galley. The gold that poured into merchants' coffers was proof of the trade's worthiness, and a source of respectability, and as the holds were scrubbed and sweet when they returned full of sugar, tobacco, cotton and rum, there was no savour of the foul basis of this fortune, and the whole trade was thought as sweet as the cargo that landed on Bristol Key. In addition, the trade was justified by saving pagan souls from the fires of Hell, the profits were taken as proof of God's approval of the scheme.

*

It was in the autumn of that year, the city was flourishing on the bounty from the trade and the side benefits of privateering, as well as the new wealth from the manufacture of brass and other goods, that a stranger arrived at the door of the Trow.

It was after midnight, all were settled in their beds ready to be up early for the tide, Simon and myself being the only ones still awake as we damped down the fires, emptied slops and secured doors. I was preparing to walk home to Hannah and a warm bed, when as I pulled the Trow's heavy door shut, a shadow emerged from the gloom.

'Hold fast there, is there no harbour here for one who slipped his mooring long ago?' said the man in shadow.

'We are closed up, you may find some hospitality at the Shakespeare or the Hatchet if you care to look, or we will be open again at six. A good night to you, sir,' I replied, coolly.

'And I thought the Trow gave a warm welcome to all men; it must have changed under Queen Anne!'

'We are a most welcoming establishment, sir, if you care to visit during more regular hours, but even innkeepers require sleep, and that is where I am bound to now.'

As I moved to pass him on my way to what I will always think of as Mistress Cleary's house, a hand grasped my arm with a grip that insisted I stop.

'Do you not know me, Porter, whom you taught a lesson with a heavy tankard right here where we stand, or is that just small beer to you now?' he hissed.

'Teach – can it be you?'

'Aye, it is, but keep your voice down, for I have enemies in this town that would not have me walking free. Can we go inside away from the eyes and ears of the shadows?'

'Simon has bolted the door and retired, he will not easily or willingly open up and the noise would wake half the street. Why not come with me instead?'

'I would follow you to any safe harbour, Porter; be my pilot.'

So we walked in silence, just visible by the few lanterns

that were placed to prevent too many of our sailors drowning in their livelihood. Teach was a moving shadow keeping to the darkest patches of shade. As I came to the door, he reappeared at my shoulder and whispered, 'Is this not the Cleary's house?' to which I replied, 'Aye, it is a long tale and I will lay it out for you inside.'

I let us in, and led him through to the kitchen, where we could converse without waking the household, and where we might find some sustenance to aid our talk.

As was our routine now that we had three children, Hannah had settled Edwina and the boys, laid out a meal for me on the table, then taken herself up to warm the bed. She knew that the day at the Trow was long and not infrequently extended by tides, tardy arrivals and drunken departures. She would often wake from her first sleep as I returned, sit with me as I ate, then settle me with her own comforts before we shared the second sleep together. Now I needed to talk with Teach without disturbing her and I had been doubly careful with the doors to be quiet.

I lit a pair of candles and set them upon the table, found a loaf of bread, some cheese and a bottle of port to go with the pot of stew that had been left for me. I sat upon the bench, leaving the one fine chair for Teach.

I now got my first look at him. He wore a large hat without ornamentation, like a puritan's, with a brim so deep it concealed his eyes; a heavy travelling cloak concealed his body from the shoulders to near the ground, and what lay in between was buried behind an enormous beard, pitch black and curly, from high on his cheek bones, down onto his chest, from one ear to the other. He saw me staring and chuckled, then lifted off his hat and tousled up his long curly black hair, and then shed his cloak to reveal a dark brown velvet doublet and britches, as fine as any merchant's, though of a strange fashion. He sat himself down with a sigh of satisfaction, drew over the bread and tore off a handful, then poured us both generous portions of the wine.

'This is fine tucker for a man who has not eaten all day; your good health, Porter! I will tell you all about myself once you have satisfied my curiosity on a few vital points, if that suits you? The first of these, and I suspect the most vital of all, is how I am sitting at the board of Mistress Cleary with my old Quarterdeck chum, John Porter?'

'I will tell you gladly, though you may not be happy with all aspects of the story I have to relate. The first element of this is that Woody, your old friend and later enemy, did not take advantage of your sacrifice to marry Hannah, but instead he abandoned both her and their daughter…,' he leapt to his feet, cheese in one hand, his other a fist, spluttering in fury which I urged him to restrain.

'It is all right, Teach; she is, I trust, better off without him. He married an admiral's daughter, and after losing much of his father's fortune, he has now embarked upon a desperate mission for fame and fortune, sailing round the world to raid Spanish gold, with another man adept at losing fleets and courting disaster.'

'And how is it, pray tell, that she is better off?' he asked.

'Because she is married to me, and mother to our two fine boys, as well as her daughter whom she named after you, all of whom are at this minute asleep above our heads.'

He stared at me for a minute or more, with an intensity that I have never experienced before or since. His eyes reflected the candles, and he looked at me with a hard and unreturnable glare so that I felt increasingly ill at ease, until at last the eyelids narrowed a little, crinkles appeared at the corners, and he held out his open hand towards me.

'You have done the honourable thing, when both I and that dog Rogers ran from it. I congratulate you, Porter, and say you are the best of us all, and I know you will be rewarded in this world, and any other, for your good heart,' and he shook my hand with a grip that could anchor a ship.

'But tell me how this came to pass, it must be a pretty tale?'

So I told him all about Woody's behaviour after Edwina's birth, about the Storm and Mistress Cleary's death, our rescue of Hannah, working together at the Trow, even about that walk back from Pill to secure supplies for the winter. He leaned forward, slapped his thigh on hearing of our gallant efforts during the tempest, laughed at Jack's rescue, beamed at hearing his antics whilst entertaining Edwina, and looked a little misty as I told of the day that Hannah became my wife.

'You have had quite a time, and I would say you have the greatest tale of all the 'Deckers, if it wasn't for the one that I have to tell. But you are by far the luckiest of us all, of that I am certain,' and he slapped my shoulder firmly. 'I would have no other man than you look after dear Hannah, she needs someone solid and I know that you are a true Bristol diamond.'

'Now, before I relate my own story, tell me how fare's my own family; would they welcome home their prodigal son?'

So I had to tell him of his father's death, and his

mother's reduced circumstances and her frail health.

'I feared such might have happened, that is why I felt compelled to make this visit. Father was a good teacher, but a fool with money, and too trusting of those who deserve no trust. It is just as well that my current line of work puts a lot of gold my way, and that I can spare a pretty penny for the comfort of those back home. Before I forget, take this and put it to good use for the comfort of all Hannah's children.'

He lightly tossed a leather bag onto the table, where it made a heavy clinking sound. I opened it to find upwards of forty gold coins, of various designs, many that I had not seen before, but also a collection of guineas faced by several monarchs amongst them.

'This is too generous, Teach, I don't know what to say.'

'Just say that you will use it well and discreetly. There are those around who would make me pay a high price for disrupting their trade with Spain and France, even when it is my patriotic duty to do so, and I am under Royal license. I have an arrangement with Captain Jennings, and he will hold my share and pass it on to whomever I want, and I will put that to my mother's disposal now. But I do not think that I can see her, it would distress us both too greatly and be a waste of tears. So I will leave it in your hands to pass on this second bag, and news of her financial salvation, if I may?'

'I would be glad to be of service to you. But what is it that you have been doing that yields so much gold, and which makes you so many enemies so far away?'

'Ah, Porter my lad, that is a tale which requires a full glass and many hours to tell. Settle yourself down, and I shall begin…'

*

As you may recall, I sailed on the first voyage of the Beginning, on the new venture of the triangular trade from Bristol. As Captain Barker later related to me, the whole business is driven by the wind, not just as the means of propulsion but the direction of the prevailing winds dictates the route and the form of the trade undertaken in all of its aspects. For if a Bristol ship wants to reach Newfoundland, it can either fight against the westerly trades every step of the way, or it can take the course past Africa and have the wind with it the whole way, there and back. A ship could go to Guinea, then across to the Caribbean, and still be on the Banks sooner than if she had tried to get there directly. It makes no sense for a merchant to sail legs with his hold empty, so instead of carrying worthless ballast he would rather carry something he can sell at the next port and use the profit to buy stuff required at the port after that, and the opportunities along this route allow him to change poor quality cloth into gold in three easy stages, turning a profit on each. There is not much we would want to carry from Guinea, their main goods are gold, ivory and fruit, none of which can be bought for cloth or last the journey, or be needed in the Indies. But what they do have is a ready supply of pagans, and Factors willing to turn those raw savages into docile slaves. If it was not for the triangular course of the winds, the Africans could sleep safely at night without fear of the slavers, and the merchants of Bristol would wear a lot less silk!

All of this sounded eminently reasonable to me as the Captain explained it as we sailed south, almost as if God had set up the winds as a factory to turn these pagan savages into useful labour for our Christian plantations. But when we arrived in Guinea and I first saw those shattered souls who were bought and sold, inspected and mauled, like so many cattle; who were packed into the hold with as much care as if they were bolts of coarse cloth; I began to doubt the truth of the matter.

This gave me great unease, and over the months of the journey west before the winds towards the Indies, that unease grew. Each day, I was involved in checking for the dead and sick; any I did find were then thrown overboard like so many bruised apples. The dreadful cry of surprise, the leaden splash and the silence, each time weighed heavier upon me. I took to ignoring all but the dead, or those that were so feverish that their condition would increase the suffering of those around them, but still the toll mounted. The other sailors did not see our cargo as being any more than complaining cattle, or awkward timber, and had no consideration for them as fellow beings; their hearts were as hardened to this work as their hands were to the ropes. Some even indulged themselves by showing especial cruelty to the slaves that peaked their spite, perhaps because they looked like some old enemy of theirs from home, or for other motives too dark to mention.

After those months crossing the ocean, losing perhaps one in eight of the cargo over the side as we went, maintaining the rest on near starvation rations so that they stayed docile and kept the cleaning to a minimum, we landed them into the auction pens. There I could see the ends to which these slaves were to be put, and although it was less cruel than the confinement of the voyage, it was to be a life of constant fear of the overseer's whip, of drudgery, of hard forced labour until death released them. The only care was for the value paid at auction: lives would not be unnecessarily taken as this would be a loss of value on the books, but at all turns the soul was to be starved, the spirit crushed, and the body mortified if that was needed to maximise production of sugar or tobacco. At the pens, we fed the slaves, cleaned them and dressed them to realise a high value. They tasted the whip and soon learnt that compliance was the less painful option; subjugation of the soul is more easily borne than punishment of the flesh.

When I saved Barker from that buck who attacked him for molesting his wife, it was only on impulse. If I had thought harder, I might have relished the sight of this man who had caused so much pain in the name of profit, bearing a mortal punishment from one he sought to crush. But as it is, I stopped that man and saved the Captain, and his gratitude enabled me to hatch my plan to free Hannah's hands, and to remove myself from that sickening trade forever.

But in that at least I failed: for years, the only work I found was associated with the trade, because nothing there is done without the stain of slavery. No food is grown, or cooked, no crop sewn or harvested, no goods packed or shipped, without the involvement of black flesh under threat of a whip. Still the plantation owners complain about the wicked costs, how they barely turned a profit, yet they pay not a penny for the labour upon which all their fortune depends: they pay more for whips than they do to the people who grow their produce, more for candles to show their piety than they do to ease the pain of their workers. It is an economy of evil and cruelty, that is blind to all but the price commanded by tobacco and molasses, that aims to live like a little England in the tropics, but is built more on the backs of slaves than Rome ever was.

When the new Queen came to the throne, and we came to be at war with France and Spain, I found my way out. I joined Jennings on one of the first privateers, and I can tell you that the air was wonderful on that first day as we sailed away from the stench of slavery into the wider reaches of the Caribbean; clear sparkling, turquoise waters, and all hands paid for their labour, with a fair division of any bounty should we waylay the enemy. Jennings owned the boat and fitted it out with guns, grappling irons, swords and pistols, and other boarding equipment, yet he allowed fully half of any bounty to be divided between the hands. This made for a keen crew, with watchful eyes, up the masts and on the prow, eager to capture their first prey.

At the start, we knew exactly where to look as only days before Jennings had been peacefully trading with the very same ships. Now in possession of our letters of marque, we could seize back what we had already profitably sold. Those first prizes were easy to take, no ships were as heavily armed as Jennings' Prospect, nor as swift, nor had a captain as familiar with the waters, for he had traded there all of his life. We took ships easily, killing only the most belligerent, who would have seen us dead instead, setting the crews ashore in some remote but not inhospitable spot, before landing the goods back at our home harbour, and refitting with the proceeds. We quickly grew to a flotilla of four boats, with the Prospect still the swiftest and most fearsome, but the others none too shabby, and we found it increasingly easy to take lone ships when they could see that they were outgunned and surrounded, often not firing a shot other than one across the bows.

Within the year, we must have taken two dozen craft, upgrading to the new ship if it was better than one of our own, otherwise just taking the goods and gold, and spiking their guns before letting the forlorn enemy crew sail away once more. If the enemy captain chose to put up a fight, we would hold him prisoner and humiliate him whilst putting the rest of the crew ashore, then we would scuttle his ship. We would then either release the now shipless captain to make his way in a rowboat with no clothes or oars, or take him to be prisoner on one of the English islands. There were some occasions on which we badly used the captains, Jennings encouraging it so that we built a black name for ourselves, and this meant more crews would surrender peacefully rather than risk our wrath.

Jennings knew that most crews, even captains, had no stake in the cargo or the ship, they merely worked for the owners, and so they were reluctant to put their lives at risk to save the profits of another man. So he chided us to build up our monstrous image, to evoke fear and panic in the hearts of any that saw us, making all prefer to surrender rather than risk a fight, and the consequences of defeat. I became a mascot of sorts, growing this black beard of mine, to which I added ribbons, and hung gun fuses from my hat so they smoked and sparked, and I roared murder from the bows as we approached any we fancied to take. It was all for show, of course, we would rather turn a profit than be bathed in blood, but we were willing and able to fight if so required.

After two years, we all had fair shares laid by and could pick and choose which prizes we pursued: even the cabin boy had a house and servants on Jamaica! Of course it was not all plain sailing, we were sometimes chased by the escorts of richer ships, or hunted near our home port, and any encounter with French or Spaniards ashore might turn bitter, but our reputation tended to make for very short battles, and a strangely civil dealing with the enemy crew afterwards.

It was only when we attacked the richest prizes, carrying gold from Mexico back to Cadiz, with naval escorts and marines, that real danger and bloodshed ensued. One such ship was La Cordoba, a sweet little frigate that would have easily out-sailed the Prospect but because of her hold pregnant with gold, and surplus of guns, she lay low in the water and wallowed badly when she turned. She was accompanied by two smaller ships, packed with marines, and some returning dignitary as super-cargo, and it was because of him that fought rather than just submitting to our will when we approached.

We had known this fleet was to sail from an agent in the harbour of Caracas. Jennings had us wait for the fleet behind the island of St Lucia. He posted lookouts on the peak to signal the approach of the Cordoba which happened on the third day of our wait, when the crew were becoming restive and bored with the usual make-work chores of scrubbing decks, tidying ropes, and even whittling.

A flag was waved by our lookout, where we could see it against the forest canopy but hidden from the Spanish. We rapidly prepared, priming our guns, unfurling the sails, and weighing the anchors. Two of our fleet went round the island to the East, rounding the headland and turning as if to intercept the Spanish fleet, which caused the escorts to go on the offensive and move ahead of the Cordoba, hence engaging our smaller ships but leaving their charge unguarded. Our ships were ordered to run before the escorts after firing a volley at maximum range, leading the Spanish further away from their duty. As soon as we heard this fusillade, we cut out around the island to the West, coming neatly on the tail of the heavy gold ship which was near defenceless because of its inability to manoeuvre. We fired our warning shot across its stern, and began our carnival of acting on the bow and yard arms. I was on the bowsprit, beard bristling with fuses, hair tied with blood red ribbons, one hand on the sheet and the other swinging a cutlass, yelling that I was the infamous Barbo Negro and they better heave to or bear the consequences.

They did not yield, instead they ran and turned at full speed, with their gun ports open, ready to deliver a broadside. She heeled over badly due to her load, and must have started to take on water before a single shot was fired. When they did fire, the ball went well over our masthead due to how far she had rolled. Before their captain could correct this error, the boat was down and sinking, taking all that gold and a full complement of crew with it. The water is deep on that side of the island, and by the time we crossed the site we could only see her topsails as a brighter patch in the infinite deep blue of the sea. Few of the crew escaped, all from the open deck, none from below.

So many more were trapped and drowned as that gold sailed to the bottom of the sea, we could hear their screams and knocking as it descended. We picked up the survivors and gave them all a tot of rum, apart from the reckless captain whom Jennings had whipped and salted for risking his ship and crew for another man's wealth.

The rest of our fleet returned, with the two escorts now controlled by our men, having turned and outgunned them on the far side of the island. Jennings transferred the enemy, including the broken captain, upon the most badly damaged escort, and cut them loose. We had not won the prize we so desired, but we had done our duty by preventing that gold filling the war coffers of the Spanish, we had dropped many of their guns into the depths, and demoralised many of their sailors.

We retained the belongings of that nobleman, leaving him with only the clothes of a common sailor, and a fury that could have coddled eggs. We kept the other escort for our fleet, so that we at least gained something from the venture. We would have preferred to have the Cordoba, as it was a fine vessel, but we had to satisfy ourselves with that dignitary's clothes and jewels. This suite was his; doesn't it fit me well?

Because of that adventure, we were actively sought out by the Spanish navy, whose wages were now in Neptune's pocket, and if it was not for the guile and skill of Jennings, we would have suffered badly for it. Instead our continuing liberty only increased our reputation, and when the Spanish had twenty boats hunting us to the East, we were taking prizes off the coast of Belize. When they laid a trap for us in Cuba, we slipped away under the cover of a nighttime fog, and were coming down like a wolf upon the French fold a hundred leagues away while the Spaniards still awaited us at the mouth of an empty river.

Our enemies never understood that Jennings valued his crew more than the wood of his fleet. When seemingly cornered, more than once we would leave them besieging an abandoned ship, or sacrifice one ship to free another.

Our closest scrape happened after many months of angering the enemy. By chance we were moored at night in a deeply incised bay off a lee shore, when a fleet of Spanish warships closed off the mouth of the bay. It was evident that at first light we would be attacked and captured or sunk, and we had no opportunity to manoeuvre or escape before dawn. Jennings had the crew abandon the ship and row to shore, with muffled oars and no lights showing, taking advantage of a moonless sky. We then carried the boats across the island and assembled again under the trees at the edge of the beach.

We could see a single brig held in reserve, silent and dark as its crew slept in preparation for a busy day fighting "El Capitano Hennings". He had us put our boats in the water again, we rowed noiselessly out to the Spaniard, boarded her and captured the crew without a single shot, and only bruises and bumps inflicted upon the enemy, who had awoken to find knives at every throat. We could not release the crew because they would raise the alarm for the rest of the fleet, so instead we secured them in the hold and sailed away towards Jamaica where they were detained by the Governor.

In this process we managed to exchange our wormy old vessel for one of the sweetest and swiftest to ever come out of Cadiz, and to earn the Jennings the title of "El Zorro", the Fox. Soon we were being accounted responsible for all the Spanish losses at sea, even those that we knew were due to other privateers, storms, reefs or incompetent captains running aground, or running off with their masters' gold. In fact, we spent the next few months living it up in Jamaica, maintaining and upgrading our fleet, and dallying with the French off the American coast. Sometimes we attacked under the Spanish flag for the devilment of it, hoping to drive a wedge between those two unlikely bed-fellows.

We were soon up to a fleet of five, armed to the teeth, and swifter than all but an unloaded slaver, and we had a safe home port guarded by the Queen's finest. The Navy always bristled until they saw Jennings' flag flying at the masthead of our ever changing fleet.

To enhance his reputation, Jennings had a dozen standards made, each black with a white fox head over crossed swords, which he carried with him from ship to ship. He had one made up into a waistcoat so that he always had it with him, no matter if his fleet had two oars and only space for him and the ship's cat.

The regular navy does its own part, protecting our harbours, mounting attacks on enemy ports, conveying soldiers to the mainland and escorting larger merchant ships well out into the open sea. It is left to us privateers to inflict damage upon the trade of the other side, which we do admirably and to our great profit, but the tars are evidently resentful of our success and wealth.

The French are sickening already in their possessions, but the Spanish are more determined, and too reliant upon American gold funding their lifestyle at home to consider giving up. It is a dangerous game, of course: privateer boats have been seized, or sunk, some have been turned against us, and many of the crews have died at sea or on the gallows. Captain Jennings has kept away from real hazard, whilst making a fortune where the pickings are surer and safer, and he has steered us clear when things have turned stormy.

*

'It is a great life for a black sheep with no ties, like myself. I did have a little speech prepared to persuade you to join us, but I can see you have found a good anchorage and far greater bounty by your good heart and honest labour, than any of us who fight under the black flag. You have Hannah and the children, and all the joys that they entail. Even if you are the adopted son that will never inherit, you have all the wealth you could ever want asleep within these four walls tonight. I bless you and thank you for it; I know you have corrected the harm that my and Woody's follies have inflicted, and all is well,' Teach said.

'Now, I have filled my hold with good food and wine, and need to drop anchor, so I bid you a good night, my dear Porter.'

My old friend pulled his cloak around himself, tugged his hat down over his eyes, and lay out full length on the bench, and was soon asleep and snoring fit to alarm the neighbours. I damped down the fire and climbed the stair to Hannah, leaving Teach to the flickering of a candle and the glowing embers in the kitchen. I undressed as quietly as I could and slid into the bed, where Hannah had warmed it better than any pan could, she shifted to fit to me without waking, and I was soon asleep to dreams of the high seas, and daring deeds.

It was late when I awoke, and as the year was old the dawn delayed and misted. 'What kept you so late last night, John, it is not like you to be so tardy?' Hannah asked as she awoke beside me.

'I would have been here earlier than usual, my dear, but I was detained by an old friend; can you guess who it was?'

'Was it Peter, visiting from his Butchery in Bath?'

'No, my dear, it was not Butch but instead …'

'Don't tell me, surely it was not Mr Jones, but he is quite the regular visitor, welcome though he is, so not an excuse for irregular hours.'

'No, it was not Slate, it was…'

'Well, then, I cannot guess who could detain you at such an hour, and would not be put off to the morning, nor do I think much of it!'

'You might change your mind, for it was Teach, Edward that is, who has been abroad these ten years and dead to us, in name at least.'

She gasped and sat up quickly, 'Dear Edward, where is he now? You should have woken me at least, oh how I want to see him; the children must meet him too, of course.'

'He is asleep in the kitchen, if he has not already woken and eaten all the food in the pantry.'

Hannah hurriedly put on a robe, and we descended quickly, full of anticipation, to the kitchen. On opening the door, we found the room to be deserted, and only the debris of our late night repast was testament to the truth of my story.

'Where is he, surely he is still here?' she asked anxiously.

'I think he has left us a note dear, under the bottle; shall I read it to you? It says:

'Dear Porter, and Hannah who will surely read this too, I thank you most heartily for the hospitality that you showed me when I appeared out of the night, and I am most glad to have talked with you once more. I realise that my purpose in visiting, to persuade you to join me in the life of a privateer, was misguided and moreover the worst thing you could possibly do. I am jealous of the happiness you have found, it radiates from your eyes and is carried in every word you speak, and I trust that it will continue for the rest of your lives, may they be long. I hope that you will find some good fortune to secure yourselves in later years, so that your grandchildren can share in your perfect happiness.

I have as usual skulked off like a coward; I do not think that I could bear being made to feel welcome in your home and family only to return where I must, far away. So I will disappear again, you would not find me if you tried, so best not to waste your time in looking.

Be of good cheer, my hearties. Know that I am doing

what I believe to be right, and be as happy for me as I am for you.

Farewell, your friend as always,

Teach'

Hannah was shocked and dismayed, 'You must find him, John. Go immediately, and I will find the other Quarterdeckers to help you, as soon as I have summoned Mistress Griffin to see to the children.'

So I ran out, barely prepared for the cold autumn fog that awaited me. I sought Teach in all his old haunts, but found no one that had met him, nor seen any person of his peculiar appearance. The remaining 'Deckers, Fuller, Crusty, Jasper and Spadger, helped in the search but none had heard from Teach. It seemed that his mission to Bristol was to seek me alone, or at least first, and he had changed his plans overnight. A couple of times I thought I saw a familiar figure in the mist, but these just melted away as I approached. I cannot be sure that any one of those phantoms was him, but I sensed that he watched my pursuit with mild amusement, before finally departing unseen.

The final apparition, which I was sure to be Teach, was crouched near the new square in the shadows as evening came on that sunless day. This time as I ran towards it, it did not disappear, and I challenged it.

'Teach, what are you about, leaving us like that?'

'Yuz not seein akrut, Porter, tiz but I, Jack,' the figure revealed. He had been minding his business when a bundle of rags was dropped in front of him. When he examined it, he found it to be a fine set of clothes, with two guineas in the pocket.

He had not seen nor heard his benefactor, but he was now wearing the large hat and cloak that Teach had worn on the previous night, and below I could glimpse the suit of that Spanish ambassador in all its splendour. So Teach had managed to continue being a guardian to Jack, and at the same time frustrated our search for him by ditching most of the elements of his appearance by which he might be described or identified. For all I knew, he may well have removed that magnificent beard, which any trapper might have been proud to wear, or possibly have hunted down and sold as a fine pelt on Hudson's Bay.

It was hopeless, and so dejectedly I returned to the house once more, by way of the Trow where I had to explain my unexpected absence to Simon. He became quite animated, in exchange for the angry frown he wore when I first entered, 'So that was Teach, was it? I did not recognise him myself, when he came in here a few hours ago, he said he had something that he thought belonged to you, and he left it in my keeping. Here it is.'

He handed me a small box that I recognised as coming from our kitchen, we used it to hold our tiny store of sugar, but now it felt unusually heavy. When I opened it, I saw that it contained twenty or more gold coins of a Spanish design, enough if not to buy a house then at least to build one. Simon had no idea where Teach had gone afterwards; as he had still been dressed in his fine clothes, we had no clue to his new appearance.

I took the box and returned with it to Hannah, who had been back in the house for some hours to act as a central point for information from the 'Deckers, to no avail.

'Hannah, my love, he has been as good as his word and disappeared. I have had no sighting of him all day and have only certainly crossed his trail twice, and both of those in the last hour without any further hint as to his course, but he left this at the Trow,' I said as I handed her the box, and she gasped at what it contained.

'This will see us comfortable for some time, John, but it pains me that this gift is truly his final farewell to us. What a good but misguided man, always making unnecessary sacrifices for the happiness of others. We must endeavour to keep his good name alive, amongst his friends and beyond.'

So Teach left us once more to our domestic bliss, and our daily labours at the Trow, and we heard not a word from him for years, nor any much detail of the war with the Spanish and French in which he was engaged.

Teach's gold was put to good use by us: we took some to ease his mother's life a little, and the rest to ensure that the children had as good an education as we could find, even Edwina. This was most economically provided by bringing a tutor to the house, as at that time the only teaching for girls was at the Red Maids and that was only so that orphans could learn to sew and keep house, that they might find employment and security in life. Later on, all of them had places at Mr Bedford's school at the Temple. Our children learnt mathematics, latin, read from the Bible in English, and they studied modern works such as those of Shakespeare and Donne. They also had some French and Spanish, in case we should ever be at peace long enough for trade to begin with those countries again. Without Teach's gold, none of this would have happened, and the children would have been condemned to follow as lowly a life as that of myself and Hannah, though it has to be said she is far better read than I am.

*

One addition I will make here. Further to Teach's

assertion that I was the adopted son who would never inherit, and must look sharply for some new source of wealth to secure my old age, a sad turn of events brought that very thing to pass. Not many months after Teach's visit, Simon received bad tidings. His only son, Roger, had been at sea for many years and had always planned to make his fortune before returning to Bristol, rather than risk being a cellar man or bar tender for the rest of his days. We had not heard any word of him for a considerable time; he had never been very communicative and messages often went astray as they crossed the world, even from the most diligent correspondent.

Just before Christmas, a man came to the inn who had evidently fared badly at Fate's hands. He was perhaps only thirty years of age but appeared to have almost twice those years, had a darkly tanned skin that bore several silvery scars, and he had the hollowed eyes of one who has known starvation and never truly recovered from it. He spoke with an accent that I had rarely heard before, a soft but cracked Scottish brogue.

'I am seeking Captain Hawkins, might you know where I could find him? It's yourself, well that is the first good luck I have had in a very long time. I am afraid that I bear ill news for ye,' he revealed.

'Sit yourself down, sir, we have no whisky but I expect that brandy will serve you well enough,' Simon offered.

The sailor thanked Simon, and then continued, 'Aye, anything to chase the chill from these bones, and to damp down the fever I carry with me wherever I go, will do me well enough. To get to the heart of the matter, without ado, I have to tell you that your son Roger is no more, I buried him myself with these blasted hands of mine.'

Simon went white and rocked a little, I helped him to a

chair and fetched him another glass of brandy. It was not until he had taken quite a gulp, spluttered at the burning, and squeezed his eyes shut for a moment, that he finally spoke again, 'Sir, please tell me how this occurred, and how you knew my son?'

'Cap'n, I will answer the last first of all, as it is an easier recollection for me to bear. I first met Roger upon a boat trading in the Indies, he was the bosun and like to be master in a year or two, I was to help him with the navigation of those islands. Being of a similar rank and age, we got to yarning and liked each other well enough. Then as the old century drew to a close, I aimed to return to Scotland where a new company was being started to compete with the English East India and African companies, and much good fortune was promised by that venture. Roger felt that this might lead him to greater things than the small trade around the islands, so he came along. We both enrolled in the exploit, and were all eager to sail to Africa or India, but by the time we embarked we were instead dispatched to start a colony in Panama, in a place called Darien, although it was going to be named New Caledonia when we had settled it. We were to make our fortunes by controlling fast trade between the Atlantic and the Pacific, cutting many leagues off the journey around the toe of the Americas, saving months and many cargoes that would as like have been lost to the sea.

There were fifteen hundred of us onboard the fleet that sailed from Leith, keeping our heads down so the English might not guess our purpose or destination. By the time we reached that so-called Golden Isle off the coast of Panama, there were already a few dead from fever and scurvy, but the rest set to with a purpose to clear the jungle for a fort, trading post and harbour, as well as land to feed us. It all looked rosy, but the crops we planted failed, disease of all kinds ran through the colony like a firestorm in that wretched, steamy heat, and all our attempts to break a path through to the Pacific were frustrated by endless mountains, rivers and trackless swamps. On top of all this, no traders called in at our port, being either ignorant of its existence, or warned off by the Spanish who claim all trade along those coasts as their own. Within a year, most of our number had died of hunger or disease, or attacks by the natives, or perished trying to escape. The fever took Roger, hale and hearty one day, pale and gibbering on the second, dead by the third. I buried him on clear ground overlooking the harbour so he could see the ocean, and said what words I could of comfort and commemoration, before collapsing into a fever of my own.

To my shame I survived, and with a fifth of our original number we sailed for home, abandoning that awful place and all our beloved dead. Even that was not the end of the folly, for before we had returned, the stupid lying letters of good news that we had sent home at the beginning of the misadventure, had caused another thousand misguided fools to set out to join in our good fortune, and wreck themselves upon that accursed shore anew.

I am sorry that I have nothing to give you of Roger other than the tale of his demise, but I brought back only that and the broken body you see before you.'

The effort of this story clearly exhausted the unnamed man, tearing both at his body and his heart.

'Sir, what you say pains me greatly, but I am glad that he had as good a friend as you with him at the end. Please stay with us here until you have gained some strength, and perhaps you can remember more of my son to warm my memories of him,' Simon suggested, as he fought back his own tears.

In so saying, Simon closed one chapter of the tale of the Trow, and opened another one, for in a conversation with me some weeks later, after the sailor Angus had set out again for his home in Scotland, Simon made it clear to me that he now held me as his son and heir, and that I should consider myself his equal in all respects.

With Teach's gold, and the happy consequence of Roger's sad death, I had indeed found some small fortune to keep me in old age, even if the taste of this good fortune was almost too bitter to bear.

6:Wanderers Return

We again settled into our life of parenthood, serving at the Trow, and loving each other, with little to disturb its pattern. More than a year after last seeing Teach, we heard that his mother had died in her sleep, still clasping a locket given to her by her husband which contained a lock of her son's hair. At least both of her men were close to her heart when it finally failed in its duty. As we expected, there was precious little estate left to pass on to Hannah, and that smallness made it easier to accept, knowing that Mistress Drummond's few resources had been spent easing her own discomfort and not conserved for our sakes. She was buried at St Michael's with her husband, as so many of our friends and relations have been over the years, with that locket safely in her grasp, over her heart.

We had no way to communicate this news to Teach, I doubt if he ever heard it by other means, and this made him seem to be even further from us, more a story than a real man.

In the autumn of the following year, we learnt that Woody's expedition had finally returned but had chosen to anchor in London rather than Bristol, to the great annoyance of its merchant owners and investors. Woody's luck continued to run badly as it seems that he, of necessity, had called in to the Dutch colony of Batavia in the East Indies, and in doing so had violated the monopoly of the great Company that laid claim to all trade in that region. After much strife and legal argument, he was forced to pay six thousand pounds to settle the case, far more than he had hoped to earn himself from his three years sailing around the world, with much hardship entailed. The merchants managed to double their money and were well enough pleased with Woody, who had taken the largest risk and was again faced with huge debts run up in his absence by the incontinent spending of his wife, and by his failing business concerns. He returned to Bristol at the end of the year, a wearied and broken man.

He came soon to the Trow, no more the arrogant captain of business with a fleet of his own, but as near to collapse as any man I have seen.

'Porter, if I may still claim the honour of addressing you by such a familiar term, I come to you as a fool who has run after dreams of wealth and returned only in rags. I have spent years trying to grow the fortune and fleet that my father left me, and I have been reduced to selling almost all I own. I could do with a friend who is neither a creditor nor a trickster, to put my feet on the path again, and I can think of no man who better deserves the name of friend than you, even though I have never deserved the friendship that you have shown me.'

'Woody, I am not a man to turn away a cry for help, but you must know that you have wronged the people I love most of all, and it is hard for me to forgive that in any man. But you look terrible, so I will bring you a plate and a glass and we shall see if hospitality can overcome hostility, as you tell me your tale.'

He sat humbly in the corner, warming himself at the fire while he waited for the food and drink that I brought to him. He did not look like a man of my thirty years, but more a man of Simon's age, and badly used at that. His hair had thinned and was greying, his face had a fading tan tending towards jaundice, with striations and scars, deep lines but no marks of habitual laughter, more the set of deep sorrow and strain. He had a terrible mark in his left cheek, puckered pink and angry, and his whole face was pulled towards this wound. He was ill-shaken and care worn, and though it was now December he still wore clothes both old and unsuited to the cold. I drew myself up a chair near the fire, and let him choose how he wished to tell his tale.

*

They had set off full of vigour and hope, more than three years before, but from the outset they were cursed with ill luck and bad planning. After the first mutiny they had to replace much of the crew, and thus had a body of men that did not work as a team and in fact often did not even have a common tongue by which to communicate. There was another mutiny when some of the hotter hands wanted to attack a Swedish vessel, and Woody had to deal harshly with all of those men or they would never have got south of Spain, but that was the cause of later resentment rather than respect. He regretted ever having listened to that damned Dampier, who was trying to recover his fortune by burning through Woody's; he was a poor help and his reputation for ill-treating crew was well known to all hands before they had even left Bristol.

Dampier was as bad luck to the voyage as if he had slaughtered every dolphin that crossed their path. When they reached Tenerife, they recognised that they had insufficient equipment for doubling the Horn or following Drake's passage, so they provisioned with wine to warm the blood and turned many of their blankets into extra clothing for that cold and inhospitable journey. But they failed to reach the passage, the storms in the Southern Ocean blew them far south, maybe further than anybody else had ever been, and they would have worried of freezing to death if they were not already terrified of the wind, and of waves higher than their masts. There may be land down there, Woody did not know, but he saw plenty of floating bergs like those of the far north which break off the continent up there, and these others may have hailed from some austral land of which they had no sight.

By the time the fleet had returned to calmer latitudes, they were running out of provisions and the crew was rife with scurvy, and they had long run out of the last of the limes with which they made the water palatable. Woody dared not pull into any Spanish port in that weakened state, being on a mission with letters of marque to raid the wealth of Spain, so they soon were desperate for a source of fresh food and water.

At this point Dampier provided his sole benefit to the mission, for he pointed on the charts to where a tiny group of unconsidered islands lay off the coast of Chile, where they could safely drop anchor and resupply. He had last been there on his own round the world cruise, shortly before he lost all his ships to his own incompetence, burrowing worms and the rocks of the continental coast. The fleet pulled into a large sandy bay and the crew gladly went ashore to find what sources of food and water were available. There they found a river as sweet as nectar which had the men bending their knees to God in thanks.

Woody decided they should rest there to heal the sick, which was most of their number, and to melt the ice out of their bones. They had been on that beach for a couple of days when into the middle of their encampment walked the oddest creature Woody had ever seen. It had the shape and carriage of a man, but was covered in goatskins from head to toe and looked wilder than the original owners of those skins; where might have been face was all beard; and it carried on a muttering argument with itself. It carried a musket in one hand and had slung a satchel of sorts made from yet more goatskin across its shoulders. This contained much of the creature's possessions: powder and shot, a knife, a small block of tobacco, the remnants of a pipe, a steel and flint, a small flask, and a well-thumbed Bible.

The newcomer was wild-eyed to see Woody's crew, and spoke in a cracked voice that at first they could not understand, and so they believed him to be some aboriginal of the island. When it spotted a bottle of madeira it gestured wildly and was most grateful when they offered a portion of it, and with that liquid easing its throat they at last could make out that it was indeed speaking a form of English, although with a strong accent of Scotland.

The man, as he was now revealed, began to make Woody understand that he had been living alone on this remote island for years, with only the goats for company, from which he derived food, clothing and the marginal sanity to survive. He had lived on his wits and the small amount of provisions with which he arrived, before he was able to establish a sustained life based upon the goats and some meagre crops that he had grown from stray seeds that landed with him.

Just as the man had finished revealing his story to Woody, fully emerged from his hermit-hood thanks to the wine, Dampier arrived to complain to about the arrangements of the camp upon the beach. It was all Woody could do to stop the ragged goatskin man from leaping upon Dampier and filleting him with his knife; it took fully four of the crew to pull him away from the ashen faced adventurer, and they then had to pin the goat-man down to find the cause of this primal upset in his emotions.

It transpired that the aboriginal hermit was one Alexander Selkirk, who had been master mariner on Dampier's previous expedition, until they had called in at these islands. Selkirk had demanded that the ships pull-to and let themselves be thoroughly careened for the tropical waters had caused to grow upon them such a wealth of weed and barnacles that they handled poorly, and in his experience where you got both of these you also find burrowing worms which could turn the sturdiest oak into sponge in very short order. He feared that the hulls might already be so unsound that they could fail in the more trying conditions of Cape Horn and all hands would be lost. Dampier had refused to accept such a delay to his plans and poured scorn upon Selkirk's opinion, which left the Scot with no choice but to request to be put ashore rather than drown in those rotten hulled ships. So it was that he was marooned on that isle with only his sea trunk, enough powder, shot and provisions for perhaps one good hunt on a Shropshire Sunday, and a Bible with which to make peace with his maker. He was left to make what life or death he could on that tiny rock, with no hope of rescue, while the blessed William went off to pursue Spanish gold.

It was of great comfort to Selkirk, and embarrassment to Dampier, that not many weeks after this marooning, the fleet did indeed sink and wreck upon the coast of Peru, and Dampier had to make his way back in a stolen boat with some remnant of his crew before being thrown into prison as a pirate by the Dutch, and he eventually returning to England to face disgrace. It was this sequence of misfortune that led Dampier to dishonestly persuade Wood into mounting that new expedition.

Selkirk was not going to forgive Dampier for his idiocy and arrogance, nor forget the years of isolation and privation upon that lonely isle, and he was truly minded to remain with his goats rather than join any mission that counted Dampier in its number. With a good glass of madeira inside him and all the assurances that Woody could give him that his old captain had no commanding role in the current venture, Selkirk finally decided to give up his solitude for the chance to converse with people again. He also missed other blessings of civilisation, not least of which being cheese of which he had fantasised but failed to manufacture from the milk of his goats.

Selkirk was a strange one: he had been a buccaneer and a privateer for as long as any man, and rose to the post of sailing master under Stradling; he knew how to handle a ship in calm and tempest, and how to judge the soundness of a craft; he could spot a heavily laden enemy ship by the way its masts moved even before its hull came over the horizon, and he could plot a course to intercept with the greatest advantage to his captain given the state of wind and tide, yet he knew almost nothing of how to relate to other men or command a crew.

After four years of his own company ashore, with only his wits, the Bible and some feral goats and cats for company, Selkirk had become an island himself, wholly self-reliant and largely silent, apart from muttering to his God under his breath. When he had a ration of drink, he changed into a charming and humorous creature who entertained all with his tales of taking prizes from the Spanish, of the ports he had seen and the women he had wooed, all in a rolling Scottish brogue which became almost incomprehensible as the bootle emptied. Once in his cups, he would become maudlin and curse his fate, claiming that he should have stayed at home and become a master cobbler like his father rather than chase blowsy Spanish ladies all over the seven seas.

With Selkirk on-board, Woody had several quick successes, Dampier sulking in the background all the while, taking the prizes easily and even adding some of them to our fleet. Woody then foolishly tried to take a coastal town, but the citizens were wily and hid all their wealth, only yielding up the sort of trinkets shipped to Guinea in exchange for slaves. This so angered the crew, who had anticipated rich pickings, that they dug up the graves in search of treasures and were cursed with sickness and death for it.

After this, they had weeks without sighting any vessel larger than a fishing smack, neither did they sight any settlements along that sun-bleached coastline. Woody feared that the men would rise up again, and he was preparing to sell his life dearly from a stronghold in the fo'c'sle, when there was a call from the masthead.

They engaged Our Lady of Desengunyo and overtook her without any substantial fighting, so surprised had she been to find an English fleet off the Pacific coast. She was so heavy with gold and goods that she wallowed when trying to manoeuvre, like a fat matron in all her skirts. Dampier was full of his own greatness for this, but in truth it was Selkirk who plotted the course so that they could surround the Lady leaving her no chance of escaping the embrace.

They did not count on the Lady having a heavily armed ladies-maid that had become detached, and having unsuccessfully challenged Woody's attentions to the mistress, she fled leaving the Duke in more tattered robes than usual.

Although the engagement with this maid was brief, it had a long lasting effect upon Woody. There must have been at least one able musketeer on that boat, perhaps up in the crow's nest, for he picked Woody out on the bridge and fired a large ball at him. If he had not at that moment turned at another sound, Woody would surely been killed. Instead the shot struck him in the cheek, below the left eye, and wedged in the roof of his mouth. Woody was knocked off his feet, blood flooding his mouth and boiling out of his face, but he continued to command for several more minutes until the Lady was taken, and the maid fled, before collapsing upon the deck.

He awoke in his cabin, the carpenter-surgeon unable to do more then staunch the flow of blood and crudely sew his face shut with a sail needle. He had no tools nor skill to remove the ball, his only experience beyond woodwork being in the amputation of damaged limbs, in which at least some of his patients had survived. Woody was in tremendous pain, and regularly had to spit out blood and fouler humours; his eye was swollen shut and he had no strength to stand, but he still directed the deployment of the wealth captured from the Lady, over a hundred thousand pounds in gold, jewels and fine goods. Woody then determined that they should turn for home before anything else could befall them.

Woody put Dover in charge of the Lady, with Selkirk to guide him, and you can be sure that it was Selkirk who steered the craft and not that apprentice financier. Four vessels now set course for home, damaged and low in supplies but with gold enough to justify the voyage. Woody lost track of the weeks after that due to fever caused by his awful wound.

They called in at Batavia to resupply, for which they had to trade some of silks, and in that process they violated the Company's monopoly, and hence caused all kinds of trouble for Woody. The pain that was his companion every day, was cured by a skilled Dutch surgeon, who extracted the ball and closed the wounds as cleanly as he could. At the Trow, Woody placed the offending article in all its horrid glory upon the table, still bearing the marks of his blood upon its surface.

The surgeon made as good a job as he could, but I could see that there would be few fair ladies swooning for Woody ever again, though some might faint at his monstrous appearance. His wife had screamed on first seeing him as he returned, and did not readily believe it was Woody. None of this voyage had brought him any joy, for after it he was in such deep debt that the house in Queen Square must be lost, and his reputation was lower than it had ever been. Even his backers, who had made a pretty penny from the venture, refused to see him and resented that their piles of gold were not even larger.

*

After paying out this tale, Woody said, 'I, who cared so much for my name, fortune and good looks, have lost all of them on one foolish throw of the dice, and now I am like a wreck floating into harbour. What am I to do to keep my family fed and a roof over our heads?'

He looked at me then, tears streaming down his devastated cheeks, a shadow of the arrogant youth, who still held my childhood friend in his eyes, but only as a faint echo. The firelight flickered on the horrid ball of lead extracted from his skull, flattened by the impact, gouged by the surgeon's tools, its dull grey sheen as evil in purpose as anything I had ever beheld.

'Woody, God knows I have enough reason to cast you back into the night and damn your soul: the way you treated Hannah and abandoned your child, chased Teach away to the ends of the earth and set yourself up as better than all of us. But it also occurs to me that without these scandalous actions, I would never have married my beloved wife, nor would I have my children or the shelter of my own roof, and all of these should make me eternally grateful if I could only forget the wrongs that brought them about. I am conscious that my daughter carries your blood, and for the sake of that blood I should show you some mercy.

'I am not a rich man, and much I own is locked away in wood, brick and mortar, but I can spare you some kindnesses. I can let you have a small loan, though you may never tell anyone of it, and I can offer you some advice. If you come back again in the morning, I will be able to advance you ten pounds, which should help you in some small way.

'The advice I will give you is in two parts. Firstly, you must swallow your pride and try whatever you can to reduce your expenditure and attempt anything legal to increase your income, even if this is not to the taste of the husband of an admiral's daughter. You must let-out or sell your fine house in the square, you should readily find a taker as it is now a most fashionable address, and you can then move somewhere more suited to your resources. You must then make as much out of your recent adventures as you can without risking any capital by embarking on another cruise.

'I would propose that you do this by writing a book that is both informative for other navigators who might follow your course, and also entertaining to the general public. The first might be most taken with your sojourn into the southern seas, the preservative effect of limes for health, the coast of South America, and opportunities for provisioning thereabouts. The second, larger audience will be excited by storms and battles, your bravery in continuing when badly wounded, and the ships filled with gold. They will be amused by your account of Mr Selkirk, half man and half goat as he was, like some God fearing faun, or Pan himself, and they will be mightily impressed by your journey right around the world without losing either ship along the way.

'If you commit yourself to sitting down and writing such an account, then we can provide you a space here in which to write, away from the pressures of your much reduced home, and when it comes time to publish I may be able to help you there too. Now this is not much and I cannot offer more, does its taste suit your palate?'

He looked at me long and hard, again with tears in his eyes, then said, 'Porter, it is true what I have heard, that the best heart in Bristol belongs to John at the Trow. I will gladly grab hold of this lifeline that you have thrown to me, and I will do all that you have suggested, with a good heart. Your counsel is wise, and though it is bitter for me to leave the square, I know it will make a great difference to my fortunes. I will return tomorrow with pen and paper and will humbly start my journal, while my wife bewails our fate at home. I will not forget this kindness, I truly know how much it costs you to offer it to a wretch like me.'

He rose then and clasped me to his chest, and I could feel how thin and insubstantial he had become. He left with a lighter step than that with which he had arrived, with the slightest twitch of the old arrogance to his shoulders, which made me smile, as he still looked more captain of the road than commodore of the fleet.

I could not keep this arrangement secret from Hannah, of course, nor would I have even tried. She saw Woody at the Trow the next day as he sat bent over a muddle of papers and she did not recognise him until I revealed his identity. She let out a little cry and put her hand to her mouth: was this really her former handsome beau, the man who had so swayed her with romance that she had willingly given her virtue to him, this now shabby and aged man with the ruined face?

I had explained the pact that I had made with him, and why overall I felt gratitude or pity rather than resentment towards him; his betrayal of her having been the enabler of our own happiness together. She was not totally persuaded by my words, but on seeing this devastated wreck of a man, her natural compassion overcame her former resentments and she graciously dealt with him, as kindly as she would be with any other customer, if not more so.

For his part, Woody was humility itself, asking my opinion on a turn of phrase, or on how much detail to include on his choice of provisions, relations with the crew, or on his marooned friend Selkirk. For the most part, he sat in a corner by the window where the light was better during the day, then returned to his new and more humble abode before he might have to resort to expensive candles. Even the cost of paper and ink stretched his meagre resources, but I was glad to supplement them now that I could see the merits of what he was producing. The work was to be both useful to any person planning a similar expedition, and at the same time be interesting and exciting to the general reader, and we both had great hopes for its success. He worked at it for several hours every day, when he was not needed to settle his own much diminished business affairs, which mostly involved the selling off of all his assets.

During this process, which took a number of months, I made the acquaintance of another visitor. One day, just as spring was coming in, a sailor of odd habit came into the Trow and requested a glass of rum to warm his bones. When I brought it to him, he asked if I might "Ken where I can find Cap'n Rogers," and when I pointed him out at his table in the corner, he hailed Woody loudly and strode over to him with a roll to his gait.

'Landlord, ye put yon man's drink on ma slate – I owe

him a lot and now I have the means to make amends. I dinnae suppose ye have any whisky aboot the hoose? Nae problem, rum will serve reet enow.'

I brought over a bottle to Woody's table with two glasses and received a gold coin of unusual design in return, 'That should cover it an' all its wee brothers to come, jest see a man disnae go thirsty,' said Woody's guest.

As I turned to leave them, Woody grabbed my arm and pulled my down onto the bench, 'Porter, I would like to introduce you to the goat man of Juan Fernandez, the saviour of our voyage around the world, and raconteur extraordinaire, Mister Alexander Selkirk. Alec, this is Porter, a childhood friend of mine who has seen past my many wrongdoings, to come to my aid in my time of need.'

'Glad to meet ye, Mister Porter, an' even gladder ta see that the Cap'n has some friends ashore, for he seems to have such terrible luck, an' I ken an awful lot aboot luck an' providence, d'ye hear?'

'Porter has kindly helped me get back onto an even keel, he has provided me this space to write up my journal in the hope that it might rescue me from poverty, and my name from disgrace. I have just reached that part of our voyage where we dropped anchor off your island, so perhaps you can tell us again how you came to be there, and how you survived alone for so long, whilst I make some notes on what you say?'

'Och well, now ye have got me onto my two favourite subjects, to wit the greatness of Alec Selkirk esquire, and the folly of that idiot William Dampier, may his black heart moulder forever!'

He winked at me as he said this, uncorked the bottle and filled his glass halfway, then topped it up with water, a taste he had acquired whilst on naval vessels.

*

I had been a buccaneer and privateer ever since I ran away to sea, for more than ten years, when I first joined the crew of Dampier, that self-aggrandising, fossicking buffoon. I signed as sailing master, being in charge of the deck, the sails, the management of the craft and vitally the navigation, but not the mission of the ship. It is the most important role for the safety of the crew and vessel, but never has the glory of the captain or commodore. But that has never fussed me as long as I got my share of the bounty an' we stayed with our heads above water.

I was on the Cinque Ports under Straddling, that fool Dampier was on the St George. We had fought both storms and Frenchmen around the Horn, when Dampier's folly raised the alarm and all our enemies were alerted to our presence. We failed to take a port in Panama which we had attacked, but then we took a rich prize on which I was to be captain, before Dampier decided to set it free again. These and other incidents made Straddling rightly despise Dampier and he cut off on his own, leaving me on that idiot's boat.

We called in at some islands off Chile for water and food, and in that calm clear water I could easily see that the hull badly needed to be careened and overhauled if it was to survive. It was like a magnet, drawing in all the boring, rotting and accreting elements that wait in warm waters for the sweet flesh of a northern boat. But Dampier ignored my advice, just as he always did, refusing to heave to for a few weeks to make good the damage, and he was recklessly determined to carry on raiding coastal towns and pursuing Spanish boats. I told him that all his precious boat was fit to do was sink at its anchor, and that I would rather take my chances on a wild shore than try to swim half an ocean when his boat finally foundered.

Instead of this giving him pause for thought, and reason to consider the wisdom of my counsel, he said 'Very well, you shall see how soft a posting it is on this very island' and he set me ashore with my kit and a few items to aid my survival, mostly smuggled to me by others who held me in some regard.

Dampier refused to take me back even when I begged on bended knee, and they sailed out of the bay a few days later, the ships still encrusted in all the foulings of that warm sea, leaving me to my own very limited devices.

It is of little comfort to me to know that his boat did indeed fail and sink under him soon after, and the few that did live were captured and thrown into gaol. The idiot himself survived and did not learn anything, not humility and certainly not wisdom.

I was in despair upon that reef, certain I would die alone and be forgotten, with no hope of a Christian grave, and less of rescue. I dwelt on the beach eating shellfish and weed, using a small stream that ran into the sea for fresh water, terrified of penetrating the interior or of leaving the beach and missing a sail on the horizon that might mean redemption. I scanned the horizon everyday with my glass, had a fire ready to send flames or smoke high into the air as a signal at a moment's notice, but no ship did come, the horizon remained unruffled. When, to my reckoning, the year turned and my beach became host to countless noisy and aggressive sea-lions, I had to retreat into the jungly interior, losing hope of readily spying rescue and resigning myself to a lonely fate.

At first I struggled to survive, but then I found signs of wild goats, which not having seen humans before, were easy for me to approach. I captured a number, and these supplied me with milk, a modicum of meat, and later when my clothes failed, garments for my body and shade for my head. Though I could only crudely fashion them, having no scissors, thread or needle, they kept me warm and dry and decent in the eyes of the Lord, and allowed me to approach wild goats and other creatures more easily. There were roots and leaves that I cautiously learnt to use, having nearly poisoned myself once with a leaf that I took to be cabbage, and I carefully applied these to add savour to my food, producing for myself a decent enough mess which gave me strength and the will to continue. Rats might have driven me mad, was it not for some previous visitor having released some cats upon the island, who would tolerate me and in fact relished the opportunities that my food presented by attracting the aforesaid rodents. The cats were kept to this arrangement by their liking for the goats' milk, which I supplied to them as an aperitif for rat.

I had few enough tools to begin with, but fashioned a large knife from the remnants of a barrel, and husbanded my powder so that I might shoot wild goats rather than deplete my own flock too often. When I ran low on powder, I chased prey with my knife, and thus one day nearly ended my lonely sojourn by following a goat right over the edge of a cliff. The hand of Providence held me even then and I landed on that large she-goat, breaking he back and not my own. After that, I determined to make greater efforts to increase my domesticated herd rather than risk my life in pursuit of a mouthful of meat. My father was a tanner and cobbler, and although I had thought that he only taught me pain and resentment, I now blessed the knowledge I had unwittingly learned from him. I knew how to treat a goatskin so that it did not rot and instead stayed flexible, how to sew it with a needle fashioned patiently from a nail.

I read the Bible every day and it comforted me, and kept my language alive. Without it, I would have turned as mad and feral as the other inhabitants of the island, though they all bore four legs. I thought myself to be rescued twice, but each time they were Spaniards and I had to hide to avoid a painful death at their hands. On one occasion I was almost captured, and but for my lithe climbing of a tree, my scorched and dirty skin, and my hide clothes, they would have spied me up there. It was not until four and a half years had passed that an English boat hove into the bay, and by that time I had given up any hope of rescue and often spent weeks away from the coast.

To my surprise, a foraging party was led to the smoke of my camp fire and Mr Dover greeted me as if we had just met on a thoroughfare in London. I was overjoyed but ill able to say much, having not spoken aloud for many of my fifteen hundred days on that isle. I was taken to their camp and found there Commodore Rogers, and also that damn fool Dampier. He had forgotten all about me when he suggested pulling into this bay to find food and water, and that lack of consideration was the only service he has ever done for me, because if he had remembered he would surely have steered clear. The crew were weak from scurvy, and I as governor of that island took it upon myself to bring them fresh meat and vegetables to rebuild their strength. When they were all back in fine fettle, Cap'n Rogers made me second mate and we departed that land which had been my lonely home for so long.

Later I was made captain of a captured prize, before we sold it back to the Spanish at a handsome profit. I readily took to privateering again, and like to think that I brought some good fortune to the venture. I am just sorry that Cap'n Rogers suffered so much to bring others such good fortune, I owe him everything for rescuing me, and I hope I have brought him some ease since, as I know that he has suffered gravely both in mind and body, whereas that fool Dampier has escaped with skin and fortune intact.'

*

Woody looked both happy and tearful at this extolling of his merciful virtues, and said this of Selkirk's own qualities:

'You can see, dear Porter, when looking at Alec here, how solitude and retirement from the world may not be so insufferable as many might think. Indeed I believe that it made him a stronger, wiser and more considerate man than many I have met, even when he was dressed in goatskin. If it were not for Alec, I would have been bankrupt many times over rather than just half-ruined as you see me now. You two are my dearest friends, and if only Teach was alive here, I could die content. I will return to my journal tomorrow, and I will, if I may Alec, include as much of your story as you are happy for me to relate. I would be grateful if you could answer my questions regarding your time on that island?'

'Of course, Commodore, now enow yapping aboot that blessed island, let us get famously drunk so that even the pagan gods would be outraged!'

So they began, and I left them to it as soon as was seemly, apart from bringing them another bottle of spirits an hour or so later. I felt that Woody deserved a rest from his labours, and I had supplied him nothing stronger than small beer in the weeks that he had been sitting at his pen. I sent the pot boy Toby around to Woody's house to inform his wife that he was likely to be sleeping at the

Trow and not to fuss, and she sent a reply that she knew her husband was indebted to Selkirk and did not begrudge him this *one* night of indulgence.

Around midnight, the corner fell silent apart from snores like the rending of a ships timbers, and the odd muttered gaelic oath, a-cursing rats, cats, Spanish dogs, and that fool Dampier. I left them with a jug of water to hand and a couple of old blankets in case they were needed, and returned to bed with Hannah, having a tale to tell.

In the morning when I arrived, Selkirk was already up and hustling for breakfast, Woody was just blearily coming around from his stupor. I got him fed and respectable and delivered back to his wife Sarah before too long. He returned again in the afternoon, slightly chastened but eager to crack on with his journal and Selkirk's part in it, which he now had firmly in his mind.

He worked diligently on his manuscript for months, letting us see parts of it at times, and asking our opinions. Simon and Slate gave views on what would be of interest to sea-farers; Selkirk, when he was present and sober corrected factual errors in the account of the second half of the cruise, and more generally besides. Woody was well pleased with it and growing in confidence, when he received news that the captain of the Duchess had put an account into print before him. This threw him first into a red rage and then a blue funk, thinking that his only path out of penury had been blocked, his labour had been stolen from his hands. He dropped his pen and did not pick it up again, yet so ingrained was his habit, and so afeared of his wife knowing of his further failure, that he still came and sat all day in his corner, nursing a pint of small beer.

One day I was passing near this ship-wrecked man

again when he burst out, 'Dash it all, I am ruined, what is the use of pretending otherwise?'. He knocked over his tankard as he bundled up his papers and moved to cast them all into the fire. I had not the time or position to grab him or block his way, so I threw the jugs of beer that I was carrying into the grate with a splashing clatter, extinguishing the flames, before his book could be burnt upon them, releasing in the process a great acrid, yeasty hiss and a cloud of steam. He collapsed upon the floor in front of the hearth, sobbing mightily, as I retrieved the block of papers which were fortunately only smudged and stained at their edges.

As he calmed down, he turned to me with a wry grin and said, 'Once again, Porter, you have saved a friend from foolishness with the unconventional use of beer! I thank you, but I am still in despair. Perhaps it would be better if you looked after these, while I seek some other form of employment?'

This struck me as an even more desperate act, but I agreed to hold onto the papers until he needed them again, if only he could resist the temptation to despair. First thing the next day, I sent for a copy of Edward Cooke's book from London, to see if there was still any merit in Woody completing his own account. This cost me no little effort and expenditure, but I could not stand by while a state of fear ate away at Woody's soul.

After the better part of a month, I received a heavy package containing two volumes by way of a relay of contacts between Bristol and London. Opening it I could quickly see that this account of the cruise around the world was a much poorer thing than that which Woody had embarked upon, and seemed to devote many pages to the cities of Mexico and other parts of South America whilst skimping on detail of surviving the Southern Ocean, rescuing Selkirk, and winning several prizes, possibly because these fell to the credit of others rather than to Cooke himself. In fact a lot of it felt like it had been copied from accounts of other explorers of those lands rather than expressing any new experiences or discoveries of the author. It would not be of general interest to the public, nor of great service to any subsequent navigator.

I hurried around to the small house that Woody was renting near the Shambles, where his wife Sarah met me at the door with a cold attitude, trying to prevent me from seeing the truth of their much reduced circumstances, and thinking me in some way responsible for her husband's low spirits.

'Mistress Rogers, I must speak with Woody, the Commodore, immediately. Is he not here?'

'Mr Porter, he is indisposed and I will not have him being disturbed by you. You have done too much to raise and dash his hopes and I cannot bear it. Surely he has suffered enough without being taunted by all and sundry. He is my husband and I will protect him from idle chatter.'

'He will want to be disturbed for I have brought him a vital tonic which will surely cure him of that which ails him.'

'I doubt that there is anything that you or your kind can do to help him, a great man fallen foul of Fate, I shall not let you in.'

I was in a quandary: should I abandon my mission, or should I barge past this impossible and haughty woman in her own home? At that moment someone came out of the room behind her, I barely recognised him with his shaven head bound in a simple scarf, no flowing locks nor luxuriant wig, looking more a wreck of fifty years than in the vigour of thirty.

‘What is all this damned noise, woman, can a man not wallow in his misery without being deranged by idle gossip and caterwauling? It would drive me to drink, if only I could afford it!’

‘Woody, please come here, I have a present that will surely lift those clouds from your brow.’

‘Porter, what are you doing here? Come to gloat at my misfortune again?’

He came to the door and I handed him the volumes written by Cooke. He listlessly opened the cover of the first volume, and on seeing the title page almost threw it aside in disgust, but even then stopped himself when he read its long and self-important title. He quickly turned to the contents page, and thence to several indicated sections of the books, his actions becoming less listless and more animated with every passing moment, his expression changing from that of resigned despair to one of eagerness and laughter.

‘Why this is a terrible book, it is written by a man who has as little control of language as he had of his ship, a man who barely knows larboard from starboard, the East Indies from the West Indies, a junior who knew little and says less, who has taken this opportunity to lay claim to the fame and glory earned by others. It is laughable; I hardly recognise the voyage he describes, and I was on it!

What a fool I have been, I have wasted weeks in selfish despond, fearing this schoolboy essay. Porter, let me hope that you still have my papers safe? Just let me fetch my hat, wig and pen, and I shall be wanting my seat in the corner for a few more weeks yet!’

I assured him that all he needed was waiting from him

at the Trow, and as he scurried off to make himself look more respectable, now merely tripped and stumbling rather than fallen or downtrodden, I turned to go but his wife placed her hand on my arm.

'Dear Mr Porter, I have gravely wronged you. I had thought that what Woodes had said of your character must be born out of some silly childhood loyalty, but I can see now that you are his greatest friend, his only true one. Please forgive my sharp tongue, this has all been very trying and I have had no reason, or desire, to learn resilience to hardship before. I doubt we will ever be in a position to repay it, but we are in your debt forever.'

I could see then the strength of this woman, who was trying to protect all that was most precious to her: her husband and children, having recognised the empty triumph of title, fame and possessions.

So Woody returned to his opus and duly it was completed, and while he edited that draft, we engaged engravers to copy maps from the best Spanish ones available and to add to these annotations from Woody's own charts used on the voyage. In order to make it an attractive book for the more wealthy reader, or those looking to speculate on future voyages, and hence to command a higher price for the key information contained in the book, we had it made available in fine calfskin or Morocco leather, and Woody added an introduction extolling the virtues of the South Sea trade, comparing its scale to the vast wealth derived by the Spanish from Mexico and the lands further south: a river of gold that flowed to Cadiz.

Woody travelled to London with his precious manuscript and engraved plates, carrying with him money lent to him by myself, Simon and Selkirk, and he hoped to engage a publisher or at worst to publish it himself to recoup his costs. In the end, his book proved to be hugely popular in all its forms, sales being driven by its appeal to merchants, speculators, navigators and the wider public in need of tales of adventure, for which there was a great appetite.

*

Despite the success of the book, Woody did not enjoy any fortune derived from it. His father-in-law, the Admiral, had died leaving little, most of it to his second wife, and owed thousands which were never retrieved. Woody's crew sued him over an unfair split of the spoils from the cruise, and all of this drove him even further into debt. He had to finally sell the house in Queen Square, and soon after the birth of his fourth child by Sarah they became irrevocably estranged, their household fell apart and Woody was again adrift. By that time his friend Selkirk had, by means of drink and nefarious deeds, burnt through much of his own gold and was a regular in the cells of the watch. He was arrested for rowdy and violent behaviour and given the choice of gaol or shipping out, he chose the latter. To add to Woody's woes, his new child fell suddenly ill and died soon after; he felt truly alone, a failure, and there was nothing more I could do to help him that time.

7:Succession

The war came to an end with signatures on a parchment in Utrecht, with Britain benefiting in many ways. Bristol may have gained more than many cities through its control of both the wine trade and a large fleet of slavers, who turned shoddy goods into gold without any dirt ever being landed at our quayside.

Another consequence of the treaty was that all those patriotic men who had raided enemy ships in the Caribbean as privateers under license, would become illegal pirates or freebooters overnight should they continue in that line of work. It would be months before Teach and his comrades heard of the treaty, and thus they unwittingly put their heads into the noose while believing they were still operating in their country's best interests.

Woody was now desperate: he needed a scheme to raise his fortunes, yet had nothing to stake but his name and the reputation he had gained from the previous profitable expedition, and from his account of it. One day, he came into the Trow with a feverish glitter in his eyes, and he called me over as soon as he spotted me.

'Porter, come celebrate with me, I have hit upon a sure scheme for regaining my fortune and I have already found some sponsors for it.'

I fetched him a French brandy, the first we had openly stocked since the end of the war, and sat down with him.

'What is the greatest benefit to the world of trade, and what is the greatest threat?' he asked.

'I know little of the wider world, but I know that hot weather is good for selling ale, and a rainy night is bad for it,' I replied.

'Porter, you need to see more of the world, beyond the Mendips and the Avon! But the fine weather of the world of trade is provided by cheap labour, and there is no labour cheaper than that of slaves. The rain that dampens world trade is adverse losses, and there is nothing more adverse than the scourge of piracy. So what I aim to do is to mount an expedition to the island of Madagascar, with the aim of purchasing slaves there to sell-on, under the Company's purview, in the East Indies and hence turn a handsome profit. While I am there I will see what can be done about the pirate rats that infest the place. If they can be brought under our flag, or failing that be crushed, then I plan to establish a British trading colony on the island, and to use those handy fellows to safeguard it.'

'How do you know you can get slaves from that island, Woody?'

'That is easy, my friend, the place is ruled by a despot who has enslaved half the population, all those of a different blood, one tribe lives like gentry while all others do their bidding or die. It is a ready market, we just need to take some sophisticated goods from here such as fine cloth, Mr Darby's fine brassware, musical instruments, books and the like, and the ruling class will give us all the slaves we desire in return.'

'It all sounds a bit unlikely to me, Woody, but you might be right,' I said.

'I have no choice, Porter, it is this or I will need to find a barrel to live alongside your friend Jack.'

'In that case I wish you well in this venture, and God's speed.'

This scheme must have appealed to enough merchants and bankers eager for a profit, for soon Woody was decked out in a new uniform and leading a little fleet out of the harbour and off to the Indian Ocean in search of another fortune. Selkirk was at the helm on the first of his missions against the pirates, and this job would keep him at sea for many years, and away from the cells and hard liquor.

*

Ever since Queen Anne had come to the throne, there had been doubts about the succession, and after seventeen failed pregnancies it was clear she would produce no heir. Parliament cast about for a Protestant relative and in the end had to settle on Sophia of Hanover, but even she died before her turn came, so then her son George was chosen as heir. Perhaps the Government felt that they could use this change to move power out of Royal hands and into their own, but the people were not all as satisfied with the arrangement. Many disturbances occurred including a riot in Bristol, because protest is as natural as breathing to us.

The riot has quite some relevance to the rest of my story. On the evening of the coronation of King George, an angry mob assembled at the Custom's House in Queen Square, then proceeded to Tucker Street, attacking another crowd it found there that seemed to be celebrating the Royal occasion. The mob was shot at, then trampled Mr Thomas, a peaceful Quaker who had attempted to calm them, and finally returned to the Custom's House. A ball was in full swing there to commemorate the coronation, and the mob broke windows and scared the fine ladies in their best gowns, before finally dispersing when the cider jugs ran dry and the militia were rumoured to have been called.

The Corporation, afraid of such riotous and rebellious behaviour, called for a special assizes, but this itself was greeted by another mob when the magistrates first entered the city. Eventually the assizes panel sat and imposed some minor penalty upon the rioters that could be found, the ringleaders having had plenty of notice and assistance to flee. The son of Baker Stevens escaped punishment for shooting a rioter dead, and the Baker himself attempted to get compensation for his ransacked premises.

The news of the riot spread beyond Bristol, even to London, and this excited certain political and journalistic interest: if such riots could happen in England's second city, then what for the capital itself?

One journalist came to investigate, and he was already widely known for his writings: he was the author of The Storm which we all had enjoyed reading to see how Bristol's woes measured against those of others. It was a cold December when a man concealed in a carriage coat, scarf and broad-brimmed hat came to the Trow. He approached the bar and ordered a mulled ale to fend off the chill, and then asked if he could talk privately with the owner of the establishment. Once seated in the private lounge, kept for certain paying guests, or at other times for the family of the house, he began.

'Captain Hawkins, my name is Defoe, you may have heard of me?'

'Aye, Mr Defoe, we most enjoyed your account of the Great Storm, which as you know had a tremendous impact on our city and caused much suffering here, and we have read other of your works since with interest. What brings you to our fair city and how might we be of assistance to you?'

'First, I am glad that this is a private place for I need to ask you questions without fear of us being overheard. Let me state that I am writing various pieces for which I need information which is not yet widely known. Some of these pieces may only be seen by certain of my private readership, others may contribute to pamphlets or books for the wider public. Whatever you tell me will be kept anonymous and you need not fear any consequences, indeed I rarely record or give any names in my works just so the people who talk to me can do so with confidence, unless such people specifically ask to see their names in print, which I do not often accede to anyway. Furthermore, I may choose to do nothing with what I learn from you, it all depends upon the quality and usefulness of the information, and if it combines to make a story that needs telling to the ears that listen to me.

I have come for information on two very different topics, being the recent riots associated with the arrival of our new monarch, and also, if you know anything about the curious tale of one Mr Alexander Selkirk, who was mentioned in a book by Captain Rogers of this city. Perhaps you can help me with one or other of these matters?'

Simon looked at me, I shrugged, so he began.

'On the first matter, I do not have much direct knowledge, most I heard third or fiftieth hand. I do know that Queen Anne was well liked in this town, having visited here and knighted the Mayor and so forth. We had a long association with the Stuarts, and did not have much issue with them apart from the wrath of the Roundheads that they brought down upon us, and we did not worry which were Catholic or which not. We have many different flavours of the worshippers of Christ in this city and more appear every year, and we rub along well enough. Many were displeased to hear that we were to have a German King, at least the Stuarts spoke English and preferred to live here rather than in Scotland or Hanover. So some in Bristol felt that celebration of the coronation was an affront, and took exception to our new Custom's

House being used for that purpose, and those few stirred up a drunken rabble to express views with fists and stones.

As for the unfortunate incident at Stevens the baker, I cannot rightly see the cause of it. He may have expressed some positive view of the new king, or had a special royal knot loaf on display, or cast aspersions upon the old Queen, but I think it more likely that the leaders of the mob already had some grudge to settle and when the baker refused to feed the ravening rabble, they cut up rough. His son had recently returned from the sea and decided that force was needed to protect life and property, so he took his pistol to them. Mr Thomas, as quiet and God-fearing a man as I have ever known, was foolish enough to believe that he could quell their anger with some words from the Bible. Some of the rioters did not like Dissenters and he was shoved aside, fell and was trampled, though accidentally I believe. I will not believe that any there meant to kill him.

As for the assizes, they were a farce from beginning to end. They neither tried those responsible, nor then punished those found guilty. I do not know what purpose they served other than to satisfy a side of Government that wanted to assert its view without risking another rebellion.

That is about all I know of the affair, I don't think John here can add any more to my account,' Simon stated.

I responded, 'Indeed not, if anything you have said more about it than I had already known, for that day I was busy in the cellar and knew no more of events in the street than the sound of feet trampling over the hatch. I do know rather more of Woody and his account of Alec Selkirk's little spell abroad, having known both of them and heard the matter discussed between them at length, both when they were sober and when they were drunk.'

Defoe now interjected, 'I would surely love to hear that story from one who is close to the facts, but for today I need to pursue the matter of the riots, not to confuse the two matters in my mind. I will repair to my lodgings at the Star, and make some more enquiries upon the way. Tonight I will write up what I have learned and the impressions I have formed, and tomorrow, if I may, I will return bright and early to hear all John has to say on this other matter? I will of course pay for the disruption to your business, perhaps by renting this room for the day, and having my meals here at a price that suits your needs. I suggest that a guinea might suffice?'

'That is a pretty price for what little you ask, and we will be happy to oblige you in your researches,' answered Simon.

So it was, early the next morning, that Mr Defoe turned up again just as our first customers, the porters and shore-men, left after their breakfast and a long night on the quayside. He brought with him many papers, including a copy of each of the books pertaining to that voyage, both Woody's and Cooke's, as well as an account of Dampier's previous venture on which he had marooned poor Alec in the first place. These were carried through to the lounge by the pot boy from the Star, who looked around the Trow with disdain. Defoe settled in there and arranged the books and papers according to some scheme known only to himself, ordered a large breakfast and jug of coffee, and requested that I sit with him as he ate so that he could begin to take my account, first putting the promised guinea on the table and pushing it across to me.

Defoe began, 'Now John, I have read all of these worthy tomes, but I need to know things beyond what is written there, to help shape my understanding, and I trust that you will be able to provide such knowledge and impressions that will help me to turn these dry words into a living picture of events as they occurred.'

'I will endeavour to do that for you, Mr Defoe, as I have met most of the actors in these events, and have known some of them for many years,' I answered.

'First, please tell me of Captain Rogers, how was it that you first met?' he prompted.

So I settled down and related much of what is written here, or at least that which pertains to Woody, whilst trying to remain truthful and avoiding matters of deep emotion. I avoided any mention of his past involvement with Hannah. The telling of this tale, interrupted as it was by Mr Defoe's frequent requests for clarification, and searching questions on character, motivation and consequences of actions with a moral dimension, extended over two whole days, and another guinea.

I found the experience quite draining, both in the sense of being mentally tiring but also I was being emptied of a story that had been filling my mind for much of my life. Afterwards I felt strangely relieved, concluded to some extent, no longer tied to the threads of my past as firmly as I had been only the week before, nor as bound into courses set by the actions of others, or where society as a whole expected me to be anchored. These sensations gradually faded over some weeks, but I still recall that feeling of cold detachment that I gained during that interview. Perhaps that is how Mr Defoe felt all of the time?

The questioning progressed over those days, relaxing slightly in its formality and tone of inquisition or examination, as we became used to each other and as he gained trust in my testimony, whose veracity and consistency he was constantly testing. After the first couple of hours, Defoe reached up and pulled off his long brown wig, of the style favoured by the Stuarts, and dumped it without ceremony amongst his papers, without a word, revealing a large, bald pate surrounded by a circlet of grey hair cut very short for comfort. In this tonsured state, surrounded by piles of papers and open books, he resembled a monk searching for God amongst the scriptures, and he did this earnestly, until he called for wine or beer after many hours.

When Defoe had finished for the day, his manner changed completely: on closing his notes he would lift his eyes and smile, becoming affable and charming, rather than coldly incisive, and would gladly become the raconteur and gossip about people and events that had impacted upon his own life. From these talks, Simon and I learnt much about the background to events of which we had only distantly heard, such as the rebellion led by Monmouth in which Defoe had taken a part in Somerset and been lucky to escape with his life, the various intrigues and machinations surrounding first the act of Union and then the struggles over the succession, including the farce of Darien, the Scottish bankruptcy, the Jacobite sympathies both north and south of the border, and much else besides. In this area I felt that he was hiding something, and I perceived that he was not just an innocent observer during his period researching a book in Scotland, being instead part of some shadowy attempt to influence events. For the most part, where his views did not impinge upon the political clashes between the Tories and the Whigs, they were as straight, reliable and open as those of any man alive in England.

For the first two days he had pursued all aspects of Woody's life as it was known to me, he then turned to asking me for my impressions of Selkirk. I told him that Alec was a strange mixture: reliable and skilled, of amazing mental strength and endurance, resourceful, and as loyal a friend as any man could wish for, but he was also fiery, quick to judge and slow to forgive, particularly when in his cups, as I had seen him often. I told him the story of Alec's first going to sea after falling foul of the strict Kirk and town authorities of his home, and how he had similarly escaped penalty in Bristol after a drunken episode, by signing up to hunt pirates. He was even then pursuing that endeavour with Woody, somewhere off Africa. It was quite the most fashionable naval mission of the day, because it defended the interests of the trade in slaves and the gold that flowed from it. Selkirk had been accepted despite, or possibly because, he had been a privateer himself.

Defoe asked me a few more questions about Alec's adventures upon the island, to clear up how he had survived, both in practical and spiritual terms, but this was a very different form of questioning, not with the same focus on objective facts and dates, but looking for impressions of character, feelings and emotions. I could not tell at the time what use he intended to make of this information, but I could see the fruits of it some years later published in the account of one Robinson Crusoe, mariner, as usual not under Defoe's own name.

As for the detailed information about Woody, I never found any product from this, either under his name or otherwise, and I suspect it was summarised for private consumption by his masters in London. At most I could detect some amalgamation of Woody's and Teach's stories in the character of Captain Singleton, but that is just my opinion. This brings me to the fascination that Defoe had for my other friend, who was inevitably mentioned during my account of Woody's life. He had not known of him before, and was quite taken by his mixture of being an outward gang leader and outlaw whilst being highly moral, trustworthy, loyal and more devoted to liberty and justice than any man I knew, and certainly more than many of those set to defend those things. I did not reveal the secret of his true identity, referring to him as Teach throughout, and perhaps this explains why he became quite such a man of legend under that name later on, for I am sure that Defoe related a distillation of Teach's background to his masters, and that this coloured their views when they subsequently were making decisions in his direction.

Defoe was fine and gossipy company, when not working in his official capacity, but every now and then he would pause as if he was mentally making a note of some casual point that arose or of a particular turn of phrase, ever the journalist or novelist, sometimes the agent. I told him of Teach's disgust at the reality of the trade upon which he embarked on leaving Bristol, and his determination to get away from it as soon as he could. He was most taken by the eagerness of this man to act for Queen and Country in his role of privateer, and intrigued by how this strange chain of friends – Teach, Woody and Selkirk came to join and leave the great pursuits of those years: slave trading, privateering, piracy and pirate hunting. How could such men, seemingly so different in outlook, background and prospects, cross each others' paths so easily and so often, the threads of their lives running parallel, then tangling in some Gordian knot?

On the evening of the fourth day since his arrival, Defoe came to thank us for the hospitality that we had shown him, and for the aid we had provided in his various projects, and then he took his leave of us to travel back to London by way of a meeting with some merchant friends in Bath. He left with us an inscribed copy of the Storm, which sits even now upon my shelf.

*

Some months after this, we heard that Woody had returned to England, landing in the capital and proceeding directly to lobby at Court and Parliament for his venture. He had fared reasonably well in that distant isle of Madagascar, finding enough trade to pay his costs, and he had even been able to negotiate for many of the pirates there to stop attacking British ships and to come under our flag, allowing that great island to part of a fruitful trade for the first time. He had turned a profit, which for once had not been swallowed up by debt, seized by his partners or crew, or otherwise taken from him.

What was taken was far worse: his grand scheme to pacify the pirates and open a whole new line of trade into the Indian Ocean, to be the founder of a new empire, and to make a fortune from it, had been undermined by the malign presence of the East India Company, whose monopoly it might circumvent. They saw this new source of wealth not under their control, and a whole ocean closer to home than Hindustan and the Spice Islands, as a far greater threat to their fortune and monopoly than the predations of a few mangy pirates. After all, what piratical losses they could not recover from the coffee house insurers could be compensated for by raising prices over which they had sole control, but there would be no such redress if a competitor undercut their prices with fresher and faster goods.

Unfortunately, the Company's Royal licence for the monopoly protected them, preventing Englishmen from establishing competing positions in most of the world, and the Company exercised all rights and powers they had within and beyond that licence, being the civil, judicial and military power in all of Hindustan. The petition that Woody had raised, signed by the pirates of Madagascar, offering to turn them from piracy in return for clemency, fell upon deaf ears at King George's court. It did impress key advisers to the king, several of whom already held Woody in some regard, and out of this came a new scheme that this time looked to the West Indies, rather than to the East.

There was a governor of the Bahamas, a powerless man with title but no influence or force. He governed only in name on behalf of the absent Lords Proprietor who sat in London and counted any revenue that arose, though there was precious little of that. This governor in particular had no power against the 'nest of rascals' that infested those islands, many of whom had previously been blessed and acclaimed privateers, but who were now deemed to be accursed pirates, even if their activities showed precious little difference to the disinterested observer. The governor was now out of his wits, and happy to hand over the reins to any new regime. Woody negotiated with the Lords and sub-leased their rights to the islands for twenty-one years in return for a peppercorn rent. In return Woody would have all the powers over the islands, becoming the new governor, and he would try to repeat the success he had had with the Madagascan pirates with their cousins in the Caribbean, turning them from theft to the path of innocent trade.

All of this I learned from his own mouth at the start of 1718. He had arrived back in Bristol in high spirits, to ready himself for his new venture, and during this time he briefly visited the Trow. It was a cold winter's day, the fires were roaring, the windows were streaming and misted, and anyone entering the inn was accompanied by a freezing blast, and more icy glances from those already snug inside. When Woody entered in his great travelling coat, as broad and full of himself as he had been in his teens, it was not to a universal welcome but instead to a chorus of 'close a door yer gurt idjit, youz freezing uz.'

This was soon forgotten when he offered the whole room a drink to celebrate the change in his fortunes.

'Porter, come toast my success, my star is in the ascendant and I will follow it to my fortune!'

I asked him to explain and he told me what I have outlined above, and then continued:

'Those scoundrels of the Company would have me ruined to protect their blessed monopoly, but I have my own friends in high places and have secured a deal which will make me rich, and I will have my very own monopoly. King George has just declared me Captain General and Governor in chief of the Bahamas and I will have full power there, and own all those islands produce. I have with me letters patent that give me limitless power in the exercise of my duty and monopoly, and further I carry a document which will pardon any pirates that come into the fold by September of this year.

'Any who don't, of course, may be hunted down like the dogs that they are, but I believe that they will turn away from that path and become valuable citizens under the law once more to the benefit of the prosperity of all, myself in particular. I have come home to settle my affairs here as I will be away some years, perhaps for the rest of my life.'

I was concerned by this turn of events, for it meant that the success and happiness of Woody depended upon the downfall of my wayward friend Teach. I tried to deflect him as far as it was possible for a man of my station when pitted against the will of the King.

'And how do you propose to conquer these men, who

have fallen into piracy after defending our country from its enemies?' I asked.

'I will approach the key players, such as Vane and Blackbeard, and convince them, or destroy them. It is key that I tackle the men with the blackest hearts first, for my success as paramount governor. I am determined to drive piracy out of their hearts, or to drive the pirates out of the islands, and I will have the Crown's assistance in doing so. I shall not need cannon, I trust that I shall bring them to the law and loyalty by the power of reason and scripture. It is a blessed mission and I know that God is on my side in this. Wish me well, Porter, for tomorrow I return to London to lay my plans, assemble a fleet, and depart to my new empire!'

'Woody, of course I wish you well but I would also remind you that whatever else we have heard about this Blackbeard, he seems to be well respected amongst his kind and fearless. It would take more than religious tracts and even the odd borrowed naval ship to change his ways, surely?'

He did not answer, but just stared at me as if I had slapped him, then nodded with a grunt, took his hat and moved to the door. Holding it open to the icy blast, and much complaining from within, he said finally: 'Porter, I have owed you much and am grateful for it, but I now close this door for the last time. I bid you a final farewell.'

He was gone into that winter's night, leaving only a cloud of cold air and silence which soon dispersed, with a certain amount of muttering 'Bout time too, anna good ridden chew' as the men returned to their drinks.

*

I read in the Post Boy that Woody had assembled a fleet of seven ships and three navy escorts and with these he had set out to his province. He took with him soldiers, settlers and printed tracts with which to persuade the piratical inhabitants to turn from their wicked ways. That he sailed from London and not Bristol demonstrated his social and political ambitions had caused him to sever his links with his former home.

There the story rested, for we heard little in our city of events so far away. Life continued much as before for us, with only a few notable events. One involved the city's ducking-stool, which Woody had used to enter the moat on that fateful day in our youth.

The stool was employed for the last time to try to bring a nagging and scolding wife to heel. The husband of the lady in question truly deserved the scolding as he was a lazy drunk, and the mayor Mr Mountjoy foolishly decided to make an example of the woman for reasons of his own. For Mr Mountjoy was not the king of his own home, he was hen-pecked and chided by his wife from dawn to dusk, and it was said of him by coarser citizens that there was precious little joyful mounting in that household.

Mountjoy, having despaired of his wife's sharp tongue at home, stormed out and walked around town in a foul mood, ignoring the salutes and greetings of his fellow citizens, his mood darkening by the minute. When he reached the area of the hot wells, he heard a woman's voice, berating her husband for being a 'good for nothing, faint-hearted, wretched sot' at which point a small man was ejected from a house by a large wife whilst she continued to chide him for being lackadaisical when running household errands, and incapable in the bedroom.

Incensed by this close reflection of his darling wife's comments upon his own character and abilities, Mr Mountjoy saw an opportunity to relieve the suffering of a fellow being whilst teaching a lesson to two scolds at once. He summoned a passing officer of the watch and required him to arrest Mistress Blake, to appear before the magistrate (Mountjoy himself, of course) at the earliest opportunity.

When Mistress Blake did appear before Mountjoy the following day, far from being cowed and chastised by the ignominy of arrest, she in fact put up a vigorous defence:

'Who does he think he is to talk of a man being master in his own home, when it is well known that he dare not even sneeze without begging the permission of his wife?'

Amongst the hilarity, shared by all but Mountjoy himself, the mayor grew furious and sentenced Mistress Blake to three dips of the stool, to quench the fire of her tongue. He chose the ducking-stool because he assumed that the noisome waters of the Frome would stop up that woman's nagging mouth and leave a bad taste there which should remind her not to fall back into her critical ways.

In front of a huge and raucous crowd, Mistress Blake took her three dunks into that foul channel of water without a struggle, word or cry. Yet being released from the stool, she stated that she would 'be even with that hen-pecked man who only has the courage to duck another man's wife'.

She duly impelled her husband to sue Mountjoy for damages, which were awarded in full, and set so high that no magistrate would ever sentence a woman to ride the stool again. Mountjoy dared not show his face in public for a long time afterwards, and this brought him far more of his wife's company than he would otherwise have desired.

The stool was bought by a tradesman and the wood used to make snuff boxes, rumoured to protect the owner from a nagging wife. Yet as neither Mountjoy nor Blake had felt such benefits from the wood when it was serving its original function, nor did the sale of this mystical product succeed as intended.

*

Our daughter Edwina had grown into a fine woman, with a fair face and full figure, long dark curls and wits to match any man's, and to preserve her virtue for a worthy suitor. She helped us in the Trow between and after her studies, and was spotted there by a young man who worked for Mr Darby. They met and fell in love, decorously and without undue haste, and were married at St Nicholas. This man, Michael Cargill, was a buyer of raw materials for Darby's work in the North. He was only in Bristol on occasion and more often in Coalbrookdale and its surroundings. He took Edwina there with him and they settled in a cottage away from the smoke, but they found that they could almost read at night by the light of the flares and furnaces in the sky. Whenever he came to Bristol to buy coal and ores, he brought Edwina with him, so the family was not as finally separated as we had feared. In due course, Edwina bore Cargill two children and their visits became less frequent, but more noisy.

Our first son, Simon, was apprenticed to a printer and binder in Broad Street, whereas Jack learned his trade with us at the Trow.

I am sorry to record now that soon after all our lives seemed to be thus happily settled into their grooves, that first Jane and then Simon Hawkins, who had been present from the second of my birth, and had become my parents in deed before they were my parents by deed, both sickened and died. There was nothing any apothecary's physic could do for them, no lessons from Harvey or Hippocrates that could save them, and certainly any strength or resolve that the old sea captain still had soon left him on the death of his beloved wife.

Once again we trooped to St Michael's, again we heard about ashes and dust, and again we had to swallow down the poison of loss. The church could not hold all those wishing to show their respect for Simon and Jane, who were buried together in a single grave, and the docks that morning stood still and silent as there was not a single hand to pull a rope or roll a barrel. All were remembering those two good people who offered everyone a warm home and a settling draught after a hard day's work.

So I am finally come into my estate, owner and landlord of the Trow, and how it does not please me I cannot say. For my fortune has come of great loss: of my mother, of Roger, Jane and Simon Hawkins, of all those who might have better claim than me upon the Trow. Yet I know that I must drink from this glass to its bitterest dregs, for the duty that those people's love has placed upon me compels me to stand and face the storm, and never to break.

8:The Prodigal

By the end of the year we were at war again, with Spain on one side and ourselves, the French, the Austrians and the Dutch on the other. Ironically, after the previous war which was ostensibly about the French wanting to control the Spanish monarchy, this time it was the Spaniards trying to seize the French throne: disgruntled cousins seeking to displace their more privileged and decadent relatives. As always, this was not really about which particular silk draped arse sat upon which gilded chair, but about countries with imperial ambitions, or at least wide trading and colonial interests, trying to out-do each other and clip the wings of the other side.

This had impacts not just in Europe but also in the Americas, and we heard that Woody was having to fortify his colony against possible Spanish attack whilst at the same time trying to pacify the pirates who were also a large part of his citizenry, or at least trying to convert them back into being privateers that they might fight once more against Spain on England's behalf. I don't believe that anyone thought too carefully about the consequences of encouraging, arming and licensing such men in the defence of Britain, no one thought about how they might be employed after the war inevitably ended. The issue of creating pirates may not have even occurred to the relevant powers, eager as they were to tap into a private navy at low cost.

Sure enough, two years later the war did end and more pirates existed than there were before, few of the privateers deciding to go back to more innocent pastimes after having tasted the rich fruits that theft on the high seas had brought to them.

Woody's trials did not end there, for he had become

massively indebted through the costs of fortification, having in some cases to borrow from the very criminal citizens that he had gone there to eliminate. He had failed to turn a profit from trade due to losses to the Spanish, and to piracy before that. Three years after his hopeful departure, he returned to London hoping to build new support for his venture and monopoly, both political and financial. Instead he learned that a change of heart had happened, his contract had been revoked, his company dissolved, he was to be replaced as governor, and all his debts were to be called in forthwith.

Woody was thrown into debtor's prison, where he languished short of food, drink and friends until after some months he managed to convince his creditors that he had no means to pay them nor any prospect of acquiring such means, and also that he had in no way profited or gained from their funds, all having been spent in defence of the islands and in the interests of Britain. He was forgiven his debts, having no prospect of honouring even a part of them, and he returned once more to Bristol the next year, a more broken man than before.

Almost as if it was the same night on which I had seen him last, he returned in the Winter's dark to an inn filled with those eager for warmth and afeared of draught. If it was the same night then some magical horror must have occurred to him outside our door, for his frame was now bent, his face lined and his scar livid against his skin, which had a yellow pallor, and his hair was thin and grey. I truly did not know him as he entered, he had the appearance of a man in his dotage, and badly used at that, rather than a man bearing only the same three-and-forty years as myself.

'Porter, it is so good to see a friendly and familiar face again; do you not know me?'

'Woody – can that be you? You have so changed since I last saw you, and to tell you the truth, I never expected that we might meet again after that night. But I am a big man with a thick skin, and I say welcome to you, as all are at the sign of the Trow. What brings you back to Bristol – I thought your interests all lay elsewhere?'

He looked at me sorrowfully and said, 'My interests are but dust; all has been taken from me including my pride, and I have even less than I started with, hardly more than the clothes I now wear.

'I feel that I am in some Greek myth, such as Sisyphus eternally pushing his rock up a hill only to have his labour reversed overnight and to have to begin again next day. Or Tantalus, always able to see sweet riches but never able to grab even the tiniest piece, or perhaps like Prometheus having his liver pecked out every day by an eagle. No matter how promising a venture I set forth upon, all comes to ruin, and the more it promises then the less I am left with, yet I am compelled to repeat the cycle forever.

'I am hollow, and that hollowness echoes to all the pain I have felt and caused. I will come to that in time, if I may, I have other things that I must convey to you and I hope that it may gain me some absolution for my many sins.

'First, let me give you this, my greatest burden, and then please fetch us a little refreshment that I may tell you my tale, and you can judge whether I am deserving of either your hospitality or your pity.'

At this, he produced from the folds of his cloak a satchel and he removed from this a bundle tightly wrapped in oilcloth and bound with a hempen cord. It was about the size of a household Bible, and showed some signs of age. Upon the wrapper was a scrap of parchment bearing a few words in a hand that seemed vaguely familiar, and elsewhere the wrapping had dark brown stains. I turned it round to read the inscription, and saw the words 'To be passed to Governor Woodes, for his eyes only.'

'Please open it Porter, I have previously only penetrated this outermost wrapper, and since resealed it for its protection.'

Curious to find out what this could mean, I untied the cord and slipped it from the parcel, then pealed apart the edge of the cloth which had fused into a seal upon itself. Inside was a similar layer of wrapping, with a layer of parchment thrust beneath a fine ribbon. Woody nodded to indicate that I should open the missive, which read:

Governor Rogers, my previous friend Woody,

I entrust the enclosed item to you knowing that I am unlikely to live out this day. If in fact I do survive, then perhaps some other day we may treat as friends once again. I do not expect you to believe me when I say that my actions were for the most part performed for the purest reasons, only occasionally allowing anger, or loyalty to my crew, or greed, to cloud my judgment. I know that you have sworn to eliminate my kind and my trade, and I understand that this in itself comes from virtuous roots. I shall not rehearse my reasons for following my line of work here, nor shall I criticise you for yours, indeed I wish you every success in it.

I call upon you to perform one last act of friendship for me, and that is to pass the enclosed to my good friend Porter at the Trow. He will know what to make of it, and what purpose to put it to, and I trust you may render him some assistance in whatever course he chooses. I would say more but my hands are needed to clasp my pistol and sword, and I must seal this letter before it is too late.

Yours, in memory of past friendship,

Teach

I had to wipe a tear from my cheek, knowing that this parcel was the most certain sign that Teach was dead. I then carefully cut the ribbon with my pocket knife, it evidently being untouched since he had sealed it as it lay cleanly in its imprint upon the oilcloth beneath.

I unwrapped it to find another parchment and a heavy leather bound book, with no marking upon the cover. Feeling the import of this next letter, I invited Woody through to the lounge, where we sat either side of the table. I opened the message, and saw written there:

Dear Porter,

I trust that yours are the first eyes to see the enclosed book after mine, and that you will make best use of it that you can. I have entrusted it to our old friend Woody and I believe he will do his best to deliver it into your hands; if he does not then I must satisfy myself with dying an obscure and pointless death.

Know now that you have always been my best and truest friend, and that there is none that I would trust more, nor for whom I could wish more happiness. Though you have remained moored at the Trow all these years while I have adventured in warmer waters, I know that your heart is calmly sailing and your spirit free and true.

As you read what I enclose, please remember that I blame none but myself for what has unfolded, and I regret not one thing that has happened, save running from Woody when I should have stood my ground and explained. But even that I cannot really regret, for it brought you to the safe harbour of Hannah's love, and that I would never wish to reverse.

I know that these will be the last words that will ever pass between us, and yet I cannot find the right ones to express my gratitude and respect for you; just know that wherever we both are, I am always your friend and truest brother.

Farewell, my hearty,

Teach

Woody was trying to hide his curiosity for the contents of the letter, but I retained it as I pulled the large book to me and opened the cover board, to find inside inscribed the following words, in Teach's hand:

The log of the Revenge
A ship of Pirates
Under its Elected Captain
Edward Teach
Known as Blackbeard
In the years of Our Lord
1717 – *1718*

With the second date hastily added and somewhat smudged. I closed the cover again, for I wanted to know how Woody had come by this parcel, and what he might know of the fate of our dear friend Teach. Woody turned his eyes to me, and indicated he would like to read the letter, which I passed to him conscious that it might cause him some discomfort, but also that it showed the true colours of our old playmate. Woody read it carefully, with a frown, and in silence, finally handing it back to me with tears in his eyes. He clasped my hand in both of his and said hoarsely,

'Never were truer words written, I had only guessed but now I know that he was a good man worthy of our friendship and loyalty, and I have failed him and you many times. I hope to make some amends for this, if I am only granted the time by both God and yourself.'

'Woody, that you have brought this book and letter to me is as large a reparation as I could wish for. Please tell me how you came by this parcel, and what you know of the fate of our friend.'

So once again we sat in the lounge with a jug of ale and some vittles, and he started to relate his tale to me, in that room that had heard so many outlandish stories from distant places over the years.

9:Woody's Tale

As you know already, I was granted license, letters patent and monopoly over the isles of the Bahamas, to bring them back from waywardness and piracy, to legitimate trade under the King. In so doing as Governor, I had high hopes for my own prospects, and fortune. I raised a fleet of seven ships and was granted an escort of three navy vessels. We carried over one hundred soldiers, rather more of colonists, plus a variety of craftsmen, to establish a proper settlement and colony rather than a ramshackle camp of freebooters. We also took plenty of food and equipment, as well as my secret weapon: all the latest and best religious pamphlets with which to buy over the souls of that rabble, for I truly believed that hearts that had once fought on our side against our enemies in good cause, could be won over once more by scripture to the side of God.

It was a fair voyage, travelling first south then west to follow the same trade-winds used by the slavers. As we came in sight of the harbour at Nassau, in those warm blue waters, we saw moored there two ships, one flying the pirate standard, and the other standing alongside evidently a recent prize, its torn French flag hanging from the mast. I signalled for our fleet to block the mouth of the harbour, so our ten ships fanned out to form the blockade, with the naval ships to the fore. Although the guns had a good range they still could not reach the pirate sloop, and the navy ships had too deep a draught to enter the shallower waters where it was moored. To break this stalemate, I sent an envoy to the enemy to discuss terms. After some hours the pinnace returned with the lieutenant shaking his head:

'Governor Rogers, Captain Vane presents his

complements, but regrets to state that we have nothing that he wants, least of all, and I quote, "the reported and distilled words of a god," so he trusts we will not take it unkindly if he declines our hospitality.'

Almost as this last word was spoken, both of Vane's ships started to move towards our line, having an offshore breeze to their back, and every scrap of sail upon their yards. The French ship was out in front, and tearing towards us with no sign of veering, Vane's flagship was behind, firing small amounts of shot at us from guns mounted on the deck, being unable to make a broadside whilst holding its course. With the Frenchman half a league off, we could discern only two men upon its deck, and one of those was lashing down the wheel, the other seemed busy about the foredeck and hatch. The watch at the head of our mast shouted down so all could hear quite distinctly 'He is setting a fire, and there are many barrels upon the deck.'

At this we knew what was afoot: Vane was sending the French ship amongst us as a fire-ship, it would like collide with us and soon after explode sending burning pitch or even Greek fire onto all nearby. We broke the line, scattering one way and the other, turning our full firepower against the trojan vessel just as we saw its skeleton crew cut loose from the stern in a jolly-boat. Vane knew what he was doing, the decoy came amongst us and disappeared in a great ball of flame and debris, with a thunder clap fit to burst the ears, and a hot wind accompanied by slivers of oak that punctured our sails and peppered any skin exposed to it, a whole league of sea seething with foam and flame. The splinters felled some of our men like assassins' daggers. Amidst this tumult, fire, smoke and confusion, Vane calmly picked up his agents from their row boat, slipped through our line and escaped into the gathering gloom.

So having seen the mettle and mentality of the pirates, we were abashed but not ashamed. We had learnt valuable lessons, and the bay was now empty of anyone but ourselves, the town of Nassau undefended. With the Navy guarding the mouth of the harbour, I took our seven smaller ships and landed parties ashore, where the soldiers soon secured the town and fort, only having to subdue a few remaining piratical criminals too old, sick, limbless or drunk to resist.

I established myself as Governor and rapidly set out to work on the two projects that were vital for the success of my plan: the strengthening of the defences of the town, now that we held it, and the pacification of the resident and visiting pirates. Those left ashore were a wormy bunch, no longer fit to be at sea winning prizes, and without much persuasion they agreed to accept the King's Pardon that I carried with me and to become law-abiding citizens. How honestly they made their pledges, I cannot tell, for these men were never the kind that one would seek to trust in any contract, but having them nominally converted from pirates to colonists began a new chapter for the island of New Providence.

All was not well, and I had enemies and untrue hearts on every side. First, I lost two of the navy boats, who departed for New York without listening to any order, request or plea on my part. Then a terrible fever swept through our camp, and the town, sparing the former pirates but taking almost half of the total strength of colonists. It was like the Angel of Death sparing the Israelites but taking the Egyptians, though I could discern no mark of blood upon the lintels, nor knew of any witchcraft by which this could have occurred. I then discovered that the Spanish were turning back to their old aggressions and aiming to drive the British from the Americas, starting with the islands of the West Indies.

I attempted to treat with the Spanish, sending envoys to Havana seeking to find an accommodation with them, but instead of delivering this message, and delivering us from a new war, these ships turned spontaneously to piracy before they ever reached Cuba. At least they then mostly attacked Spaniards in preference to their former colleagues.

Now down to five vessels, we lost our final naval escort, who promised to return shortly, but never did, and I believe the captain had no intention of doing so even when he made his oath to me.

With Spain likely to attack our tiny island, we urgently needed to strengthen the fort and harbour defences, and I turned most of our diminished strength to this task, soldiers working as labourers alongside colonists and those ex-pirates able, sober and willing enough to be of use. We truly got little aid in this from the converted reprobates, through ill-faith or just as a demonstration of the uselessness that had left them stranded on the island in the first place. We were at full stretch protecting the seat of the colony, without much prospect of outside assistance.

It was at this moment that I received a note from Vane, the same pirate we had encountered when we first arrived, stating that I should depart forthwith for he aimed to retake the town with his own force combined with that of Blackbeard. He even had one of our own boats that had turned coat on its way to Havana. Things were coming to a desperate pass with our weakened numbers, impending attacks from both the Spaniards and the pirates, and I was coming to my wits end. As summer ended, not that there really are seasons, as the great swirling storms of that region were beginning their dominance, I heard that Vane was in a bay of the island of Abaco, barely thirty-five leagues to the north of my fort. I was not the first to hear the news, of course, and overnight many of the black-hearted, erstwhile pirate residents of Nassau decamped and set off to join him in whatever worm-eaten tub they could take.

Already outnumbered, I was in little doubt of our fate should both sets of enemies attack together, although I took some comfort from the fact that their mutual loathing would make such an alliance unlikely. The only course open to me was to use those pirates who had accepted the King's pardon to draw the strength from Vane's fleet. So I met with two of the now settled captains, Cockram and Hornigold, and asked them to pretend to have relapsed into their old ways. They would sail into the Vane flotilla and see what could be done by way of persuasion, negotiation, subversion, or even sabotage, to sew the seeds of discontent and division and hence break up the fleet. They undertook this mission gladly, but I could not be sure how much trust to place in either of them, I might just have been adding two more powerful ships to my list of enemies. Hornigold was eager to intercede with Blackbeard, having been his commodore in years past, and he still had great respect for the villain.

These two were gone for many weeks, and throughout that time I drove all available labour to prepare for the worst. We laid in what supplies we could, dug fresh wells and buried hundreds of barrels of water to help keep it fresh in that stifling heat. We baked biscuit as hard as brick, salted fish and meat, sharpened blades and forged more from whatever steel we had to hand, divided our powder and shot so that it could not be all overrun at once or destroyed by fire, dug redoubts in which to place our cannon and to slow the advance of any attack. We even carved more cannon shot from the local rock, which was for the most part poor stuff. All this in preparation for an attack and siege that might arrive with no more than an hour's notice, or no notice at all if it came on a moonless night.

Six weeks after they departed, my envoys returned to find the island under martial law, feverishly awaiting the blow of one hammer or another. Hornigold had not been able to convince Vane that he had returned to piracy, and also failed to draw Vane out of Green Bay and into open battle, but he had managed to capture one other ship and its crew and to bring them over to our side. This partial success demonstrated his good faith, and I dispatched him to try to recapture those ships I had sent to entreat with Havana and which had turned to the bad.

Another month passed, with many sickening from the tension of awaiting their fate, before Hornigold returned having found only one of the traitors' ships, drawn it into battle, captured the defeated crew and scuttled the ragged remains of the vessel. Ten men of this crew still stood, three more having died in the fight, and I put those ten on trial for their treachery. I was convinced that one, the youngest of them, had been drawn into the conspiracy with no choice on his part, and he had been unable to resist without sacrificing his skin. I knew he came from a good Bristol family, so I pardoned him for his part in the betrayal and consequent piracy. The other nine had no excuse, and many offered none, so I sent them to stretch the hemp without any qualm or revision, all of them being blacker of heart than Vane himself.

I was determined to use those men as examples to any reformed citizens who might waver in their loyalty to the crown, so I had every man of the island brought to witness the execution, with a body of marines behind them to require their attention to the proceedings. Those eighteen dangling legs were left there for a full three days, before the flies and stench became too much of a hazard for all around, and they were then dropped without ceremony into the trench that I had had those condemned men dig on the evening before they died. The effect of this show was to crush all outward resistance to my power and to quell much of the rebellious sentiments held within the breasts of the islanders too.

When we held the winter festivities, in temperatures akin to the hottest English summer, I had to control the supply of alcohol in order to limit rowdiness and rebelliousness, and to ensure we could still repel an attack should it come at that time of peace. There was a minor uprising started by those resentful of my rule, and moreover of my ruling over their rum. The majority had no fire left to take up this cause, so I had just the leaders flogged on the site of the gallows, to remind them of the consequences of further rebellion. After that, they all fell to and became, if not model citizens, at least a part of our society and a useful component of our defence.

In the spring, I heard that Spain was openly at war with Britain and I feared an immediate and crushing attack would fall on my island from Cuba to the South. I borrowed what money I could, much from reformed pirates such as Jennings and Hornigold, and used it and other credit to supply the fort and prepare for invasion. I did this because I clearly had no time to send to England for further resources, and I trusted that I would be reimbursed and praised for this initiative.

We were ready for the hammer blow, and I heard that a mighty fleet had been dispatched from Havana aimed to crush us, but it never arrived, and through circumstances that seem strange to me even now. In this war the French were our allies, whether through common cause or expediency I am unclear: they had long been intent on weakening the Spanish hold in the Americas with an eye on seizing a portion of that fountain of gold that originates there. The French had sailed into the sheltered harbour of Pensacola on the Gulf of Mexico, and had swiftly taken the Spanish town there. Part of the small Spanish fleet based there had escaped and headed for Havana, and it intercepted the armada aimed at us. The loss of that major asset on the southern coast of America was of greater and more immediate importance to the Spanish than our minor island, so the whole fleet diverted in that direction.

Meanwhile, Vane and many of his allies had returned to their favourite sport of attacking all Spanish interests, and they mostly left British interests alone, a state of affairs I was content to see exist. I was happy for the pirates to be my shield, rather than a dagger at my throat, so my major worry became the repayment of my debts for the defence of the town and its few hundred sea-rotted ex-pirates.

Finally, after a year of hostilities, the Spanish arrived at the mouth of our harbour and encamped on Hog Island where they could control access to the bay if they used it wisely. We had had years to prepare and fortify, we had cannon with which to mount a fusillade of the island, and could deploy boats with a shallow enough draught to approach the island from the town-side and attack them at night, whereas the enemy boats drew too much water to approach us any closer than that pitiful lump of rock on which they had camped. My marines, and the pacified pirates soon managed to drive them off and we returned to peace.

My final concern for our security, a raid from Vane,

had also been diffused. He had run aground during a storm when running between battles with the Spanish, and there he was captured whilst he was defenceless and marooned. He was soon hanged, and the most militant brand of piracy died with him.

Having successfully, and with some distinction, defended New Providence, placated the pirates of that island and brought them to the rule of God and King, I expected to be recompensed for my considerable financial outlay, and thus saved from the ignominy of bankruptcy. But the war had passed, all threat to the colonies had been removed, and none at court or amongst the Lords Proprietor, felt any duty to honour my debts, and I was cut off with neither funds nor credit.

I fell ill; I feared it was the same fever that had run through the town in previous years and taken so many of the colonists as easily as a storm takes a feather, and I retired to Charles Town in the Carolinas to recuperate. Whilst there, I fell into a quarrel with one Captain Hildesley over the appalling treatment I had received from my naval escorts after our arrival at New Providence. This led to us fighting a duel, for he felt I had impugned his honour, he having been on one of the vessels concerned, unbeknownst to me. He had since become the captain of the first navy ship permanently based in the area, and had more pride and pout than a courting pigeon. He was younger and much better trained with the sword than myself, and he must have relented, through pity or mercy to leave me with only another scar upon my face rather than running me through.

Once again I had to recover my strength, having lost both honour and dignity, and I determined to return to London to re-establish my funds and credentials as Governor of New Providence. After a long voyage, not just metaphorically licking my wounds, I rushed to court only to find that I had been supplanted as governor, my contract for twenty-one years had been consigned to the fire, and all my rights had been voided as if they had never existed.

To add further insult I was immediately called upon to honour all of the debts and obligations that I had undertaken. Of course I was quite unable to do so, and had not the means to pay off even one-hundredth part of what was owed, and all appeals for leniency and justice fell upon deaf ears and closed minds. I was thrown into debtors' prison and left to rot or starve. No other party, neither the government, the Lords Proprietor, nor my erstwhile business partners, could be compelled upon to pay even a shilling of my debt, and I had only despair to draw upon.

So it was as I sat in that cell with a score of other debtors, some who had roast meals brought to them every day, and others who scrambled for stale scraps, that I felt this was the very bottom of my slough of despond, and no shaft of hope could ever shine through those bars, no ladder of rescue would be offered to me.

I was wrong, for just as freedom began to feel like some forgotten dream, I was visited by two gentlemen who introduced themselves as Mr Defoe and Mr Mist. The former quickly told me that he had heard of my incarceration and felt that it was the height of injustice, just as the King was reaping the rich rewards of peace in the Indies, that the man responsible for it was cast into prison for bearing the costs of the victory, which should in all righteousness have fallen to the Crown.

Defoe declared that he had followed my career over several years, and had made quite a sum from the book he had written which grew out of Alec Selkirk's adventures, and of course none of that would have come to light were it not for my voyage with the Duke and Duchess, and my account of it, which I wrote in this very inn. Mr Mist was largely silent but did confess to being a printer and sometimes writer, who had most admired my book, and envied Defoe his success with his adventure novel.

Defoe mentioned how he had visited you here, and how much he had enjoyed interviewing you, Porter. The two gentlemen vowed to do whatever they could to gain my release, without exacting any promise from me. They departed, leaving me in much improved spirits, but as time passed and I heard no more from them, I fell back into despair.

That condition continued to sap my soul until not two days ago when I was suddenly called to the cell door, and from there brought forth into the yard full of straw and filth, and thence through the wicket gate in those great studied doors. There I was set free and handed a parchment bearing a court seal, which said all debt was deemed cancelled and I was free to live without a blemish on my soul or name.

Still in a daze, I was met outside by those same two gentlemen, lords amongst men, who clasped my hands and smiled upon me. They had gathered my sea-trunk containing my paltry possessions, hired a carriage to take me to the postal route to Reading, and gave me a purse to cover my expenses. Still they asked not one thing of me in return. Just as I was mounting up into the carriage, and Mr Defoe was seeing that my trunk was safely aboard, Mist whispered to me that he would greatly appreciate some of my time to discuss all I knew about pirates, and he would arrange for us to have a talk after I had truly recovered from my tribulations, if I would only contact him at the address upon the paste board that he handed to me as he shook my hand.

Mist is interested in publishing a definitive study of the pirate species, something that he felt would be to our mutual advantage. I readily agreed to this, and said I would be available to him at the Trow, for I had no bed to call my own any more. So I arrived here by stage to Bristol, and straight to your door. I came here because I realise you have been a true friend to me far more often than I deserve, but also to discharge a debt of honour placed upon me by our old friend Teach, on his dying day. This I have performed in half by placing in your hands this parcel, the other half is to tell you what I know of the circumstances leading to my possession of it.

As you know, Edward took the name Teach, which we had used as a nickname as children, to conceal his true name of Drummond and hence protect his family in Bristol from any scandal or repercussions of his actions. He was also spurred into taking this action so that he could pretend to be dead and allow me to marry Hannah; it was an honour that I foolishly declined, though I am sure you are very glad of it. I had believed Teach's lie until I met him one night in Nassau. Under that name he became a privateer with Jennings, serving his country well, gaining a fiery reputation with those who witnessed his satanic appearance in battle. Out of this grew the myth and legend known as Blackbeard, or Barbanegro as the Spaniards called him. When the war ended, he carried on in his battle against Spain, but was now called a pirate and a traitor rather than a hero, and his warlike strength and reputation grew far beyond any we knew before.

Teach based himself at New Providence, indeed he established it as a free state for pirates and their camp followers. But I knew nothing about Blackbeard being our very own friend Teach, believing him to be long dead, having perished on that voyage with Barker. When I landed at Nassau, I heard considerably more of the legend of Blackbeard, but no more about the real man. For sure, every person on that island had respect for Teach, some out of loyalty and others out of fear, but all I could ever see was his cold footprints and his shadow, which was cast across the whole Caribbean.

When I received word from Vane that he intended to retake the island with Blackbeard's aid, I was mightily afraid and many around me quaked and paled at the prospect; but still I knew little of the man himself. Then one night, while I awaited the return of Hornigold from his second mission, I was following my habit of walking around the streets of the town well after midnight, unable to sleep, worrying about attacks from pirates or the Spanish, and the mountain of debt that I had accumulated. I was also enjoying the brief respite from the heat that only the deep night and its breezes could afford me, when I was waylaid. I had reached the most distant point of my nightly perambulation from the safety of the fort when I was grabbed, gagged and dragged down a deep alleyway beside a noisy inn. I was forcibly sat upon a bale, with my arms pinioned behind me, and a loathsome neckerchief pulled tight into my mouth. A lantern was held close to my face so that all I could see around me was impenetrable black, my eyes no longer accustomed to the darkness. Out of this gloom came a darker shape, which spoke to me thus:

'Ah, so it seems we have caught a Governor in our net, my hearties; let us see what strange kind of fish this is. It is dressed as fine as any salmon, but has a face like an old pike that has seen many battles! I have heard much of your exploits, Governor, here and abroad, and I believe

you must truly be the most unlucky man alive. For a sailor of fortune to lose one fortune after another, it must bite hard. And here you are setting yourself against both pirates and our old enemies from Spain, and you might well feel that the last trace of your luck has deserted you. Well, perhaps that might change tonight. Perchance your unfortunate life will end, or maybe it will just be your ill-luck that ends, for a while at least.

'I have heard that you are seeking after one Blackbeard, but all your efforts have failed to locate him. Tonight, Fortune is smiling upon you, for Blackbeard is right here. Now, don't struggle and shout, for there is no one within earshot who would not applaud you being thrown back into the ocean, gutted or otherwise, and I wish to have a civilised conversation with you, a little "tatertate," as the Frenchies say.

'Now if you agree to sit still and talk calmly, I will request that my comrades release your arms and tongue, and restrain themselves from cutting any of them off. But if you try to escape before I am done, they may feel compelled to show you the kind of tender mercy that you would show to any one of them if they stood before you at the assizes. Do we have an understanding? Slacken your hold on him, Israel, he cannot nod or shake his head without fear of cutting his own throat! Good – I see you agree to the conditions; so lads, release him into his own cognisance!'

'What do you want of me, you dog?' said I, and the shadows around me stiffened and growled, but the voice in front just chuckled.

'Well, now, Woody, is that anyway to talk to an old friend, who this very night may save your life and let you free to live it as you wish?'

'You are no friend of mine!'

'Am I not – do you not recognise me now? Am I so hirsute and villainous that none may know me?'

At this he lifted the lamp so its light fell upon his face, with the other hand he removed his hat, giving a courtly bow into the bargain.

'I present to you Edward Teach, known hereabouts as Blackbeard, but most just call me Teach, and you may remember calling me by that name, though it did not always please you to do so. You can call me by any name you choose, other than scoundrel.'

'Teach – but you are dead these twenty years, how can this be?'

'Mere subterfuge, to give me my liberty and you the freedom to marry Hannah. Yet I know that you squandered that chance, much that my friend Porter may bless you for your callousness in that respect. I have been fighting for my country and my principles ever since, with a little light piracy on the side, you might say, to cover my expenses. I can see that piracy will soon have had its day, for once the wars with Spain and France cease, as they must surely do, there will be no space for a pirate in this sea with three navies upon our tails, and I for one would then have no trade to pursue. I can see that your agency in pardoning pirates is laudable, and will save many of our number from the noose, or a watery grave, whether they deserve that mercy or not, and knowing them as I do I can truly say that many don't deserve such a reprieve.

'Why, you might even persuade me to put down my pistols and to shave off my beard, once the Spanish are quelled once more. But enough of me, I believe your mission is a fair one and I am prepared to allow it to

stand, and to this end I intend to deflect Vane from his plans to attack this island. This is not an altogether selfless act, for I do not trust the man and would not have him governor here in your place, and perhaps this will count in my favour should I choose to lay down my pistols later on.'

'And what should I owe you for this favour, Teach?' I enquired.

'Well, I guess payment is in order for such a generous offer as this, but as you have less money than the damnedest drunk lying on the floor of that inn, I cannot reasonably ask you for gold. What I do request is that you remember this favour, and those I have done you before, and that you move heaven and earth to return them when the time comes and you have the power to do so. Will you swear to do that, on what honour you have left?'

'If you send Vane away, I will truly owe you and will remember to repay in whatever way is needed.'

'That is a fair deal, Woody. Now if things were different I would suggest that we repair to the hostelry and drink it dry, but I do not think either of us wants to be openly seen in the other's company. So I will bid you farewell, and wish you a luckier life than you have had up to now.'

At that, the lamp was shuttered and I was blind once more, the shadows shifted and then I was alone. When my eyes had adjusted, I hurried back to the fort and drank half a bottle of brandy before my nerves were calm again.

I had a search made, but there was no sign of Teach upon the island, any trace of his boat was indistinguishable from those that routinely visited the island and plied the waters around it. I believe he did hold to the bargain, for Vane never did attack, and I think it was Teach that turned the blow towards the hated Spanish, and that led to Vane's capture and execution, which no doubt grimly pleased Teach.

I heard no more from him, and a few months later I heard that he had been captured and killed off the coast of Carolina, though no detail was available to me. Some weeks later, I received a visit from HMS Pearl and its heroic captain Lieutenant Maynard, and he was most eager to boast of his encounter with Blackbeard, and he even showed me where he had hung the severed head from his bowsprit for some time after their fateful meeting.

I will tell you more of that anon, but for now I will say how sickened I felt that our friend, and more than once my saviour, had been butchered by this man whom I had to praise and fawn upon in public. Amidst all his boasting and bragging, he said that he respected my stance against the pirate vermin and for that reason he felt compelled to give me a part of the spoils, though by rights it should all fall to the Crown, or to himself. What did he offer me? Not gold, nor jewels, nor even Blackbeard's sword, and thankfully not some gory souvenir hacked off in fervour. No, it was this parcel, covered as it is in spots and smears that might well be Teach's own blood. I do not believe he would have been so generous if Teach had not addressed the parcel to me, but perhaps his honour prevented him from opening it, and he hoped to be allowed to see its contents once I had received it.

I realised that this was the one last opportunity to return Teach's favour, and I took it as a sacred trust that his executioner should not benefit in any way from it. When I had a chance to open it in private, I found that only the first layer was for my eyes and I have respected that and preserved it for you as I received it. I have gladly held it close to me through all my tribulations until such time that I could deliver it into your hands, which I have done today. If you feel, in the fullness of time, that I can be allowed to look at its contents then I would gladly receive that trust, for I must admit to being curious beyond words as to what is contained in that book. But for now I know that I have discharged in part the huge debts that I owe to Teach, and to yourself.

I will tell you now what Maynard related to me, but please remember that this is the account of a man who was ambitious and eager for promotion and frustrated at that being withheld from him, telling of his brave exploits against pirates. So there may be more gravy than meat in the pie that he fed me.

Soon after waylaying me in that alley, Teach began to think about taking the King's pardon, and to that end he tried to find a way to retire with most of his gains and without most of his enemies. To this end, he persuaded another pirate called Bonnet to take the pardon first, to test that it was given in good faith and not being used as bait in a trap, but in the process he made an enemy of Bonnet and was only saved from his wrath when that man was captured and hanged after he relapsed into piracy.

Teach settled on the coast of Carolina, and took the pardon himself, but only after shedding much of his fleet, by dint of stranding two ships on sand bars, and marooning the more rebellious members of his crew. Having taken the pardon, he then invited Vane to join him and they held a massive council of pirates near a place called Ocracoke in that colony, where much drinking and wildness occurred for the best part of a week. I do believe that this action is what drew Vane's attention away from New Providence, and I am heartily glad of it. Teach had plans to take a commission as a privateer should the war begin again, and was biding his time on the coast. But such a large concentration of cut-throats and vagabonds in one place would never be peaceful or tolerated, and although Teach had made friends with the attorney and governor of Carolina, those in charge of neighbouring Virginia and more distant Pennsylvania were far from comfortable with his presence. So plans were hatched to destroy Teach, even if he remained at peace in Carolina.

Two navy ships were ordered to approach the bay where Teach was residing, with the majority of the crew and their captains going overland to try to capture Teach where he was off the shore of Bath, the ships being taken around the coast under Lieutenant Maynard to block the mouth of the inlet should Teach try to escape. It turned out that much of his pirate crew were ashore in Bath, or settled in the surrounding countryside, or causing mayhem further afield, and Teach was aboard his boat Adventure entertaining some local dignitary. Maynard had arrived at the mouth of the waterway and moored on the seaward side of an island there. He learnt from some small boats coming out from Bath that Adventure was moored on the inland side of the same small island. In the evening he could hear the sounds of carousing coming from the pirates, a wild sound being carried on the breeze. Maynard decided to wait until first light to make his move, afraid of running aground on one of the many sandbanks in the area if he tried to move into the open inlet in the dark.

Someone must have been on watch on the pirate vessel, despite the freely flowing rum of the night before, for as Maynard brought his sloop Pearl through the mist towards Adventure, Teach was seen running across the empty deck with an axe in his hand with which he severed his anchor cable, and cried out clearly for all to hear

'Damnation to the lot of ye! Cowardly puppies!' The Adventure swung round quickly in the current and as it came beam on it fired a broadside of twenty cannon at Maynard's ship, killing a third of the crew and stripping away the masts and sails. Losing control of his ship, Maynard sent most of his remaining crew down below, leaving the dead and dying in a lake of gore upon the deck. The Pearl then ran aground on a sand bar, dragged by the ebbing tide, and in an effort to free it they started to offload heavy items, including several cannon and much of their shot.

Adventure bore down on the Pearl, whether to attack or to go round her to reach the open sea is not clear, but then it too ran aground and set fast a few yards away. Teach saw that Pearl's deck was covered with the dead and assumed he could finish the job and make it safe for him to wait for the next tide to float Adventure. He decided to board her with his skeleton crew of less than twenty, including half a dozen blacks that he had released from a slaver many years before, and who had gladly joined his cause. This small band fought bravely against those of Maynard's on that slick deck, Teach being in close combat with Maynard, firing their pistols at the other, Teach breaking the lieutenant's sword with a blow from his cutlass, cursing the naval man to Hell with every breath, believing himself to be the wronged party, he who had accepted the King's pardon and then been murderously attacked when peacefully enjoying his retirement.

As the battle went on, Teach's crew were gradually reduced in number, and he became isolated at the stern with Maynard. At that moment, the lieutenant cried out an order and the rest of Pearl's crew barrelled up onto the deck and into the melee, rapidly capturing or killing all of Teach's crew, leaving only Blackbeard himself in combat.

He fought on against Maynard and would have won if they had been alone. One of Pearl's crew slashed Teach in the neck, and as he struggled to stem the blood as it choked him, and to keep Maynard in his sights, Teach weakened and fell to his knees and was then put upon by ten or more of the sailors. In a few seconds, his head had been severed from his body and held aloft to prove his death, like our old King's had been. Maynard examined Teach's body and found that he had continued to fight despite having received five wounds from bullets and twenty or more from swords before he fell.

The remnant of Adventure's crew were sought out, including one who had been tasked with exploding the powder store if all else failed, and they were put on trial. All of those were hanged, apart from one who proved to be the very dignitary that had been the guest of honour on the previous night, who stated that he had been coerced into taking part in the action. The black crew members were not suffered to share the same trial with the white pirates, being deemed to be bad escaped slaves, but they still shared the same fate, on separate gallows. Teach's body had been thrown into the Ocracoke inlet, and his head affixed to the bowsprit of Pearl, so that Maynard could prove his success and reap the rewards of capturing Blackbeard's flagship.

Yet reward Maynard gained none: all the bounty found upon Adventure, or in various stores, warehouses and caches that Teach had left ashore, was seized by the governors of Virginia and Carolina, and even the small amount that had fallen into the pockets of Maynard's men as they searched Adventure was sought out and clawed back.

Maynard hunted through that ship for signs of treasure within minutes of seeing Teach killed, but found there only to be papers and the parcel we have here. Of the other papers he made what advantage he could, including a letter linking the attorney and governor of the colony to Teach, proving their friendliness towards him and hinting at a closer and more financially rewarding link, and this paper was used to displace both these persons from their positions. But this did not prove advantageous to Maynard either, who had deprived his superiors of the glory of Blackbeard's capture.

*

Woody then concluded by saying:

'The parcel, he brought to me when he found he was to receive no part of the two thousand pounds raised from the sale of Teach's goods; he gained no reward, nor any promotion. He expected some favour from me, but I had none to bestow upon him, nor would I willingly give any to the man who had murdered Teach. I have kept the parcel with me, unopened, even though its contents might have relieved some part of my debts, for I felt that there was a sacred trust placed upon me by Teach, and my gratitude towards him, and yourself, required me to keep that trust. I would be most grateful to read it, should you allow me to do so, but I understand if you do not feel so inclined.

'Now, I have no place to lay my head tonight, and I still have a few coins from Mr Mist, so may I stay here at the Trow, until the course of my tomorrows is a little clearer?'

10:End Papers

Once again I played host to Woody. This time he slept in my small, old room in the eaves, at his own insistence, rather than anywhere more comfortable. He looked to be beyond exhaustion, all of his struggles come to nought, his only wealth a few coins given to him in charity by some stranger, his face having the weight of perhaps an extra twenty years, scarred on both cheeks, eyes reddened, a man truly defeated by life and his own ill-luck.

I had hoped, beyond reason, that Teach would someday return to us and settle to a peaceable occupation; that his guile and wit, his gift for disguise, would allow him to escape his enemies and the destiny of his profession, and bring him home to us, to spend his greying years scandalising us with his stories before a roaring fire. Now I held his last words in a wrapper stained with his own blood, and all hope was gone. There was no chance that it was another, not my friend, that fell to Maynard's attack, no possibility he had evaded and survived.

That night I sat down and read his journal, to know all I could about the years we had been apart, to try to understand how my boyhood friend had become the most notorious of pirates, a man of legend, and to decide the most appropriate way in which to remember him, perhaps even to memorialise him.

As I read, at turns I was fascinated by the endeavour he described, made sorrowful by his heartbreak, laughed at the folly of others, and at last brought to that final night, feeling the same tension that must have gripped Teach. I may not have understood why he did all those things, but I understood them to be truly the actions of my long lost friend.

I have spent some time to write my account in the final pages of the log so that the whole of Teach's life may be remembered. I do not think the time is ripe for this to be placed before the public, it would not serve his memory well. I may let Woody read Teach's account, that he may know the true man, and not just the villain of rumour and legend. Then I shall seal the log away until the times are more auspicious.

There is now a hole in my life that shall never be filled, and I must use what wit I have to carry on, and to endeavour to ensure that the name of my friend is never forgotten.

I leave his words to speak for themselves.

John, called Porter, adopted Hawkins,

this 21st day of January 1722

Part 2

The Log of the Revenge
A ship of Pirates
Under its Elected Captain
Edward Teach
Known as Blackbeard
In the years of Our Lord
1717 – 1718

1717

I, Edward Teach, being elected Captain of the good ship Revenge on this tenth day of September, do set down here the facts that led to that event.

First I will state how I, a son of Bristol, came to be in this district of sea in the first place.

As a young lad of nineteen, I had some trouble at home, and I determined to escape it, and my past identity, by taking a ship to the New World. As it happens, the venture that I joined was the first run of the Triangle route out of Bristol, under one Captain Barker. All I had seen of the trade at home was the riches gained from the goods it brought back from the West Indies, and how the merchants were jealous of their London counterparts who made the most profit from them.

I had seen some black men kept as periwigged footmen and curiosities by the richer merchants, in more finery than I had ever owned, and I thought the trade noble if it took savages and made them into such fine creatures as those. It must have been well-founded and to the benefit of all, I thought. I lost this vision rapidly when we moored off the coast of Africa, and the stench of Elmina drifted across to us, worse than any plague pit.

That journey across the Atlantic, with the moaning of the slaves, packed tightly on their shelves, the dropping of the dead and sick over the side, and the other practices that showed me that the cargo was considered to be lower than pigs and cattle, all of it turned my stomach. On landing in Jamaica, I took advantage of the Captain's gratitude to me for a service that I rendered him, so that I managed to leave the ship and shed my born name forever.

The infection of slavery is everywhere in the islands,

and I could not escape it for two whole years. I was desperate, but then war broke out between England and an alliance of France and Spain. Suddenly there was an opportunity to fight for my country, earn a living from it, and to escape the taint of slavery. I joined Captain Jennings on his privateer ship, and we spent years pursuing Spaniards around the Caribbean.

We were like a branch of the navy, better armed and more aggressive and daring, but perhaps lacking in training and discipline, and in the finer points of etiquette at the captain's table. Under the direction of the admiralty, and on our own initiative, we hounded and harried the Spanish at sea and in their harbours, we tangled up the French, cut their lines of trade and supply, and wasted their energies. We earned the contempt and jealousy of our naval masters, and they banked up the fires of their hatred for us, awaiting a time when we might be less in favour and become their prey rather than their partners.

The time did come when finally the parties to the war came to sign a treaty, and ended all hostilities. Some of our number went back to their cotton, tobacco and sugar, to peaceful trade and cruising around the seas, aided mightily by the golden bounties that they had seized over the dozen years of that war. For many, this change of life was neither easy nor tasteful, and I was in that number alongside Jennings and others whose names are now well-known abroad.

Unwelcome in the naval harbours of Jamaica, we shifted our base to the small island of New Providence, where we lived in a republic, brother pirates under a code, our elected captains determining law and punishment, all equal under the black flag. The harbour welcomed pirate vessels and those caught as bounty, but its shallow draught gave no welcome to our heavy former allies from the navy.

From this protected base, we could easily cruise to the straits of Florida and take our pick of the boats trading there, or which were heading to Europe burdened with goods.

My preference was to only take Spanish or French vessels, and to honourably leave our friends bound for England alone, but not all the crews held the same allegiances, or the same moral code as I, and would prey upon anything slow enough for them to catch.

After a while, Jennings decided to take his considerable wealth back to his large estate on Jamaica and to retire from the life of a rover, and in doing so take his ship to use for trade rather than sport. Not yet being in a position to retire, nor wishing to be becalmed upon New Providence with the lame ducks and rum sots that infest the place, I joined up with Captain Hornigold, and he was glad to have me, being by then well acquainted with my reputation for swiftly won battles, with little loss of life or blood on either side.

Hornigold had his flagship, Ranger, and a sloop he had captured from the French called the Maid of Orleans, which he gave into my charge. We made several sorties, taking first a Spaniard out of Cuba with a hold full of flour, which had some value but little interest for the hands, and then a few days later we ran down a sloop from Bermuda carrying a hundred barrels of Madeira wine. Hoping to sell most of this, we made for Nassau, but the crew fell upon it like wolves on a fold of lambs, and drank much of it down in one mad night, like a cup of milk, and even more the next morning to slake their raging thirsts. Having now gained a taste for this liquor, the crew desired to find some more forthwith, and so we came to take an English boat off Virginia, and harvested its lake of wine before, to my shame, scuttling her and sending all her other fine goods to Neptune.

With the crew once more too foxed to stand, Hornigold and I picked out the most mischievous and rebellious of the culprits, had them whipped in the scuppers, then dunked in the sea with a rope round their ankles, until all sense of pleasant drunkenness had left them, to be replaced by the fear of God and Captain. Only by this form of punishment could we bring any semblance of discipline to the crew, a thing vital if we were to survive against any trained opposition.

After some months cruising, we came back to Providence bay and whilst anchored there were approached by another vessel under the black flag. This was a buccaneer crew under one Stede Bonnet, who had set up and funded the whole venture himself from his earnings as a farmer on Barbados. He was sick of the agricultural life and eager to share in the adventure and spoils of our roving nation.

Buying a ship and hiring a crew of cut-throats does not make a man into a pirate captain, and he had only earned the spite of his men through high-handedness, irrationality and ineptitude. His crew demanded a change of leader and were one step from gaining it through murdering Bonnet. It was this vessel that came alongside, the common men wanting to join under Hornigold's flag, the only gainsayer being Bonnet who had been secured by the roughest of his critics, to restrain his towering temper. It was clear even to him that the best bargain he was going to strike was continuing to have the right to breathe fresh air above the waves, and he relinquished his boat to us and became just another hand upon the Ranger.

This last happened just yesterday, and since then I have been placed as captain on the ship which was paid for by

Bonnet's wealth and lost by his fecklessness and folly, I being so elevated by selection of Hornigold and acclamation of the hands. This good ship is the Revenge, and this book shall be its log, and my history.

12th September

Much merriment followed my election as captain of Revenge, and every last drop of Madeira, and all but the vilest of our other grog, has been guzzled. The dregs were poured onto the decks to give the ship a drink to toast its new master, or laced round the scuppers and lit to produce a blue ring of flame to dance around us in the dead of night, before being doused to save us all from being burned to ashes. Not a hand stirred yesterday, but today I had every weary, sore-headed pagan up in the rigging, or a-scrubbing the filth from the decks, or careening the hull of its be-fouling skirts of weed, worms and snails. Now Revenge is a beauty again and ready to strike fear into all who cross our path. We have a new flag stitched by sailmaker Roberts, which bears the head of a fearsome bearded pirate grimacing over crossed swords; he says it is a portrait of me, but I see no likeness there.

15th September

We set course for the Florida straits again, mid-channel between the mainland and Grand Bahama. The lookouts at the top of the mast can see a horizon of three leagues, and now with three ships spaced out we can survey much of the width of the straits. When the Ranger sighted a sloop heading south to double the peninsula, we close up in pursuit of it, and being lighter, newly careened and sleekly nimble, we reached it an hour before sunset. On seeing the standards at our mast and bow, and myself right out on the bowsprit with one hand on the sheet and a cutlass in the other, sparks leaping from the fuses under my hat, they dithered between running and surrendering, knowing not which action would lead to more pain. We swiftly cornered her, fired shots across the bows, and were soon aboard her using our hooks and ropes. We took the ship and cargo, which this time was composed of food, wine and other goods bound for the Spanish in Pensacola, accepted those crew who wished to join us as freebooters, and landed the others on the Keys, with no worse than the odd bruise from rough handling for those that struggled.

Now being a fleet of four, we returned to Nassau where we sold or bartered the goods, drank the wine, and initiated our new colleagues into the arts of piracy.

22nd October

Much as the grand snakes of the tropics eat but rarely, and then laze about their digestion, so most pirates spend their days enjoying the fruits of their brief labours, and only turn out for more work when their stomachs or purses are empty, and the barrel is dry. So it was with us, having a fine time on the proceeds of a day's work, until well into October. Then we grew restless and hungry, so we set out once more.

We played our game of stringing the fleet out across the strait, casting a better net with four vessels than we could ever do with three. All hands were eager and ready: while the watch at the masthead scanned the horizon, and others kept an eye on the neighbouring ships in line to see if they signalled a catch, all others were in preparation for the coming events. The gun parties cleaned and supplied each gun, checking the restraining ropes, greasing all that needed to be free, tightening all that should be fixed. The boarding parties cleaned and primed pistols and muskets, sharpened blades, and prepared their appearances so to strike terror into all who saw them. I replaced the fuses in my fighting hat, beribboned my beard, put black around my eyes, white powder to my skin, and oiled my hair until I had attained an horrific aspect.

All then not engaged in watching, took their food and as much sleep as could be found amongst the engines of war, to be well rested for action. It was truly a thing to see, all these men made up like ghosts and monsters in a mummer's play, sprawled in their dreams upon the decks or on bundled ropes.

Around noon we were woken by shouts from above; the watch had spotted signals from Ranger which indicated that two prey had been seen and were heading for Havana. All hands were roused, the sails were unfurled and set for speed, our course determined so we would close with Ranger before we could sight the prey, or they us. Two hours later, our pack was clear and gathering, the two targets not yet aware that wolves were on their tails. Another hour and all four of our fleet were within shot of the target and closing fast. We saw clearly that they were heavily ladened sloops making slow progress, they fired a shot apiece to ward us off, but one volley from us filled the sky with smoke and fire, and sent balls through every sail on the pair, and they wisely pulled to and surrendered.

We took all the goods carried by the Robert and the Good Intent, both British boats but going about Spanish business, conveying silks, brandy and other luxuries to those fine houses of Havana that had grown fat from the slave market there. We had no need for two extra boats, so we moved all their witless crews into the Good Intent and release her, keeping the Robert for ourselves.

This day's work has led to a change in our fleet. Captain Hornigold was for leaving those ships alone as they flew the Jack, yet his crew was hungry for conquest, overruled him, and threatened to depose him. I am no great lover of taking British boats, but I also see that the men have expectations and less moral niceties than their captains. They formed a fo'c'sle council and moved a note to take the ship from Hornigold, which within the pirate code they are perfectly at liberty to do. For some time, those loyal to the Captain were arrayed in the cabin with him, having enough pistols and blades to overrun Cuba.

Before this mutiny could overheat and bloodshed ensue, I called a parlay on deck. Having great respect for Hornigold, I had no wish to see him deposed, or split open, so I argued for a third way. I suggested that the bounty be split early, and for all those loyal to the captain to join him on Ranger and retire from the field. Argument went back and forth for hours, it was lucky that I had locked away all the booze so it could not get any more heated. Finally it was agreed that Ranger and the smallest sloop would depart with a reasonable share of the spoils, Hornigold retiring from the pirate trade altogether.

Following this split, I was confirmed as captain and promoted to commodore of our fleet of three, being Revenge, Robert and the sloop we now call Falcon. Hornigold sailed to Nassau, planning to open an inn with his share.

28th November

We have lain up for weeks enjoying our winnings, this time mostly anchored off an uninhabited island south of Nassau, not wanting to cross our old Captain's path for a while. This, combined with incognito visits to the dives and cat houses of Havana, kept the crew distracted and happy. But restlessness and poverty again roused them and we began to cruise south until we had reached St Vincent. With only the three ships we could not cover a breadth of sea like the Florida strait, but we should so easily pick up vessels trading along the chain from Havana down to Brazil, and on this day we did just that. We spotted a Frenchman plying its way northwards, moving slowly due to its sizeable displacement, so we engaged it. It showed no interest in stopping so we overtook it and fired a broadside across, taking out the hind mast and holing the sails. It soon became apparent to them that surrender was required and they pulled up.

We had a struggle on the deck, but the French crew was small and unused to fighting other than in pub brawls, my men were drunk with the excitement and the last of our brandy. She was named the Concorde and was on the second leg of the triangular route, carrying slaves towards the market at Havana. We took her and what little real cargo she had apart from the slaves, and set her crew free upon our sloop the Robert. I could see Concorde would be a mighty ship once all the slaves and associated paraphernalia were offloaded, with plenty of room for guns and booty, and our ever-growing crew.

The French grumblingly took our Robert and baptised it Bad Meeting, and sailed off in her yelling that they would have their vengeance upon us, though it was hard to hear this over our laughter. We had of course stripped it of its guns and other assets before letting it sail away; we did not leave even a single hammock for the French to take their ease. These assets were then strapped and piled upon the deck of the Concorde as the hold was still full to bursting.

With some difficulty, being a mast down and heavily laden, we manoeuvred her out and sailed further to Bequia. We set in as close as we could to the shore as we dared, then broke out the slaves and ferried them to the beach, this task taking us near on two whole days to complete. We struck off their chains, and left them with all the provisions we could spare, and indicated that they would be wise to swiftly disperse lest the slavers attempt to recapture them. Whether it was due to a lack of a shared language between us, or the shock and strain they had experienced from capture to release, but few moved from the sandy strand, instead sitting in many separate huddles, silent, or rocking and crying, or pleading for us to return them to the ship and back to their homes an ocean away, which we could not do.

I cannot say how this affected me, having seen the whole process with Barker and having been sickened by it then, but I could do nothing and there was little sympathy to extract from the crew, some of whom were angry that we had not taking all of these lost waifs to the slave market and turned a fortune from this black gold. So we departed, taking with us only a dozen slaves who happened to speak a tongue understood by some of our crew, and who showed the spirit and fight to join us in our roving lives above decks.

The men have worked hard clearing the foul detritus from the former slave decks and reusing the wood of the shelves to build partitions and cabins in the vast hold. We have removed all trace of the shackles and shelves, and above a dozen bodies of the captives that the French had not cleared when we captured them, and which must have been there for days; it is little wonder that the hold's former inhabitants were subdued.

We have created new sea-proof gun-ports at balanced points along the sides, and lowered the Robert's guns into the hold. The vessel being now capacious and swift, we have plenty of room for crew and booty, and she is a fine vessel. I have named her Queen Anne's Revenge, in remembrance of our good queen whose dynasty failed, to be replaced by a foreign king to whom I owe no loyalty.

She will strike fear into all who see her, being fast and black and bearing over thirty guns, more than the other two ships combined.

Before we had fairly finished this work, we encountered a powerful vessel, Great Allen, that took it upon itself to attack us and rid the seas of pirate scoundrels. What made a merchantman think it could out gun three pirate vessels, I cannot guess, but it was a hard and bloody fight, our sloop was badly damaged, Great Allen had shredded sails, splintered decks and fire in the bows. My men were incensed, hot to slaughter all upon the attacker who had the effrontery to take on Blackbeard and his band of cutthroats. But I tempered their anger by saying that only the captain and owner of the Allen were to blame for the day's actions and the orders that had guided them, and that the best way to hurt those gentlemen was to take away what they cared for the most: the ship and its cargo. So we herded her to a deserted island some leagues from St Vincent, offloaded the crew onto that isle, with the captain tarred and feathered, for which I sacrificed a pillow I most liked: even I cannot deny the men some sport! We took all the cargo, a rich haul indeed, which even then only filled a small space in our echoing hold, and then moored the Allen offshore in full view of its erstwhile hands, poured pitch across its decks, and then from our fifty guns sent a barrage of ball and flame into her, that set her alight and then sent her to the deep in under ten minutes. Let that be a lesson to all those who think they can oppose us with impunity, let them be thankful that they had eyes to witness it from a safe distance.

5th December

After our encounter with Great Allen, we headed north again along the chain, working our way back towards Nassau with the aim of selling our goods there, or in

Havana. As we neared Anguilla, we ran across another merchant, the Margaret, sailing low in the water beyond Scrub Island to the East. We happily drew around it, fired our usual greeting volley of balls and chains through the sails, using some of our remaining stock of slave manacles for this, and made our most fearsome faces and terrifying warlike noises, as is our wont. Margaret healed to, being but lightly armed, heavily outgunned and far too loaded to try to run to Anguilla. I took her men and Captain Bostock onto Queen Anne's Revenge and entertained them there, while my men took all of value from the captured ship.

After eight hours, Bostock tired of my company, so I let him depart with his much slimmer Margaret to St Kitts with our blessings, and a tale or two to tell to any who would listen. After all, it is handy that merchants know that their lives and ships will be spared if they cooperate, but if they decide to fight then they need expect no quarter to be given, and their skins and hulls are in peril.

I sold Bostock a tale about our being bound for Hispaniola to ambush a fleet carrying Spanish gold; he was so greedy for stories of our wrongdoings and of our treasure, that we were happy to oblige him by inventing much that we had not done, nor could ever achieve. We used a large and gaudy cup, much prized by the captain of the Allen, as evidence of the boundless wealth we had accumulated, and invented several extra attacks, just to increase our reputation. I am sure that the blowhard will spread the news of this across the Caribbean, much good it will do him, but it will divert any pursuers from our tail, to have them chase us around an island two hundred leagues from our real location.

I had from Bostock confirmation that a Royal pardon is being offered to pirates, should they cease their operations, a story I had only heard whispered before, and that this shall be brought to us by one Woodes Rogers, famed for his cruise around the world. I was most surprised to hear the name of my childhood friend and compatriot from the lips of this silk clothed buffoon, and it gave me pause for thought.

After Bostock had departed on the Margret, we sailed within his sight around the southern side of Anguilla to indicate our course was set for Hispaniola, and then we ran into another pigeon off St Eustatius. The men were still afire for a fight and I could not control them: they ransacked the boat in minutes, threw those who did not cooperate into row boats, the rest joining our numbers, before we set light to the rotten hulk which they had been sailing.

We doubled back for Nassau, and I retired to my cabin while the crew celebrated another good day's work by seeking the bottom of a barrel or two.

I have been thinking for some time about where all this will end: can I be a pirate when I have fifty years under my belt? Do I wish to follow this life until it is my death? Now that we take ships of all nations, what is the defence for my actions? Am I not just another brigand of the sea who will steal from all without loyalty, and piss that wealth away? How has the school master's son come to this, he who sacrificed his life on high principle for the happiness of others? Now that the man who should have been beneficiary of that sacrifice is coming to seize my island sanctuary, offering a pardon to peaceful pirates and destruction to the rest, what course should I set?

6th December

Sailing north, well out to sea, crew mostly sick in the scuppers or singing in their hammocks. I have puzzled all night over what I should do and am now determined to exit this life of piracy, but need to plan how to do this and keep my skin whole while taking a fair share of the spoils into my new life. As Woody is not yet arrived, I have some time to lay the ground for my retirement with actions both at sea and on shore. My largest problem will be the men, with over two hundred of them under my command, though that term implies a sight more control than can ever be exerted upon such an unruly bunch, I must plan very carefully. I am sure that some who are loyal to me, and who have accumulated a goodly portion, by not spending it all on wine and women, will be open to hanging up their cutlasses. There are certainly some who will not retire because it is brigandry that they live for, not the leisure that it might fund.

I have amongst my crew many men from Bristol, though they never knew me under my original name, and have not seen me without this voluminous beard, so they do not know who I really am. Some of these men are Tom Price, Hal Virgin, Dick Harris, Bill Child, Bert Goss and of course Israel Hynde. Only the last of these has tried to shed his true name as I did, having taken to the surname Hands and attempted the nickname Basilica, though most of us call him Israel as even he forgets what it means, or why he adopted it. These men, and our new black colleagues, might form the kernel of a new band that I could take out of piracy. Israel is hard to predict and control and I do not know his intentions in life, but he is also as able a captain as I and will be vital to my plans.

I must plot carefully. First, of course, I must fill the hold with gold so that the men get their share and they don't feel aggrieved when I leave with mine. To this end I will put Bonnet in charge of Revenge, Hands on the Falcon and I will remain on the Queen Anne.

10th December

We are returned to Nassau, all men are ashore involved in spending their gains on pleasures of the flesh, and only a small skeleton crew are left behind to maintain the ships.

12th December

I have taken the smallest ship, the Falcon, and my trusty band of mates from Brizzle, to take a pleasure cruise. We are in fact aiming for Carolina, where I have a feeling we might meet a warm welcome in certain quarters.

14th December

Having landed under an English flag and false name in Charles Town harbour, we have proceeded incognito to find out about life in the town and in particular of the Governor, a man called Eden. For disguise all I had to do was shave off my beard and wear a colourful waistcoat, for my reputation as Blackbeard is such that being bare headed and clean shaven is enough to make me into another man altogether. I took the name of Thatcher as just different from my own nom de guerre that I would be unknown, but close enough that slips of the tongue would not prove fatal.

Mr Thatcher and party have been well entertained, being most welcome with our fine clothes and bulging purses, and we have met both the Governor and his minister, Tobias Knight. This last character I have many hopes of, for I can see that he must have been cut from much the same cloth as I and he has retired into a position of respectability and luxury, at the right hand of power. For who else but a pirate would take a name that evoked the three nights of chastity before consummation that the church expects of a worthy marriage?

When Knight met me he had the glint in his eye of a man who is surprised that no one can see through his game, and who had met a player of the same kind. He may even have called me "Mr Teacher" once, to signal that he knew my true provenance and was happy to play along, to our mutual benefit.

I am sure that for the right price this man will help settle the Governor on granting us a pardon, no matter what our past transgressions might be.

15th December

We have been invited to join Governor Eden at his home to celebrate the birth of Our Lord, and we are happy to use the Falcon, currently dubbed "The Maid of Ayr" for the purposes of subterfuge, to transport the Governor and his retinue to his mansion in Bath, off the Ocracoke inlet, some hundred leagues north-east of Charles Town.

20th December

Having made good progress betwixt merry makings at the captain's table, we entered Bath creek, off the Pamlico River, at dawn today. We are now moored below the Governor's own house. It is fair land around here, with hills and farms like those around the home of my youth, and a good mooring for ships right up to the shore. Perhaps I should settle here, in the namesake of a city near where I was born?

6th January 1718

Having spent a very enjoyable Christmastide in and around Bath, we should make ready to depart. The Governor is not wanted back in Charles Town for some weeks and plans to travel there on horse-back, to gain some knowledge of how things fare in the further reaches of his domain, whilst his chattels travel back by cart. I shall now relate what has passed here these last three weeks.

The Governor, Mr Eden, or Charles as he became known to me, is a lover of good things, be they wine or music, fine conversation or the company of pretty women. Yet all this fine living is a strain on his finances, and his waistline. His income is prey to the fickleness of tax collection, the revenues from which are dominated by a few large towns, which are often slow and mean with their returns. How can a fine man, with a large establishment, hope to keep up appearances when his purse is near empty?

Eden took me to be a rich merchant, my clothes and manner did not betray me and the fine vittles upon the "Maid of Ayr" did nothing to disillusion him. He took me into his confidence, damning the burghers of Charles Town in particular for enjoying the benefits of being the seat of government while not paying above half of the duty and tax that was owing to provide for said institution. They complain of paying for naval ships nearby, and a hundred other services that they perceive to be of no value. They would retain all their taxes and let all that depends upon them go-hang, or rather drown in their muddy streets, open sewers, or fall foul to any of the pestilences of a *civilised* life. Eden would have them brought up short, and made more respectful of their Governor, as are the citizens of Bath, but he could not see how to bring this about.

On another occasion over Christmas, Mr Knight came to me at a ball being given by the Governor, and while all the others there were engaged in minuets and more relaxed country dances, he stood beside me and started a conversation out of the side of his mouth, thus:

'Forgive me, dear Edward, please do not give be *black* looks for *beard*-ing you so about the matter of your good *fortune* in trade. For I know that whilst *roving* and *ranging* around the seas, you must have met many people, and I would like you to *teach* me all about it. I am sure that it must be a *cutthroat* business!'

He clearly emphasised several of the words so that I was in no doubt that he knew that I was the famous freebooter Blackbeard. Given there was a price upon my head, we were standing in unarmed in our best silks at the Governor's mansion, with several of the local militia at hand, why was he addressing me in code rather than having me clapped in irons?

I responded in kind as best I could, 'Why, Mr Knight, I can see that you are not a man to delay your *curiosity and pleasures for three days*. I feel that we might well have a *lot in common*, being both men who choose to have a private word in a *private ear*. Perhaps we should step outside for a while, to see what our stars might indicate?'

We repaired to the grounds of the mansion, there to appreciate the fine moonlit view of the creek where the Maid rode at anchor, and beyond it the wider estuary out to the Atlantic. My, what a fine sight it was for a sea-going man!

'Now, Mr Knight, please speak plainly or hold your tongue, if you value it!' I declared.

Unabashed he replied, 'Edward, we both know that you are none other than Blackbeard, who is famed for marauding these waters, and beyond to the coast of Brazil. Let me state boldly that I care not what you have done, for I am very much cut from the same sailcloth, as you have surmised, but I have been settled here for some time and now am the Governor's trusted counsel, collector of duty and a big man in the colony. It was not always thus, however, and it was only through luck that I found Charles' weakness for fine living, and his inability to pay for it, and I invested my fortune in securing both his future and my own. Now all that is endangered because those fellows of Charles Town pay too little of what they owe.'

'What has all this to do with me, pray Tobias?' I asked.

'We have all heard rumours of a pardon for pirates, and it will surely fall to Charles to grant it to any who submit to him, and this may be preferable to asking any other Governor or even that man in Nassau, when he arrives. Any man wanting a pardon will also desire a safe berth in which to retire, and that is far harder to find than a parchment and a seal. So I submit to you that you might be well advised to curry favour with Charles and devote some part of your wealth to his happiness,' he stated.

'And Tobias, what do you hope to gain from this for yourself?' I enquired.

To which he responded haughtily, 'Edward, all I want is in the best interest of Carolina and its Governor, but I cannot deny that I have a very comfortable sinecure here and it has many enjoyable perquisites which would be endangered should Charles' finances weaken to a critical point.'

'So, what can I, as a good citizen, do about this state of affairs?' I probed.

'I can think of two actions that would secure you Charles' permanent gratitude, and safety in your retirement, for that is surely why your are here without your famous facial covering. The first of these is to purchase from Charles the title of the steading that adjoins these grounds. That should alleviate his immediate financial worries and give you the opportunity to further your interests with him and to put down roots here. I did much the same thing a dozen years ago, and see how well it has done me!' he expounded.

‘That sounds a fine scheme, and one that fits with my plans and desires. What is the second item that you have in mind?’ I prompted. He then laid out his plan:

‘We need to increase the revenues from Charles Town, and to do this the merchants of that burgh must see the value in government and the services that it provides. So I suggest that you mount an attack upon the town, blockading its harbour and exerting some severe taxation of your own upon all craft that try to cross your line. This will not only recompense you for your investment in Charles, but also demonstrate to those rebellious and stubborn burghers that they need the protection of the navy and Governor, and that paying for their services is far cheaper and surer than the alternative: a pirate siege. In return, Charles will grant you a pardon irrespective of the terms being brought from London by Mr Rogers. You may then retire to Bath with impunity, and live the life of a rich country gentleman, hobnobbing with your powerful and grateful neighbour whenever you wish it. What say you Edward, is this to your taste?’

I admitted that the scheme had its attractions, but it would take quite a fleet to perform this trick at Charles Town, and that would require cooperation from my fellow corsairs, some of whom might be less amenable to the proposed deal. I said I would sleep on the matter, and consult with my closest compatriots. We then returned to the ball.

One further item of interest arising from that evening I should note here. I was accompanied in one of the country dances by a fine young woman, Elizabeth, daughter of a neighbouring farmer Mr Everard Bowyer. She was such a shapely lass, fine of face, graceful of movement and intelligent of conversation, that I was quite reminded of my past brief marriage to Hannah. So taken was I by her that I could not help but ask her for another dance later on, and my eyes followed her at all other times. Perhaps if I did as Tobias proposed and settled here, I could ask for her hand in marriage? Whether Mr Bowyer wants an outlaw for a son-in-law is unlikely, but once I am pardoned then I will be just an exceptionally wealthy merchant, with a rich line of after dinner conversation.

Later, I sounded out Israel on Knight's scheme, for I need at least one ally within my crew who is conscious of and complicit in my intentions, and he thinks it is a truly bonny plan. He has not yet chosen to retire, but he is as old as me and as likely for the gallows, so needs to weigh the consequences of other pirates taking the pardon, leaving more resources to hunt him down. In the morning he came to me and gave me the nod, and his hand upon it.

I sought out Tobias, who looked as if he had been on tenterhooks all night, for I found him waiting in a pretence of casual idleness, not far up the path from the landing stage, eager for my answer, and very happy and relieved to receive it. He insisted on conducting me directly into the Governor's presence, where we immediately went about enacting the first element of the plan, seeking to purchase the steading known as Eden's Piece, which was both a surprise and a great joy to the Governor, for he is always conscious of how empty his coffers are. As yet he is unaware of my true name or profession, so the papers will be made out to the name of Thatcher, which I may have to bear for the rest of my days. I gave him a purse containing some hundred guineas to seal the deal, and now hold the title to the parcel of land where I hope to make a good home for myself, and perhaps my new wife, if I capture young Elizabeth.

I then spent some time with Tobias alone, to plan out the second element of the scheme. Before departing this shore, I went to pay my compliments to Mr Bowyer, and thus to see the lay of the land. He was so confused to see this moneyed and silk clothed merchant at his table, his gruff and bluff manner were not immediately conducive to broaching the matter of a union of our houses, so we conducted our audience with plain opinion on the price of cotton, interspersed with long silences. His wife, however, when she witnessed this awkward meeting decided to join us, quite furrowing her husband's brow by this indiscretion.

She was so captivated by the prospect of my wealth that she practically wed me to her daughter there and then as she declaimed how she had always wanted a son and one that would grow into a fine rich man like myself. The girl herself was called to meet me by her ebullient mother, to make formal introductions, and she was charmingly blushing to have attentions paid to her by such an eligible bachelor. So I concluded that it would be an acceptable match and the wedding might be executed when I next return to Bath, albeit in some months time. I did not reveal these thoughts to any of the Bowyers, however, I merely ascertained that I would be very welcome to visit again.

Now we are at sea again, making for Nassau, and I have put away my razor and have a week for my beard to have some semblance of growth, or none will recognise me there. Fortunately, in my case, it grows so fast that if I am clean-shaven in the morning, I appear quite the ruffian by supper.

14th January

Having arrived in New Providence once more, I can see my crew have not spared themselves the joys of the Christmas season: they are for the most part bleached or burnt, flabby, bleary and debauched. The ladies of the town need a respite from the crew, and my men need to find their mettle again before we can get back to serious business, so I will make them exercise the ships around the island until their hands are raw and their stomachs firm.

21st January

I have our little fleet whipped into some semblance of shape: the three ships under myself, Bonnet and Hands are working sweetly again. Now we need to select targets carefully with an eye to growing our reputation, and our flotilla, before making an attempt on Charles Town. I reckon we will need eight or more ships to close off the harbour effectively, and we therefore must take targets that are suited to the task in mind. We may not need to add to the number of men as much as we need to increase the yardage of timber, for we already have over three hundred of the most determined freebooters in our band, and we have enough cannon ports to make the siege stick.

While we were happy celebrating the festivals, half the navy have been on exhausting manoeuvres to catch us, hundreds of miles from where we were too comatose to care. How that buffoon Bostock must have whipped up a fury after seeing that gaudy cup! Next time that wolf is cried, they will be much more reluctant to respond.

We have set course for the rich pickings around Arguilla and Martinique, the cruise will take a week or so and we will keep well out to sea to avoid any unnecessary attention from those frustrated tars before we reach our fishing grounds.

28th January

On station near St Kitts, where with our three ships across the strait towards Antigua we can sight any who are following the chain of islands from Florida to Brazil, or any arriving on the trades from Africa. We have only seen small craft so far, none yet to get our blood hot, or which suited our purpose.

29th January

Engaged a French sloop but it refused to yield and the crew were beyond my control, especially once Bonnet had launched a broadside at the enemy. We took the other side and let fly with all thirty-six guns of the Queen and in seconds took their vessel beyond seaworthiness. Only then was a white flag evident, I think it might have been the captain's own shirt stripped from his back by less recalcitrant ship-mates. We took off all the men and the meagre cargo, before sending the remaining matchwood to the bottom of the channel. The prisoners were a poor showing, or stubborn, and of too great an enmity to be persuaded to throw in their lot with us, so we put them ashore on the most barren promontory of St Kitts.

25th February

Several more engagements have occurred, often not sought by ourselves, from which we have half-filled the hold with valuables, and have drunk and eaten very well to boot, but have no more fleet than we did at the start of the year. We have hogsheads of brandy, barrels of sugar, chocolate, coffee, all of the provisions we could wish, plus chests of gold, coin, jewels, and bales of fine cloth, but still not one extra ship. We shall head for Belize to see if we can find a better haul there, rather than continuing with the small fish of these waters.

3rd March

Having landed at Turneffe to take on water and fresh supplies, using some tiny part of our fortune to buy what we needed, we then sighted a fine sloop making its way towards Jamaica. We surrounded her and demanded surrender, which we promptly received. I approached the good Captain Harriot and suggested that he might like to join with us. He pondered this briefly, but was soon won over by the sight of the wealth stored in our hold. His worthy men and the aptly titled Adventure now make up the fourth of our flotilla, and their erstwhile cargo of rum is being spilled down near four hundred throats. I have put some of my men aboard to run it along buccaneer lines, to ensure discipline and loyalty, with which Harriot is not best pleased. He may become accustomed to this yoke, or he will be put ashore on some quiet island along the way.

5th March

First action with our fleet of four off Honduras. Today we have taken another ship, almost as big as Queen Anne, not much damage was taken as there are very few ships that can withstand a siege by four other vessels, armed heavily and manned by ravenous and successful rovers like ourselves. With our number of guns, our swift and concerted attack, and fearsome aspect, few can resist us. The more in our pack of wolves, the easier it is to bring down our prey, and the less risky the game becomes, for us at least. It is now almost like the childhood game of tag, where the more that are pulled onto our team, the swifter it is to grow at each new tag. We now number three large ships with a total of sixty guns, and two capable and fast sloops carrying ten apiece.

20th March

Over the last two weeks we have added four more sloops to our number, the last of which we took with only a single warning shot, more for form than necessity. We now have a fleet approaching the size required to execute our Carolina project, though I will wait a while longer to see what other fish may bite.

21st March

Bonnet has decided to go it alone, not wanting any involvement in the plan at Charles Town, so has taken his Revenge off to the southern part of the Honduran coast to skulk and sulk.

29th March

To our surprise, we sighted Revenge approaching again from the South, flying a strange and tattered flag, not the usual one for which Bonnet had paid a pretty penny when he traded farming for piracy. We hailed them and drew together until our gunnels were a yard apart. She was a sorry sight, like a cat that had been mauled by the neighbourhood tom. Bonnet was bedraggled and had been evidently voted out of his role as captain once more. I have accepted him as my guest on the Queen Anne, much that it pains me to see both his failure and to have his moping face around the ship again.

I put up John Richards, and he was elected, as captain of the Revenge, and the whole body of crew are happy to once again be part of my flotilla. What had occurred to bring about this reversal of fortunes? It seems that Bonnet was keen to demonstrate how great a captain he was, not suffering from the timidity and cowardice of his former commodore Mr Teach, and he had picked as a rich looking prize, the Protestant Caesar, a large merchantman of four hundred tons and many guns: a veritable warship in commercial clothing.

Not only did he fail to take this maiden, but his clumsy approach had allowed her to slap his face and tear his fine vestments. This was too much for the men, who tolerated him only on the assumption that he was a successful and aggressive leader, and not a foolhardy idiot and bully, so he lost their faith and his place at the top table. Bonnet was slung aside while the crew made frantic manoeuvres to avoid being captured or sunk by the indomitable spinster. Bonnet is once more a useless and depressed guest, a ghost at the feast; I will need to see if I can shed him along the way as he is wont to bring others into his misery and discontent, forgetting that it was his own blind belligerence that led to this pass.

9th April

The crew of Revenge, up to now a generally reluctant and malcontent bunch, have become more joyous than I have ever seen them, drunk or sober. For today we ran into that self-same Caesar who rejected their advances before, just south of Cuba as she sailed towards Jamaica. With our mighty squadron of eight, we easily surrounded her and took pleasure in paying her back for the humiliation she had inflicted upon Revenge. We had her crew in irons upon the deck, when generally we would have them entertained unbound in the mess with a pipe and a glass to calm their nerves. We had them watch as we shot away every spar and mast of the Caesar, before using our own version of Greek fire and chain shot to further wreck her. We finally opening a huge port below the waterline at the stern using our largest guns so that she sank without dignity backwards beneath the waves. Her men, now cowering, we left on Little Cayman to await rescue, and to think upon the vengeance wrought by Blackbeard.

Revenge's crew became Richard's men heart and soul after this, and Bonnet is a wraith onboard, whispering of retiring from a career he has failed at; I hope to lose him as soon as may be, for he has become a liability to me.

12th April

Beyond Grand Cayman, we engaged and took a small turtling boat, as much because it lay in our way as for any reason of treasure or aggression. We consequently dined finely upon the turtles that it had caught, so we gratefully escorted it to Cayman Brac, having wined the crew and fed the captain all kinds of false stories about our plans and deeds; he will spread the tale that we are bound for St Kitts to await Spanish gold.

15th April

We encountered a Spanish sloop out of Havana, freshly loaded with gold and goods bound for Cadiz. With our fleet so large we now find that we meet negligible resistance: no captain worth his cabin would try to outgun or outrun us, certainly not when out of sight of the shore. We absorbed the vessel and crew, added the gold to our hoard, with some portion set aside for our new latin crew-mates; this is far more than they would expect had they reached Spain, and this extra incentive has helped to calm and regulate the hotter blood of our new recruits. Some of them, however, are not willing to partake in this pragmatic betrayal of their former masters, so we will be forced to strand them somewhere soon.

20th April

The non-compliant Spaniards proved to be quite a handful and had to be accommodated in irons to keep the peace on-board: some of their old shipmates would have gladly slit their throats for the insults that were hurled at them for joining our side. We dropped anchor off a long thin island which parallels Florida, not far from where a Spanish treasure fleet is said to have sunk, three years back, in a great tempest. The Spaniards believe that this shore is haunted by those thousand sailors who drowned that day for the sake of a foolish captain and the King's gold. We left our troublesome guests on that bank, knowing the tale is in their minds and will give them precious little sleep. We trust this anguish will chasten them, and that they will bless us for our mercy in leaving them alive rather than dead. We were careful to misdirect them by stating we are now bound for Antigua. We don't want a naval fleet to find us athwart the harbour at Charles Town.

22nd April

Now as commodore of a mighty fleet, I need to check the lay of the land before we proceed. I have sent all but the Falcon off to Nassau, to sell their cargo, restock, refit as best they can, and to have some leisure without too much debauchery, whilst I sail on with my trusted band along the Carolina coast. If all is well, we will gather with them again near Charles Town in three weeks time.

25th April

Disguised as a rich merchant aboard his ship the Maid of Ayr, we visited Charles Town to take careful note of the waterways, defences, inshore fleet, and to ascertain the schedule of expected arrivals and departures for the next few weeks, on the pretext that this might help me get ahead of the pack at the best prices, wily merchant that I am. The approach to the town is through a wide estuary guarded by two islands named after Messrs Morris and Sullivan. The waterways are extensive and navigable many miles inland, but there is nothing of interest for us beyond the town itself. At the pinch-point between the two islands, the channel is less than a league across, easily defensible with our fleet of ten vessels, upwards of five hundred men and eighty or more cannon. With the fleet nose to tail across the mouth, there will be less that a hundred fathoms between any two ships, and we can close that gap by movement or shot far more swiftly than any enemy can hope to cross our line and leave our range.

With our fleet of three, we would have struggled to control the situation, but with our current embarrassment of resources, we may be stumbling over each other's feet! I have learned of the regular traders that ply to and from the port, but they rarely amount to much individually, for the Spanish treasure never comes here for fear of being impounded or taxed, preferring the risks of being wrecked or stranded offshore to that of yielding wealth to other nations.

While here, we once more ran into Mr Knight and he carefully avoided too high a degree of intimacy with us, but let it be known that Governor Eden was in town and planning to depart north to Bath again within the week. Thinking it wise that neither of these gentlemen be around when I bring our fleet to visit, I suggested that we might take a cruise along the coast, to which Knight readily acceded. So once more I am playing host to two of the most powerful, and dishonest, men of the colony.

30th April

Having arrived once more in Bath, I am now guest of the Governor in return, and he is courteous to me but much distracted. It seems that his financial worries continue despite the funds he gained by selling the farmstead to me. He is fearful of disgrace and dishonour if his debts are called in and his finances subjected to a close inspection, not being such that he desires them to be examined at all. At an intimate dinner for just myself, Knight and Eden, the Governor poured out his woes. He quite ruined the fine food with his complaints that if only the burghers of Charles Town would pay their taxes he might have no further worries; both himself and the government would be flush with funds and able to perform their duties without distraction. Then Knight put down his half drunk glass of madeira and stated:

'Charles, it might well be that our friend Edward here has it within his power to solve all of your problems at one stroke.'

Eden blustered in reply, 'I know that he is a fine gentleman, and he has many admirable qualities, but I struggle to see how a man of silks and trade can help me turn this situation around when an army could hardly do so!'

'Ah, but that is because you know your guest only as Mr Edward Thatcher, merchant, and not by his more usual name of Teach, a man of infinite resource and well known success at extracting value from recalcitrant merchants,' reposted Knight.

I started at this, but he waved me down, and smiled at me. I still put my hand to the small pistol I had concealed under my coat, just in case.

'Teach, surely I know that name? Why, isn't there a pirate fellow with a name like that?' queried the confused Eden.

'Indeed there is, dear Charles, this gentleman who has shown you every possible consideration and assistance is none other than the infamous Blackbeard, the terror of the Caribbean!' Knight revealed.

It was Eden's turn to start and fluster. He paled, gibbered and looked fit to fall into an apoplexy.

Knight seized his moment, 'Now, now, Charles, you are surely not afraid of the man who has conducted you twice to your house and dined at your table, drunk your wine and replenished your coffers. We both know that you are used to dealing with pirates, or recently retired ones at least. Edward here is a loyal subject of the crown and a sworn enemy of the Spanish, and has in the past done as much for his country as any sailor alive. He is now desirous of finding a way to retire honourably from the roving life, and has set his heart on making a new one here on the land that you sold to him, and perchance to take as a wife a respectable local girl. To do this he needs to be sure he will not be pursued, and for that he wants to ensure that he will receive the King's pardon and clemency, something that lies within your power to grant. In exchange, he is willing to perform one last great act of service to you using all the resources at his disposal. Might this suit your purposes?'

'It is true that I have had to deal with such gentlemen in the past, but only when I judged it to be for the good of the colony, as you well know. But what service can Blackbeard perform for me that might merit my granting him absolution for all of his considerable past sins, when we know full well he has been active since January which violates the terms of the pardon already, even if he should desist from piracy today?' asked Eden, regaining some of his former bluster.

'Perhaps Edward should tell us what he plans, as I am sure that he has his scheme clearly in mind?' suggested Knight.

All of this time, Knight conducted the conversation as if he was the intermediary between a proposal of mine and the Governor's tender heart, and not the instigator of the whole affair. He indicated for me to divulge all that I had devised. I hesitated to tell the most powerful man in Carolina, the very one charged with its defence, of my plans to attack its most valuable port, to lay siege to it and squeeze it until the pips appeared, but it seemed that the only way to fully gain his confidence and gratitude was to fully implicate him in the conspiracy, so I laid out my plan before him.

'Governor, I have now at my disposal a fleet of ten boats, five hundred men and enough guns, shot and powder to defeat the Navy Royal. I plan to lay a line of siege across the outer limits of Charles Town harbour, and waylay all who attempt to enter or leave it. Any who are stubborn may be sunk, but I plan to peacefully relieve them of any burdensome goods and entrap them in the anchorage. By this means we can hold out for some time without any word reaching the Admiralty ships. Having thus held the gates to the sea for a week or more, we will find a pretext to close in upon the town and put them to such a fright, and squeeze them some more. Once our demands of tribute are met, we shall rapidly disperse, but leaving the threat of a repeat performance whenever we feel so inclined. This brings me on to the next element of my plan,' I began.

'And pray, dear Edward, what could be the next step after holding a whole town to ransom?' asked Knight, playing the innocent.

'I intend to retire from ranging these waters, and to become a gentleman farmer upon the adjacent steading, living a peaceful life of luxury funded by my past career, and in the company of some of my closest friends,' said I, turning towards the Governor.

At this, Eden again lost all his high colour from his cheeks; he was happy to have the services of pirates harassing the wayward citizens of Charles Town, to aid his political ambitions, but less pleased to be obliged to hobnob with us on a daily basis, or to witness whatever Bacchanalian rites we might be in the habit of performing.

‘But I cannot have the most infamous of all pirates as my closest neighbour, especially after he has just threatened the seat of government with cannon and sword!’ he exclaimed.

Knight then interceded, ‘Charles, do not fret so, this is ideal. After Edward has attacked, but not actually harmed Charles Town, the whole colony will be as eager for action as it is incapable of delivering it. But you, the great Governor, will secretly negotiate with the most dreaded cutthroat of them all for his surrender, and make wise use of the pardon to permanently remove the threat of his return to rampage our coast again. It is more than a dozen naval ships could ever hope to achieve. You can then enjoy the glory of having brought safety to the region without risking a single life or capital asset, and you will have our most splendid friend Edward to warm the cold winter nights with tales from the high seas. What could be better?’

Eden looked nonplussed, then an expression of idiot cunning crept across his face like a poacher creeps past the gamekeeper. He no doubt began to perceive the advantages to which he could turn this situation, and perhaps even ways in which to betray me and wash his hands of any associated filth, but then Tobias interrupted his reverie:

‘And now, so we all know where we stand in this matter, I have drawn up a very simple memorandum for all parties to sign and keep, to give each other confidence that the others will perform their part,’ stated Knight.

This was obviously aimed at Eden, for just as there is little which the normal process of law can do to enforce a contract upon a pirate, there is similarly little that a Governor can do to save himself from proof of collusion with said pirate in attacking his own taxpayers. Eden's expression changed to that of a rabbit who has heard the fox bark in the darkness and who has no hole in which to hide himself.

Knight handed each of us a parchment with a large amount of neat copperplate writing upon it, which the Governor took as distastefully as King John must have Magna Carta. It read:

This thirteenth day of April in the year of Our Lord 1718, the parties hereunder signed do solemnly contract and swear that whereas

Edward Teach, pirate, shall lay siege to Charles Town in the colony of Carolina within one month of today's date for a period not less than five days and shall exact a penalty upon the merchants of that town of not less than five hundred pounds

Charles Eden, governor, shall duly grant said Edward Teach under His Majesty's Pardon freedom from all pursuit and persecution for all of his crimes heretofore and also any arising from the execution of said siege, on condition that said Edward Teach shall declare a permanent retirement from said line of work to wit piracy

Tobias Knight, attorney, shall witness each party to deliver upon this contract and all three parties shall keep all work of this agreement secret while any of the other parties remains alive and for twenty years thereafter unless said parties have been found to have breached this contract

Any breach of this contract will remove all benefits and protections from that party that performs the breach

Hereby signed and mutually witnessed by

Edward Teach, Charles Eden, Tobias Knight

I was quite amused that either Eden or Knight believed that they could hold a man such as I am to any contract, but I was very happy to go along with the farce of it, and it seemed to give the Governor some comfort for he trusted in paper more than in the firmness of a handshake, or the steadfastness of a heart.

6th May

We have spent a pleasant time here these few days, made all the easier by Eden taking himself off to visit the remotest parts of the colony, including Durham and Salem, so that he was away from the impending action and all responsibility to counteract it.

Meanwhile, I have had several pleasant meetings with Elizabeth, who is most taken with my now regrowing beard, not having seen it at all when we initially met, most of these encounters being under the most diligently watchful eye of Mrs Bowyer. I did, however, manage to arrange to meet without any supervision for an hour or more at a barn on the edge of my property where it adjoins that of her father's larger steading. For the most part we talked, at first quite formally, but then in an increasingly friendly and openly familiar manner. I have not revealed to her the real nature of my business, for I do not want to give her any cause for fear or doubt, but otherwise we conversed as if I was the commander and owner of a merchant fleet of quite remarkable profitability.

Having thus whiled away some time in open discussion, I declared myself quite enamoured of her and desirous of making her my wife. She was surprised at this sudden turn of events; she blushed and averted her gaze before turning back to me with the sweetest smile to say that she was pleased by whatever pleased me, but her hand was not hers to give and I must gain the approval of her father, the daunting Mr Bowyer. She then condescended to smile warmly and allow me the privilege of kissing her most fervently for a while, before pushing me away and demanding that I see her father if I dreamt of taking any further liberties.

Being by now most sorely provoked, and desirous only of making this infuriating creature my wife, I resolved to visit her father once more, as soon as Elizabeth had been able to return to the homestead to give the appearance of having merely taken the air along the boundaries of the property.

It was a bare hour later that I was admitted to the home of the Bowyers, sat as it was upon the crest with a view of the Bath inlet to the front and the rolling Carolina hills to the rear. Mr Bowyer was as gruff and plain as any man I have met, having descended from Yorkshire stock two generations hence.

'To what do I owe the honour of Mr Thatcher interrupting my ease?' he challenged.

Not to be put off I stated, 'Mr Bowyer, I am a wealthy merchant but newly arrived in this area, and I have found it much to my liking. I have the steading adjacent to yours, bought at not inconsiderable cost from the Governor of this colony. I have determined to settle here with my fortune, which shall yield me not less than a thousand a year. All I am missing is a wife with whom to share this good fortune, and I had despaired of ever finding one, until I met your fair daughter Elizabeth. I declare that I am quite besotted by her and desire to make her my own as soon as may be.'

He harrumphed and then stared at me, quite silently, for upwards of a minute, during which time I had to resist the impulse to run away like some naughty pupil caught out by his schoolmaster, or alternatively to declare that I was the scourge of the Caribbean and I would have his daughter with or without his blessing, or that of the church. He grumbled once more, then said,

'You certainly have wealth and prospects, and my wife has nowt but good words to say for your humour and manners, and though I don't value those things, I do highly value her opinion, on things not relating to money. So I declare that I am satisfied with this match, and I give it my blessing, provided you are still of the same mind in June when the nuptials shall take place.'

I assured him that nothing could weaken my resolve to marry his daughter, that I had work calling on my attention for the remainder of May but June would be most satisfactory. At this point Bowyer called for his wife and Elizabeth, and announced to them that he had agreed the union, on which Mrs Bowyer near fainted away, and Elizabeth's smile made my heart thump.

I was quite drunk by the time Bowyer's cart dropped me back at the jetty, with a date of mid-June set for the celebration of my wedding. I wonder how the cantankerous old grump will then take the news that I am a famous, and only recently retired, pirate?

15th May

I have arrived once more in New Providence, thrown a few of the more drunken crew into the blue waters of the bay, and forced the rest into making the ships fit for our next adventure. I summoned the captains of each vessel to assemble in the cabin of the Queen Anne's Revenge to be briefed on my scheme. I did not, of course, say anything about my imminent retirement or betrothal, but instead pitched the project to their interests thus:

‘My hearties, we are now such a fleet that I believe it is time to change our tactics and pursue larger fish, to suit our strength. In the past we have had to rove the seas, waiting to pick off the weak, the misguided and the lost, the slow and the isolated, whilst steering well clear of retaliation from the navy or the shore. But we now have such force that we surely have nothing to fear even if we were to encounter the whole Navy Royal. We can now turn our attention to targets ashore, and I believe that the first of these should be the ripe peach of Charles Town, which should fall easily into our hands.’

There was much astonishment, and some consternation and grumbling at this, but I continued to outline how we could pull off such a project, by holding the mouth of the harbour and thus lay siege to the town with impunity and at very little risk, and how we could expect much reward from this venture. This pleased several of the older and wiser captains, but one or two of those assembled there remained dissatisfied with not being forceful or bloody enough a course of action, and stated that they wanted to continue their roving ways by laying waste to the town and having their choice of the womenfolk.

I robustly responded to this, ‘We will not act like barbarians to satisfy your base lusts and urges, we will use our strength wisely to exact a tax upon the rich merchants of Charles Town without earning ourselves the hatred of every man in Carolina. With the money you earn from this, you may buy yourselves the attentions of every damsel in Havana, for the rest of your sordid lives, be satisfied with that.’

They muttered resentfully, but accepted the view of the others there, and we proceeded to the details of the plan. I made sure to remember those awkward elements, and I will shed them at the earliest opportunity that presents itself, for they are a liability to my own future happiness, I am sure of that.

17th May

We have set out for Charles Town in two parties, one circling in from the North, the other approaching from the South, and by this means we shall sweep the sea clear of any opposition and perchance drive much useful shipping into the harbour ahead of us.

22nd May

As dawn broke, I saw that we were in place all across the bay, with the shaded bow lights of each of our fleet dotting across the waters clear from Sullivan's Island to the opposite headland, for all the world like a king's naval review. The trap was now set, and yet the town was ignorant of its fate, for the only boats we had encountered on our approach had either fled, been absorbed into our number, or in one case summarily sunk by one of the hotter headed captains.

Within two hours our first customer approached as a heavily laden sloop bound for Havana came into view. It was brought to a halt by a solitary ball through its foresail, the master tacked swiftly as he found himself surrounded and cutoff from retreat. As we had previously arranged, the plunder went to the hold of one of our larger vessels, leaving the smaller ones light enough so that they could manoeuvre swiftly. We held the sloop's crew below, and added the vessel itself to our wall of wood across the estuary, which also prevented any word getting back to the town of our presence or intentions.

By mid-morning we had taken three outgoing ships and two incoming ones, our facilities for guests were rapidly filling, as was our treasure hold. The last of the vessels to try to run our line as it came out of the town was the Crawlay, bound for London, with some of the great and the good of the town aiming to spread its fame in the home country, and to gain wealth from so doing. Amongst the gentry was Councillor Wragg, one of those named by Knight as being resistant to the demands for payment of tax by Governor Eden, and this statesman was incandescent with rage at our audacity and impudence at impeding his mission, or so he declaimed. I had not expected so useful a prisoner, nor so vociferous and vocal a one, so I had him confined in our darkest and leakiest hold to cool his emotions and to teach him some humility, during the remaining hours of daylight.

When I went to visit Wragg at two bells of the first watch, he was soiled and sweaty in his silk suit, and most eager to please me. First I questioned him and his companions as to the vessels currently in port, and those they expected. They were keen to help, but stated there would be little more for another week on their regular schedule, and there would be none at all if our presence became more widely known. As this corresponded well with my other information, it was clear that it was time to put the next element of my plan into action.

I addressed Wragg, 'Now, Councillor, it happens that some of my crew are mighty sick, and although we carry several saw-bones to treat them, we have little of the appropriate medicines. So I require a full apothecary chest for each of my ships before we contemplate departing this place. If this is not readily and speedily provided by the town then I shall have no choice but to send the heads of all those I have captured to the Governor, and make a viking funeral of all the boats I have taken and the others that remain in the harbour. All of this can be avoided if the town provides promptly for our simple needs.'

He anxiously replied, 'Commodore, let us not be hasty, I am sure that Charles Town can provide whatever herbs and medicines you may require with all alacrity. There is no need for any bloodshed.'

'Well, let us hope that this proves to be true, for your sake,' I said finally in my best growl.

I had him sign a requisition and affidavit, and I sent these with one of his ship's men, a Mr Marks, as emissary along with Israel Hands and Henry Virgin, whom I had briefed carefully and confidentially on how I wanted them to act. The two pirates took one of our long-boats rigged with sail and oars, and departed with Mr Marks as Night brought out her stars, dappling the slowly swelling waters of the bay which we encompassed with our fleet with sparkling diamonds.

I had instructed my two men to be infuriatingly incompetent, which came not naturally to either of them as they were the best sailors of all, but they had diligently studied more foolish tars as they punished their waywardness and now they put that learning into practice, and made fair play of it. They almost capsized the long-boat before it had left the moonlight shadow of the Queen, putting Mr Marks in a fair flurry of anguish for his own life and those of his colleagues who depended upon his mission. I heard later that Israel got to within a few hundred yards of the port, after much wasteful tacking and backing across the vast bay, then jibed badly and upset the boat, ensuring that Mr Marks plunged into the briny whilst reserving only a wet foot each for himself and Henry. Once righted again, they limped into port and Mr Marks had to present the now sodden requisition to a suspicious harbour master.

I had given them two days to collect the supplies, not

because I expected it to take any fraction of that time to complete, but to enable Israel and Henry to cause sufficient mayhem to frustrate all of Mr Marks' good intentions. So it was that two full days passed, and then one more, before a message was sent out to me that delays had occurred including the capsize, and more time was needed: just as I had wanted. I sent back a reluctant agreement to wait for a final two days for our simple demands to be met, then drew most of the fleet into the harbour proper, with close on fifty cannon lined up to sink the whole town if it proved necessary to focus their minds on the task in hand. This, of course, caused considerable panic as could be clearly seen from my deck: shutters were put up on all the windows, many fine people were to be seen fleeing in hastily donned clothes carrying only the most portable of their wealth, servants running with handcarts behind with random assortments of their household possessions, and what militia could be summoned stood cowering on the water's edge with a hotchpotch of weapons and uniforms, like children dressed for play.

After a further day, a boat was rowed out to us by a handful of terrified citizens, Mr Marks ashen-faced in the stern, Hands and Virgin rolling in the scuppers, bawling the most vile and noisome songs ever learnt by a sailor. Once on board, Marks explained that the Governor had but lately arrived and caused the medicines to be assembled within the hour, thus achieving more in that morning than all the burghers of the town had managed all week. Then the pirate escorts could not be found, so Eden caused the town to be scoured for the two wayward buccaneers now wailing vile ditties whilst lying upon the deck, and they had been found surrounded by drunken and bloodied companions in the most disreputable inn of the district.

I thanked the good Mr Marks for his service and agreed to release the prisoners and their craft forthwith, but release none of their valuable goods and possessions, which I retained as tribute. Wragg I returned in his underwear to the longboat on which Marks had arrived, now a thoroughly bedraggled and humiliated figure. We exited the bay as a fleet, without a scratch upon us, and dispersed, some to New Providence, more to Havana and other ports where to sell the goods as soon as may be, and spend the gains on whatever vile entertainments are to hand.

While we had awaited the return of Mr Marks, we had received word that the new Governor of Nassau was on his way and it was confirmed that this dignitary was to be none other than my old friend Woody. I have mixed feelings about his arrival: to succeed he must defeat the pirates and throw them out of their republic, and thus will end the life I have enjoyed these many years; but on the other hand I rely on the instrument of pardon that he carries to enable me to retire to Bath, to marry and for my dreams to proceed. I know that I owe Woody no debt of gratitude and no favours, but my link to him may well prove useful if invoked in a surreptitious manner. I need to have the authorities well disposed towards me if I want to enjoy a retirement without constantly anticipating a noose or a dagger.

29th May

I have seen and heard enough to know that I will not be able to take the whole fleet into retirement, and I am also concerned that the terms of the pardon exclude acts after January this year, so our little show of strength at Charles Town may be my death sentence, though no blood was spilled there. On top of this, a large part of the crew are so far engrossed in and enthused by the business of piracy that they cannot be expected to become respectable or law-abiding men, and I dare not mention any intention to take the pardon to any of that kind. I have taken Israel fully into my confidence, and offered him a place at my homestead in Bath, which I intend to rename Avonview instead of Eden's Piece, and to give him an introduction to fair society there, if he only gives me his help in this matter, and he is agreeable to the scheme.

I still have a sizeable crew who will not be manipulated into surrender, so I will need to pare down our numbers quite substantially. For this purpose I have devised a plan that I will put into action this very day.

30th May

Today we have entered Topsail Inlet at Beaufort, with the idea of mooring up and careening our vessels to remove the buildup of weed and worms that have gathered on their hulls in these warm waters, which slow us down and threaten the strength of the timbers themselves. Having seized some admiralty charts of this area, I am quite sure that there are many risks of grounding in the inlet and I intend to make full use of these, whilst appearing to be an innocent victim of Nature, the tides and the mobile geography of the area.

31st May

When the morning tide, as near a spring tide as can be anticipated, retired and ebbed, Queen Anne ran at full pace into a sand bar and became fast there, the jolt being enough to knock the main mast off its footing, cracking the mast and splintering the hull. We were taking on water fast, I ordered that all valuable items be moved from the Queen onto Bonnet's old ship Revenge, seemingly hoping to lighten the Queen and enable its escape. The other ships in our group threw on ropes to try to drag the Queen on the falling tide, but to no avail. Indeed Israel managed to reduce our useful fleet still further by ramming Adventure onto the same bar in a mad and quite inspired effort to free the Queen. We saw the tide fall rapidly, leaving these ships high and dry, creaking under the strain of their own weight. Only having the Revenge, a recently acquired Spanish sloop, and a smaller sailing boat which we took at Charles Town, we could not berth all the crew, so we ferried many to shore, promising to return for them soon, but making certain to leave them with a reasonable portion of the takings, to keep them content.

Once this task was completed to the point of having a crew complement for the two larger ships, we only had to shed Bonnet and his die-hards. Bonnet has always had ambitions to be commander of a great pirate fleet and he questions my every decision, and despite his record has a section of the men who are loyal to his bloodthirsty and risky style of work. So we have conceived a plan to remove Bonnet from the picture, which runs thus: firstly, convince him that war with Spain is imminent and that he could make far more money, with less risk to himself, if he turned legitimate privateer and reserved his efforts for attacking gold ships rather than making enemies of all the navies of the world. Secondly, that to become a privateer he must first relinquish his title as pirate and that requires receiving the pardon from a well-disposed governor. While he is about this fool's errand, we may redeploy our fleet to best facilitate my transition from pirate to planter, and friend of powerful politicians.

I met with Bonnet and readily convinced him to become a privateer. He was all for taking the whole fleet to Charles Town or Bath and waylaying the Governor, but I eventually persuaded him to take the smallest of our vessels with a skeleton crew, so as to not appear threatening to the man that he wants to pardon him. Having thus dispatched Bonnet, the remainder of his crew got to learn that he was off to surrender, and this produced in them a fury. Israel had to be careful to use just the right amount of poison words to bring this event about without it turning into a riot and mutiny. Meanwhile, in other ears, Israel had whispered the story that Bonnet's men were planning a treachery against us and were not to be trusted or heeded. Thus it was that Revenge, Bonnet's command, has been boarded, emptied of everything from powder to spare ropes, gold, silks, charts and even the fine cup we took from that truculent captain so long ago. The crew has been trussed up and marooned on a low sandbar, with a small chest of food, a couple of long boats and a liberal dose of black eyes and bruises. Not needing a stripped-down boat, we left the Revenge moored near Beaufort, with little more than its masts still standing.

Thus we are down to one ship of loyal men, and we sail from the inlet with lighter hearts.

1st June

Of my once mighty fleet, the accounting is now thus: five smaller vessels are off trading the goods we captured at Charles Town, and I assume that this will give each man a sufficient pension if husbanded well that I need have no more concern for them, and they can have regard to their own souls. The Queen Anne lies wrecked and the Adventure stranded upon a sandbar at Beaufort, and the Revenge is stripped bare and abandoned; thus we are left with the Falcon bearing a crew of fifty in total, all loyal to me. On the rising tide this night we floated the Adventure and transferred all the goods to it in silence, then scuttled the Falcon in its place, though it flew the pennant of the Adventure. So we slipped away to sea under the cover of darkness, leaving the wrecks of two ships and the empty husk of a third, with none ashore any the wiser of our actions or our course. We now sail for Bath, taking a wide path to avoid the returning Bonnet who must hug the coast due to the minuscule size of his vessel.

3rd June

We have arrived once more in Bath, with our fair ship now titled the Maid of Ayr, though somewhat different in size to the previous holder of the title, laden with fine things. I am fit to become a member of the local gentry, happily married and settled with my feet upon the soil at last.

Israel had been keen to see around the farm, and stated that it was a grand place and he intended to have one just like it for himself. I went to call upon the Governor, who was flustered to see me. Bonnet had been there but a few days before, full of brass about how mighty a pirate he was and how the King must welcome him into the fold as a privateer in defence of the realm against the Spanish horde. This attitude had not endeared him to Eden, who knew better than most the very minor role that Bonnet played in my fleet, but he still granted him the pardon, being careful to emphasise that any return to his former ways would put Bonnet's head in the noose.

I assured Eden that even if Bonnet wanted to start as a pirate again he would be severely hampered in that ambition by his total lack of equipment, crew and skill.

'I am glad to hear that, Mr – er – Thatcher, now what may I do for you?' he enquired.

'You may deliver on your half of the bargain: I held Charles Town to ransom, I shook it until all its coins fell upon the ground, now you must give me the King's Pardon so that I may peacefully retire.'

I could see fear and uncertainty in his eyes, and this again turned into that look of idiot guile and cunning that he wore instead of shrewdness and wisdom.

He haughtily replied, 'I do not believe, sir, that we had any form of bargain. You have committed a great crime that indisposed and terrified citizens of this colony, and though that may have brought the wayward elements to heel, it does not merit my granting a pardon to a man who is still an obvious and active menace …'

He may well have intended to continue speechifying and blustering awhile, as if he was talking to his council, but I briskly thrust him against the wall and lifted him clear of the floor by his throat.

'Perhaps you have for the moment forgotten our little contract, drawn-up and witnessed by Mr Knight, for the very circumstance that you suffer from a loss of memory, courage or morals. I am not in the mood to go through the legal niceties of suing for a breach of promise when I have a ship moored below here, with cannon enough to raze this mansion to a pile of dust. I left your enemies in Charles Town without a scratch, because they treated me with honesty. No one crosses Blackbeard and survives to boast about it, and certainly not corrupt little rats like you,' I emphasised, inches from his face.

I dropped him and turned on my heel, and was striding to the door when he hoarsely called out to me.

'Mr Thatcher, Edward, please, you have misunderstood my little jest, there is no need to take any drastic action. Of course you may have your pardon and my blessing with it!' he wheedled.

So it is that this day I have received from the hand of Governor Eden a parchment bearing his seal, witnessed by

Tobias Knight, that grants to me and several named members of my crew, and by extension all those loyal to me, a Royal Pardon for all acts of piracy before January 1718, and any other acts deemed relevant by the said Governor prior to September of that year. I gladly took this and returned to Adventure, where I showed it to Israel. We each had a large glass of rum and then introduced the matter to the crew. Some small number grumbled about their loss of livelihood, but most were very content with their share of the booty, and the removal of the shadow of execution dock from their future. We caroused well into the night, and I trust that the sound of our singing gave Eden little peace in his sleep. In the morning not a man was fit to climb the rigging, even if there had been a need.

5th June

I have this day moved into my homestead, with Israel left in charge of Adventure after he had visited my home and complimented its fineness. Last night, I had a small band of my trusted crew, including all six of the former slaves that we rescued from the French slaver, bring all my chattels and most of my portion of the booty to the house. After most had departed, I and my African colleagues proceeded to bury a large part of the wealth in several caches scattered about the grounds. I trust those who helped me to never reveal the whereabouts, their loyalty to me is unswerving and they are justly rewarded for it, but it was so vastly dark, the path that I chose quite convoluted, and the amount of brandy imbibed afterwards huge enough that any memory of the night that they do retain will be of little value. The caches are hidden well, and too deep for any plough to find. There is easily enough wealth left above ground to keep me even if the farm never produces a farthing of profit, and the rest would allow me to restart my settled life several times over, if necessary.

7th June

I again visited Mr Bowyer and his fine daughter. We set a date for our nuptials two weeks hence, after I had produced evidence that I was wealthy enough to afford such a marriage. This proof included presenting Mistress Bowyer with a fine necklace of emeralds, and one of sapphires to Elizabeth; both of these jewels had been bound to adorn the neck of some Spanish princess before I came in their way. To Bowyer himself I gave a fine French clock fit for one of the many Kings Louis, with which he was seemingly pleased, despite his gruff manner and comments of it being 'too grand and fancy for a farmhouse'. Elizabeth was more beautiful than ever, and the sapphires made her eyes shine a brighter blue than I have ever seen. I cannot wait to marry the wench and bring her to my home and bed. I still have not revealed to them my true past profession, and I won't until the deed is done.

14th June

Much of my crew is now dispersed to Bath and beyond, Israel has had a bid accepted upon a steading a mile beyond my own, we shall surely make a fine old pair of farmers, and woe-betide any that come poaching or scrumping upon our lands! I see my Elizabeth almost every day, to arrange the ceremony, or the details of our future lives together, and she grows more perfect in my eyes with every glance, every graceful movement, or wise word, each modest attention she pays to me; and the few kisses that I can steal from her sweetly inflame my passions as I have never known before.

I have received word that Bonnet arrived back at Beaufort with his newly minted pardon only to find Revenge stripped and bobbing, deserted in mid-channel, with his crew marooned upon the shore. He has sworn his vengeance upon me, but I have no fear of him, and he has set out southwards to seek me when all the while I am happily ensconced in the place from whence he had just departed, and where he dare not return in fury.

20th June

I am to be married tomorrow, an old pirate of eight and thirty years wedding a fine country lass of nineteen. It may not be the match she dreamt of, but I believe that we are not only well suited but also in love, as much as I can comprehend the term. This night, I will have the remaining crew to my house for my final raucous carousing as an unwedded and disreputable man, before settling to a life of quiet, sober, utter respectability.

21st June

Having sung our loudest and bawdiest tunes until near dawn, then collapsing into a bare four hours sleep, I was looking every one of my fourteen thousand days when I stared in the mirror this morning, deciding how to make Blackbeard resemble a fitting groom for a country princess. After a large mug of coffee, a plunge into the horse trough outside, which displaced much water, a number of surprised frogs and quite a few oaths from myself, and a rum with a pinch of gunpowder stirred in, I managed to change the ancient wraith that awoke into some semblance of a man once more. With the aid of my newly hired servant, Buxton, I dressed in my finest silks and tamed my hair and beard so that even if I did not look quite like a lord, at least I may not have been mistaken for a vagabond, or a pirate.

We assembled at the church in Bath, a small but charming building not much older than myself, all of wood washed white, with a view over the inlet. The bride arrived on her father's arm, and was so fair that I heard a few unseemly comments pass between the crew before Israel caught their eye with a murderous look. The service proceeded as might be hoped, with no incident, and when it came time for the bond to be sealed, Elizabeth gave me a kiss that I would forego an Armada of treasure ships to receive again.

At the breakfast, there was the usual making of speeches which might be seen at any country wedding in the Americas, or in most of the world, I hazard. There was one little matter which I felt compelled to get in the open before I could settle to my new, sober life.

I opened my speech thus, 'My friends, old and new, I am truly the happiest man alive to be stood here today beside the beautiful woman who is now my wife. I have to thank several people for this happiness, and you must forgive me if I mention some of those who have contributed to this marvellous day. I have here my old friend Israel, who is as firm a compatriot as any could hope to meet in a dozen lifetimes. There is Mr Bowyer, who has allowed me the hand of the lovely Elizabeth. There is the girl herself, for being the most wonderful prize at the end of this journey of mine. But there are others who may not be known to those here present, or whose role in my life is not widely understood. There is the new Governor of New Providence, one Woodes Rogers, without whom I would probably be teaching latin to the ungrateful boys of Bristol. There is Henry Jennings, who taught me my trade, and there are the many merchants of all nations, but principally the opportunistic French and the damnable Spaniards, who have traded their wares with me along the way and made me the wealthy man that you see today.'

There was increasing mirth amongst my old crew who assumed I was going to keep up my image of respectability and loved the coded way in which I was alluding to the true nature of my business, whilst cocking a snook at my audience, telling it all in an obscured manner.

I continued, 'But most of all I have to thank the two august men present here today, Mr Tobias Knight and our very own Governor Eden. For without their wise words and aid I would never have come to settle here, nor have met my lovely wife, but instead have remained a rover to my dying day. Now to reveal the key to what I am saying here, I will ask the good reverend to read the entry I made in his register not an hour ago. Please tell all here gathered what I have written there under Elizabeth's name, Mr Hodgson.'

He was somewhat surprised at this, the register normally being a pedestrian read that few find to their taste, but having borne it with him from the ceremony at my insistence, he opened it to the latest page.

He stuttered, 'Why, Mr Thatcher, there seems to be something a little amiss here. You seem to have signed by the name Edward Teach, and given your profession as "rover, retired"!'

'Indeed there is no mistake Reverend, for that is the name by which I have been known for many a year, that was of course when I was not being called by that other name: Blackbeard,' I explained.

There were gasps, not least from my darling wife, and a look of furious consternation on the face of my dear father-in-law.

I continued my exposition, 'As I have said, I have Governor Eden to thank for persuading me to give up my former life, and to settle to that of a gentleman farmer in this fair county, and it is to him that I am grateful for the granting of the Royal Pardon for all my past misdeeds. For I stand before you now, no longer Blackbeard the pirate, the scourge of the Caribbean, but plain Mr Edward Teach, gentleman of Bath.

And so I now propose a toast, to my beautiful bride Elizabeth, and to the beneficent Governor Eden.'

There was a mightily confused chorus, with many of the guests still reeling from the news of my true identity, some stumbling or giggling over "beneficent", the Governor speechless and aghast at the revelation of what he thought was the darkest secret, Knight biting his fist to suppress a guffaw, and my crew raucously toasting the bride and eager to try their luck with any of the other wenches present. Bowyer went from puce to ashen pale as he realised how totally hog-tied he was and how impossible it would be to escape from having such an infamous man for a son-in-law.

1st July

For more than a week I have been becalmed in Bath, in the arms of my wonderful wife. Each day begins with wonders unknown to me before, the love of a good woman who is not daunted by my name, past or aspect, who will be my master as well as my mistress, who commands the ship on which we sail each night, causing the sheets to billow and strain to drive us along our course, whose cries would drown out the storm, whose whispers caress and lull sweeter than any zephyr-like breeze. I thought I would find a comfort and a helpmeet, but I have discovered a most worthy companion, and commodore of all my desires. I have only one wish in life and that is to see it out with my dearest Elizabeth, and perhaps to sire a crew of little pirates in the fullness of time.

Bowyer continues chill to me, he is not yet accustomed

to the truth of my identity. Governor Eden left red-faced from the breakfast as soon as was fitting, and has not been seen since by any I know. Knight came to see me, shook my hand and winked, but said no more. He must have played Eden in a like way in the past and appreciated that my greatest defence was the truth, and my direst vulnerability would have been to conceal it.

The good townsfolk of Bath have demonstrated no such leeriness, but instead are positively drawn by the tales of my wealth, and by the glamour of having such a celebrated and infamous personage in their midst. I am sure that each one of those who have shaken my hand will send letters out so no friend or relative of theirs will be left ignorant of it. The shopkeepers and tradesmen are keen to offload all manner of expensive luxuries and tat upon me, for a prime price, assuming I will be stupid with my fortune as many a drunken pirate has been before me.

I have spread a little largesse for the show of it, and Elizabeth has kitted out the homestead with finer cloths and glassware than I have ever had need for, but not without driving a bargain hard enough that the vendors might think that she had been the pirate, instead of me!

7th July

Still in Bath, still blissful, still in wonder at the luck I have in a wife.

15th July

Bliss calms the sea from horizon to horizon, a doldrums of calm and wonder, but any dish without spice or salt or leaven, no matter how sweet, may start to become tasteless to the tongue. I plan to take a little cruise soon to keep my sea legs, to stop the Adventure from rotting at the quay, and to show my wife a little of my former life.

22nd July

I arranged a cruise from Bath to Ocracoke Island, where the bay finally becomes the ocean. Along for the ride were Knight and my darling Elizabeth, with the best of my crew at the ropes and Israel at the helm. Not long past dawn we all assembled in the yard, and from thence proceeded down to Adventure, no longer masquerading as the Maid of Ayr, and standing proud under her given name. While my wife organised for provisions to be loaded and for breakfast to be served to all upon deck, I went around the whole ship to inspect it for leaks and rot, frayed ropes and loose fittings, running my hands over all the familiar wood and remembering wistfully the life of a rover. I gave the crew the rough edge of my tongue, as they expected and appreciated, and it was greeted with an ironic tugging of forelocks and wringing of hands. Something will have to be done about them if we ever come out of this retirement, but I will not have anybody whipped with my wife aboard. For the time being I just had the most mocking of them put into the pilot boats where they had time to row out their disrespect as they dragged us against the tide out of the inlet, to where we could catch the wind. This took some of the stuffing out of them, and made their soft lubberish hands red enough to remember the lesson.

Once in mid-channel the sails began to fill and I allowed the tug-men back onboard, they grumbled but were mighty relieved to allow the wind to take the strain. Elizabeth was full of smiles and gay repartee, her eyes shining at being out on the water in a legendary pirate ship, bound for points unknown, to her at least who had never ventured beyond Bath. We had the wind full astern and made a good pace before it, so that we could make Ocracoke by noon.

We dropped anchor on the estuary side of that long

narrow island, and then came ashore in the long boats. We made quite a party of it: the crew settled upon the sand, some helped to dig the fire pit and erect the spit upon which Cookie was to roast the pig 'borbecu' style, as that scoundrel Dampier had it. I led Elizabeth, Knight and a small party of daintier folks over the crest of the island to view the rolling green majesty of the Atlantic beyond. This gave my wife her first real view of the ocean that had been my home for many years. This saved her from witnessing the last moments of the giant porker that we had brought along for supper, who had been most bemused by his one and only journey by ship. The pig had been quite remarkably amiable and cooperative in the long-boat, but his suspicions had grown through anxiety to fear and storming rage on seeing our preparations for his leading part in the evening's proceedings.

Elizabeth was most taken with the endless parade of waves across the surface of the sea, the white surf and foam being thrown upon the strand, and the constant crash and suck of the waters that broke there, as the wind had now turned to a brisk easterly. She had never seen that open vastness before, having been no more than a mile beyond the circle of her home and the town of Bath in all her nineteen years, and had never so much as touched the sea. She insisted that we walk upon the shore, and being surprised by the wash coming up to our very shoes, she removed her own and insisted that I join her in like fashion. We walked along, leaving briefly behind a twenty-toed story of ourselves, before the tide of history erased all record of our passing. We were soon wet to the knees as the surf boiled in upon us. Knight remained on the edge of the dunes, just below where the coarse grass started, studying the horizon with a glass I had lent to him, perhaps reliving his own sea-faring past.

Elizabeth asked, 'Would it not be fine to bob and frolic in the sea as easily as the mermaids do, my love, like those over there?'

'No, my dear, I think those creatures are but the seals that live in the sea and bask upon the shore, they are not fish nor people but more like a sea-going dog, they bark like them anyway. And I, like most true sailors, cannot swim well and have a deep fear and respect for the sea. No captain I have ever sailed with would trust a man who could swim away from the ship rather than risk everything to save it. Only the terror of a watery grave can truly drive a man on who finds himself in mortal danger upon the sea, even if it might cost him an eye or a limb. I am happy to bathe in water, but only ever inshore, or in a tub, and always with my feet firmly upon the ground, never where Neptune could claim me for his own,' I explained.

My sweet wife gave a shudder, I do not know if it was due to the cold of the water lapping at her ankles, or some vision of the revenge that might be wrought by the ocean gods upon those impetuous enough to ride upon the waves. Whichever it was, she soon steered me to the warmer sand, then back to the peak of the island amongst the dunes, where we sat amongst the grass and could see both the ocean and the bay. She read from her small book of poetry while I rested my head upon her lap, her hand playing in my curls. The sun dropped to beyond the crest, casting first red rays across the wave peaks, then leaving us in a rapidly approaching darkness, black all the way to Africa, the bay behind still glinting with golden waves, with the silhouette of Carolina beyond. We dusted off the sand, adjusted our dress, and returned towards the fire-pit upon the other strand line. The crew were sat in a circle around the pit, their faces flickering between black and orange in the glow, apart from the few who were already drunk and asleep in the dunes.

Cookie was busy carving generous portions of our former shipmate Mr Pig, and passing these on hunks of bread to the waiting disembodied heads, which soon shone with grease dripping from their chins, or bejewelling their beards. A space was made in the ring for Elizabeth and me, Knight slotted in on the far side of the pit, looking directly across at me. Once all were sated upon pork, bread and rum, Elizabeth asked me a question and the ring of diners fell silent to hear my answer:

'You ask me to describe the life of a pirate, you say it must surely be exciting. Well, I do not rightly know how to put it into words, for I never did decide to become a pirate, one day I was an honest and dedicated defender of Queen and country, the next day, at the stroke of a pen thousands of miles away, I had become a rogue and an outlaw, despised and persecuted by all. I have loved the life of a rover for twenty years, but only more recently have been despised and feared as a pirate. A lot of the time I am an honest merchant, I sell the goods in my holds at an honest price and do not deceive anyone about them, although I do have difficulty selling empty barrels that formerly held madeira; their contents seem to leak away mighty quickly on my ships! We have many trusted partners who buy our merchandise, and many a fine mansion is founded on the profits that we have made. The only difference between us and other merchants is that we pay not a groat for our stock other than by way of our own blood and sweat, and thus we can offer our customers discounts on the goods that fall into our nets whilst sailing upon the deep. Although we have been known to drive a hard bargain with our suppliers, we are known to be fair enough to let them escape with their shirts and their skins,' much chuckling could be heard around the pit, and I could see Knight toasting me across the way.

'I do not worry that we pay too little for our stock, for much that we take has been made by the sweat of subject nations or by slaves, none of whom chooses to be the source for trade or is rewarded for it. I cannot feel like a criminal when we are just diverting the profits of another man's thievery. We are Robin Hoods of the high seas, the wolves of the ocean, the knights of the caribbean. Long may all merchants fear us, or at least those of us who have not become honest farmers!'

There was a hurrah, then somewhere in the flickering gloom a voice started into a wavering shanty, and a chorus joined at the refrain. Soon we were all singing, even my wife, with ever more outrageous verses being added by the deckhands, which at first had shocked Elizabeth before she started to laugh at them as loud as any other there. So it continued until we had burnt all the wood and it was too dark to go hunting for any more, at which point I slipped away with her into the dunes where she shaped herself beside me most sweetly under a moonless sky, bejewelled with the necklace of the milky-way. It was so dark that it appeared we were in a world of black velvet scattered with diamonds, with only a few fragmented lines reflected on ripples to show where our invisible world merged into the water all around.

25th July

We have returned to Bath and Elizabeth has fully satisfied her wonder for all things naval, and she now wants to concentrate on being mistress of the steading, manager of the house, and director of the farm. She spends many hours of each day consulting with and directing the servants and hands, setting to rights the many faults she perceives in the establishment, from the cloths upon the windows to the hedging of the fields, to the determination of crops and livestock we should have. It is as if she has absorbed all of this from her parents, household management from Mistress Bowyer, farm operation from the indomitable Mr Bowyer, and has awaited only the opportunity to deploy this expertise in practice. Perhaps if she had had siblings, particularly a male one, then she would not have received all of the attention, and she might have been left to her dolls and sewing, but as she is alone of her generation she has benefitted from unlimited attention and education. I appreciate all of this skill and insight, of course, but it would appear that I am needed only to finance this venture, and to accompany her to bed when the day is done. Not quite what I had envisaged my life to be when I ceased to be the most feared man afloat!

Pirates around the world try to retire from the cannon and the blade, to establish themselves in island hideaways, such as Morgan on Jamaica, our own New Providence, Sainte-Marie off Madagascar and so on. Yet most of these salty rovers, with missing eyes and hands, barely a full set of limbs between them, would have felt as helpless as I did, with my young wife running the operation and I only sitting there with an open purse.

30th July

Another week has passed becalmed, with me feeling more of a cabin boy than the terror of the seas. The social round is dull: Elizabeth insists that we dine with her parents twice or more each week, and I am sure we have retraced every line of possible conversation a dozen times already; with another evening spent in visiting neighbours or relations. All other days take my wife's time from dawn until dusk in the running of the steading, and I am not countenanced to see my friends or colleagues from my roving days, not even Israel who is to be our neighbour. I have bought and read every book from the shops of Bath that does not concern animal husbandry, crop rotation, the predictions of the almanac or the pronouncements of God, and I am dragging my anchor chain, wanting wistfully to slip away on the tide.

3rd August

All came to a head today, and my vision of ever extending bliss has become mortally tainted. Bowyer came this morning to take his daughter to town on a mission of which I had been kept ignorant until that moment. She came to me and requested that I give her fifty pounds so that she might purchase cattle for the farm. I was surprised at the size of the sum and questioned her upon the price and the number she was needing, especially as I was not aware that the steading was particularly suitable for dairy or meat rearing purposes. It gradually dawned on me that we were not discussing a purchase of a herd of oxen, but in fact the acquisition of a number of slaves, fresh arrived from Africa for use on the farm sewing, tending and harvesting tobacco and other crops such as sorghum. I was dumbstruck: had I worked for so many years to avoid any involvement in this filthy business, to now retire and live off the sweat of my own battalion of slaves? Elizabeth and her father laughed at my surprise and naïvety, how else did I think my crops were to be grown to compete with those of other farmers? Did I think I was going to produce them all by myself, or to pay some band of peasants to do the work? Would I have white men toiling in my fields when these animals were available and suited only to this task, without pay, with no more than the sorghum porridge that they themselves must grow as food, and cheap rags to cover their foul bodies?

I exploded: I stated baldly and without restraint that I knew these slaves were just as much real men as Bowyer, perhaps more so as those loyal to me were better men than most I had known, and I numbered several ex-slaves amongst my most trusted friends.

My wife contradicted me, 'Edward, you are mistaken, these animals may mimic the ways of true men just as a mynah bird or parrot may copy a voice, but they are dull and aimless creatures and only of use as labour in our fields. Do not mistake animal cunning for humanity, they are without soul or mind and are lower than the horses and cattle in Creation.'

'Elizabeth, I forbid you to do this. If our crops cannot be tended by free men then I will leave the fields idle and fallow. I will not have any slaves upon my farm, or in my house, if a black man cannot look me in the eye as an equal then it shall not be me that binds him. You shall not have one penny to buy slaves on this day, nor on any other,' I reiterated.

Bowyer himself then put in, 'You are a fool, Thatcher or whatever you call yourself, and you insult all who are here by pretending that these creatures are any more than cattle. You have received my daughter's hand on false pretences and sullied my name. If she is to stay with you then that is her look-out, but you are no longer welcome on my land or under my roof. Good day to you!'

Bowyer stormed out and Elizabeth burst into tears and ran to her sewing room, from whence she managed all the affairs of the household and did precious little needlework. She slammed the door so it rocked the building.

12th August

Elizabeth has not abided in the same room with me for over a week, a fine state of affairs for a newly married man! She communicates only through notes passed by the servants, and I have no company in the house. I have been returning to Adventure each day and have slept there for the last two nights. I have tried to approach her to explain my position and to justify it, but she has repelled all my advances, thrown my gifts to the floor, even those of great value, and turned her back upon me.

I am heartbroken at the loss, but I can see that it is my own false expectations and unrealisable dreams that have led me astray: at no point had she pretended to be anything other than her father's daughter, and a product of this land and the way in which it is worked. I do not know how to make amends, and my long cherished fantasy has turned from the sweetest wine to the sourest vinegar in my mouth.

14th August

I visited Knight at his place further up the creek last evening, in a boat rowed by my faithful friends Jacob and Adjukay, both as black as the night we rowed through. Although Knight was friendly and hospitable to me, he could offer no comfort in my woes.

He said, 'Dear Edward, what did you expect? You have married the daughter of a planter and all she knows, all she owns, rests upon this way of life, and could not be sustained by your daydream of hired hands and tenants working the land. This is not the way of America, nor ever shall be, we make the best use of our natural resources to realise our profits, and these dumb cattle play their parts and are glad of it, if cattle can be said to realise any form of emotion. You must relinquish your fantasy and live in this real world, or sacrifice all the good things that you have accomplished.'

He of course meant that I should bow to Elizabeth's wishes, acquiesce with her view, and work my farm with slaves bought with my portion of treasure, but I heard the opposite message. I perceived that my retirement in Bath was a dream, and I should return to the reality of a roving life, where it mattered not a jot the colour of a man's skin if his hand could ably wield a sword or steer a ship, and if only a loyal heart beat in his chest, nothing else could matter to his shipmates.

I must admit that I returned from Knight's house in a stormy state of mind, and when we encountered another small craft on our way back to Adventure, I was taken by a great thirst, and I demanded a bottle from the man who was tending his crab-pots by the light of a lantern at the stern. When he refused, I boarded his craft and acted the grand buccaneer, until he fearfully gave me his pathetic flask of whisky, which I drained in front of my silent companions, who sat almost invisible in the rowboat, with only their teeth and eyes visible in the candlelight. We must have terrified that poor fisherman, but I had no desire to keep in with the neighbours any more.

18th August

My crew have, in many cases, run through all goodwill and credit amongst the people of the district, and there are now more than enough of them retreated to Adventure for me to run a ship as I did in former days. I have spent some time contemplating my position and I have decided upon a new course. In the last few nights I have retrieved most of my booty from the caches around the farm, even if the total has been somewhat depleted by my wife's taste for rich comforts. I have put aside a goodly purse that should see her through the rest of the year if she uses it wisely, and have had the rest brought back onboard. I plan to sail at dawn on the ship that is my one true home, and never return to the steading again. I sleep tonight for the last time in that establishment for which I had such dear hopes.

19th August

I rose at four and crept to Elizabeth's room, where I found the door firmly locked and barred. She would not answer my knock and call, so my farewell to her was but a brief note attached to the purse which I laid at the foot of the door. I slipped out into the morning dew, the sky starting to lighten from deepest black to subtlest lapis upon the horizon, and I followed that well worn track down to the bay for the last time. All was ready when I arrived, the ports and hatches secured, the hands in the rigging ready to deploy the sails, the pilot crew ready to lead us away from the jetty. We slipped out on the ebbing tide, opened the sails to be filled by the wind's sweet breath, we heeled to and cut the water as well as we have ever done, so by the time the sun was clear of the horizon we were well out towards the open sea. I buried Edward Thatcher where I had removed my treasure; Blackbeard had returned.

20th August

One element of my plan was to apply to be a privateer for the Crown once more, and for this purpose last week I visited Eden.

I asked the Governor for his permission to convert to this profession, finding the life of a farmer to be too dull for my tastes, though I did not mention to him any of my troubles with Elizabeth or my intention to leave the area altogether. He was only too glad for me to depart to St Thomas, rather than having such a desperado as his neighbour and as a permanent ghost at the feast. So we head for Jamaica and a prospect of legal and profitable employment that fits our skills and experience.

27th August

Having sailed at full speed directly to Jamaica, we

arrived in Kingston harbour this morning, and were much surprised to find a sizeable naval fleet riding at anchor. I carefully carried my pardon with me as we rowed ashore, and again I had the ship shown as 'Maid of Ayr' rather than bear its more infamous title which might lead to awkward misunderstandings. In the longboat with me were only the most respectable members of my crew, hardly an eyepatch or truncated limb amongst them, in their finest clothes, albeit these may have been involuntarily handed down from their original owners. We endeavoured not to appear to be a bunch of desperate former pirates invading the heart of British power in the region.

We proceeded from the quay to the Governor's mansion where we had a considerable wait to allow the man himself to breakfast, powder his wig, break wind and so forth. During this time there was considerable whispering in galleries and indications that many unseen persons came to witness Blackbeard at bay. At last, we were admitted into his glorious presence. It transpired that Sir Nicholas Lawes was himself freshly minted in his new job and was determined to make his mark on history and then hightail back to England as soon as glory was assured, despite already having sixty-six years under his capacious belt.

He held forth, 'Mr Teach, I see from this parchment that you have gained a pardon for all your previous crimes as a pirate from the Governor of Carolina, despite your infamous siege of Charles Town in that colony not a month before, and well after the official limit for the pardon. I cannot tell what reasons Eden may have for this benevolence, but I am damned if I am to offer you any similar indulgence by admitting you into the ranks of my privateers. Once a blackguard, always a blackguard I say, and I shall not trust you as far as I can piss. The only offer

I am prepared to make to you is that if you helped me to hunt down the rest of your species, then I might just admit your good faith and preserve you from my navy. I am just as determined to sweep your kind from the seas as the Governor of New Providence, and I shall not have the likes of Morgan back in Jamaica, even though he previously sat in this very chair. No matter what service a privateer might have done for his country, all that is erased and forgotten the first time he takes a prize under his own flag.'

My blood boiled at the arrogance of the man, and I only narrowly restrained myself from ensuring he never reached seven and sixty, but instead I said at last,

'All I ever wished was to continue in the service of the Crown, but if it is clear that I am thought to be lower than the poorest limpet upon the most rotten naval sloop, then I will not further my dishonour by betraying my brothers at sea. I refuse your offer with all my passion. Good day to you.'

And I swept out, leaving him to bluster and swear in my wake. We made it back to Adventure as swiftly as we might, and fled to the open sea with the alacrity of a ship that is outgunned fifty to one.

31st August

Sailing first east then north, we ran across the path of a Frenchman beyond the Inaguas. It was speedily taken and found to be packed with Jamaican rum and sugar. We split the cargo between the new vessel and Adventure. Just as we were completing this, another ship, flying the Fleur de Lys, crossed our path, and again we pursued and took her with but a few balls fired. We put all the French onto the smallest vessel and left it adrift with its sails hobbled, and turned north as a fleet of two, being Adventure and the new incarnation of Revenge, with Israel at the helm.

15th September

We have been prowling the coast up towards Delaware Bay with little opportunity for engagement. Where there is no navy, there is nothing larger than a fishing smack to capture, and where the crop is more bountiful the navy is ever present and alert, so we have had slim pickings and are missing our warm home waters. So we turn once more for Ocracoke.

20th September

Having arrived at Ocracoke inlet once more, we were hailed by a boat flying the Governor's flag, and challenged over our new acquisition, which foolishly still carried its French pennant. I was summoned by Eden to an Admiralty court and challenged on this new member of our fleet: had I returned to piracy, in which case my life was forfeit, or was there some legitimate explanation? I stated that we had been on a pleasure cruise, being gentleman farmers and labourers all, not pirates. The ship in question had been found abandoned without a soul aboard, and we lay ropes upon her and claimed salvage, to protect other vessels from the danger of collision as she was unlit and adrift in a busy shipping lane. There was some debate on the plausibility and veracity of this story, much of which pivoted on the value of its cargo. At last a judgment was made, and I was able to retain the new Revenge as a salvor's prerogative, but her cargo was forfeit to defray the costs of the court, meaning that Knight and Eden gained eighty hogsheads of sugar as payment for their vigilance and steadfastness in the defence of the colony. May they both choke upon it! At least I had removed half the cargo before we were apprehended by these paragons of virtue.

22nd September

Wanting to realise our gains before the machinery of the courts could lighten our purses further, we sailed to Nassau and discretely disposed of the cargo for ten shillings on the pound, no suspicion being raised despite these vessels never having been seen there before. Having concluded our business, we started to make quiet enquiries about Woody around the taverns, only to find that he was as hell-bent on bringing all pirates to heel as Governor Lawes, and was currently much afeared of Vane. He had sent my old master Hornigold north to try to trap Vane at Turtle Bay, but knowing both men I was certain that Vane could evade Ben even if they were locked in a wardrobe together.

1st October

We have been here incognito for over a week, and all of us can feel the tension emanating from the Governor's mansion. No news has been heard of Hornigold's mission, and several retired pirates have sailed to join under Vane's flag. I have intelligence that Woody expects to be attacked imminently by either the Spanish or a great pirate fleet, possibly both. All hands he has under his command or influence are put to strengthening the fort and outer defences, and martial law has been declared. I do not like to think of my childhood friend being threatened by my kind, and I feel if nothing else I must do what I can to avoid a massacre occurring here.

2nd October

Last night, we waylaid Woody as he pursued his regular nightly prowl of the town, in supervision of its curfew. We caught him near the Hooked Hand inn, and held him in the dark, playing tricks with lights and shadows to keep our faces hid, and to amuse ourselves without inflicting any harm upon him. He was scared but forthright, and as arrogant as ever; a brave show, I must say, given his position. When I revealed first that his captor was Blackbeard, he was put to his mettle, but when I revealed that legendary buccaneer was none other than the long lost pal who had shared his adventures, and his intended wife, he went white and stammered. I do believe he had more fear due to that wrong he had inflicted upon me as a boy, than of the cutthroat pirate I became. It was that look that made up my mind, that decided me to make a final act of reconciliation to the boy who had first saved Hannah's dog, then broken her heart. I offered, on the spur of the moment, to draw Vane off and perchance to convert him from piracy, or at least divert his focus from an attack on Nassau. I did this so he might know forgiveness and redemption, even if those things are now beyond my own reach and hopes.

I don't think he believed me, but he was relieved to hear that I was cutting his risks rather than his throat.

4th October

We sailed north to Green Turtle Cay, and there we found a fleet of pirates not seen since the heyday of Morgan, maybe not even then. There must have been fifty ships anchored there, under the flags of Vane, Deal, Calico Jack Rackham and a dozen minor captains, like an Armada or the Spithead review for the King of pirates, and that is exactly how Vane saw himself.

I was greeted warmly by Vane, as a king might greet his favourite knight, and it was during that first shared bottle of rum that he rebuked me for betraying a brother pirate, with a glint in his eye. It seems that when Bonnet returned with his pardon, to find his crew marooned and his ship hollowed out, he flew into a fury and swore to have my blood. He chased out to find me but turned south rather than north, a move typical of his perception and skill as a tactician, and he only realised his mistake after weeks of searching an empty sea. Bonnet then got distracted at the sight of a pretty french vessel off Cape Fear and fell back into his piratical ways. Soon afterwards, he encountered two naval ships, one following the coast, the other coming out of a river's mouth, and was captured while he was busy sorting his silks from his fine French brandy. He is to be dancing at the end of a rope before the year is out. Vane is none too sad at this loss, in fact it rather amuses him.

By the second bottle of grog, Vane was hatching a plan for us to join forces and retake New Providence, and by the third I had persuaded him of the foolishness of having a permanent pirate base in the Caribbean when the ships of three navies were on our tails. I then invited him to visit me at my favourite haunt, a spot he had not yet seen, the tip of Ocracoke Island. So it is planned for the grandest pirate carnival and barbecue to take place on that beach where I had loved Elizabeth, in two weeks time.

16th October

We returned to the vicinity of Bath, to lay in stores for our grand party of buccaneers, with much rum, madeira and brandy being brought from our own stores on-shore, and when that was not enough more was purchased from warehouses and chandlers. Those shopkeepers may never have had such customers as these, many short an eye or a limb, salty dogs and desperadoes, but on their best behaviour spending my money, picking delicately through crockery and cutlery, linens and silks, picking out the finest accoutrements for our festivity. They bought cloths for the tables, candelabras and chairs, finger bowls and vases, as fine as any I saw at Eden's mansion. We also acquired flour, potatoes, pigs and calves enough to fill a farm, gleaming pots and pans fit to blind a Persian army, spits and all manner of paraphernalia to make the cooks of the largest palaces jealous.

All of this was ferried to Ocracoke, which we treated as our own province, all comers avoiding our ship anchored at the point, with the Roger flying and her gun-ports open. No doubt word has spread of our presence in the bay and of our preparations for some mighty pagan feast, and someone will stir up the militia to try something desperate if we dawdle here too long.

17th October

We spotted the topsails of Vane and his mighty armada coming over the horizon at dawn, and within the hour they filled the offing with timber and canvas. By noon they were at bay around Ocracoke, my little kingdom, and their cutters had carried to the beach more supplies and bizarre things that they had acquired from reluctant donors at sea: hundreds of barrels of rum and madeira, chests of coffee, a four poster bed with elaborate carvings of an immodest nature destined for the Governor of Mexico and his new love, a dozen brightly coloured silk dresses for a cat-house in Havana, a gold covered throne taken from some temple in the southern colonies, and all manner of musical instruments and games, paintings and other diversions.

All of these were setup upon the shore or amongst the dunes in a series of areas and encampments, as if some great palace had been built here then blown away, leaving its contents upon the sand. By dusk the animals had been slaughtered, the sea in the bay filled with their blood, and they were set to roasting on a dozen spits.

Long trestles and benches had been set out for the generality, and a fine round teak table and matching chairs were set upon a Persian carpet in a sheltered circle in the dunes, for those most favoured by Vane. Where the crew ate off wood or bread trenchers, we had the finest Meissen plates, gold cutlery, crystal ewers and goblets that shone like diamonds. A chandelier was suspended from ropes between A-frames, with a hundred guttering candles dripping wax upon all below. There we sat with manners that varied from courtly to feral, Vane casting angry glances at those slurping, burping, taking food in their hands or wiping fingers upon the fine lace cloth; he kicked away the legs of the chair of any he felt to be too disgusting. Even as we descended into howling drunkenness, Vane tried to give himself airs, despite his wig being askew and smouldering foully from an encounter with a candle.

The crew tables were in full swing, the men so drunk that they donned those fine coloured dresses and danced lewdly upon the board: there is always some pirate who will put on a dress, it seems, normally the ugliest of all. The roar of celebration and debauchery was muffled at the captains' table, being some distance away in the dunes and concealed even more by a scratch band playing the tunes of Purcell and the latest by Handel, or at least some approximation rendered almost incomprehensible by the mismatch of instruments, the lack of skill of the players, and the gallon of rum that circulated amongst them. All the pretended gentility dissolved into chaos and unconsciousness, as did the raucous rowdiness of the common herd, until as dawn broke again there was not a head held aloft.

So that we did not leave ourselves exposed to attack, we left fully a quarter of our number on guard on the island and on the ships, and though they had but water to accompany their repast that first night, they had their turn for dissipation on the next, their places of penance and watchfulness being taken by those whose heads were sorest from the night before and who had foresworn all drink forever when they awoke in the sand.

23rd October

So we proceeded for the best part of a week, until every last drop of liquor had been drunk, every animal became no more than a pile of gnawed bones, the chairs and benches splintered, the four-poster rocked to destruction, and not one pirate amongst us sure whether it was Thursday or Doomsday any more. On the last hectic evening we were joined by Knight, who brought with him a party of doxies and a warning that Eden had heard mutterings from his brother Governors near and far about him tolerating an outlaw horde on his doorstep. These mutterings were likely to become musterings if we did not depart rapidly. A political poodle he might be, but Tobias knows when a pirate should pick up his britches and retire with dignity. So this day, once every bottle had been checked to be empty of all but sand and flies, the mighty Armada began to disperse, with vows of friendship, to half the points of the compass, no doubt with a raging thirst and heads full of clanging bells.

In that week of drunken revelry, and counsel lit by a French chandelier, lubricated by the best liquors that another man's money had bought, and a rover could steal, what did we discuss? The first night was mostly boastfulness, unlimited tales of conquests and victories, treasures plundered and fair damsels taken, not half of it true and not a quarter of it to the credit of those that spoke, but all to the delight of an audience who knew a thing or two about tall ships and taller tales, of bravery and rampage, and each story was savoured as the fine treat that it was, even when it was more fantasy than substance.

On the second night, we turned more to our pasts, those secret identities from our homes. I shall not record one word of those shared secrets here, any more than I would write down the truth of my own, lest this book fall into the hands of those that might wish harm to our loved ones or pursue them for the wealth we have purloined. By the third night we were addressing our hopes and plans for the future, and it was then that Vane reiterated his plan to retake Nassau and to become the king of the pirates in the Caribbean.

I ventured a counter view where we could enjoy all our victories against the Spanish as privateers once more, then peacefully settle in New Hampshire or Florida as pardoned and wealthy men, as our hair grew grey and thin, with time to enjoy our riches without fear of the sword or the gallows. I painted a rosy picture of my own retirement, none of my audience being any the wiser about how its reality had not fulfilled my dreams. As slowly the bottles emptied, and the spits held only skeletons, the other captains began to nod and I could see that they were dreaming of their own retirement hearth, tended by wives or maids, their booty around them in gold plates and fine goods, candle flames flickering on it all. Even Vane became diverted by this vision before he toppled backwards into the sand, brandy spilling from his glass, and dead to the world.

So it went till they departed, with Vane deciding to try his luck further north until the war with Spain finally started for real, when he intended to turn to privateering.

I am glad to be alone once more upon the Island, the desolate sand that I have loved before. I will take a little cruise and then decide what my course should be, whether it is to return to Bath and make amends with Elizabeth, or to set sail for more distant lands and truly rove again. I am in complete indecision and need to be out on the deep water with the deck rocking beneath me once more before I can read the wind and set a bearing for my life.

5th November

We spent a week cruising around the outer islands, not being welcome to visit Nassau or Charles Town, or many other places, just putting Adventure through her paces, running before the wind, tacking back and around, practising drills and manoeuvres that we have used dozens of times before, to outpace and outflank our prey, yet in the whole time we have engaged no-one, being as law abiding as if we were a ship full of constables. Although we performed all of this as well as we had ever done before, it had an unsatisfying dryness and coldness of spirit about it. Not many of us seemed to the will to continue in our old ways, yet we also did not have anywhere to call home, nowhere to feel safe and loved.

Those men that lusted after blood for its own sake have been shed along the way, either because that lust made them incautious and too heroic to think and thus they have fallen to ball or sword, or they have danced for the hangman. Any of that number who survived I stranded at Beaufort when I cut Bonnet adrift, because such men kill their friends as readily as they kill their enemies, through their vainglorious carelessness. Now the crew are like a reunion of retired soldiers, with tattered coats and tarnished medals, trying to recapture old glories which may have been illusory, and their heart is not in it any more.

The party at Ocracoke was the last great show of pirate strength; we have departed the stage, leaving the real villains to run things while they wear the wigs of judges and governors, eat the feasts of bankers and merchants, with their black flags hidden from public view.

This night we lie becalmed well offshore, with no light but the stars, chasing their flickering reflections on the swell, and we toast the defeat of the Papist plot with rum and improvised fireworks, and shots of flaming pitch and rags. We cranked a cannon up to a high degree and the balls of flame followed a long arc out and up, reflected in the black mirror of the sea, before meeting their doubles in a puff of steam in some distant fold of water, and so passed several hours before sleep overtook us all.

12th November

We pulled back into the bay behind Ocracoke, no more purposeful than when we left it. The men have dispersed, some to seek a place to retire, others to seek oblivion and to forget that they have no plans, and others to lay in provisions for a voyage that we may never take. I had a feeling of foreboding about our return here, and perhaps that led to my irritation when Israel insisted on remaining with me on board when I wanted him to supervise the work ashore. I meant to assert myself and fired my pistol into the deck at his feet, but the ball must have hit a nail and it kicked up into his calf, opening a lengthy gash, and releasing from him a long and rich stream of invective. I gruffly apologised but continued to assert that he should do what I say and leave the ship, and he did so to avoid further incident, with a wounded look in more senses than one.

Israel left with more than half the crew, who may be gainfully employed there or spend their time seeking the bottom of a barrel. I have hurt myself in this for he is a link to the city of my birth and my closest ally and friend. Perhaps I should retire to the original Bath, or even to Bristol itself, and pretend there to be a fine American merchant who has made his fortune in the Indies. Even this speculation is pointless, I have a premonition and certainty that I shall die on the water, or under it, at the hands of my enemies.

There remain with me a crew of two dozen, several originally from Bristol, and six others being the slaves I liberated when first we took the Queen Anne, and these men are as loyal and sturdy as any you might find on the finest ship of the line. It is a source of pride and joy to me to be their captain by acclamation, rather than force or some order from on high. I know they would follow me into Hades to steal the Devil's pitchfork, but I do not want harm to come to them due to my lack of vision, my indecision, or for my failing faith in this life.

I have just now been interrupted by Knight, who has rowed out to meet me. He has brought tidings that forces are being gathered against me, and for me to be prepared. It seems that the party I hosted for the great pirate armada has fanned the flames of fear amongst the Governors of Pennsylvania and Virginia, and now that my fearsome crew are dispersing across the land, it has brought them to the point of panic. Tobias says I must be ready to fight on land or sea against navy or militia, and I must abandon any idea of settling in Bath, and any hope of aid from Eden. I thanked him for this information, saw him safely ashore, but do not know whether to believe this threat to prepare to face it, or to run away with most of my men stranded ashore.

18th November

Despite Knight's anxious warnings, all has been quiet here for a week, and I cannot help feeling his mission was to save Eden's embarrassment by inventing a phantom attack. I had the men clean and oil every weapon, coil every rope and generally make ready for ambush and war, but you cannot remain shuddering in anticipation for time without limit. I have let half the men out into Bath to relax and to bring back more provisions on their return. The rest of them are here with me and I have given them the task of careening the hull with cables, to keep them busy, and to make us swifter if we need to escape. This is never as effective as a dry dock but it will suffice, and it keeps them all from worrying.

20th November

The shore party has not returned on time and I suspect that they have been delayed or waylaid by the Pennsylvanian Quakers. I am now sure that there was some justification to Knight's concerns and if they do not return within two more days we will have to cut and run, and let them save themselves.

21st November

Still no sign, and I have a feeling of dread that I was foolish not to leave this place long ago, and now all is lost. We will have to depart tomorrow, whether the men return or no. I so wish Israel was here to give me counsel, but he must at least be laid up with his injured leg, if he has not been captured already. I dreamt last night of Bristol in my youth, of all my old friends there and our many adventures around the town, the rescue of Hannah's dog, the entanglements that led to, the lifelines of Porter and Woody, Hannah and myself, all plaited and tangled together into some Gordian knot, that none can untie or even sever. Yet we are now cast to the corners of the world, with Woody prince in my former realm of New Providence, Porter and Hannah at ease in Bristol, and me cowering from unknown enemies near the pyre of my shattered dreams.

Having remembered these good friends and the interweaving of our lives, I am determined not to disappear without a trace, yet there is little I can do now without a friend ashore whom I can reach or trust. So I will place my hope and faith in the honour of the British navy, and in the good name that my old friend Woody has amongst them still. I will now seal up this log so that it is safe against prying eyes and the elements, locking away the truth of my life and identity in it. I will address it to the two men in the world that I might hope truly remember me with some love and gratitude, for them to do what they will with it. I wish for it to be delivered into the hands of Porter, the boy whose heart has always been truer than mine, and to get it there I will trust that Woody will hold his honour more highly than his curiosity. If it should happen to fall into the ocean, then I hope that it may wash up as flotsam on some distant beach and be of amusement to whatever castaway may find it.

But if it is read by any for whom it is not intended then I damn them and their black hearts and I guarantee that I will find their souls and chastise them throughout eternity, as only a man called Blackbeard could.

I finish this log on this twenty-first day of November, in the year of our Lord 1718, and consign it to the care of my friend John, called Porter, at the sign of the Trow, in Bristol. May God smile upon him, as much as He has frowned upon me.

Edward Teach, called Blackbeard,
pirate of renown

Glossary

Bristolian Dialect

Bristolians have their own dialect, with a distinctive accent and vocabulary. The accent has been called "half way between a farmer and a pirate" and that is where Bristolians of the early eighteenth century stood, with many of the famous pirates hailing from a city founded on the trade of agricultural produce. There follows a guide to some of the dialect that appears in this book, if you keep the farmer-cum-pirate accent in mind it may help matters of pronunciation and comprehension.

Bristolians often run words together, drop initial H's and many T's, soften L into W, lightly roll some R's (notably the end of Jasper), add L's to the end of words ending in A, and have some distinct verb forms that may date back to the Saxons or Vikings.

Aw: all

Babber : friend, baby, darling, depending on contextBarrow : barrel

Bissen : am not

Blige : exclamation akin to the Cockney "cor blimey"

Brekfuss : the first meal of the day

Brizzle : what Bristolians call their home city and by extension its dialect

Burra : but a

Cannava : can have a

Cappin : captain

Cawd : cold

Duz : "does" or "do"

Ee : "he" or "him"

Fort : I thought

Frim : for him

Gawd blessem : God bless him

Ginormous : "giant" or "enormous"Giss I : please give to me

Goner: dead person

Gudun : good one

Gurt : great

Immy : in my

Ize : "I am" or "I have" depending on context

Jasper : a wasp; the boy is called this perhaps due to his striped smock or a similar first name

Jeerme : do you hear me

Jeswait : just you wait

Less I go : let me go

Merical : America

Nuvver : another

Spadger : a sparrow

Summon : something

Umble : humble

Wadya : what do you

Whoz : "who is" or "who has"

Youz : you are

Yurtiz : here it is

Zider : an alcoholic beverage made from apples

Zit : “is that” or “is it”

General Glossary

Alderman : a city councillor

Almshouse : a charitable institution providing housing to the poor

Assizes : a county session of a court of law, under judges who travelled around the country

Avon : the main river that flows through Bath then Bristol and out to the Severn Estuary

Backs : the secondary part of the harbour, on the Avon, where the main Key was on the Frome

Batavia : modern day Jakarta on the island of Java, in Indonesia, then a Dutch colony

Buccaneer : a pirate

Cadging : slang for begging or asking for a service for no money, as a favour

Captain of the road : a tramp

Carpenter surgeon : a man skilled at working wood who was also called upon to extract teeth, and not infrequently to amputate limbs

Channel : the Bristol Channel, the estuary of the River Severn

Coffle : a small group of slaves shackled together, sometimes by a rigid bar between their necks

Company : the East India Company, that held a British monopoly over trade in the East

Corporation : the body that ran the city, subsequently the city council

Corsair : a pirate

Cromwell : Thomas C. - in charge of the dissolution of the monasteries under Henry VIII; Oliver C. (descended from Thomas's sister) – leader of the republican forces against Charles I

Curry : to groom a horse

Cut-purses and lifters : forms of pick-pocket

Dunkery : a high hill to the south of Bristol

Elmina : a Portuguese built port on the coast of modern day Ghana, a key slave trading port

Factor : a business agent, an intermediary in the slave trade

Firkin : a smaller barrel, holding about nine gallons

Flotsam : detritus floating upon the sea

Freebooter : a pirate

Frenchman : a ship sailing under the French flag

Frome : a smaller river that flows through Bristol and forms the main section of the harbour

Fuller : a person who fulls or softens cloth, possibly by mashing it in a tub of stale urine with his feet

Gentleman of fortune : a pirate

Good King Harry : Henry VIII

Gun fuse : a treated length of cord used to light the powder hole of a cannon

Haymarket : an area where originally hay and oats were sold for animal feed

Horsefair : an area where horses were traditionally soldIn his cups : drunk

Indenture : the legal agreement between a master and his apprentice, torn into jagged or toothed parts that would match up, hence the name

Jolly-boat : a small row boat carried by a larger ship

Key : original spelling of Quay, the harbour side

Keys : the Florida Keys, a line of small islands stretching out from the mainland

King Road : a section of river near the mouth of the Avon where pilots or cutters met larger ships

League : a unit of distance of three nautical miles, about 3.5 miles, 5.6 kilometres

Letters of marque : licenses to act as a privateer attacking enemy shipping for gain

Levels : the Somerset Levels, and area of drained marshland used for grazing, and prone to flooding

Marsh : a square area between the harbour and the Backs that had formerly been marshland but had been drained and become a fashionable recreational area

Offing : the part of the sea visible before the horizon

Overseer : one who supervises, controls and drives slaves, often with a whip or other weapon

Papist plot : the gunpowder plot of November 5th 1605

Pill : a village with harbour along the Avon towards the Severn, which supplied pilots to boats

Pitch-and-pay, pell mell, box and dice : games of chance, a

small street in Bristol is named after the first, a larger one in London after the second

Porter : a strong dark style of beer similar to stout made with roasted or even burnt malted barley, a fore-runner to stout

Post Boy : an early local newspaper

Priory : a monastery.

Quarterdeck : the raised rear section of a ship's deck where the captain stood

Quartermaster : an officer responsible for supplies

Quayside mud : before the harbour gates were fitted to create the floating harbour, boats would settle into the mud and had to be strong to cope with the strain of doing so, hence "shipshape and Bristol fashion"

Ranger : a pirate

Rover : a pirate

Shambles : a street where pork butchers worked

Sheet : a rope used to control a sail attached to a lower corner

Small beer : a weak form of beer, with very little alcohol but often cleaner than the water supply

Spiking the guns : inserting an iron spike into the powder hole of a cannon to make it inoperable

Spile : a wooden plug or bung used to block the ports of a barrel

The Horn : Cape Horn, the southernmost tip of South America

Trow : a kind of cargo boat used on the Wye and Severn rivers

Tun : a large barrel for beer or wine, holding about 252 gallons

Weare : the bank of the moat

Y Fenni : the Welsh name for the town of Abergavenny

Background notes

Chapter 1

Other guilds existed in Bristol besides the Merchant Venturers: weavers, dyers and fullers, all those who drove the cloth trade from the backs of Cotswold sheep to the docks of Bristol, but the real wealth was with those men who traded that cloth in France, Portugal and Spain in return for wines, silks and other luxuries to sell across England. This body of men formed a guild, the Merchant Venturers, who mounted ever more ambitious expeditions to find markets for fine wool cloth and to bring back more exotic items to excite the jaded palates of the English.

Small beer was a weak brew but often consumed in preference to water, because it was boiled during its manufacture and hence more likely to be safe. Use of such beer continued well into modern times, particularly in the allowance of beer for furnace men at foundries where it helped to counteract water lost though sweat.

Before the lock gates were added in 1809, transforming Bristol docks into the Floating Harbour, the harbour was subject to some of the largest tides in the world and this left boats stranded, often at steep angles, upon the mud. The ships would need to be strong to withstand this, hence the saying “shipshape and Bristol fashion”. Crew would rather not sleep on the boats and ships because of this, bringing much trade to local hostelries.

Boats coming towards Bristol harbour had to rely on a rising tide, and would not find much use for their sails on the winding course of the Avon through the Gorge. Larger boats often unloaded onto lighters either out in the Kings Road or along the Avon without ever reaching the harbour. In addition to the tides, ships would be towed using ropes to the towpath where men or horses would pull them along while the tide assisted, and at each ebb tide they would securely moor up to await the next rising tide. The journey from the Severn to the harbour could take a week for a large ship.

Bristol at the time was the second most important port in England, and specialised in certain trades: long distance fishing, export of wool cloth, and later other manufactured goods, import of wines and later goods aided by the slave trade including sugar, rum, cotton, chocolate and tobacco.

Bristol was surrounded by fields and orchards, and the Downs were grazed by sheep and cattle, beyond these was mostly thick woodland. From these, the largest trees, the broadest oaks that had seen William conquer England, had long been taken by branch or trunk to make the skeletons of ships and timbered houses, or the great tithe barns of the monks, and the smaller trees had been trimmed for fires or coppiced to make fences and wattle walls; but despite this the forest was still dark and extensive. Bristol was fuelled in part at least by coal from Kingswood, and this helped to preserve the forests.

The sheep on the Downs had been the main source for the wool that fed the cloth industry on which Bristol's trade was built, but by the eighteenth century far more was needed than could be fed by the capacity of the Downs and this wool came from the Cotswolds and Mendips down the drover tracks to Bristol.

A barrel of wine might arrive on the Key in the morning from Bordeaux, then be rolled down King Street and be off to Wales on the falling tide, or else be on a cart to a manor in the Cotswolds, or to sweeten the acrid waters in Bath, or be rolled up to the cellars in Wine Street made from the catacombs left by the friars, or be consumed in one gulp by a busy inn like the Trow.

Other goods were taken from the ships by hand or crane onto sleds, pulled by ponies. The iron runners of the sleds scored the cobbles and could crush the unwary, and explain at some of the cast iron kerbs we still see in the centre of the city today.

The merchants of previous centuries had left great fortunes to almshouses belting the city, remembering their names and their piety to posterity through eternal charity and solemn masses. This practice was a lot less common in the eighteenth century although Colston founded one on St Michaels Hill, and greatly expanded QEH. Many of the later merchants are memorialised by grand houses and estates beyond the reek and cry of the docks.

Chapter 2

The grill the Quarterdeckers found covered the 'sally port' inside Bristol castle. This was a way for defenders of the castle to access the moat and come up behind any attackers unawares.

Towards the end of the seventeenth century, there was a growing anxiety and turmoil in the port: Bristol felt itself to be the equal of London, though it was many times smaller, and resented that the London merchants had a monopoly on the bounties drawn from the trade in slaves. The Royal African Company held the letters patent for this monopoly, and even issued its own coinage, the guinea, to raise funds and to distribute the gold it harvested from West Africa. That the King's brother had been the founding member of this company can only have helped to strengthen its monopoly, and the way it shaped thought in the capital. The Merchant Venturers were angered by being cut out of this fountain of gold and they campaigned and lobbied to get access to the dark continent. They put their own candidates up for Parliament and gradually won their way. The merchants could already trade with the colonies but could not make a good profit from it: there was little the colonies wanted or could afford from Bristol, yet much we wanted back, so to trade we would need to send out our gold in exchange for simple goods such as sugar, rum, tobacco and cotton, and no merchant was happy shipping his gold abroad.

With a licence to trade in slaves, the business would become hugely profitable: merchants would buy shoddy goods such as poor quality cloth, knives and rough alcohol in England, ship them to Guinea and buy slaves in exchange, then ship those to the Caribbean and America where they could be sold and the proceeds used to purchase the raw goods that were so in demand back at home. Not only did this avoid sending the merchant's gold abroad, but it meant making three profits rather than one and taking advantage of the trade winds that ran west from Africa and north east from the Indies. This profitable triangle was what they dreamt of, and schemed to achieve. That it pivoted on selling holds full of slaves that were lower in their estimation than cattle, and treated accordingly, mattered nought. The goods in the hold whether cloth, slaves or sugar were just numbers on the ledgers, and only the health of the last was of any concern to the merchants who would have to bargain the best price for it at the exchange.

Chapter 3

The merchants, hoping for great wealth in the offing from the new slave venture, paid to regild the high cross standing in the High Street near St Nicholas as a down payment on their fortune. To make way for more hectic trade, the houses on the bridge were cleared away after hundreds of years of being a landmark, removing a throttle point on the roads from the city. The merchants who had previously vied to live on the bridge now had ambitions to be in the new Square or further up towards Clifton, both smarter and less odorous areas; the space on the bridge was needed for more carts and sleds. The first house made entirely from brick appeared on the Key, which was thought to be a folly even by those who own timber frame houses twisted like saplings or ships in a gale, and were at great risk of fires such as the one that erased half of London soon after the King returned.

Chapter 4

It was estimated that the one night of storm had cost the city a hundred thousand pounds, or what might be earned by an average man in two hundred lifetimes, or a year's earnings for every man in the city. Financially, the majority of this loss fell on the richest merchants who lost their stock but not their homes or their lives, but no one in the city was left untouched and very many suffered greatly, or mourned deeply.

Daniel Defoe advertised in the London Gazette for people around the country to send him accounts of the storm and its consequences for themselves and their localities.

Chapter 5

A new venture was founded in 1702, the Bristol Brass Company of Mr Abraham Darby, based at the old Baptist Mills. Demand for all forms of cast and finished brass was growing at such a pace that Darby could easily have taken on a hundred partners, or retired a rich man, but instead he focused on improving the works and how they were used, always increasing the output and quality of these golden goods, whilst reducing his costs and turning both the air and river black with soot from the works. One of his earliest products was a malt mill, used in the production of beer, and hence despite being an abstemious Quaker he helped the working man have a drink when he sorely needed it. He also made brass pots of such delicacy that all the ladies of Bristol demanded them. This industry was initially fed by mines on the Downs, disfiguring that pasture with pock marks of mines and mounds of spoil, extracting ores for lead and tin, and calamine for brass, which were also shipped up the Severn to the other works Darby had opened in the Midlands. As this changed the landscape, it also transformed the fortunes of the city and the way it worked: Bristol was selling some of the earliest products of the Industrial Revolution and this put some Quakers at the forefront of the city's society, a position that some of the more established merchants resented.

Many long voyages, insisted on taking barrels of Bristol water with them as it was reputed to stay sweet longer than any other, and this was drawn from the springs that fed the conduits running under the city streets, built centuries before to feed the Abbey and monasteries of the city, before Henry VIII ran the monks out and the merchants took over. These springs ran all year round, whether in driest summer or coldest winter, and meant a Bristol man could have fresh water at St Johns even when he could not afford a pint of small beer at our table. The St Johns conduit still runs beneath Park Street (there are little markers in the pavement) and until recently the water still appeared out of the fountain on Nelson Street.

The hot-well was also established as a source of curative waters, to rival those of Bath, with accommodation and entertainment growing up around it to lighten the spirits of those consuming this flavoursome brew, and to lighten their pockets too. It was said that it cured the gout or consumption, and "increased the flows" when those of Bath were said to decrease them.

One consequence of the foolhardy venture to Panama was that it almost ruined Scotland, reducing it to the status of a bankrupt, from both the loss of its national pride and the mass of the country's wealth that had been squandered on this failed exercise, all that gold poured into a fetid foreign swamp. The result of this was the Union by which the Scots agreed to come under the yoke of the English, and one shilling in the pound on their losses, and were grateful even for that. Elements of this have been conveniently forgotten in the intervening centuries.

Chapter 6

Partly due to Woodes Roger's book advocating trade in the South Seas, a great speculative bubble in the stock market began in 1711 and burst in 1720 – some of the debt from this is still on the Government's books.

Chapter 7

The great powers of Europe met in the Dutch city of Utrecht and signed a treaty and by doing so ended the protracted and bitter war over who should rule Spain, and more importantly which country could claim ownership of the colonies in the New World and the East Indies. Britain gained certain rights and by doing so weakened its enemies, limiting the power of the French in the Americas, gaining vital bases such as Gibraltar right on Spain's doorstep, as well as extending its rights to trade in slaves. This in turn stimulated an explosion in the activities of the merchants, at last able to trade with the continent again and eager to make the most of the triangular route.

Teach's old mentor Jennings decided to retire to his considerable plantation estate in Jamaica, which he had greatly enlarged with the proceeds of buccaneering, and lived there without fear of being pursued by the authorities for many years. Other privateers were seen as Britain's enemy, being a barrier to wider profit and a threat to new allies and trading partners. Many had skills in the job, and such a taste for it, and saw it as their duty to continue it even if a parchment had been signed on the other side of the world.

Suddenly, Britain's enemies were not the Spanish and French but the pirates who had previously been our unpaid navy, and all men labelled as pirate were seen as equally condemned whether they held letters of marque or not, whether they had defended England's interests or had attacked them. This meant that the bloodthirsty rogues inhabiting Libertatia off the coast of Madagascar were seen as no worse than the likes of Teach.

Queen Anne, niece of Charles the second, had over the course of her reign seventeen pregnancies without producing a single surviving heir. This had understandably wrecked her health, and left the country without an obvious or acceptable monarch in waiting. Her Stuart line would cease unless we accepted a return to a Catholic king, and Parliament refused to recognise such a monarch; yet if they did not then Scotland would recognise them and the Union would split.

This problem had simmered for years, Anne had insisted that Scotland unite with England and accept the English accession, the proud nation repeatedly refusing. This desire of the Queen's was finally achieved only when the Scots' adventure in Panama had bankrupted them, they then had no choice but to agree to a union. But by that point it was clear that no new king was going to be produced by Queen Anne, and Parliament then had to cast about for anyone who could be seen as both having some legitimacy as a successor and who would fit with the Protestant requirements they had laid down. This search identified Sophia, Electress of Hanover, a cousin of Anne, who was duly selected as the heir apparent to the British throne. This would have settled it, but by the time Queen Anne died, Sophia herself had succumbed to the force of Destiny, and this left her son George to become our new king, ending forever the Stuart line and beginning what became the House of Hanover.

This pleased Parliament sufficiently to have a new, though by no means young, and above all Protestant king upon the throne, who might be open to the influence of the wise heads of that esteemed establishment. The predilection of the new king for long, nay interminable, periods back in Hanover was enabled by the establishment of an active Prime Minister and cabinet, and hence the disaffection of a foreign king laid the ground for our current democracy.

All was not well, however, the selection of a foreign king soured the relationship with Scotland for a generation, making the division between the Tories and the ruling Whigs deeper and more vicious.

Daniel Defoe on several occasions worked as a Government agent to find information not readily available to visible figures of authority. He was born Daniel Foe, so his modified surname was quite unique at the time and quite recognisable, even if he often published anonymously or under pseudonyms. Even his most famous book is published as if he was Robinson Crusoe himself. He backed the wrong side in the Monmouth rebellion and narrowly avoided the gallows, quite possibly by offering his services to the Crown to spy upon the fractious Scots and other troublesome elements that he had up to then been actively supporting.

Some of Defoe's books and pamphlets were not objective journalism or satire, but drifted into the acts of an agent. He wrote in support of the opposite camp but used positions and opinions so extreme that they would discredit those he pretended to support, making them into fools or fiends.

Chapter 10

There were two books published after Blackbeard's

death that may have derived from his story or used Woodes Roger's expertise, these being "The Life, Adventures and Piracies of the Famous Captain Singleton (Defoe, 1720)," an account of an English pirate in and around Africa, and "A General History of the Robberies and Murders Of the most notorious Pyrates" (1724). This last was supposedly written by a Captain Johnson, who had previously been associated with a play about pirates, but it seems likely that Nathaniel Mist, Daniel Defoe or both were the creators of this work. As neither of them had great experience of the Caribbean, it seems likely that they would have consulted someone like Rogers who had a working knowledge of the subject. As Mist was a Jacobite, it is also quite likely that Defoe was spying on him even when he worked for him on his weekly paper. Not long after the publication of the History of Pyrates, Mist fled to France to avoid punitive fines for allegedly libelling the King.

Log of Revenge

One pirate who survived and flourished was Blackbeard's old chief Hornigold, who retired to his estates and took the King's Pardon, living off the accumulated bounty of both privateering and piracy.

The term "tobias night" comes from the Book of Tobit or Tobias 8:1-3 (part of the apocrypha, although this designation varies across the Christian churches). In the story, a woman named Sarah has lost several husbands on their wedding nights because they were killed by the demon of lust, Asmodeus. Tobias is encouraged by the angel Raphael to marry Sarah and is told how to drive the demon away, in which task he succeeds but this delays consummation by several nights. Subsequently people came to believe that postponing the consummation by up to three days demonstrated a proper respect for God and a restraint on the urges of the flesh.

Author's Note

Let me come clean: there is no log, there is no letter, if Blackbeard buried any treasure, I don't know where it is (my lack of Porsche's and private jets testifies to that).

What I have tried to construct here is a plausible history, a yarn spun from the raw stuff of the past, woven into a fabric that wears well, if a bit coarsely. The beauty of writing about people dead for three centuries is that often there are large enough holes in the accounts to allow the writer of fiction to introduce a narrative where originally there was just a person, living day to day, driven by their own faulty ambitions. It also helps that they are unlikely to sue for defamation, though I think I have treated them pretty fairly; more fairly than history has anyway.

Woodes Rogers was indeed a very unlucky man, but whether that was his fault, or coincidence, or forces working against him is hard to tell; perhaps all of these acted at different times in his life. Blackbeard is a far more shadowy character and I have had much more liberty to play with his story, although most of the actions in the Caribbean are based on contemporary accounts; he certainly had a more enlightened view of his freed slaves than was fashionable at the time, and it seems that he avoided unnecessary violence where possible, preferring to menace with the weight of his fleet and his horrific appearance, rather than to enter into close combat. But a saint he was not, and I hope that I have not painted him as such. The other historical figures that cross these pages all visited Bristol, or crossed the paths of Teach and Rogers, though the details went unrecorded until I recreated them here.

I was quite delighted to find that Israel Hands, the evil

cutthroat of Treasure Island, really existed and sailed with Blackbeard, in fact was his close friend. Whether he is the same man as "Israel Hynde of Bristol" is my speculation, but there was quite a band of pirates from the city, so it might be so. It appears that Teach wounded Hands to get him off the ship before the final encounter with the authorities, and this no doubt saved his life. Hands was captured, then took a pardon in exchange for testifying against corrupt officials of the colony; this implicated both Knight and Eden. So perhaps saving Hands was Teach's ultimate act of revenge. Hands did not come out of it that well: Captain Johnson records that he died in penury in London, but at least not by the noose at Execution Dock.

It is my speculation that Captain Johnson was a collaboration between Rogers and Nathaniel Mist, it is convenient to the tale and has some plausibility. There is certainly evidence that Mist was the author, and Defoe gets mixed up in there. Defoe knew a lot about the Caribbean, but had never been there, that is perhaps why he transferred Crusoe to that area from Selkirk's isolated island in the Pacific. Mist had been a sailor in the West Indies, but was busy being arrested for sedition in London for publishing his weekly paper during the action of Blackbeard's log, so it seems likely he had help filling out the details from someone who had been on the scene. Defoe, by the way, had been instructed to spy upon Mist while he worked for him on the paper, a hangover of the settlement that preserved Defoe's own liberty after he had written seditious pamphlets of his own some years before, and chosen to be on the wrong side of the Monmouth rebellion.

Events I record in Bristol largely happened as written in the log: there was a lobby to break the monopoly of the Royal African Company, to allow Bristol to trade in slaves, and the first ship out was under Captain Barker and called the Beginning; there was a terrible storm in 1703 which wrecked large parts of the city and had the appearance of an almost Biblical plague; there was a mayor who came off worse from attempting to punish a nagging wife; Defoe, Selkirk, Hogarth and Robert Louis Stevenson all visited for roughly the reasons given here.

If I have committed a gross factual error, I apologise. All I was doing was spinning a tale, and some threads will snap and tangle even for the most careful worker. I trust that what remains will inform and entertain those that read it.

JB, May 2015

Acknowledgements

I would like to most sincerely thank all those people who have spent their time putting information that I have used onto the web. In particular the editors and contributors to Wikipedia, the nameless and selfless saints who have scanned in so many of the books written by the protagonists of my story and put them where I can find them, and those others who have exposed the kinks of Bristol's history which I have gratefully plundered (see the references below).

I would like to thank Hellie Kenwright for her insight and comments after fighting her way through an early draft.

My endless gratitude I owe to my wife Judith, who has *not* been squeezed under any floorboards in any public houses to my knowledge, and to my children who have tolerated their father being locked away with this book. I trust they will forgive their fictional appearance in it.

References

I used quite a variety of sources to inform and inspire the text, and this is by no means an exhaustive list. The outline of the lives of Teach, Rogers, Dampier, Defoe and Selkirk can be found in the relevant Wikipedia pages, but in addition you might find these of interest:

Defoe's 'The Storm' can be read at bit.ly/defoe-the-storm

Defoe's 'A Tour Through the Whole Island of Great Britain' at bit.ly/defoe-whole-gb

'Life aboard a British Privateer in the time of Queen Anne' by Woodes Rogers, at bit.ly/woodes-privateer

'A Voyage to the South Sea and Round the World' by Captain Edward Cooke, can be found at bit.ly/cooke-south-sea

'A Cruising Voyage round the World' by Woodes Rogers, at: bit.ly/woodes-cruising

Millerd's Map of Bristol in 1673 : bit.ly/millerd-1673

Bristol in 1747 : bit.ly/roque-1747

The Bristol Ducking Stool : bit.ly/bristol-ducking and the Trow page bit.ly/bristol-trow both by Paul Townsend

Bristol's early MP's : bit.ly/bristol-early-mps

Bristol's mayors: bit.ly/bristol-mayors

'A Chronological outline of the History of Bristol' by John Evans, at bit.ly/evans-bristol

'The Annals of Bristol in the Eighteenth Century' by John Latimer at bit.ly/latimer1800

I would recommend both 'Treasure Island' and 'Robinson Crusoe' be read on good old-fashioned paper. Come on, splash out, *cos youz wurf it*!